STEPHEN KING
FROM **A** TO **Z**

DISCARDED

Lodi Memorial Library
One Memorial Dr.
Lodi, NJ 07644-1692

STEPHEN KING
FROM A TO Z

AN ENCYCLOPEDIA OF
HIS LIFE AND WORK

by George Beahm

Property of
Lodi Memorial Library

**Andrews McMeel
Publishing**

Kansas City

ADG-8046

Stephen King from A to Z copyright © 1998 by George W. Beahm.
All rights reserved. Printed in the United States of America.
No part of this book may be used or reproduced in any manner
whatsoever without written permission except in
the case of reprints in the context of reviews.
For information, write Andrews McMeel Publishing,
an Andrews McMeel Universal company,
4520 Main Street, Kansas City, Missouri 64111.

www.andrewsmcmeel.com

REF
813. 54
BEA

98 99 00 01 02 QBD   10 9 8 7 6 5 4 3 2 1

The review of *Bag of Bones*, written especially for this book, copyright © 1998
by Michael R. Collings. The artwork by Stephen E. Fabian, copyright © 1998 by
Stephen E. Fabian, is reprinted with his kind permission. The extract from *Conversations with Anne Rice*, by Michael Riley, copyright © 1996 by Michael Riley, is
reprinted with permission.

This book has not been approved or authorized by Stephen King,
his publishers, or his authorized representatives.

Library of Congress Cataloging-in-Publication Data

Beahm, George W.
   Stephen King from A to Z: An encyclopedia of his life and work / George Beahm.
      p.   cm.
   Includes bibliographical references.
   ISBN 0-8362-6914-4
   1. King, Stephen, 1947-   —Encyclopedias. 2. Horror tales, American—Encyclopedias.
3. Novelists, American—20th century—Biography—Encyclopedias. I. Title.
PS3561.I483Z55   1998
813'.54—dc21   98-22006
                                                                          CIP

Attention: Schools and Businesses

Andrews McMeel books are available at quantity discounts
with bulk purchase for educational, business, or sales promotional use.
For information, please write to: Special Sales Department,
Andrews McMeel Publishing, 4520 Main Street,
Kansas City, Missouri 64111.

for Donna and Rex

"But the writer's job is to write, and there are no brand names in the little room where the typewriter or the pen and notebook sit waiting. There are no stars or brand names in that place; only people who will try to create something out of nothing, and those who succeed and those who fail."

—**Stephen King** "On Becoming a Brand Name," in *Fear Itself*

Contents

Foreword

Stephen King, Beowulf, and the Necessary Landscapes of Darkness

Michael R. Collings

Not long ago, as I was reviewing materials for my "Survey of English Literature" course, I received the following reminder of how precarious—and sometimes how pretentious—our grasp of what is important often reveals itself to be:

> It seems inconceivable that the poet of Beowulf should have intended to sublimate his evil dragon into draconity, making what has reality in the Bible into something abstract or symbolic, something acceptable to a twentieth-century audience willing to swallow monsters only as myths or symbols. Moreover, however we ourselves may wish to read Beowulf, of one thing we can be pretty sure on the evidence of the manuscript: the Anglo-Saxons read the poem as an account of Beowulf the monster-slayer, and preserved it with other accounts of monsters. . . .

> Most of us now think tales of monsters a low order of literature, unless redeemed in the handling. The poet of Beowulf handles his story with literary artistry; he has made the story rich with spirituality. That has led some modern critics to look away from the reality of the monsters, to make them be wholly the powers of darkness towards which they tend.[1]

For a moment, and almost simultaneously, I was struck by two important perceptions: first, that what we think is important—and the reasons we might assert for that importance—may be as fluid and ephemeral as the flow of cultures and histories; and second, that in some important ways, Stephen King has more in common than one might initially suppose with the anonymous author of the greatest surviving Old English epic and of the indisputable monument to English literature, *Beowulf*.

Both writers, for example, love monsters—for their own sakes (the monsters', that is) and for the sake of the insights the figures of monsters can give into human existence.

Both are also supreme storytellers, embodying their monsters with the strength and fascination that elicit—over a thousand years later—heroes strong enough to do battle with persistent darkness; human enough to fall into occasional moments of error that become both cosmically comic and pitiably tragic; and persistent enough to continue the battle, against whatever odds, until the darkness gives way—however fragmentarily—to the light.

And both were entranced by the darker undercurrents of their landscapes, both literal and metaphorical, real and imagined—and in particular with the creatures that survive far beyond the bright shadows of the mead-hall or, in the case of King, in the cultural icons of a highly technological, avowedly scientific, frequently morally ambiguous world: in automobiles; in sterile, secret laboratories; in the open wounds of mines that scar the larger landscape; in our increasingly lethal devices of death.*

There are some significant differences also, of course. King does not write in the highly so-phisticated, highly artificial (a good word here, in its meaning "to create" or "to inform with shape and meaning") dialect of the Anglo-Saxon poet. Instead, he has chosen an art form—the prose novel—historically associated with the rise of the lower classes from anonymity (and from their primary purpose as dragon fodder) to a condition of wielding remarkable political and economic power, a form at times considered almost synonymous with straightforward, unadorned, penetrating narrative that communicates not only the excitement of the moment but the standards and values of a culture. While occasionally indulging himself in the myster-ies of poetry, King more typically explores his landscapes through the medium of a prose that is frequently (and at its best) stripped of self-consciously academic or literary pomposity, that speaks to the rhythms and bluntness of common thought, and that sears itself into his readers' imaginations.

Nor is King in any sense an anonymous figure, nearly submerged in the intricacies of his stories. Unlike the author of *Beowulf*, who remains (for us at least) frustratingly shadowy, a persistent presence behind his story but rarely and usually only tangentially an overt part of it, Stephen King is an integral part of the culture he dissects. His identity is well known—at least his public identity. His name and face are familiar, even to the annual ebb and flow of facial hair that reveals itself in dust-jacket photographs. We know where he lives (and few writers have lived in more appropriate settings). We know his likes and dislikes, his interests, his fears. Especially, we know his fears.

He is, in short, as much a cultural icon as the form he has chosen and the monsters he sur-veys. His name figures prominently on multiple millions of book covers, ranging from tat-tered, well-read, hand-me-down paperbacks to volumes that rank among the most expensive and most sought-after limited editions. And if the books are not enough, there are the films . . . and the audio- and videocassettes, and the annual appearances on Halloween specials, and the commercials, and the, well, the appurtenances of personality-dom, everything from T-shirts to allusions on prime-time sitcoms to guest shots in comic strips. His name has become synony-mous with the landscapes he has mapped; his personality occasionally seems to merge with the darknesses he has made his own.

The centrality of Stephen King to popular culture has also given him unusual power, power to help form and shape the world he simultaneously reflects. He can explore landscapes of imagination and reality that many authors cannot. He can attempt new terrain, especially as his interests relate to publishing. Recently, he has examined, among other innovations, the possibilities of:

♦ A serialized novel such as *The Green Mile*
♦ The dual publication of novels by an author and by his pseudonym, by two respected pub-lishers, in hardcover format, each book not only telling its own tale but in some important ways telling and at the same time revising the story the other novel tells

* This is not to ignore, of course, their mutual interest in the strange and the exotic: in remote hotels not that far removed in purpose and plan from the glittering halls of Heorot; or in the inexplica-ble relationship between the stories of a distant past, whether retained in word or in picture, that can come alive and alter the present and the future.

♦ Four books in a continuing high-fantasy, epic, Western, past/future, postapocalyptic horror-adventure tale conceived in 1970 and still going strong

By moving beyond the conventions, beyond expectations, he can remain consistently a spokesman for his time and his place nearly a quarter century after his first novel appeared.

He has become, in simple, a landscape within a landscape, both that which creates and that which is created. He writes books, and is at the same time the subject and content of multiple books. He imagines monsters that take their place beside the "real" monsters of the world we have created for ourselves; and by doing so he gives us a better understanding of both the process and the outcome, of the metaphorical and of the literal.

Now, to return to the beginning: Over two centuries after the *Beowulf* was finally transcribed and thus (no matter whether accidentally or not) preserved for later generations to ponder, to wonder at, and to enjoy, in the early eigth century, the Anglo-Saxon Chronicles for the year 973 reported the following:

> In this year dire portents appeared over Northumbria and sorely frightened the people. They consisted of immense whirlwinds and flashes of lightning, and fiery dragons were seen flying in the air.[2]

Dragons still flew then, long after the story of Beowulf and his monsters had passed into folklore and legend.

Perhaps, courtesy of Stephen King and the unique landscapes he has carved out for himself and for us in the unmapped wildernesses of Castle Rock, of premillennial twentieth-century America, of the untrammeled human imagination, they may fly still.

Notes

1. E.G. Stanley, *"Beowulf" in Beowulf: Basic Readings*, ed. Peter S. Baker (New York: Garland, 1995), p. 6.

2. Kevin Crossley-Holland, ed. and trans., *The Anglo-Saxon World: An Anthology* (Oxford, England: Oxford University Press, 1982), p. 39.

Introduction

Stephen's Kingdom

George Beahm

Stephen King's oft-quoted dictum, "It is the tale, not he who tells it," emphasizes the importance of the story, not the storyteller. But to my mind, it is the tale *and* he who tells it.

The two are inseparable.

In my previous books on King's life and work—in two editions of *The Stephen King Companion*, a previous biography *(The Stephen King Story),* and a recent biography *(Stephen King: America's Best-Loved Boogeyman)*—my attempt was to cover what Joyce Carol Oates termed the three King personas: the man, the writer, and the phenomenon.

Though those books covered a lot of ground, there was a lot of information that never made it into print, because the opportunity had never arisen.

To adequately chronicle King's life and career, an additional book was needed—a catchall book in which the odds and ends could be chronicled, without the usual constraints of narrative flow (as in a biography) or thematic unity (as in a companion-style book). The answer: an A-to-Z look at King, intended as a reference work, but one designed to be read, not merely consulted. The entries are written in an accessible style, and of course, because of its design, it's perfect for dipping into at random, like picking chocolates out of a sampler box.

From a theoretical point of view, there's no limit to the detail or the number of entries this book could contain. From a practical point of view, there are clearly limits: How much do you *need* to know versus how much do you *want* to know?

Instead of writing a book that would appeal principally to King's die-hard fans who have explored every nook and cranny in Stephen's kingdom, I wrote this book to appeal to his general readership.

I would appreciate hearing from readers with suggestions on additions, deletions, and, most important, corrections, so that material will be on hand for another edition, if and when. See the entry *Phantasmagoria* for my addresses.

I am especially grateful to my friends at Andrews McMeel Publishing, who have outdone themselves in putting this book on the fast track. Two people deserve special mention: my book editor, the indefatigable Donna Martin, whose editorial acumen has been instrumental in shaping the vision for all of my books at the house; and Matthew Lombardi, who worked behind the scenes to shepherd this book in-house through its preproduction gauntlet.

I am especially grateful to the members of SKEMER (the Internet discussion group "Stephen King Electronic Mailers")—too numerous to mention here—who combed their King collections to find book blurbs by him, saving me invaluable time and uncovering material that would otherwise remain undiscovered. These are some of the best people I know, and my long-standing association with them is one of the great joys that has come out of exploring Stephen's kingdom.

Three SKEMERs deserve the keys to the Kingdom for their ongoing efforts to help me on this project: Michelle Rein, Kevin Quigley, and Rich DeMars.

As for the usual roundup of suspects, I am also grateful to my wife (chop the broccoli!). I am similarly grateful to Colleen Doran (beware the gryphons!). And to Michael R. Collings, Ned Brooks, Stephen Spignesi, David Lowell, Stuart Tinker, Bev Vincent, Charlie Fried, and all of my other friends whose patience with me and my endless questions apparently knows no bounds; for them my respect knows no bounds.

Thank you, one and all.

George Beahm
Williamsburg, Virginia
March 1998

Abbreviations & Miscellaneous Notes

Abbreviations

ABA American Booksellers Association

ALA American Library Association

BDN *Bangor Daily News*

HWA Horror Writers of America

LJ *Library Journal*

NAL New American Library

NYT *New York Times*

NYTBR *New York Times Book Review*

PW *Publisher's Weekly*

SK Stephen King

UMO University of Maine at Orono

On Entries for King's Novels

The information given is for the first edition published in the United States, whether from a small press or a trade publisher.

STEPHEN KING
FROM **A** TO **Z**

Ackerman, Forrest J.

Former publisher of *Famous Monsters of Filmland*, to which a teenage Stephen King submitted "The Killers," a short story, which was rejected. Years later, after King became a brand name, Ackerman published the story.

Ackerman is the author of *Mr. Monster's Movie Gold*, for which King wrote the introduction, in which he said that Ackerman "stood up for a generation of kids who understood that if [horror] was junk, it was *magic* junk."

Advance at Scribner

At Scribner, in sharp contrast to NAL, King will get only $2 million a book, but almost 50 percent in a profit-sharing deal.

That's a far cry from the $17 million he was reportedly asking for *Bag of Bones*, which industry insiders said was a money-losing deal if structured in the standard advance-against-royalties agreement.

Simon & Schuster, who owns Scribner, calls the new arrangement a "copublishing venture," which is not unusual for one- or two-book celebrity authors, but very unusual for novelists. (In time, another Simon & Schuster author, Clive Cussler, would follow suit.)

Advance, book

The "front" money paid to authors before the book is published, a loan against earnings. The book has to "earn back" the advance before the author gets any further money, called royalties.

When the brouhaha erupted over King's departure from NAL to Scribner, he said that his advances at Viking were approximately $15 million per book (according to a *New York Post* story).

Over the years, King's advances have ranged from a symbolic one dollar to tens of millions of dollars.

Advance reading copy (ARC)

For major promotional pushes, King's publishers have printed, usually in trade paperback, copies of a new book for distribution to key reviewers and bookstores.

Because of the expense, this kind of star treatment is reserved for books that, in the eyes of the publisher, warrant special promotional consideration: For instance, thousands of advance reading copies of *Thinner* were printed and were distributed free at the American Booksellers Association convention in 1984.

More recently, *Rose Madder* (1995) got such treatment: thousands of ARCs were sent out to bookstores. A major thematic departure for King, *Rose Madder* likely benefited from this promotional push, since the publisher didn't want the book to be viewed as just another King supernatural novel. This one has a more serious theme: spousal abuse.

The Aftermath

Unpublished short novel, written in 1963. (Douglas E. Winter puts its date at 1965 or 1966, but 1963 is what King had written on the manuscript itself, which I feel is probably the most accurate.)

The most ambitious work written during his high school years, this 50,000-word short novel, though clearly juvenilia, shows a budding talent.

In an introduction to Harlan Ellison's *Stalking the Nightmare*, King comments on such works: "They don't call that stuff 'juvenilia' for nothing, friends 'n' neighbors. . . . There comes a day when you say to yourself, Good God! If I was this bad, how did I ever get any better?"

Against the Wind, by J. F. Freedman

SK: "A rip-snorting, full-throttle novel that mixes bikers, murder, a bloodcurdling prison riot, and a powder-keg murder trial. The result is a high-octane blast that makes *Presumed Innocent* look tame by comparison. J. F. Freedman has made an auspicious debut with this compulsively readable tale of crime and punishment. It kept me up late into the night!"

Agency (film)

Creative Artists Agency represents King.

Aliases

Only two, Richard Bachman and John Swithen.

Alpert, Michael

Poet, college friend of King's, book designer.

Alpert designed and shepherded through production all of the Philtrum Press publications to date, including *The Plant* (three installments); *The Eyes of the Dragon*; *The Ideal, Genuine Man*; and *Six Stories*.

After King read *Darkwood,* a collection of poems from Constance Hunting's Puckerbrush Press (Orono, Maine), printed by Alpert, King stopped by Alpert's frame shop in Bangor and asked him to print *The Plant*, a job Alpert recalled as "fun."

Alpert: "Most commercial publications are nei-

A Is for Agent

King's first agent was Patricia Schartle Myrer of the agency McIntosh and Otis, who read *Sword in the Darkness*—King also called it *Babylon Here*—and submitted it to a dozen publishers, including Doubleday.

The 150,000-word novel was, in King's assessment, "a badly busted flush." The story, though professionally told, was grim reading—hardly entertaining fare for someone looking for an escapist read. No wonder it never sold!

In the winter of 1972–73, King began a short story intended for the men's magazine *Cavalier*, which bought his stories at $200–$300 a pop, though payment was on publication, not acceptance. The untitled story, about an ugly duckling of a girl, ran far longer than intended and was clearly not going to be a submission to *Cavalier* after all. As bad luck would have it, King had run dry—this was the only idea he had—and so he worked with the material on hand, reworking it into his first published book, *Carrie.*

After five "trunk" novels, *Carrie* would launch his meteoric career. After he submitted it to Doubleday, the firm offered its boilerplate contract, which King dutifully read and signed, after going over it, clause by clause, with his friend Chris Chesley.

At that point King needed an agent, because an author is in no condition to cast a jaundiced eye on the clauses, one of which eventually caused King to walk away from his publisher.

According to *Newsweek* magazine, King's advances on the five Doubleday books were a pittance, at a time when his books, especially in their paperback editions, were earning the publishers millions of dollars. But King didn't have an agent who could fight on his behalf, so for those first five Doubleday titles, his total advance was reported to be $77,500.

It's a truism that writers tend to be more imaginative than publishers—the talent vs. the suits—but in this case it would have behooved Doubleday to exercise a little more imagination and look down the road to see what King would eventually have brought them, based on current sales. Such an extrapolation might have shown the wisdom in keeping King by negotiating the author-publisher split to something more amenable to the author. However, the firm drew the line in the sand, staunchly refusing to budge on this issue; so when an impasse had been reached, it was clear that the time had come to change publishers, but he would need an agent to engineer the move, to ensure that the new publisher wouldn't hobble him financially from the onset.

In an essay titled "Everything You Need to Know About Writing Successfully—in Ten Minutes" (*Writer's Digest*, July 1986), King explained that when the time comes for you to *need* an agent—as opposed to *wanting* an agent—*one will seek you out*. The shoe, so to speak, is on the other foot, and you as the writer aren't knocking on the agent's door—he's knocking on yours.

In King's case, it was a matter of serendipity. At a literary party in 1976, the Kings happened to meet Kirby McCauley, who shared their interests in fantasy literature. The Kings had found a kindred spirit in McCauley, who knew of King because of 'Salem's Lot and felt that he could provide the representation to the publishers that King sorely needed.

After earning King's trust by selling short stories to major markets, so that King's fiction broke out of genre publications and into the mainstream, just as Ray Bradbury had done years earlier, McCauley came to represent King. His first task: to engineer King's move to New American Library.

McCauley called the play, and the result was that in 1977 King had his first three-book deal worth $2.5 million—a far cry from his paltry advances at Doubleday.

That deal alone catapulted McCauley—who had been laboring in the minor leagues with big names in the horror field, who were in fact small names in the larger world of mainstream book publishing—into the pro league. If we assume that McCauley was getting the standard 10 percent of gross, King's big deal translated to a sales commission of a quarter million bucks, and more when the books earned out and brought in royalties.

The relationship with McCauley lasted until 1988, at which time King did what many other bestselling authors have done: hired a lawyer instead of retaining an agent, who got up to 15 percent of the gross receipts. A lawyer, in comparison, charged a set fee for negotiating contracts, so no matter the fee, it would likely be small change compared to paying a commission on every dollar earned.

The man to whom King entrusted this job was Arthur B. Greene, a New York lawyer who doubled as King's business manager. (Presumably, this is the same one whom King alludes to in an introduction to *Skeleton Crew*—the one earning 5 percent of the net.)

King remained at New American Library until November 1997, when he left them for Scribner, an imprint of Simon & Schuster, in a move engineered by Greene. This time, however, the move was not a smooth meshing of gears, as it had been when McCauley shifted him from Doubleday to NAL. Greene handled the situation as a lawyer would, which immediately drew unwanted attention in the book trade and in the mainstream media, as well. Instead of handling it with discreet phone calls and visits, Greene's agenting of *Bag of Bones* resembled nothing so much as a three-ring circus, with King admitting that it could have been handled differently, and better, which is why he put an end to the inelegant proceedings, opting not for the reported $17 million advance but instead for a profit-sharing deal that, in effect, make King a partner of Scribner.

ther legible nor beautiful. This lack of care results from the structure of the publishing business. A large exception is the Alfred A. Knopf company, since its founder oversaw the whole operation." (Robert H. Newall, "Making Beautiful Books Is Bangor Man's Delight," *BDN*, March 4, 1983.)

Alpert, on letterpress: "This is the way the great presses do it. These are the procedures established from the very beginning of printing. Letter-press printing started out as a craft and became an industry. It's on its way to becoming a highly respected craft again. Commercial printing has no future. The history of Western culture is tied up with letter-press printing. It's a demanding calling." (Newall, *BDN*.)

Alumni Baseball Team

In October 1990, at an alumni baseball game to raise money for the cost of the University of Maine's spring trip to Florida, tickets cost $3 for adults and $1 for children. The trip was sponsored by Friends of Maine baseball, and King was the assistant coach for the team.

American Cancer Society

The ACS raised $12,000 at a Jail-a-Thon (Oct. 25, 1985). Judges Tabitha King and Linda Beaulieu sat on the bench. Stephen King was "arrested" as he got off a plane at Bangor International Airport, was cuffed, and was brought to the Cancer Society jail by the Keystone Kops.

American Express

Early in his career, a flattered King agreed to do a send-up of himself in an ad for the American Express card. In the thirty-second ad, set in a haunted castle, King extols the virtues of the card: "When I'm not recognized, it just kills me," he says, so he "carries" (ha ha) the American Express card. "Don't leave home without it," he admonishes the viewer.

With or without the American Express card, King is recognized so frequently that now it kills him *to* be recognized. Still, for those times when

you're trying to check in at the Stanley Hotel in Estes Park, Colorado, that green credit card may come in handy.

America Online, "Center Stage"

In early 1996, King gave an interview electronically, via keyboard, on AOL's "Center Stage," in which AOLers send responses in real time to the questions posed. "This is King, and I'm here. I've never done this before, so bear with me. Also, the keyboard is strange to me, so excuse the typos."

Although this was his first time in this new interview format, King proved to be as humorous via this medium as he is when answering questions in person at public talks.

Amherst, Massachusetts

King gave a talk on April 1, 1985, at the University of Massachusetts in Amherst to a sell-out crowd of two thousand fans. "An Evening with King" featured him reading "Here There Be Tygers" (from the *Skeleton Crew* collection), answering questions from the audience, and sharing anecdotes about his life. According to *Castle Rock* contributor Sheryl Mayer, "It was definitely an evening to remember."

Anchovies

When he orders pizza, King prefers anchovies on his portion.

Anchovy ice cream

In talking about the fiction of Clive Barker and Don Robertson, King has used anchovy ice cream as a way of explaining an affinity for their works. In other words, you either like or do not like anchovy ice cream; and there is no middle ground. It's the same with the two authors' work.

Angelsoft

Software company that developed a videogame of the story "The Mist."

Angus & Robertson Bookstore
(Australia)

While visiting Australia, riding a Harley David-son from Sydney to Perth, King stopped in this bookstore, pulled out a wad of cash that looked like $5,000, and bought some books. The store owner, who couldn't believe it was King, even after he said so, compared a book jacket photo to the author, but remained unconvinced until he called up King's Australian publisher, who confirmed he was in country.

If you happen to stop in this bookstore, you'll probably see their new slogan: "Buy Your Books Where Stephen King Shops."

The Annotated Guide to Stephen King,
by Michael R. Collings

Published in 1986 by Starmont House, this book is subtitled *A Primary and Secondary Bibliography of the Works of America's Premier Horror Writer.* This is number eight in the Starmont Reference Guide series.

This book was extensively revised and updated for Collings's *The Work of Stephen King* (1996).

Annual income

It's vulgar to talk about money, but the media obsess on what star performers like King earn, and feel free to report their speculations without the benefit of confirmation from the source.

Nobody really knows what kind of income King earns annually, nor is it anyone's damned business, especially since it just gives more ammunition to critics who like to talk about his advances instead of the book in question.

So where does King's money come from? Book advances, royalties, investments, interest, and participation in movie deals. In short, like any best-selling author, King has multiple income streams that collectively accrue many millions.

Now that King has changed publishing houses, it's quite likely that his income will go up, since he's not contractually tied to the limiting world of royalties. Instead, a profit-sharing plan with his publisher ties King into the performance of each book, giving him additional incentives to flog the book. (To support *Bag of Bones*, to be published in Fall 1998, King will be hitting New York, Chicago, Seattle, and Los Angeles—in addition to a book signing at a hometown bookstore, Betts—and backing those appearances with electronic media coverage. He hasn't planned this much promotion since *Insomnia*, published in 1994.)

Another Quarter Mile

A collection of poetry by *a* King (of Hayward, California), not *the* King. This King published this collection of poetry in 1979 at Dorrance & Company.

Not to be confused with *The Green Mile* by *the* King (of Bangor, Maine).

Anthrax

Rock and roll band inspired by King's fiction. The song "Among the Living" was inspired by *The Stand*; "Skeletons in the Closet" was inspired by "Apt Pupil;" and "Misery Loves Company" was inspired by *Misery*.

Appreciation

SK has expressed his appreciation for the following artists, among others:

♦ The science fiction writer Theodore Sturgeon, in *Locus* magazine.

♦ The rock and roll musician Rick Nelson, in *Spin* magazine.

♦ The dark fantasist Clive Barker, in the program book for AlbaCon III (Glasgow, Scotland, March 28–31, 1986).

♦ The mystery writer John D. MacDonald, in *The Mystery Scene Reader: A Special Tribute to John D. MacDonald.*

"Apt Pupil" (collected in *Different Seasons*)

Dedication: "For Elaine Koster and Herbert Schnall."

Though King's name has become readily identifiable with supernatural horror, he can achieve dramatic results writing realistic stories that deal with real-life horror, as in this story of a symbiotic, and ultimately deadly, relationship between an All-American California boy, Todd Bowden, and a fugitive Nazi. Bowden's fascination with the Nazi death camps puts him on the trail of the fugitive, who is masquerading as an ordinary citizen, Arthur Denker.

Bowden doesn't want to blackmail Denker; he wants the insider's scoop on what *really* happened at the camps, the "gooshy stuff." (Who is the *real* monster, Bowden or Denker?)

As Denker reluctantly recounts to Bowden the horrific history of the death camps, both men spiral downward into madness in a danse macabre that ends as all such dances with the devil must.

A real-life horror story that, King said, got under his editor's skin at Viking, this kind of story shows King's ability to write nonsupernatural horror, which because it's real can have more impact.

Astrology

King is not a believer in astrology. (Don't ask him what his sign is, unless you'd like to risk getting a rude response.) (King says his wife Tabitha calls him an "impossibly picky Virgo.")

Sounds like a writer to me.

Attias, Daniel

A first-time director who worked as an assistant director on *Firestarter*, Attias's adaptation of *Cycle of the Werewolf*, titled *Silver Bullet*, is standard horror fare. Budgeted at $7 million, it earned its money back at the box office, but it was not a critical or financial success.

Auctions and benefits

♦ A copy of *The Plant*, to benefit the American Repertory Theatre (1985).

♦ Ten holographic pages of *The Raft*, to benefit the American Repertory Theatre (1996). Appraised at $1,500, these pages sold for $6,600.

♦ To benefit Manly Wade Wellman's widow, King contributed to Confederation (a convention held in Atlanta, Georgia, on August 31, 1985) a

holographic notebook containing 89 pages of *The Drawing of the Three*; a short story, "The End of the Whole Mess"; and "The Doors." A 7-by-9-inch school notebook with a Garbage Pail Kids sticker on the cover sold for $5,200. It was purchased by Robert Weinberg and Lloyd Currey, who bought it for a collector. The auction raised $25,000.

♦ To benefit the Walker Memorial Library in Westbrook, Maine, King donated a signed galley proof of *Pet Sematary* and a signed copy of the second printing of *The Dark Tower: The Gunslinger* (Grant edition).

♦ To benefit the American Repertory Theater (1988) King donated a notebook containing holographic pages from an unpublished novel, *Keyholes*, which sold for $4,000.

♦ At an auction of Forrest Ackerman memorabilia (1988), a letter written by King to his magazine when King was 14 years old sold for $440. (The letter was donated by Ackerman.)

♦ To benefit a local children's charity at Christmas 1988 in St. Petersburg, Florida, WYNF-FM auctioned off signed King books, including *The Gunslinger* in paperback and *The Tommyknockers* in hardback; the hardbacks netted $500 each, the paperbacks, $425. The books were donated by Ed Yarb, who commented, "It was hard to donate them to the auction because I wanted them all. They were the hot items of the year."

♦ To benefit the Eastern Maine Medical Center's new children's wing, built in part with a large donation by the Kings, Betts Bookstore sold props from the television adaptation of "The Langoliers," including signed scripts, King's director's chair, dummy in-flight magazines (from the fictional American Pride Airlines), a flight bag, and other items.

♦ To benefit the Harbor House Community Center in Southwest Harbor, Maine, a boys basketball tournament was held, the 1994 Great Harbor Skip Chappelle Shootout, for which King coached a squad of Bangor High players.

Audio adaptations

There are two kinds of prose styles: one that's intended to be *read*, and one that's intended to be *read aloud*.

The distinction is a fine but important one: the former is usually academic or literary writing, and the latter is the domain of the storyteller, drawing on the oral tradition.

King is clearly a storyteller whose tales are meant to be read aloud.

Imagine sitting around a campfire with King and hearing him read "The Mist," in his Down East accent, or *Needful Things*.

This distinction explains, to a large degree, why King's visual adaptations have a greater potential for failure, but his spoken-word adaptations almost always succeed, preserving King's distinctive fictional voice: the visual adaptations take the director's vision and substitute it for your personal vision, for "skull" cinema, the movie projector in your head. The spoken-word adaptations, however, are exactly what the author intended, especially the unabridged recordings.

King prefers his fiction to be recorded unabridged and, when possible, prefers to be the reader of his own work, though he speaks highly of Frank Muller (of Recorded Books), whose deep, baritone voice is ideally suited for King's fiction.

SK: "I thought that even though I don't have a professional voice, I know what the [*Dark Tower*] story means to me, which is a great deal. . . . It seems built to be heard around a fire. A lot of fantasy is that way. . . . A good reader is fairly unobtrusive. You lose the voice in the flow of the story, and the reader is just a medium to convey the words to the ear." (Quoted in Tom Spain, "King Tapes Readings Coming from NAL," *PW*, February 19, 1988).

Note: King originally read audiotape versions of the first three Dark Tower novels; in 1997, Frank Muller recorded audiotape versions of all four Dark Tower novels as a tie-in to the newly designed trade paperback editions.

"Autopsy Room Four"
(collected in *Six Stories*)

This previously unpublished short story made its original appearance in a Philtrum Press edition.

Awards and honors

The following awards and honors are listed in Michael R. Collings's bibliography, *The Work of Stephen King*.

1977: For *The Shining* ("best novel" category), a Nebula Award nomination (Science Fiction Writers of America).

1978: For *The Shining* ("best novel" category), a Hugo Award nomination (World Science Fiction Association).

1978: For *'Salem's Lot*, selected by the American Library Association as one of its "best books for young adults."

1979: For *The Stand* ("best novel" category), a Balrog nomination (World Fantasy Award).

1979: For *The Stand* ("best novel" category), a Hugo Award nomination.

1979: For the Fifth World Fantasy Convention in 1979 (Providence, R.I., Oct. 12–14), SK was one of two guests of honor, along with Frank Belknap Long.

1980: From the University of Maine, the Alumni Career Award.

1981: *Firestarter* selected by the American Library Association as one of its "best books for young adults."

1982: For *Danse Macabre*, the Hugo Award at the World Science Fiction Convention, in the "best nonfiction book" category.

1982: For "Do the Dead Sing?" the World Fantasy Award, in the "best short fiction" category.

1982: King selected by *Us* magazine as the Best Fiction Writer of the Year.

1982: *Firestarter* selected by the New York Public Library as one of its Books for the Teen Age.

1982: *Cujo* selected by the New York Public Library as one of its Books for the Teen Age.

1982: At Necon II, King was the roastee.

1985: Chosen as the "favorite author" by the Augusta County (Georgia) Patrons of the

Awards and Honors *continued*

Augusta Library, for National Library Week, April 14–21.

1985: King listed in *Starlog* as one of the "100 most important people in science fiction/fantasy."

1985: For *Pet Sematary*, a nomination (Horror Writers of America).

1985: For *The Talisman* (with Peter Straub), a Balrog nomination (World Fantasy Award).

1986: From the Young Adult Advisory Committee of the Spokane Public Library, the Golden Pen Award.

1988: In a tie with *Swan Song*, by Robert R. McCammon, *Misery* was selected as the "best novel" by HWA, for which King received the Bram Stoker Award.

1989: For "Night Flier," in the "best novella" category, a "recommendation" by the HWA.

1989: For "Dedication," in the "best novella" category, a Bram Stoker "recommendation" by the HWA.

1990: For *Four Past Midnight*, in the "best collection" category, a Bram Stoker Award by the HWA.

1994: For "The Man in the Black Suit," in the "best short fiction" category, a World Fantasy Award.

1994: For "The Man in the Black Suit," an O. Henry award for "best American short story."

1996: For his body of work, a conference celebrating his canon was held at his alma mater, University of Maine, on October 11–12. *See also:* READING STEPHEN KING.

B Is for Bachman

I was in a bookstore soon after the hardback edition of *Thinner,* by Richard Bachman (a pseudonym of Stephen King's), was published.

A clerk and a little old lady were having a heated discussion that was on the verge of turning into an argument, with *Thinner* and Bachman/King at its center.

The clerk was trying to explain patiently that Richard Bachman was in fact a pen name for Stephen King, but the little old lady, looking for a new King book to give to her granddaughter, shook her head and stubbornly pointed to the author's photo on the flap of the dust jacket.

"That doesn't look *anything* like Stephen King!" she said, jabbing her finger at the photo of Kirby McCauley's friend, Richard Manuel.

"But Stephen King *wrote the book!*" the clerk responded.

"It can't be King. Why, these gentlemen look *completely different!*"

The clerk lost that sale, but no matter: Even though *Thinner* had only sold 28,000 (by King's count) before his cover was blown, it would go on to sell *280,000* copies once the word got out.

King could no longer hide behind the pen name.

And the little old lady was right . . . and wrong: The author's photo didn't look anything like Stephen King, but the writing was surely King's . . . and that's what started the end of the whole mess.

In an introduction to the first edition of *The Bachman Books* (its second edition has a newer and, to King's mind, better introduction), King wrote that a Washington, D.C., bookstore clerk named Steve Brown went to the Library of Congress and examined the copyright forms for the Bachman books. Brown discovered that King's name, not Bachman's (a registered pen name) was inadvertently put down as the author of *Rage*, a clerical error committed by someone at NAL who filled out the form and filed it. King probably never saw the form itself, which is why he never caught the error.

Brown, however, wasn't the first person to go to the Library of Congress to check up on the provenance of Bachman's books: A Chicago bookseller, Robert Weinberg, had done so earlier and had published his findings in one of his monthly book catalogues, alerting the fans in the science fiction community. Another book dealer, L. W. Curry, had done the same. So in fantasy circles, the word was out . . . but it hadn't gotten out in the world at large, to customers who haunted bookstores for each new King offering.

What King's mainstream customers didn't know was that in addition to *Thinner* (original title, *Gypsy Pie*), King-as-Bachman had already published four previous novels—*Rage, The Long Walk, Roadwork,* and *The Running Man*—all but two of which were long out of print, because they were published as mass market paperback originals, which have a shelf life approximating that of milk.

Why, you ask, would King even bother to publish under a pen name, when his hard-earned brand name would guarantee sales?

Because for King, publishing the books under a pen name relieved the pressure, the need, he felt—to publish, a need his publishers didn't share, since they subscribed to the Cardinal Rule of Publishing: *Thou shalt not publish more than one novel by a brand-name writer in a calendar year, for fear of flooding the market and confusing the reader.*

The solution—for both King and NAL—served both well for six years: Four Bachman books were published under cover of darkness, so to speak, in cheap paperback editions: *Rage* in 1977, *The Long Walk* in 1979, *Roadwork* in 1981, and *The Running Man* in 1982. The cover prices ranged from $1.50 to $2.50.

But the publication of the fifth Bachman book —*Thinner*, in 1984—proved to be King's undoing. Unlike the other books, this one was published in hardback and was accorded star treatment: a pallet of free advance readers copies was given away at the American Booksellers Association convention, accompanied by a breathless letter from the publisher.

By early 1985, the biggest secret of the year—an open secret in fan circles, but still unknown in the book world at large—would soon break. Here's what happened in 1985:

January: Stephen Brown wrote to King, announcing his findings at the Library of Congress.

In late January, *Entertainment Tonight* ran a story speculating on the authorship of the books.

February: In the second issue of *Castle Rock*, the editor and publisher Stephanie Leonard said that there would be "a secret revealed at last." She was referring to the King-Bachman connection, which King wanted to be the first to break.

February 9: Joan H. Smith of the *Bangor Daily News* ran the story that she had told King previously she was going to run, whether or not he confirmed the King-Bachman connection. The story's title said it all: "Pseudonym Kept Five King Novels a Mystery."

March: On the front page of the third issue of *Castle Rock*, Leonard wrote: "I don't think I have to tell anyone the big news this month. Yes, Stephen King is indeed Richard Bachman. One of the toughest things about doing this newsletter has been that I've not been able, until now, to reveal that to the readers. I have known that Stephen was using a pseudonym for years, but I was sworn to secrecy. I am relieved now that I don't have to lie or be evasive anymore. Last month I hinted that a secret would be revealed, and Stephen intended to keep it quiet until March 1, but a local paper decided they would run the story with or without his comment, as they had enough proof, and as Stephen told them, the whole thing was coming apart—he likened it to having a bag of groceries that gets wet and things keep falling out until you can't hold it together anymore. For months now he's been getting letters asking if the rumor was true, and in late January *Entertain-*

ment Tonight did a segment alluding to the connection, and that really fueled the rumors. I'm sorry *Castle Rock* couldn't have told you first, but again, it wasn't up to me."

April 9: Brown's story ran in the *Washington Post*.

Richard Bachman was dead—cancer of the pseudonym, King called it—but in the wake of the disclosure, King expressed his anger, in an interview for the *Maryland Coast Dispatch* (Aug. 8, 1988), to Loukis Louka: "I was pissed. It's like you can't have anything. You're not allowed to because you are a celebrity. What does it matter? Why should anyone care? It's like they can't wait to find stuff out, particularly if it's something you don't want people to know. That's the best. That's the juice. It makes me think about that Don Henley song, 'Dirty Laundry.' Hell, give it to them."

The initially modest sales of *Thinner* were never a concern to King, who wanted to see whether this novel would be Bachman's break-out book, though it looked unlikely. After all, it only had two print runs before the revelation was made public. But after the story made the national news, *Thinner* had third and fourth print runs of 50,000 each, with a fifth print run of 100,000 copies.

Because of reader demand—only two of the first four Bachman books were in print at the time—NAL published an omnibus collection, *The Bachman Books: Four Early Novels by Stephen King*, a collection of 700 pages of early Bachman material.

In 1987 King published *Misery*, which he felt was sufficiently Bachman in tone to consider publishing it as a Bachman book, but he changed his mind, and the supposedly dead Bachman made his next appearance in 1989.

In his author's note to *The Dark Half*, King writes: "I'm indebted to the late Richard Bachman for his help and inspiration. This novel could not have been written without him." This is a reference to *My Pretty Pony*, an abortive novel by Bachman that was reworked as *The Dark Half*.

The Dark Half is about Thad Beaumont, a writer who calculatingly retires his pen name, George Stark, only to discover to his horror that the pen name has literally taken on a life of its own, coming murderously back to life. A "creepazoid" (as Thad's wife, Liz, calls him) named

Frederick Clawson, a law student and part-time bookstore clerk who read Stark's and Beaumont's books and connected the dots, goes to extensive lengths to confirm, then confront, Beaumont with the revelation that Stark is his pen name. That revelation proves to be Clawson's undoing, since Stark pays him a visit and kills him.

But dead is dead, as far as pen names in the real world are concerned, and Bachman, unlike Stark, couldn't be brought back to life . . . or could he?

Every writer has a trunk, a repository where unpublished novels are stored. Good, bad, or indifferent, the books, for whatever reasons, are lost to the world, placed in the deep freeze.

Bachman was no different. He, too, had unpublished novels in his trunk. One of them, titled *The Regulators*, was unearthed by his widow.

In a curious parallel, Bachman's *The Regulators* was a demonic mirror image of King's *Desperation*, so it was fitting that King prevailed on his publishers to issue both books simultaneously, in October 1996.

On the jacket flap of *The Regulators*, we are told that Bachman's widow "discovered the manuscript of *The Regulators*, along with some other writings, in the attic of the Bachman residence in New Hampshire."

The jacket photo, taken by David King, was of his brother Stephen in the bedroom of their Durham, Maine home; Stephen, cigarette in hand, is seated in front of a typewriter with a copy of *Startling Mystery Stories* in its well, the magazine opened to "The Glass Floor," King's first published story.

Bachman, one reviewer put it, is "Stephen King without a conscience." Back from the dead, only an ungrateful son of a bitch wouldn't be glad to see him at all.

Of his pen name King said, "With the last Bachman novel, *Thinner*, my wife said, 'You know, it's your own goddamned fault. You knew it was like the other ones. Somebody was bound to recognize it.' If it was Joe Schmoe, nobody would have cared. Instead, you've got this guy who was familiar with the Library of Congress and works at a bookstore. He deliberately tracked down the copyrights, and our tracks were covered except for the first one." (Quoted by Edward Gross, *Fangoria* #58, 1986).

The Bachman Books: Four Early Novels by Stephen King

Hardback, 1985, 692 pages, NAL, $19.95
Dedication: none for this edition, since the individual novels were dedicated separately.
Contents
"Why I Was Bachman" [first appearance]
Rage
The Long Walk
Roadwork
The Running Man

Bag of Bones

Hardback, 1998, 529 pages, Scribner, $28.00
Bag of Bones is an ambitious novel, a turning point for King, who quite rightly terms this mainstream novel a "haunted love story."

Told in first person by the best-selling writer Michael Noonan, the novel's title alludes to the idea that people are in fact just bags of bones. True enough, but implicit in that is the notion that one's humanity is what makes the difference between different bags of bones.

In *Bag of Bones*, King has, to my mind, deliberately written a mainstream novel that will appeal to a greater audience, perhaps gaining him part of the readership long denied him, as he attempts to shake off his reputation as America's best-loved boogeyman. Though King has lamented in recent interviews that horror is not *all* he writes, this novel reinforces that aspect because of its supernatural elements. However, the treatment of those elements caters not to the horror fans per se but to mainstream readers that want a good story that coincidentally has horrific elements.

Noonan, who has lost his wife and the unborn child she was carrying, is suffering from an extended bout of writer's block. In fact, it's sufficiently severe that, had he not had the foresight to stockpile book-length manuscripts for his long drought, he would likely be turning out potboilers to eke out a living. Fortunately, his foresight has paid off, and he returns to Sara Laughs, his vacation home near a lake in southern Maine, with $5 million in the bank. (Like King, he doesn't *have* to write for a living.)

In a chance encounter on a busy main street, Noonan saves the life of a child, an engaging little girl named Ki, and becomes entangled in the life-and-death custody battle over Ki, who is torn between her mother, Mattie Devore, and Mattie's estranged father-in-law, William Devore.

A widow in her early twenties, Mattie depends on Noonan—emotionally, then financially—to help her in the custody battle. Noonan, who hadn't planned on becoming personally involved, finds himself drawn to Mattie and her daughter, but is haunted by ghosts from the past: the ghosts at the summer home, Sara Laughs, and his own tragic history.

Fortunately, he is abetted by the spirit of his wife, Johanna, who comes back not to haunt but to help him.

The result: An ambitious novel, a rich and compulsively readable book that stands on its own but also touches on other King books, such as *The Dark Half*, with its reference to Thad Beaumont.

More than anything else, the novel shows the maturation of King as a writer, in the metamorphosis of stereotyped monsters like vampires, mummies, and werewolves, to human monsters like William Devore and his nurse-aide, a diabolical woman who makes Nurse Ratched from *One Flew over the Cuckoo's Nest* look like Mother Teresa.

The novel also showcases King's ability to write an emotional story about the enduring power of love; without it, people are just, to use King's metaphor, bags of bones.

"I'm happy that the search for a new publisher has ended so successfully," King says. "*Bag of Bones* contains everything I now know about marriage, lust, and ghosts, and it was essential to me that I find the right partner to publish it."

In a letter to booksellers, King says that at 50, a writer "may have to find a few new pitches if he's going to continue to be successful. I think I can still throw a pretty good fastball when I need to, but in *Bag of Bones* I've mixed in a few sliders, a few change-ups, and maybe a midnight curveball or two. . . . I have a new publisher; I wanted to bring them the best book I have in me to write. I wanted to tell a story which would please my old friends and perhaps make a few new ones, as well. *Bag of Bones* is the result—a summation of all I know about lust, secrets, and the unquiet dead."

On a related note: Following publishing tradition, King's British publishers typically issue a signed, limited edition of each new King novel. The signature is on a bookplate pasted into five hundred numbered copies. For *Bag of Bones*, however, no British limited was forthcoming, because of a fan snafu: Premature discussions of the limited edition, made before a contract was actually signed, torpedoed that edition. (The British edition, however, preceded the U.S. edition.)

Bag of Bones

A review by Michael R. Collings

Bag of Bones is Stephen King's most recently published work, and one of the strongest tales he has published in some time. Eschewing overt social criticism while simultaneously examining a number of such social issues as integral parts of the story, this new novel harkens back to the Stephen King who wrote such memorable novels as *The Shining* and *It*, yet it also suggests that he is looking forward to new possibilities.

That initial compliment delivered, it needs to also be noted that in some important ways, *Bag of Bones* resembles earlier successes perhaps only too strongly. The tone at times seems derivative—derivative of King at his best. As occurred in *The Shining*, *It*, *The Dark Half*, and elsewhere, this story focuses on the problems of a best-selling novelist confronting writer's block. Now, while writer's problems might certainly present persistent threats for a writer of King's stature (although no one has even suggested that he himself has suffered from writer's block—if anything, he is criticized most frequently for the opposite complaint), their recurrence in novel after novel, story after story, makes it increasingly difficult for readers to empathize with the characters—especially, as in this case, when the writer in question, Michael Noonan, is worth over five million dollars. King does seem aware of the implicit complications involved in writing novels about writing novels, since he takes pains to shift his narrator-writer's chosen genre from horror to quasi-erotic romance, and then pits him against an antagonist whose half-billion fortune makes Noonan's five million seem paltry. But still, readers may have difficulty squaring precisely with the travails of a man with an abundance of ready cash, two homes, and seemingly much going for him.

A second, related difficulty lies in King's decision to use first-person narrative, a comparative rarity for him as storyteller. In general, he handles third-person with greater facility than first, particularly in a novel that incorporates the possibility—if not the probability—that the main character may be going insane. While King is particularly strong at depicting the external manifestations of the supernatural upon his characters, he is somewhat less so at depicting *internal* processes; and when, as in *Bag of Bones*, the character in question is subjected to eerie dreams, strange sounds, and largely subjective evidence that his house may be haunted, we as readers are in a quandary as to what to believe. In addition, in this case, since the narrator is also a writer whose books tend toward the erotic—Noonan refers to himself rather disparagingly as V. C. Andrews with a prick—the interior monologues at times become substantially more involved in eroticism, explicit and implicit, literal and symbolic, than the story might require. While the romance motifs impel a novel such as *Misery*, in which we are allowed to read the character's story, here we are subjected to the dreams and nightmares inherent to the writer's *life*, which is, of course, also the story we are reading. The first-person stance in a novel often invites intimacy and involvement, but in this case the intimacy does not always further the storytelling.

Such relatively technical matters aside, however, *Bag of Bones* does manage to work much of King's trademark magic. The opening chapters seem somewhat slow-paced, suggesting more the deliberative tone of *Insomnia,* perhaps, than the immersion into action of *The Stand* or *Dolores Claiborne*. Even so, they develop a sense of compulsion that, in my case at least, kept me reading—and drove me to finish the typescript version in less than two days. Once the characters, settings, and themes develop fully, *Bag of Bones* more than repays the investment in time required to read it and at the same time reminds us of why King is such a powerful writer.

There are the elements of monsters, ghosts, hauntings, etc., that are his signal pieces. In this case, the hauntings center around a century-old lakeside home called, both appropriately and horrifyingly inappropriately, Sara Laughs. Much of the action of *Bag of Bones* revolves around resolving the mysterious life and disappearance of Sara Tidwell and her extended family from the area nearly a century before, and in resolving the identity, meaning, and ultimate threat of the laughter (and other manifestations) that haunt the old house. Dreams, portents, supernatural interventions, humanlike plants (reminiscent of the hedge monsters in *The Shining*)—all of these and more people *Bag of Bones*.

But as in the most effective King novels, the superficial monsters pale in intensity beside the "real" ones. Mike Noonan's wife, Johanna, is dead because of one kind of contemporary "monster"—an internal, unseen, unknowable aneurysm that destroys her and her unborn child at the precise moment when we expect an explicitly external threat. In King's fictional worlds, as in our real one, sudden, unexpected death happens; if it is not the "Big C," then it will be something else.

Johanna's is not the only death, of course. And gradually we discover that the litany of death that surrounds Noonan—and seems focused on the landscape surrounding Sara Laughs as well—is increasingly problematical, particularly as King rather elusively begins suggesting an inordinate number of deaths of children over the past several generations. Often, these deaths suggest yet another kind of monster—the father figure who, rather than protecting, destroys. Here King touches on social issues relating to abuse that are more stridently and less effectively showcased in stories such as *Gerald's Game, Delores Claiborne*, and *Rose Madder*. The human monsters in *Bag of Bones* are no less grotesque than their counterparts in earlier stories; their victims no less innocent and despairing. But the important difference is that here, King's obvious concern for social justice is integrated with his equal (and perhaps even more critical) concern for telling the story—and through the act of storytelling, effecting rather than asserting or demanding change, he becomes even more an advocate of change.

The linked deaths themselves begin to form a pattern; and at the center of the pattern stand Noonan, Mattie Devore and her daughter Ki, Mattie's malevolent father-in-law William Devore (readers who might see a resemblance between "Devore" and "devour" are reading the novel correctly), and, inexplicably at first, two dead women: Michael's wife, Johanna, and Sara Tidwell. As the story progresses, as Michael becomes more involved in protecting Mattie and Ki from Devore's predacious attempts at gaining custody of his granddaughter, regardless, apparently of *any* cost in money, lives, morality, and dignity; as Sara Laughs becomes more and more the center of supernatural occurrences—as the dead past impinges with greater and greater deadliness on the living present, the pattern clarifies.

At that point, King moves into his most overt statement of theme in *Bag of Bones*. The past is not dead; perhaps it can (and should?) *never* die. As the biblical injunction states, "The sins of the fathers . . . ," and in the world of *Bag of Bones* those sins become explicit and living, with disastrous consequences. It is as if King is saying (and I think he is) that for any society— whether one as insular and self-contained as the community around Sara Laughs, or as expansive and diverse as late-twentieth-century America itself—for any society, the sins of the past will not and cannot simply lie forgotten, buried as it were in an unmarked grave beside a green and living tree. Instead, those sins—variously identified in *Bag of Bones* as vicious racism, rampant sexism, untrammeled violence, unbridled lust, greed, betrayal, deceit—not only survive their perpetrators but continue on to infect, at times to kill, generation after generation. Here King makes his strongest argument for justice, for equality, for humanity—and makes it paradoxically not by merely illustrating a case history but by telling a story . . . a ghost story, a monster story.

At heart, then, *Bag of Bones* is about humanity, about the bag of flesh and bones that encompasses each of us and links us with past and future. It is a *generational* story in several senses. Noonan's ability to generate, whether it be novels or children, remains much in doubt; William Devore, on the other hand, has generated too much—too much wealth, too much power, too much greed and ambition, and, ironically, too many children. One of his sons is gay and will never generate children; another is dead and yet has given life to Ki. Not content with enjoying his role as grandparent, Devore wants to possess—metaphorically *devour*— Ki; and, we discover eventually, there are several senses in which his compulsion to devour ceases being purely metaphorical. Other local families face similar problems in generating lasting progeny—and we are reminded again and again of the childless adults of *It* and of that novel's close identification of adult responsibility with adult generation.

Bag of Bones is also generational in that it talks about, illustrates, illuminates, and at times embodies the generative power of fiction and fiction making. As occurred in *The Dark Half*, here the writer breaks through his writer's block at the same time as his world inexorably disintegrates. Writing and living, literature and biography, become intertwined, at times interchangeable, and it is only part of the enjoyment of *Bag of Bones* that the story Michael Noonan tells resurrects an earlier King character named Ray Garraty. But at the end of *Bag of Bones,* the connections between life and fiction are given greater clarity than occurs in *The Dark Half,* and they are simultaneously shown to be further apart than one might expect.

Noonan's novel, we discover, is more important as a key to understanding than it is to helping him maintain his position and prestige as a best-selling writer, even though he is himself unable to realize this simple truth until almost too late. His identity, which at the beginning of *Bag of Bones* seems inescapably connected to his ability to write, develops in unexpected directions, leaving him more emphatically human and humane.

By the end of King's novel, Noonan has discovered that *his* novel is ultimately untrue to life—the best character he might create, King says, is as empty as a bag of bones. The final pages of *Bag of Bones* suggest that what King is doing—what he has done with exquisite skill for the past quarter century and more—is important . . . but there are things more important. With any other writer, the closing paragraphs of *Bag of Bones* could almost stand as a farewell to the art and craft of writing itself, to a literal closing of a career. Noonan has learned to allow people into his life more completely than he ever could before, and he in turn has entered their lives himself. This interplay, he decides, is far more important than creating yet more bags of bones to be manipulated—and frequently destroyed merely to meet the contingencies of narrative structure—in the pages of a book.

Yet at the same time, King is also asserting the critical importance of the act in which he is engaged: storytelling. It seems unlikely that *Bag of Bones* will be his swan song. He is committed, if nothing more, to completing the *Dark Tower* series; and there is little in his past to suggest that he would be willing to simply give up writing. But it would not be surprising if *Bag of Bones* pointed to a shift in direction for King, as it does for his fictional author. The monsters—both human and supernatural—are sublimated to story, and in this way, King asserts triumphantly that whatever monsters may lie in the past, whatever loss and grief and death and sorrow colors the past, the future lies in human ties, human relationships, and human love.

"The Ballad of the Flexible Bullet"
(collected in *Skeleton Crew*)

Originally published in *F&SF* (1984), the title is taken from Marianne Moore, who, according to the story's narrator, used the phrase "flexible bullet" to describe "some car or other." But he feels it "described the condition of madness very well. Madness is a kind of mental suicide. . . . Madness is a kind of flexible bullet to the brain."

In this story, one character asks another what the plot of "The Flexible Bullet" is—a story submitted by the best-selling novelist Reg Thorpe to *Logan's* magazine—and the acquiring editor replies, "It was just a story about a young man gradually losing his struggle to cope with success. It's better left vague. A detailed plot synopsis would only be boring. They always are."

That's very much the case here, since a straightforward summary sounds fantastic, even ludicrous—but King pulls it off: The purchase order to buy Thorpe's story is returned, on the grounds that the magazine is closing out the fiction department. The fiction editor, who by then has been engaging in rounds of correspondence with Thorpe and his wife as well, descends slowly into madness, gripped by alcoholism. Meanwhile, Thorpe has become increasingly suspicious of the anonymous "they" who he believes are at the center of a great conspiracy to control him. His only ally is a good-luck elf, a Fornit named Rackne who lives in his typewriter.

As Thorpe is humored, reinforcing the notion that Fornits do indeed exist, the editor loses his grip on reality and in short order loses his job at the magazine, and his apartment, and comes close to going insane.

The editor gets a cryptic message typed by the Fornit in his typewriter ("rackne is dying it's the little boy jimmy thorpe doesn't know tell thorpe . . ."), precipitating a telegram to Thorpe, who takes it quite seriously: He promptly goes out to buy a .45 automatic and two thousand rounds of ammo to protect his Fornit from all comers at his house.

When Thorpe returns home, he goes to his study, where he sees Jimmy, the son of the cleaning lady, shooting death rays into the typewriter

with his toy ray-gun, killing the Fornit, splattering its blood inside the typewriter.

Reg Thorpe then opens fire—his wife, the cleaning lady, and her son are the targets—and then shoots himself in the head.

Bangor Daily News (BDN)

King's hometown newspaper, the largest in Maine, in which numerous stories and photos about King, op-ed pieces by him, and miscellaneous articles and profiles on the Kings have appeared in print over the years.

Unlike some best-selling writers haunted by the local print media, King's relationship with the local newspaper seems to be an amicable one, though he did take exception to how they continually misspelled his name, an error they corrected after he set them straight: "My Lord! I've been living here in Bangor for five years now, and I'm still Steven King to your writers and copy editors. If you don't stop pretty soon, I'm going to spell the name of your newspaper *The Banger Dailie Noos* in my next novel." (Letter to the editor, *BDN*, Feb. 13, 1985).

Bangor International Airport

The film location of "The Langoliers" (from *Four Past Midnight*). Though BIA is a modern jetport used for transatlantic layovers, getting to BIA from points within the U.S. usually requires flying in on a small prop plane.

On occasion, King rents a private jet out of BIA for out-of-state speaking engagements. Otherwise, he would have to fly to Boston or New York, then connect to another flight; but even in first class, he'd be accosted by celebrity-struck strangers wanting autographs or conversation.

Bangor Public Library

The hometown library, one of the oldest and best in New England, for which the Kings pledged $2.5 million of $8.5 million needed for its renovation and expansion. The city of Bangor kicked in $2.5 million, and the balance was raised from the

King answers questions at the end of a talk in Bangor, Maine, at the civic auditorium—a fundraiser for the Bangor Public Library. © 1997 by the *Bangor Daily News*

citizenry through fund-raising efforts, with Tabitha King as the committee's chairperson. Built in 1912, the building needed extensive work to repair the structure itself and needed to expand to meet the needs of the community. Plans are to add a 30,000-square-foot addition at the rear of the building, principally to house a large children's room, and a 150-person auditorium as well.

Tabitha King, who attended Bangor's John Bapst High School, was an early patron of the library. According to the *BDN,* she "grew fond" of it. "I remember being very impressed with this library," she said.

Bangor State Armory

The production company for *Pet Sematary* used the National Guard Armory, located on lower Maine Street, as a staging area during its stay in the city.

Bangor Symphony Orchestra

To benefit the orchestra, bids were accepted until midnight, April 24, 1998, for the opportunity to be a character in a future King novel or short story.

Bangor West All Stars

A Little League team on which King's son Owen played. Stephen King was an assistant coach. On August 5, 1989, the team won the Maine State Little League Championship, in an 11–8 victory. Owen, normally used as a first baseman, was a relief pitcher in the championship game.

For a detailed accounting of the team's ascent to glory, see "Head Down" in *Nightmares & Dreamscapes.* For a special treat, listen to the unabridged recording on the audiocassette version, read by King himself.

Bare Bones: Conversations on Terror with Stephen King,
edited by Tim Underwood and Chuck Miller

Published by Underwood-Miller in 1988, this collection of 25 profiles and interviews was loosely organized into seven chapters. It was the first of

several interview compilations with King material to be published by the firm.

Confusion resulted in the book trade when R. R. Bowker listed it as a book *by* King instead of a book *about* King, precipitating a flurry of concerned inquiries from King's readers, who were scared that they might have missed a new King book.

Compilations like this tend to be repetitious, but the real problem is that without an index, it's impossible to find anything.

The quality of interviews varies, from filler material to the excellent *Playboy* piece, but because King didn't edit the interviews, factual errors, redundancies, misspellings and inconsistencies are scattered throughout.

Contents
1. Skeletons in the Closet
2. Building Nightmares
3. Terror Ink
4. Hollywood Horrors
5. Partners in Fear
6. Dancing in the Dark
7. The Bad Seed

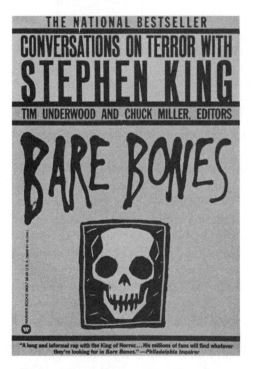

The cover to the trade paperback edition of *Bare Bones,* the first collection of King interviews, compiled by Tim Underwood and Chuck Miller.

Barker, Clive

A multitalented British writer-artist-playwright–turned–movie director now living in Los Angeles, Barker burst upon the literary scene with *Books of Blood*, inspired by Kirby McCauley's *Dark Forces*.

In an introduction to *Clive Barker's Shadows in Eden* (edited by Stephen Jones), King recounts his lackluster memories of being stuck in New Haven, Connecticut, the site of the 1983 World Fantasy Convention.

At that convention, the buzz was about Barker and *Books of Blood*.

The following year, when the King was in England, he bought the book at the bookstore Forbidden Planet in London and got hooked with that first fix. Of it he said, "Never—never—in my life have I been so completely shaken by a collection of stories." He has also said, "After reading Clive Barker, I felt the way Elvis Presley must have felt the first time he saw the Beatles on Ed Sullivan. . . . You read him with a book in one hand and an airsick bag in the other. That man is not fooling around. He's got a sense of humor, and he's not a dullard. He's better than I am now. He's a lot more energetic." (Quoted in *Time* magazine.)

Barker and King inevitably met, minutes before they appeared together on *Good Morning America*, unimaginatively double-billed as the king and crown prince of horror, on May 5, 1987.

After commenting that most horror is old-fashioned, Barker responded to an interviewer's question as to whether or not he considered King to be old-fashioned: "King is not old-fashioned. He is contemporary because he describes a real world. I'd say that old-fashioned horror lacks immediacy. King is a very immediate writer. I aim to be an immediate writer. We want our depictions to appear in the reader's mind with the clarity of a movie—that's part of our modernity. I want my images to be flashing—you know, wham! wham! wham!—whereas Poe and Lovecraft create a distance between the reader and the image. The experience is safer. You're detached." (Quoted in Murray Cox, "The Arts: Books," *Omni*, date unknown.)

Barker has also written about King. In "King: Surviving the Ride," Barker writes of his "substantial enthusiasm for the work of King" and explains his thesis that King is "the architect of the most popular ghost-train rides in the world" because, in the end, "he's selling death. He's selling tales of blood-drinkers, flesh-eaters, and the decay of the soul; of the destruction of sanity, community and faith."

A thoughtful piece from one of the most imaginative British writers in the fantasy field, Barker's essay is a studious but not academic explication of King's virtues as a writer, showing Barker's love and appreciation not only for the horror field but his obvious affection for King's fiction as well. "Anyone who is interested in the horror genre has to have some interest in King's work," he comments. "Steve has reshaped the genre in the sense that he's made it accessible to readers who would never otherwise pick up a horror book. It opened up a huge, new market to us all. And he's a superb and accessible storyteller." (*The Larry King Show*, May 6, 1987.)

Baseball

King has been involved in baseball, a lifelong passion, as a fan, a Little League coach, an assistant to a Little League team that went on to win the state championship in Maine (see "Head Down"), and an ardent Red Sox fan (King roots for the underdogs).

For the city of Bangor, King constructed a baseball field in the park behind his house, affectionately termed "the field of screams" by locals, though its formal name is the Shawn Trevor Mansfield Complex. Intended for Little League baseball games, the field is in heavy use during the spring and summer.

Bates, Kathy

Actress who won Oscar for Best Actress in 1990 for her performance as Annie Wilkes in *Misery*.

Also appeared as Dolores Claiborne in the movie made from King's novel of that name.

Kathy Bates: "I've admired King's work over the years, but I'm not a horror devotee. I read metaphysics and Jung and occasionally, Clive Barker. I'm an eclectic reader. . . . After this film, it'll start again. More Norman Bates references, and *People* magazine will refer to me as Kathy 'Misery' Bates. Everybody wants to type you. There's a human urge to pigeonhole. It's just rampant in Hollywood." (Quoted in Glenn Lowell, "'Psycho' Jokes Aside, Actress Kathy Bates Refuses to Be Typecast," *Daily Press*, Dec. 8, 1990.)

Bath Family Crisis Services

The Kings donated $50,000 on Christmas Eve to this shelter for abused women and children in Bath, Maine. The unexpected gift was the best kind of Christmas present for the shelter, the Bath Family Crisis Services director said. "We started dancing around and hugging each other in the office. That's how huge a gift it was for us."

Bathroom

When asked by the *New York Post* where he got his ideas, King cited the bathroom, because, as Stephanie Leonard has pointed out, "he takes hypertension medicine and spends a lot of time there!" (*Castle Rock*, June 1985)

Batman: The Dark Knight Returns,
by Frank Miller

SK: "Probably the finest piece of comic art ever to be published in a popular edition."

"Battleground" (collected in *Night Shift*)

Originally published in *Cavalier* (September 1972), this is a revenge story that predates the use of animated toy soldiers in Disney's *Toy Story* by over two decades.

John Renshaw makes a hit, on Hans Morris, the founder of the Morris Toy Company. The hit is successful, but now the tables are turned: Renshaw receives a package from Morris's wife, a "G.I. Joe Vietnam Footlocker," the kind of green toy soldiers sold in the back pages of comic books.

The soldiers were sent on a mission: To kill Renshaw, and use their miniaturized munitions to complete the hit and finish off Renshaw with a thermonuclear device.

BBC

Abbreviation for the British Broadcasting Company. On February 20, 1997, the BBC aired a radio dramatization of *Pet Sematary*.

"Beachworld" (collected in *Skeleton Crew*)

Originally published in *Weird Tales* (1985), this story has the trappings of science fiction but is in fact a horror story: FedShip *ASN/29*, with its crew of three, crashes on an alien world. Of the three crew members one dies in the crash, another struggles to survive, holding on until the rescue beacon can bring another ship, and the third goes slowly crazy, literally consumed by, and consuming, the sand of which this dunelike world is composed.

Beahm, George

A writer who, in the finest tradition of the creepazoid, specializes in writing about Stephen King's life and work, including *The Stephen King Companion* (1989); *The Stephen King Story* (1991); *The Stephen King Companion* (1995, version 2.0); and *Stephen King: America's Best-Loved Boogeyman* (1998). Also publishes an unofficial King newsletter, *Phantasmagoria*.

In response to a query from a fan who was wondering why SK does not care for George Beahm, Peter Straub responded: "I am treading on dangerous ground here, so will have to watch my step, but I'd like to offer a few thoughts. It was my general impression that Steve King maintained a sensible abhorrence of those useless & parasitic folks who tried to make money or a name for themselves by trailing after him, however idolatrously, and sorting out the crumbs he happened to drop. The books were what mattered, not trivia. From a posting I read here [at alt.books.stephen.king, on the Internet] about King's use of my childhood history in *It*, Beahm's remarks have not always been strictly accurate. But besides that, just try to imagine how you would feel about any person who in effect spent a great deal of time rummaging through your garbage and peering into your windows with magnifying glasses. And King is from Maine, a state where people have a highly developed sense of privacy."

Bedtime stories

According to Tabitha King, when their children were young Stephen King read them bedtime stories, often improvising and using different voices. *See also* LIVING WITH THE BOOGEYMAN.

Beer

A favorite King beverage, though in recent years he's drinks "lite" beer.

Being edited

As King readily points out, being a best-selling author means that there's a reluctance to tinker with the story. As King told Lynn Flewelling (*BDN*, Sept. 11, 1990), "At this point, nobody can make me change anything. It's like where does a 10,000 pound gorilla sit? The answer is anyplace he wants."

Benefits

In conjunction with AM radio station WZON, King sponsored an advance showing of *Creepshow II* on May 14, 1987, to raise money for the American Red Cross local flood relief effort. Two shows were screened at the Bangor Cinema 8, raising thousands of dollars to help Bangorians who were hard hit by a March 1987 flood.

King made an appearance in front of the audience at both showings, thanking them for their support, and urging them to dig deeper, to donate more.

Bestsellasaurus rex

According to King, he became "a big, stumbling book-beast that is loved when it shits money and hated when it tramples houses." A metaphor for how the booksellers see him, the term appeared in "The Politics of Limiteds—Part II," a King essay that to date has appeared only in *Castle Rock* (July 1985 issue).

Best-sellers of the '80s

In a list of the top twenty-five fiction bestsellers of the eighties, compiled by *Publishers Weekly*, King had seven titles:

The Dark Half No. 2. (1.5 million sold)

The Tommyknockers No. 3. (1.4 million)

It No. 10. (1.1 million)

Misery No. 15. (875,000)

The Talisman No. 17. (830,000)

The Eyes of the Dragon No. 22. (750,000)

Skeleton Crew No. 25. (720,000)

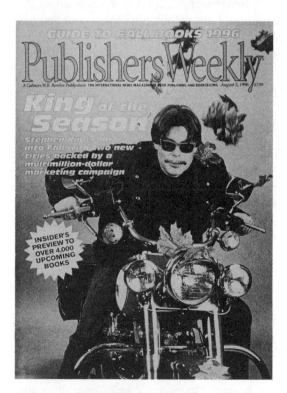

The cover to the fall announcements issue of *Publishers Weekly*, the journal for the book trade, which featured an interview/profile with King. (Note: King is astride a Harley.)

Betts Bookstore

A bookstore in Bangor, Maine, run by Stuart and Penney Tinker. The store is best known for its King offerings, notably its signed material and

Stuart Tinker, proprietor of Betts Bookstore in Bangor, Maine, awaits the imminent arrival of the SKE-MERs, an Internet King discussion group.

limited-edition books, and for being the place to find virtually anything by or about Stephen or Tabitha King. The bookstore mails out a regularly published newsletter, supplemented by a Web site.

Write to: 26 Main Street, Bangor, ME 04401
Phone: 207-947-7052
E-mail: *Bettsbooks@aol.com*
Web site: http://www.acadia.net/betts

"Big Wheels: A Tale of the Laundry Game (Milkman #2)"
(collected in *Skeleton Crew*)

Part of an aborted novel, *Milkman*, this vignette is classic King, evoking the small-town, blue-collar world that characterizes much of Maine: Rocky and Leo are out cruising, not for chicks, but for a place that will inspect Rocky's ailing Chrysler, due for a state inspection that it obviously cannot pass.

Rocky, as his name implies, has had a hard life, not the least of which is the time spent in the slammer. Spike, a milkman, not only cuckolds Rocky but knocks up his wife as well, which is why Rocky got a gun and went out looking for Spike, stopping only when the police got to him first and relieved him of his weapon.

Rocky's sidekick is Leo, who works with him at the New Adams Laundry.

Fortunately for Rocky, he stumbles across Bob's Gas & Service. It's Bobby Driscoll, an old acquaintance, whose own life is mired down in an endless nightmare of routine, trapped by his work and his marriage.

It's old times again when Rocky meets Bobby; they talk about happier times in the distant past, reinforcing Bobby's unhappiness with life in general and specifically his wife.

As Rocky and Leo head out, drunk on beer, a truck pulls out of a side road with the lights off. It's Spike Milligan, but *this* time he's off his route, making an unusual nighttime delivery. After he's made his delivery—scaring them shitless by his eerie appearance, causing them to crash into another car coming the other way—Spike decides to make a final delivery . . . to Bob Driscoll's house.

Bijou, by David Madden

This novel is "one of the books I admire most in the world," says King, who lamented in "The Guest Word" (*NYTBR*, Oct. 24, 1976) that Madden had made only $15,000 for his book, whereas King made considerably more on his novel *'Salem's Lot*, approximately $500,000.

Bishop, Jim

English professor at the University of Maine at Orono.

Bishop, Jim *continued*

Burton Hatlen: "Jim Bishop was the first person Steve King met on campus who was responsive to his work."

In "The Student King," Sanford Phippen writes: "Jim Bishop . . . remembers 'Steve's big physical presence' and how King was 'religious about writing.' He also remembers that King always had a paperback in his pocket, and knew all these authors that nobody else had ever heard of."

"Steve was a nice kid, a good student, but never had a lot of social confidence," Bishop added. "Even then, though, he saw himself as a famous writer and thought he could make money at it. Steve was writing continuously, industriously, and diligently. He was amiable, resilient, and created his own world."

Black Magic & Music

A benefit for the Bangor Historical Society, put on by King and Brad Terry & Friends of Jazz, at the Bangor House Ballroom on March 27, 1983, at which King talked about his new novel in progress, *Derry*, later titled *It*. The novel is set in a thinly disguised Bangor.

Blaze

Unpublished novel by King.

Completed on February 15, 1973, this 50,000-word psychological suspense novel was dedicated to King's mother.

A literary bounce of sorts off Steinbeck's *Of Mice and Men*, this novel tells the story of an infant kidnapping and the mildly retarded man, one of the two kidnappers, who comes to love the child.

Submitted to Doubleday simultaneously with *Second Coming*, the original title for *'Salem's Lot*, *Blaze* was wisely passed over in favor of *'Salem's Lot*, beginning the process of King's brand-name identification with the horror genre. See King's afterword to *Different Seasons* for his perspective.

"Blind Willie" (collected in *Six Stories*)

Originally published in *Anateus* magazine, this story was reprinted in this collection.

Bloch, Robert

A writer King has cited as a personal favorite, Bloch (1917–1994) was one of the dedicatees of *Danse Macabre*.

For the November 1994 issue of *Locus*, King wrote "Robert Bloch: An Appreciation." Others who wrote appreciations included Ray Bradbury, Peter Straub, Ramsey Campbell, Harlan Ellison.

"The Blue Air Compressor"

Originally published in *Onan* (January 1971), this story was heavily revised for its republication in *Heavy Metal* (July 1981).

Inspired by an E.C. Comics story, this is a one-note revenge tale of a wannabe writer, Gerald Nately, who writes about his landlady, Mrs. Leighton, a big, elderly woman. When she discovers the manuscript, though, she admits it's not "such a bad story" but disparages him, citing classic American writers who, she feels, would have been up to the task; she's too big a woman, too big a subject, for the likes of Nately!

Upset, he stuffs the hose of an air compressor into her mouth. Rapidly expanding, the already big Mrs. Leighton grows even bigger, then explodes.

Nately, whose ego has been deflated by Leighton, gets the last laugh.

Blue Oyster Cult

On a promo-only audiocassette release of this group's song "Astronomy," King contributed a forty-two-second introduction.

Blue, Tyson

A contributing editor to *Castle Rock*, columnist for *Cemetery Dance*, and author of *The Unseen King*.

Blurb

A blurb is a short quote solicited by the publisher from a big-name writer whose pithy and enthusiastic comments are prominently positioned on the covers to help sell the book. The bigger the name, the more valuable the blurb as a commercial commodity, which is why they're called "money quotes." King has written blurbs for numerous books.

The journalist Curt Suplee observed that King's blurbs are "both bankable and prolific."

King publisher Stuart Applebaum called King "one of the great blurb-meisters.... He's like a guy who says he's gonna quit smoking but always wants one last puff."

BMG Video

The original recording of "The Rock Bottom Remainders," performed at Cowboy Boogie in Anaheim, California, on May 25, 1992, became a collector's item after the videotape showed King improvising the lyrics to a song, prompting its publisher to force its removal for future printings.

"The Body" (collected in *Different Seasons*)

Dedication: "For George McLeod."

For King fans tired of hearing criticisms about King the Horror Writer Who Can't Write, it's "gotcha" time: When the uninitiated see *Stand by Me* on video, they are surprised to find that Stephen King wrote "The Body," on which *Stand by Me* was based. Surprise is usually followed by the realization that King *can* in fact write something other than supernatural fiction.

The plot: Four teenage boys from Castle Rock go off to find a young boy's dead body, hoping to get their fifteen minutes of fame by being the first ones to report it to the authorities.

What's really important in this rite of passage story is its careful, loving treatment of the four boys, their interaction—complete with profanity, accurately remembered by King—and their transition from boyhood (innocence) into adulthood (experience), recalled by the narrator, Gordon Lachance, who becomes a best-selling writer.

The most autobiographical story King has written to date, and a personal favorite of King's, it is in the first rank of his fiction.

This story's connection to King was deliberately downplayed in movie theaters where *Stand by Me* was being shown for fear that his name would scare potential moviegoers away. It was a justifiable concern, since by that time numerous film adaptations of King's books had been made, most of which were average, at best.

Bomb threat?

On 3:30 P.M., on a Sunday in June 1992, an unexpected package wrapped in brown paper was delivered to the Kings' home in Bangor. The package was addressed to King and bore an out-of-state return address.

The local bomb squad was alerted. Tabitha King and her dog were escorted off the premises, the neighbors' homes were also evacuated, and the street was closed off.

When Stephen King showed up, he assumed it was a book and told the squad members, "I bet you twenty-five bucks it's a book somebody dropped off. By all means, blow it up."

"The quick, brilliant explosion scattered pages over the Kings' lawn, and the charred remains of the book were collected by several police officers," reported the hometown newspaper.

A copy of the novel *It* had been destroyed—just as King predicted. ("Killed a book," *BDN*, June 29, 1992.)

Bones and hair of dead kittens

Shirley Sonderegger told Stephen Spignesi for *The Shape Under the Sheet* that this was the most bizarre "gift" King had ever received—a ghoulish gift from someone in Bangor. "Apparently, these people had cleaned out a barn somewhere and found these bones, and who did they think of to send them to but Stephen? I showed them to Steve and we both shuddered. It was absolutely disgusting. We threw the box in the trash."

Boogerheart, Chauncey

King said that he wished *The Talisman* had been published under this name instead of his own and Peter Straub's. The fake name, King said, would have prevented readers from trying to guess who wrote what.

"The Boogeyman" (collected in *Night Shift*)

Originally published in *Cavalier* (December 1972). A worried Lester Billings lies on the couch of Dr. Harper. Billings confesses that he is, by default, responsible for the death of his three children: He did, after all, leave the closet doors open at night, allowing the boogeyman that lived within to come out and kill them. Hardly a sympathetic character, Billings appears to be, and is in fact, the murderer of his own children—he, not some supernatural boogeyman, is a *real* boogeyman.

Dr. Harper, though, is also not what he seems either. In fact, the *real* boogeyman *is* Dr. Harper, who holds a human face mask in his "rotten, spade-claw hand."

BookMarc

A bookstore-café in Bangor, where Tabitha King was asked to read from her most recent novel as part of its program promoting local writers. Feeling left out, King suggested that he, too, give a reading. In a phone interview for the local newspaper, King said, "I just wanted to be a part of the reading. Sometimes I feel like I'm not a part of the cultural community, and I want to be. People just sort of drive around me and say, 'Well, he wouldn't want to do anything like that.'"

The reading was cozy—around 130 people—and, as King explained, "It's a relief to be reading for no other reason than to be reading." He read from *Six Stories*, "L.T.'s Theory of Pets," and from Stephen Dobyns's *Common Carnage*.

The reading was held in May 1997.

Books about King

Why read a book *about* King when you can read a book *by* King? Because you want to know the story behind the story. Here's what some of the players in this field have to say about this growing cottage industry, taken from Greg Gadberry's article, "All About Steve," Dec. 22, 1991.

Shirley Sonderegger, former King secretary: "We get a couple of requests a year for help [from authors writing about King]. Steve just sort of rolls his eyes and says he isn't interested."

Douglas E. Winter, author of the first and best book about King, *Stephen King: The Art of Darkness*: "I'm troubled by the feeling of profiteering you get when you sit down and look at the number of books and the nature of them."

Stuart Tinker, proprietor of Betts Bookstore: "Books on Steve do okay. By far the best-selling book on Steve is *The Stephen King Companion* [1989], which is the choice of most, even though it's somewhat dated. *The Stephen King Story* would sell much better with a different cover—people want a visual image. . . . The revised *Companion* should do very well, if you have a good photo on the cover similar to the current one, and it has some sort of banner proclaiming "New and Improved" in bold letters. . . . *Stephen King: Master of Horror* by Anne Saidman is a great little book about Steve and also sells very well: lots of pictures, inexpensive, with very accurate information. . . . The other books on King? They sell just so-so."

SK, in a letter Spignesi on hearing that Spignesi was writing *The Lost Work of Stephen King*: "[I am] less than thrilled to be on the market again not as a writer with a book but as the subject of a book—a commodity to be pawed over like used goods at a church rummage sale."

Boris

King's pet scorpion, deceased, February 5, 1985, given to him as a gift at a speaking engagement out West. Boris resided in a terrarium over his desk. After its death, Boris was encased in Lucite.

Boxers or briefs?

At "Reading Stephen King," a public talk, during the Q&A session that followed the reading, a young woman asked, "Boxers or briefs?"

King rightly ignored her question and picked another from the audience.

Box office grosses

Here is a representative sampling:

Misery, $54 million

Pet Sematary, $57 million

The Shawshank Redemption, $28 million

King's Sleepwalkers, $28 million
Needful Things, $15 million
Dolores Claiborne, $25 million
Stand by Me, $53 million
The Running Man, $39 million
Creepshow 2, $15 million

"The Breathing Method"
(collected in *Different Seasons*)

Dedication: "For Peter and Susan Straub."

It's December 23, 197–, and the narrator, a member of a gentlemen's club that meets at a brownstone in New York, attended by a seemingly ageless butler named Stevens, tells about the breathing method (Lamaze method), and the unusual circumstances under which Miss Stansfield gives birth.

The only supernatural story in *Different Seasons*, the story is effective, appropriately chilling—a counterpoint to the coziness of the brownstone, with its fireplace and the words IT IS THE TALE, NOT HE WHO TELLS IT above it—and an appropriately macabre note with which to end this quartet of classic King stories.

Bred Any Good Rooks Lately?,
by James Charlton

This compilation of shaggy-dog stories, published by Doubleday, contained King's story, "For the Birds."

Bridgton, Maine

Small city in southern Maine where the Kings lived. Their address, RFD 2, Kansas Road, Bridgton, ME 04009, figured prominently in "The Mist."

Briggs, Joe Bob

Drive-in movie critic who thinks King's horror flicks are ideal drive-in fare. At the Third Annual Drive-in Movie Festival and Custom Car Show, Briggs presented King with the Joe Bob Briggs Lifetime Achievement Award, an engraved hubcap

that, according to Stephanie Leonard, hung over one of King's johns at the house. Hubcap-fu.

Bright, David

A classmate of King's in college, currently a staffer at the *Bangor Daily News*.

Bright edited the UMO newspaper, for which King wrote an opinion column, "The Garbage Truck." In an interview with George Beahm, David Bright shed light on King: "I was the student editor from 1969 to April 1970. I told him, 'Steve, you're more than welcome to write a column. My rules are that it's got to be here Tuesday at noon, and it has to fit the space. . . . He'd show up and type it. . . . Everybody wonders: How did King make it? There are really only three qualities: He's got a great imagination, he's one hard-working sonofabitch, and he's brilliant. There's no real magic to it, he's just good at what he does. . . . I personally think that if he wasn't an author, he'd be the world's greatest computer programmer, because he can carry around those things in his head. Most people are capable of remembering only seven things at one time, but he can carry around many more details than that. . . . The man devours literature. Whether it's music or a performance or writing, he takes great care in reading things and he's got an amazing mind for detail. He is certainly not someone writing from a vacuum; he's a world citizen."

Brodie, Deborah

Editor at Viking who edited *The Eyes of the Dragon*, recommending minor changes for consistency and clarification. Most significantly, she urged King to flesh out the references to Ben in the book, which prompted him to write a new scene about a three-legged sack race.

Brody Agency, Inc.

A Florida-based firm retained by King's Zone Corporation to license nationally "Lists That Matter," five-minute vignettes of King's personal perspectives on the best and worst things in our culture.

Twenty lists were recorded, airing initially on WZON, but few if any were syndicated nationally.

Christopher Spruce: "Taken individually, or as a whole, the *Lists* are not only amusing, witty, and humorous in the fashion that only a King can create and deliver, but they are often thought-provoking. More than anything else, *King's Lists That Matter* are lighthearted commentaries about the modern American scene by one of this country's foremost fiction writers and best-known baby boomers." (*Castle Rock.*)

"Brooklyn August"
(collected in *Nightmares & Dreamscapes*)

A baseball poem by King.

Brown, Julie

Singer who did a takeoff on *Carrie* for her music video, *Homecoming Queen's Got a Gun.*

Brown, Lance

Artist who combined Tabitha King's photo of King (from the dust-jacket photo of *The Dark Half*) with the full text (7,000 words) of "The Rainy Season." The prints were issued in two states: a signed state of 100 prints, at $100 each, signed by Brown and both Kings; and an unsigned state of 50 prints, at $50 each.

Browne, Ray

The founder-chairman of Bowling Green State University's popular culture department, who in 1987 cited King as one of the people in the field worth keeping an eye on: "I'm interested in King and what he's doing and how he's getting away with it. He seems to be a guru on everything."

Brunswick High

High school in Brunswick, Maine, where David King, Stephen's brother, attended high school.

Budrys, Algis

Book critic who reviews for *The Magazine of Fantasy & Science Fiction*. Of King, in the special King issue (Dec. 1990) of *F&SF*, Budrys said: "And once in a while—once in a great while, but then, for most of us it happens not at all—he is obviously among those of whom it can be said, in a careless moment, that he is sometimes as good a writer as there is alive. . . . Most of all, I think that trapped inside King is one of the finest writers of our time. . . . Most of all, I think he has done an almost unthinkable thing; he has not narrowed down, but rather has expanded the definition of what he is as a writer, to the point where he can say, as no one else can, that he has tried everything, and made it work in some sense."

Buick Special

The 1965 car the Kings owned when they lived in Hermon, Maine. Tabitha King called it their "piece-of-shit Buick" in her introduction to the Collectors Edition of *Carrie*. Years later, after they had become successful, they bought matching Mercedes.

Burnt Offerings, by Robert Marasco

Novel that influenced King's *The Shining*, as the editors of *Horror: 100 Best Books* pointed out: "Marasco's novel has many of the same ingredients as King's *The Shining*, but it is a quieter work, though no less chilling."

Cain, James

Suspense writer specializing in crime fiction who wrote, among other books, *The Postman Always Rings Twice.* SK: "The book which has influenced me most, without question, is a book by James Cain called *The Postman Always Rings Twice.* It's a book that every person who wants to write should be required to read. It's 128 pages long, and it just picks you up on the first page and you're yanked along. You can't stop. It's like a textbook with style and characterization, particularly in pace." (*Presumpscot Review,* 1977.)

"Cain Rose Up" (collected in *Skeleton Crew*)

Originally published in *Ubris* (spring 1968), the UMO literary magazine, this short story, written while King was writing his Bachman novels, echoes the frustration many students felt at the time, symbolized by Charles Whitman's sniper attack at a college campus from his perch atop the University of Texas tower. Foreshadowing "Apt Pupil," the story is eerily prescient: Modern-day life has become sufficiently frustrating for the term "going postal" to have become part of our lexicon, and road rage, often vented by gunfire, has become a way of life.

In numerous interviews, King has talked about the phobic pressure points of contemporary life—in short, the horrors of everyday life—saying that horror fiction is his vehicle for exploring those points.

California Book Auction Gallery

At this auction gallery's 230th sale, held on May 24, 1986, in San Francisco, King's books drew record sums, including $2,250 for an asbestos-bound *Firestarter,* one of 26 lettered copies.

In spring 1998, an asbestos-bound copy of *Firestarter* sold at an auction for $11,000.

Cameo appearances by King in films and on TV

♦ In *Creepshow,* King is Jordy Verrill in "The Lonesome Death of Jordy Verrill."
♦ In *Creepshow 2,* King is a truck driver.
♦ In *Golden Years,* King is a bus driver.
♦ In George Romero's *Nightriders,* Stephen King is Hoagie Man, and appears with Tabitha King.
♦ In *The Langoliers,* King is Tom Holby.
♦ In *Maximum Overdrive,* King is an unnamed man who, at a bank ATM, is rudely insulted by the machine, which flashes: *Fuck You.*
♦ In *Pet Sematary,* King is the minister presiding over Gage Creed's funeral.
♦ In *The Shining* (ABC-TV version), King is Gage Creed, the leader of the Gage Creed Band, that plays at the Overlook.
♦ In *Sleepwalkers,* King is an unnamed cemetery caretaker.
♦ In *The Stand,* King is Teddy Weizak.
♦ In *Thinner,* King is Dr. Bangor.

"Cannonball Cannon"

King's alter ego. A daredevil, King's alter ego gave him the power trips that he needed while growing up, which he attributed to not having his father around. "When I was twelve I was fat. I wore thick glasses. My mother made me get a crewcut every summer—I looked like a fat kraut just waiting to join the Hitler youth. I'd walk down the street and these guys would say, 'Hey there goes that fat Stevie King. Let's go beat him up!' So you'd walk around and if you had any imagination at all you'd think to yourself, 'One day, boy, I'm gonna get you down and I'm gonna punch the shit out of you, kid.'" (*Presumpscot Review*, 1977.)

Captain Trips

A virulent superflu that destroys most of the world in *The Stand*. King's trial cut on Captain Trips was "Night Surf," which originally appeared in *Ubris* but was revised heavily for its appearance in *Cavalier* in 1974.

Carpenter, John

The director of *Christine*. Carpenter had made a name for himself directing such films as *The Fog* and *The Thing* in the horror field and the action adventure films *Escape from New York* and *Big Trouble in Little China*, both starring Kurt Russell; and *Starman*.

Though Carpenter's adaptation of *Christine* is faithful to the book, the summer movie was perceived as a fast, fun ride, but clearly not standout material.

Carrie

Hardback, 1974, 199 pages, Doubleday, $5.95
Dedication: "This is for Tabby, who got me into it—and then bailed me out of it."
Contents:
  Part I. Blood Sport King
  Part II. Prom Night King
  Part III. Wreckage
Main character: Carietta (Carrie) White, student

King drew heavily on his memories of high school, reinforced by his two-year stint at Hampden Academy, to accurately re-create the caste world of high school, with its jocks and cheerleaders and student council members on one side, and the eggheads, plain Janes, and nerds on the other.

The character of Carrie White was modeled after a young girl who lived down the street from King when he lived in Durham, Maine. In a later

interview, King said that she had married a man as odd as she was, had kids, and eventually killed herself.

Those unfamiliar with his writing history mistakenly assume his first *published* novel was the first one he wrote, but the truth is that *Carrie* was his sixth novel, written on a portable typewriter that belonged to Tabitha King. Originally intended as a short story for *Cavalier*, the short novel was aborted by King, who threw the first five pages into the trash. Fortunately for him, his wife, Tabitha, fished them out, read them, and said, "Keep going. I think it's really terrific." Her story is told in detail in an introduction to *Carrie*, the Collectors Edition, published by Plume in 1991.

The result: a novel about high school hell, focusing on Carrie White, an ugly duckling who

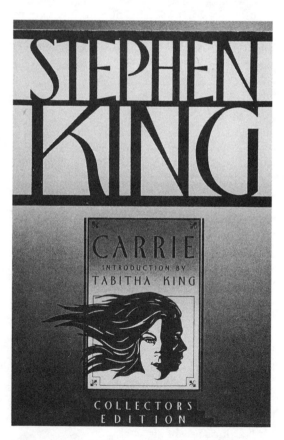

Cover to *Carrie* (collectors edition from Plume). The first book in a series that was to collect all of King's books in a uniform size and design. The series died after five books.

turned, briefly, into a swan but in the end could not escape her humble origins. In the beginning of the novel she is pelted with sanitary napkins, and, at the end of the novel, she is doused with pig's blood after being crowned prom queen on prom night.

The horror element is Carrie's ability to force objects to move by her mental will. This "wild talent," as it's called, would show up in various forms in other children who would figure prominently in King's fiction.

An impressive literary debut, as Douglas E. Winter pointed out in *Stephen King: The Art of Darkness*, the novel sold 13,000 copies in hardback but went on to sell a million copies as a mass-market paperback in its first year.

Adapted as a motion picture and a Broadway production, *Carrie* in fact carried King back to his roots—from his rented trailer in Hermon to a second-story walk-up in Bangor, Maine.

Bottom line: This is a fan favorite and after all these years still holds its own as a riveting story in its own right and an undeniably sympathetic portrayal of an unfortunate girl who from the beginning would never fit in.

King, in his essay "On Becoming a Brand Name," said, "I persisted because I was dry and had no better ideas. . . . My considered opinion was that I had written the world's all-time loser."

The original advance for the book was $1,500, but William Thompson, an editor at Doubleday, convinced the publisher to up it to $2,500, a very respectable advance for a first fiction work in 1973.

In its press release accompanying the book, written by Thompson, Doubleday hit the nail on the head: "We hope that *Carrie* will excite you as much as it has us. A tremendously readable ESP novel, it is also a quietly brilliant character sketch of a young and unusual girl trying to find her way out of a very personal hell. We think *Carrie* and King have a bright future, and we welcome this chance to share both of them with you."

Carrie was published on April 5, 1974, in a first print run of approximately 30,000 copies to generally good reviews, though most reviewers assumed it was a first novel.

SK: "At the time *Carrie* got published, I was teaching school and I'd come home and write for an hour and a half, and I felt like sort of a heel be-cause my wife was taking care of the kids, and I had all these homework papers in my briefcase that I was supposed to be correcting. I'd think, maybe what I'm doing here is being really selfish and pursuing this fool's dream. My wife was sort of submitting herself to my ambition. She's out there changing the shitty diapers and making supper—and maybe I ought to just give it up. I won't say I was serious about quitting, but I do think that if another two years had gone by I would have seriously considered shelving the whole thing." (*Presumpscot Review*, 1977.)

In a review for *Alumnus*, the alumni magazine of UMO, Burton Hatlen pointed out that this was King's *sixth*, not first, novel. Hatlen was on the mark when he wrote, "Few of our writers have such a clear sense of the demons that lurk within the American psyche. And if Steve's ability to project this vision continues to develop, he has every promise of becoming a major American writer."

What the reviewers said:

Library Journal: "This first novel is a contender for the bloodiest book of the year. . . . An interesting idea, but none of the characters is really very believable and the final orgy of destruction is terribly overdone. *Carrie* will provide a vicarious thrill for some, but cannot honestly be recommended."

Kirkus Reviews: "King handles his first novel with considerable accomplishment and very little hokum."

NYTBR: "So don't miss *Carrie*, by King (Doubleday, $5.95), a first novel and one guaranteed to give you a chill. . . .That this is a first novel is amazing."

Wilson Library Journal: "It's pure trash, but I loved it; young readers will love it—and they'll read it anyway after the movie appears."

Harlan Ellison: "I suppose my personal favorite is *Carrie*, which is not to say that he has not been better later, because I think *The Shining*, for instance, is a much better book. But *Carrie* is pure Stephen King. It is Stephen King before any self-consciousness, before any attention was paid. It's Stephen writing for himself." (From an interview in the 1989 edition of *The Stephen King Companion*.)

SK: "I'm not saying that *Carrie* is shit and I'm not repudiating it. She made me a star, but it was a young book by a young writer. In retrospect it reminds me of a cookie baked by a first-grader—tasty enough, but kind of lumpy and burned on the bottom." (At the conference at UMO, "Reading Stephen King.")

Carrie (film), 1976

King is fond of saying that he made *Carrie* and *Carrie* made him.

It's true of the book but even more true of the movie, since one of the fastest ways to build a book audience is to convert movie-goers into book readers—a technique that's helped make Michael Crichton, Tom Clancy, Anne Rice, and John Grisham brand names in the bookstore.

Though King's movies have been a mixed bag, *Carrie* is a standout, a film that has held up well over the years. Budgeted at under $2 million, the film was a top success: financially, returning $30 million; aesthetically, with Carietta White being drenched with pig's blood onstage on prom night; and as an ideal teen movie, tapping into the audience that made the book in paperback so successful.

At the time *Carrie* was made, however, there was no way to know just what kind of reception the film would get. Piper Laurie was, after all, the only name actress on the set. Sissy Spacek, Amy Irving, William Katt, Nancy Allen, and John Travolta were then unknowns, trying to make names for themselves in a cutthroat industry, trying to stay alive. Nancy Allen was also married to the director, Brian De Palma; they divorced years later.

In retrospect, it's safe to say that the principal audience may not have known, or cared, that Piper Laurie was a brand-name actress; they cared about the story, about an ugly ducking girl whose Cinderella fantasy turned into a nightmare. For teenagers who felt like outsiders who cheered for Carrie, this film hit a responsive chord . . . and they showed up in droves to see the film.

Despite the in-your-face shocker ending—standard operating procedure in a horror film for teenagers—*Carrie* the film is faithful to the book in tone, in plot, and in effect. The end result: *Carrie* was instrumental in launching the career of a

Cover to the film magazine *Cinefantastique*, showing Sissy Spacek as Carrie, drenched in pig's blood.

budding writer who would no longer have to call the phone company to tell them to remove the phone before service was interrupted.

Brian De Palma: "I read the book. It was suggested to me by a writer friend of mine. A writer friend of his, Stephen King, had written it. I guess this was [circa 1975]. I liked it a lot and proceeded to call my agent to find out who owned it. I found out that nobody had bought it yet. A lot of studios were considering it, so I called around to some of the people I knew and said it was a terrific book and I'm very interested in doing it." (Mike Childs and Alan Jones, "De Palma Has the Power," *Cinefantastique*.)

Carrie (musical), May 12–15, 1988

After 16 previews and five regular performances on Broadway at the Virginia Theater, *Carrie* shut down, losing more than $7 million and earning the distinction of being the most expensive flop in Broadway history.

Opening to devastating reviews from the *New York Times*, and savaged by other critics as well, the Royal Shakespeare Company production of *Carrie* soon gave up the ghost.

Terry Hands, the play's director and artistic director of the RSC: "Broadway is an exciting place, but it's like warfare. Don't expect to go without a helmet on. You know you're taking your life in your hands. . . . I didn't know what I was getting into. I don't know anything about the American musical. This is my first time. But all of us on the show have been incredibly, unbelievably inexperienced."

King, on opening night: "I liked it a lot. In fact, I liked it for most of the reasons that Frank Rich [*NYT* critic] did not. He and I saw the same show. We just drew different conclusions from different perspectives."

Linda Winer, *Newsday*: "Stupendously, fabulously terrible; ineptly conceived, sleazy, irrational from moment to moment, the rare kind of production that stretches way beyond bad to mythic lousiness."

Carrie's paperback rights sale

As per the Doubleday contract, for King's first paperback sale the firm retained half, and King got the rest.

David Bright, a reporter for the *Bangor Daily News* who wrote the first feature article written about King, pointed out that his newfound success brought a new dilemma: "Steve King can't quite make up his mind whether or not he should retire. For King, the book marks his first hit after three strikeouts in trying to break into the novel business. . . . His first rejection, along with a letter that perhaps he should try another field of endeavor, came that same year. King says teaching often takes up time he'd rather spend at writing."

Carrie telegram

The Kings had the phone removed before the phone company removed it for them, so when the news came that *Carrie* had been sold to Doubleday, they couldn't call him. Instead, William Thompson sent a telegram that read: CARRIE OFFICIALLY A DOUBLEDAY BOOK. $2,500 ADVANCE AGAINST ROYALTIES. CONGRATS, KID—THE FUTURE LIES AHEAD. BILL.

Cartier's

Upscale jewelry store in Manhattan. In the *Literary Guild* magazine (February 1977), Norman O'Connor reported that King had stopped off at the store to order a diamond engagement ring for Tabitha.

"I couldn't afford one at the time," King told an interviewer who asked why he had waited so long.

A Case of Need,

by Michael Crichton (writing as Jeffrey Hudson)

SK: "Fantastic . . . I loved it!"

A Casebook on "The Stand,"

edited by Tony Magistrale

Published by Starmont House in 1992, this was intended to be part of a series covering each of King's novels. A casebook on *The Shining* had been previously published, but no others saw publication, owing to the publishing house's demise in 1993.

Contents
Introduction

1. "'Almost Better': Surviving the Plague in Stephen King's *The Stand*," by Mary Pharr
2. "'I Think the Government Stinks!': Stephen King's *Stand* on Politics," by Douglas Keesey
3. "Stephen King and His Readers: A Dirty, Compelling Romance," by Brian Kent
4. "The 'Power of Blackness' in *The Stand*," by Leonard Cassuto
5. "Repaying Service with Pain: The Role of God in *The Stand*," by Leonard Mustazza
6. "Free Will and Sexual Choice in *The Stand*," by Tony Magistrale
7. "Choice, Sacrifice, Destiny, and Nature in *The Stand*," by Bernadette Lynn Bosky
8. "Dark Streets and Bright Dreams: Rationalism, Technology, and 'Impossible Knowledge' in Stephen King's *The Stand*," by Michael A. Morrison
9. "Dialogue Within the Archetypal Community of *The Stand*," by Ed Casebeer

Cash, Johnny

Country-western legend who, at concert in Bangor on October 30, 1988, was pleasantly surprised when King took to the stage and sang "Johnny Be Good." (*Castle Rock.*)

Castle Rock, Maine

The fictional town in Maine that put King on the literary map. The name of the town was derived from William Golding's *The Lord of the Flies*, one of his favorite novels. In *Needful Things*, King destroys the town by fire.

C Is for Castle Rock and Castle Schlock

Eleven years after King's first book was published, the official King newsletter, *Castle Rock*, began publication in January 1985; it ceased publication with its December 1989 issue.

Subtitled *The Stephen King Newsletter, Castle Rock*, named after the mythical town in Maine that helped put King on the literary map, was the brainchild of SK's sister-in-law, Stephanie Leonard, then King's main secretary. "*Castle Rock* will be a monthly newsletter and we will have, along with all the news, trivia, puzzles, reviews, classifieds, contests, and, we hope, readers' contributions," wrote Leonard.

The first issue was a home-brewed effort: letter size, six pages, its text set in a virtually unreadable typeface. Still, the demand for authoritative news on King proved to be irresistible, and its editor-publisher found subscribers who cheerfully paid $12 for a dozen issues.

By its fourth issue, the newsletter had turned into a professional-looking tabloid, designed by Christopher Spruce, King's brother-in-law, the station manager for radio stations WZON and WKIT, in Bangor.

In January 1989, Christopher Spruce took over editorship of the paper, but by year's end had decided to cease publication because he wanted to return to college to get a master's degree.

Unlike other publications, *Castle Rock* did not undertake any subscription drives, nor did it need to, for in-house ads in the mass market paperback editions of SK's books brought in thousands of subscribers—5,500 at its peak.

In his final editor's column, the editor-publisher, Chris Spruce, explained that he was "in a wistful sort of mood" and, pressed for time as usual, reminisced about the work and the joy that came of serving a body of readers that religiously read, and kept, each issue. "Rushing to haul the next issue together begins just about the time the previous issue rolled off the presses. It was always done in between this, that and the other thing. Sometimes it looked that way, too. For the most part, however, it seemed to come out all right. Your letters and cards over the years confirmed that impression."

Over the years at least one attempt was made to publish a facsimile reprint edition of the zine, but securing copyright permissions proved to be impossible, so the wealth of material by and about King remains in print only in back issues now eagerly sought on the secondary market.

Though others subsequently published zines about King, *Castle Rock* was unique, not only because it was the first, but because it had his blessings and insider access to information.

Stephanie Leonard: "Our goal is to keep you up-to-date on the work of this prolific writer."

Christopher Spruce: "There are some people out there who want a fanzine, but we are not interested in King's personal life; I don't feel it's a legitimate concern for us."

SK: "If you want straight stuff about me, subscribe to . . . *Castle Rock*." (*BDN*, letter to the editor, March, 1985.)

In contrast to *Castle Rock*, there was also *Castle Schlock*, a short-lived parody zine published by Ray Rexer, a Michigan policeman who felt his sense of humor about things King might help him through the difficult days, a sensibility shared by Leonard Norman, whom Rexer described as "not just your average Stephen King nut. He's like a Stephen King savant or something. He can't remember his own phone number, but he's never forgotten a single word of any Stephen King book he's ever read."

Rexer cranked up his personal computer and published the first issue, with a circulation of two copies—humble beginnings, recalling *Dave's Rag*, which was similarly published in a minuscule run. Rexer took the home-brewed effort to work, gave it to Norman, who read it, howled with laughter, and said, in the words of Leo, a King character from "Milkman #2," "This is better than getting a check in the mail! Bet your fur!"

Obviously, such a zine would have a very limited appeal, because not only would you have to know the original source inspiring the parody, *Castle Rock,* but you'd have to be conversant with the King allusions *and* appreciate Rexer's admittedly bizarre sense of humor and infectious enthusiasm for King's work.

It worked for me, and it worked for enough others who appreciated his efforts and urged him to publish more, more!

"*Castle Schlock* seems to appeal mostly to the person who's an accomplished Kingologist, a true kindred spirit, someone with a Ph.D. in Stephen King. There's a lot of inside jokes in the *Schlock* that only such a person could truly understand. For example, issue #1 mentions Stephen King's new cookbook, *Food Processor of the Gods*, an obvious take-off on a similarly named short story of King—but only to someone who's *in* on King. In another issue, a man named Art Denker advertises for sale in the classifieds three King limiteds: an asbestos-bound *Firestarter*, a leather-bound *Skeleton Crew*, and a "dead-cat" bound *Pet Sematary*. Now, this would be totally lost on someone who doesn't read King, and rightfully so—anyone who doesn't read King doesn't deserve to understand these things, and to heck with them! Let 'em go read an Updike book or something!" (The Updike allusion refers to a contributing editor of *Castle Rock* who wrote at length with complete seriousness a piece on the relative literary worth of John Updike and Stephen King—a comparison that made Maine writer Edgar Allen Beem blue.)

Here, then, is a small taste of *Castle Schlock*:

Stephen King's Face on Barn?

by "Annie Lynn Steffard"

Thousands of devoted fans have pilgrimaged en masse to J. Steven Spignesi's dairy farm in the small Michigan town of Castle Dune to view what is said to be a ghostlike image of Stephen King's face on the side of Spignesi's cow barn. Spignesi claims the face suddenly appeared one morning while he was shoveling the barn clean.

"I fell to the ground and wept," he said of his immediate reaction to the discovery, "right thar amongst the cow-floppies and all."

George Dusset, owner of the nearby Castle Dune market, said there was no doubt in his mind that the face was that of the popular author. "Just looking at that thing gives me the willies," he said. Mr. Dusset went on to say that his store now carries a full line of specialty souvenirs, including the fast selling I SURVIVED THE FACE T-shirt.

Although both Dusset and Spignesi swear that the image is authentic, another local resident claims it is nothing more than "one of them thar Smith brothers" from an old cough-drop ad showing through layers of faded and peeling paint. The resident declined to identify himself, saying mysteriously, "The pile of shit has a thousand eyes."

Well, I'd be happy to explain all the in-jokes in the excerpt above, but I'm laughing too hard to be able to type—barely. Suffice it to say that it's either very funny to you . . . or you're scratching your head, wondering what's the big joke?

"According to international parody laws" that prohibit further publication of such a zine after the original folded, *Castle Schlock* took a page from *Castle Rock* and ceased publication in December 1989, after five short issues.

The zine, wrote Rexer, "is low in saturated fats and completely safe when used as directed. Now what more could a person want in a parody newsletter?"

Not a thing, Ray, not a thing.

On April 26, 1991, Ray Rexer was killed in the line of duty.

The zine was missed, but Ray was missed even more . . . bet your fur.

Two issues of *Castle Rock*.

"The Cat from Hell" (uncollected)

This story is unusual for King because its original appearance in *Cavalier* included only the first 500 words; readers were to submit the rest of the story in a contest.

In June 1977 *Cavalier* published King's story in full, as well, making it a literary collaboration by contest.

Nye Willden, *Cavalier* editor, on the story's genesis:

> About "Cat from Hell," I came across this marvelous photo of a cat's face (from UPI, I believe) and half of it was black and the other half white. And it looked very intriguing. I thought up the idea of a short story contest to be based just on that photo. Then I thought how much more interesting it would be if Stephen would write just a short beginning to the story to kick off the contest and writers would then expand on it. So, I sent the photo off to Stephen and he wrote back shortly after, enclosing a complete short story titled "The Cat from Hell." "I can't write part of a story," he explained. "That would be like having half a baby. So, take part of the story for your contest and then perhaps you'd like to publish my story in its entirety later on as a comparison with your contest winners, or do whatever you wish with it," he wrote, which is what happened. We published the winning story, which was very good, and then the next month we published "The Cat from Hell" in its entirety.

Cat's Eye (film), 1985

Based on a screenplay by King, *Cat's Eye* is an anthology film, based on two stories from *Night Shift*, "Quitters, Inc." and "The Ledge," and an original story for the film, "The General."

Basically, there's usually no compelling reason to do an anthology film for theaters, since the individual features would be better suited for airing on television. I can readily see these three on a television show like *Night Gallery*, though with this trio of tales, only "The General" is horror-based; the other two are suspense stories.

"Quitters, Inc." is the story of a man who wants to quit smoking—at all costs. And, like the others who go to Quitters, Inc., for help, he must pay a price.

"The Ledge" is a suspenseful piece that hinges on a wager: An adulterous man is forced to walk the ledge, at night, of a high-rise apartment building. If he circumnavigates the building, he lives and is promised a bag of money and the girl.

"The General," with Drew Barrymore, is the only horror piece, with a troll-like creature that emerges from the wall to kill, sucking the life breath from its victims. The girl's cat, however, returns to save the day (and the girl, played by Barrymore), and the film ends.

The framing device: a cat that makes an appearance throughout the film, linking the disparate segments.

Gahan Wilson, cartoonist and writer: "The whole thing adds up to excellent entertainment, and I can't wait to see what King writes next for the movies, now that he's truly got the hang of it." (*Twilight Zone*, October 1985).

SK on its failure: "There are reasons for that which don't have anything to do with the movie. They have to do with the production end of it. At MGM, the whole top echelon of executives fell, and all the pictures that had been produced under those people became orphans. . . . There were no trailers, no publicity, and no promotion—that sort of thing." (Ben Herndon, "New Adventures in the Scream Trade," *Twilight Zone*, December 1985.)

Cavalier magazine

Men's magazine, otherwise undistinguishable from other such publications, except for the inclusion of King's early fiction and the artwork of the artist Vaughn Bode.

King's first sale was "Graveyard Shift," for which he earned $250. As per magazine policy, all rights were purchased, but subsidiary rights reverted to King on request of Nye Willden, *Cavalier*'s editor.

Since *Cavalier* is a cheesecake magazine with salacious ads, King couldn't send a photocopy to his mother of the story as is, so he carefully "blocked out all the ads for glossy photos and films" of young women in provocative poses, then made copies to send to his mother.

Celebrity

"Being famous sucks." (King, in an interview with *Mystery Scene* magazine.)

"The occupational hazard of the successful writer in America is that once you begin to be successful, then you have to avoid being gobbled up. America has developed this sort of cannibalistic cult of celebrity, where first you set the guy up, and then you eat him. It's happened to John Lennon; it has happened to a lot of rock stars. But I wish to avoid being eaten. I don't want to be anybody's lunch." (*Bare Bones,* 1988.)

Celebrity doodle

To benefit the Back Alley Theatre, King sent in a doodle that sold at auction for $225—the only known piece of published "art" by King, who readily admitted, in an introduction to a book collection of J. K. Potter's photographs, that he's no artist.

The cartoon shows a sun setting behind a tombstone bearing the words PLANET EARTH/ SOMEONE HIT THE WRONG BUTTON / JULY 11, 1992 / RIP. The sketch is dated June 23, 1987.

Center Lovell

A city in the lakes region of Maine where the Kings bought a 32-acre parcel, on Kezar Lake for $750,000.

Chain bookstores

The dominant players in the retail book trade: Barnes & Noble, Borders, Waldenbooks.

King, who is a staunch advocate of independent bookstores, now under siege from the superstores launched by the chains, generally does book signings and readings at independent stores, on the moral grounds that the larger stores don't need his physical presence to move the book. This was behind King's decision to support *Insomnia* on a coast-to-coast tour by stopping only at independents.

"As a writer, I love [chain stores], because they'll just wallpaper my books. . . . As a citizen, however, I feel the independent bookstore is a part of the downtown scene that makes every town unique." ("Spectacular Fall Performance," *PW,* "Bookwire," Aug. 5, 1996.)

C Is for Censorship

What's more obscene, pornography or censorship?

It depends on your perspective, of course, and that's why Stephen King and others who believe in free speech were up in arms when, in 1986, the Christian Civic League in Maine got the state legislature to put before the public a referendum banning pornography.

King is no stranger to censorship. At a public talk given in Virginia Beach, Virginia, on September 21, 1986, Kelly Powell introduced King and read off a short list of places where books by King had been banned between 1975 and 1986:

♦ Las Vegas, Nevada, where *Carrie* was challenged at the Clark High School Library as "trash"

♦ Vergennes, Vermont, where *Carrie* was placed on a special closed shelf in the high school library because it could "harm" students, especially "young girls"

♦ Rankin County, Mississippi, where *Cujo* was challenged because it was considered "profane and sexually objectionable"

♦ Bradford, New York, where *Cujo* was removed from the shelves of the school library "because it was a bunch of garbage"

♦ Campbell County, Wyoming, where *Firestarter* was challenged because of its alleged "graphic descriptions of sexual acts, vulgar language and violence"

♦ Washington County, Alabama, where *Christine* was banned from all school libraries because the book contained "unacceptable language" and was considered "pornographic"

♦ Hayward, California, where *The Shining* was removed from four junior high libraries because the book's "descriptive foul language" made it unsuitable for teenagers

Like questions about where he gets his ideas, the questions about book banning have become a staple in his life—so much so, in fact, that he feels he's been held up as a poster boy of sorts, as a representative contemporary author who routinely is banned, who must make a choice between writing his books or taking up a second career as an major figure in the anticensorship movement. He cites Judy Blume as an author who has gotten swept up in defending her books when, in his opinion, she should be writing more books.

In most cases, King is quick to point out his feelings on the matter: that you must exercise your right to make the decision on what you and your children should read, instead of letting someone *else* make that decision for you.

When it was clear that the hotly debated issue would be an all-out war, when on June 10, 1986, it was scheduled to go up for public vote in Maine, King *had* to get involved. This wasn't just another matter of one of his books being banned; this affected anything that could be construed (or misconstrued) as obscene.

King rolled up his sleeves and got to work. In a public radio debate that pitted him against the Christian League's Rev. Jack Wyman, in public-service announcements, in an editorial in the hometown newspaper, and in statements to the media, King made it very clear that he was adamantly opposed to the referendum. The road to hell, he pointed out in so many words, was paved with good intentions: Wyman *meant* well, but once the law was on the books, how could it be enforced in a fair and impartial manner without trampling on the rights of people who *chose* to read or view the kind of material Wyman adamantly opposed?

Even King's son, Joe, then 14 years old, wrote an op-ed piece for the hometown paper. In "Another Viewpoint," he wrote: "There are a few holes in the idea of an obscenity law. Unfortunately, these holes are big enough to drive Mack trucks through."

Reverend Wyman had his say, as well, in "Another Viewpoint," asserting that "hard-core and violent pornography debases and destroys lives, families and marriages. It is a cultural, social and moral blight. It lowers the entire tone of civility upon which a free republic depends. It exploits and threatens innocent women and children. The statewide law we have advanced . . . will not totally eliminate pornography in Maine nor will it end rape and child abuse, both of which have been linked to pornography. . . . Those charged with enforcing and interpreting the anti-obscenity law will, we believe, do so fairly, reasonably and with intelligent discernment."

As in all such controversies, the Christian League used as its theme, "Do It for the Children."

King felt differently, as did many others. Once a law is put on the books, it becomes a matter of interpretation for law enforcement officials, who must then enforce the letter of the law. The problem, of course, is that the *letter* of the law and the *spirit* of the law are two different things—a point that came into sharp focus when King, filming *Maximum Overdrive* in Wilmington, North Carolina, witnessed the chilling effects of an antipornography statute that took effect there in July 1985.

In the *Maine Sunday Telegram*, King urged its readers to "say 'no' to the Enforcers," because when the North Carolina statute became law, the moral climate had literally changed overnight: *Playboy* and *Penthouse* had been pulled from the shelves, covered in brown bags, and put behind the counter in a convenience store he frequented. "Nor was it just that one Zip Mart; the Porn Fairy had had a busy night. I did a check. All the girly magazines were gone from all the stores. The X-rated section of Wilmington's tape-rental stores had also disappeared. In some cases, R-rated tapes, such as Brian De Palma's *Body Double*, also disappeared."

The law was *intended* to make hard-core pornography illegal, but despite assurances from conservatives that the officials in charge of enforcement would do their job in an even-handed manner, the result was quite different: When King, at a Waldenbooks bookstore, asked a policeman going through calendars what he was looking for, the policeman replied, "Topless."

From hard-core porn to topless, to small store owners renting videos or selling men's magazines, anything that would raise an eyebrow was covered, put away, shipped back, because now the law enforcement officials—not Joe Public—made the final choice.

At his talk in Virginia Beach in 1986, King told the crowd: "I was involved with an antiobscenity referendum in Maine. The referendum question was very simply stated: 'Do you want to make it a crime to sell or read obscene material?' This is sort of like saying: 'Do you want to make it a crime to kill Santa Claus?' Well, most people said, 'Of course.' But when they went into the voting booths, I think that they thought a little bit different, and I'm happy to say the referendum was voted down, seventy percent to thirty percent, because they realized that 'obscene' is one of those words that exists in the eye of the beholder. What's obscene—what's *not* obscene? What's bad—what's *not* bad? What's moral—what's immoral?"

As for Wyman and his Christian soldiers, going onward was the only option. Conceding defeat—albeit temporarily—Reverend Wyman made a speech to his supporters, at 10 P.M., on June 10, 1986: "The campaign is ended. The election has been held. The people have spoken. And so a noble venture which was begun last fall draws to a close tonight. . . . Violent, hard-core obscenity will continue to blight our society until there emerges a public consensus as to how to effectively resist it. We continue to believe that one of the great functions of the law in a free nation is to give sanction and support to that which is morally right. And we shall continue to fight pornography and the exploitation, abuse, and pernicious greed that it represents. We take pride in the campaign we have waged and we believe the day shall come when our position on this issue will be vindicated. . . . This has been a long and difficult campaign but there are great days and great victories which lie ahead for all those who remain steadfast and faint not."

Chapman, Mark David

John Lennon's assassin, who was found not guilty of murder by reason of insanity. In 1978 or 1979 (according to King), Chapman waited outside 30 Rockefeller Plaza, where King had just appeared on the *Today* show. When Chapman saw King, he advanced with a Polaroid camera and an indelible pen in hand. After having his photo taken with King, he asked for an autograph. King obliged and signed the photo, "Best Wishes to Mark Chapman from King." "It was the guy who killed John Lennon," King said at his Virginia Beach Lecture, September 22, 1986.

Chapman is serving his sentence at Attica (New York) Correctional Facility.

Characterization

SK: "Can we believe more and more in the characters as the page numbers spiral up and up past 300, 400, 500? Do we see them grow more textured, or do we just get bored? What the writer of this sort of book wants—*needs*—to hear is, 'I hated to see it end.'" ("Books: Critic Critique," from *Adelina*, July 1980).

"Chattery Teeth"
(collected in *Nightmares & Dreamscapes*)

Originally published in *Cemetery Dance* magazine, "Chattery Teeth" is quintessential King: Bill, a salesman passing through Nevada on the way to California, stops at a roadside store to get gas. On a whim, he picks up a gift for his son, a set of chattery teeth made of metal, not the usual plastic, and considerably larger than the usual toy teeth. A comically grotesque thing, this set of teeth has the obligatory legs so it can walk and "talk," so to speak, but the storekeeper tells him it's broken and won't wind up. Bill takes it anyway. With misgivings, he takes along a scruffy young man who hitches a ride. The young man, though, pulls out a knife and makes the mistake of trying to hold Bill up. As Bill concentrates on the road and the deteriorating weather conditions, he's forced off the road by an oncoming truck, careening off the road and turning upside down.

The hitcher still tries to kill Bill, but the set of chattery teeth comes to life, chomping down in a death grip on the hitcher's nose. Then it waddles to the hitcher's crotch and takes a big bite, then turns its attention to the other occupant in the van.

Bill is shocked to see the set of teeth making its way up to him and fears the worst. The teeth, though, befriend him, chewing the seat belt that's restraining him in the van. Afterward, the teeth drag the hitcher off into the desert, only to reappear some time later at the same store, when Bill is making the rounds again.

A horrific little gem of a story, "Chattery Teeth" was faithfully adapted as a teleplay for *Quicksilver Highway*.

Chautauqua

King characterizes his public talks as Chautauquas. He typically introduces himself, chats informally, shares a few jokes, reads from one of his works in progress, then answers questions from the audience. Typically, King's talks run between two to three hours at most.

Chesley, Chris

A childhood friend of King's, Chesley collaborated on their self-published *People, Places and Things*. An excellent writer who could have written the definitive book about King's early years from his unique perspective as someone who was there from King's teen years through college, Chesley has kept a low profile, with the exception of a television appearance on *Hard Copy*, in which he escorted the interviewer through Durham, Maine, where he and King grew up.

Chesley also edited an early draft of *'Salem's Lot* and, while attending classes at the University of Maine at the Orono campus, lived with Stephen and Tabitha King when *Carrie* was sold.

When Chesley moved out to Truth or Consequences, New Mexico, he was able to get King to come out for a talk, around which the town celebrated "King Day" on November 19, 1983.

Chesley: "My thoughts are that the real King is much more interesting than the external myth that surrounds him now." (*The Shape Under the Sheet: The Complete Stephen King Encyclopedia.*)

An abandoned structure in Durham, Maine, which childhood friend Chris Chesley said was partially an inspiration for the Marsten House in *'Salem's Lot*.

Childhood residences

Because they had been abandoned by their father, Donald King, Stephen, his brother, David, and their mother, Ruth, never had a place to call home until they moved to Durham, Maine, where she took care of her aging parents.

In those early years, the Kings lived with relatives on both sides of the family in Malden, Massachusetts; Chicago; West Depere, Wisconsin; Fort Wayne, Indiana; and Stratford, Connecticut.

Children's campaign at the Eastern Maine Medical Center

The Children's Campaign, a fund-raising effort to raise an estimated $6 million needed to build a new pediatrics unit, met its fund-raising goals; it received $750,000 in three installments from Stephen and Tabitha King. (*BDN*, July 14, 1992.)

SK on their donation: "Children are important to me."

"Children of the Corn"
(collected in *Night Shift*)

Originally published in *Penthouse* (March 1977), this is one of a handful of stories King has written set outside Maine, and is one of his most horrific.

Burt and Vicky Robeson's marriage is on the rocks. Their anger boils over during a long road trip after getting lost, ending up in Gatlin, Nebraska. The war of words escalates, and as they bicker endlessly, punctuated by Vicky's endless sniping, Burt is distracted and accidentally runs over a boy.

But the boy was already dead—another victim in this godforsaken town where a primal corn god, He Who Walks Behind the Rows, holds sway. Children control the town, making blood sacrifices to their primitive god.

Inspired by William Golding's *The Lord of the Flies*, this story is first-rate King.

Children of the Corn (film), 1984

Before there was *The Lawnmower Man*, there was *Children of the Corn*, a movie so bad that King distances himself from it whenever possible, even putting it in his list of top ten worst movies ever made.

Is it *that* bad, or has King lost his objectivity? It's that bad.

Based on a horrifying story of the same name, collected in *Night Shift*, this poor excuse for celluloid has only one redeeming performance: Linda Hamilton (of *Terminator* and *Terminator 2* fame), marked for termination.

Following a string of bad movies with King's name prominently attached, this movie was simply one more clunker that alienated moviegoers.

Donald Borchers, executive, New World Pictures: "When I read the story in *Night Shift*, I was very intrigued with it because for me it provided the chance to make a statement that I really believed in. . . . Frankly, I love horror movies and fantastic stories, but I'm very depressed by seeing a story that's just a ripoff of another story. . . . I was real interested in examining the idea of dogma, the idea of blind faith, faith without questioning, and the consequences of all this." (Quoted in Daniel Everitt, "Stephen King's Children of the Corn," *Fangoria* #35, April 1984.)

Joe Bob Briggs: "I don't want to go into all the plot here, because it's boring, but basically what we got is a bunch of little brats that killed all the grown-ups in town and now they make gasahol all day and murder tourists and worship this kid named Isaac who has a Buster Brown haircut and stands about two foot six and looks like Charlie Brown with a piece of goat meat lodged in his throat. There's also a kid named Malachai who looks like Alfalfa with his hair grown out like a hippie, and Malachai likes to kill little dogs and old-coot gas-station owners. I call 'em the Cornflake Kids."

Children of the Corn II:
The Final Sacrifice (film), 1993

A sequel can come back to haunt the author, especially if he had no hand in it. Die-hard fans will note the similarity in title and, perhaps, haunt the theater to see the latest offering.

Those who saw 'Salem's Lot on television and subsequently rented Return to 'Salem's Lot were disappointed. Likewise, those who saw Stephen King's The Lawnmower Man and its sequel—neither of which had anything to do with King himself—were likely scratching their heads when leaving the theater, wondering what King was thinking when the rights to the original story were sold. (Stephen King's The Lawnmower Man was advertised with King's name prominently attached, until he forced them to remove it from all advertising.) And Pet Sematary 2 had no involvement from King—nor did Children of the Corn II, in which a tabloid reporter goes to Gatlin, Nebraska, to investigate a string of related murders—all of adults, perpetrated by children.

Let's cut to the chase on this movie: déjà vu.

Children of the Corn III:
Urban Harvest (film), 1994

Folks, if only this were the final sacrifice . . .
Enough, Hollywood, enough!
What I said about Corn II applies to this . . . this misbegotten corn-infested piece of celluloid.
'Nuff said.

Christine

Hardback, 1983, 526 pages, Viking, $16.95
Dedication: "This is for George Romero and Chris Forrest Romero. And the Burg."
Contents
  Prologue
  Part I. Dennis—Teenage Car-Songs
  Part II. Arnie—Teenage Love-Songs
  PART III. Christine—Teenage Death-Songs
  Epilogue
Set in 1978 in a middle-class suburb of Pittsburgh, Christine is King's love song to cars, rock and roll, and teenage angst. Initially a lover's tri-angle—Arnie Cunningham and Dennis Guilder vie for the attentions of the new girl in town, Leigh Cabot—the relationship fundamentally changes when Christine, a 1958 Plymouth Fury, enters the picture.

As Leigh Cabot observes, "Cars are girls."

For Cunningham (a nod to the character Ritchie Cunningham of TV's Happy Days fame), his love affair with Christine is not only unhealthy but damning—an obsessive love that turns from a love song to a death song.

"I've been very lucky with reviews over the years with the exception of Christine which was just roasted! I must have been totally wrong about that book. . . . It's like one of those dreams where you're in a public place and you suddenly realize you don't have any clothes on. That's what that experience was like. And I still don't understand what's wrong with that book, if anything is." (Quoted in Lynn Flewelling, "King Working on Book He Believes Could Be His Best," BDN, Sept. 11, 1990.)

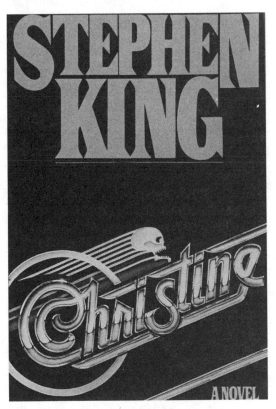

Dust jacket art for the Viking edition of Christine.

Christine (film), 1983

Only in a Stephen King movie would a lovers' triangle become a deadly ménage à trois. In *Christine*, a film budgeted at $10,000, the triangle is Arnie Cunningman (played by outsider-turned-cool guy Keith Gordon), his girlfriend Leigh Cabot (a competent but uninspired performance by Alexandra Paul) . . . and a car.

More to the point: a *haunted* car.

As in "Trucks," when the machines turn malevolent, Christine—notable for her big headlights—comes off the assembly line, ready to roll, leaving destruction and death in her wake.

There was a nationwide search to find the 1958 Plymouth Furies needed for filming, which turned up twenty-three cars in varying condition. But it proved enough—when supplemented by very convincing special effects—to make you believe that the car, after being crushed, could reconstitute itself, as the twisted metal unfolded itself back into pristine condition.

Like an undead Susan Norton in *'Salem's Lot*, Christine's dark evil was seductive . . . Arnie Cunningham couldn't resist.

The standout performance in this flick, a midlist movie, was given by Keith Gordon. Gordon gives a convincing performance as an outsider who was transformed by Christine from geek to sleek, who, when seduced by the dark side, becomes attractive in a dark way himself, to his detriment: Christine wants him for herself, and nobody—least of all a teenage girl—is going to stand in her way.

Christmas ornament

The city of Bangor commissioned beautiful Christmas ornaments of famous city landmarks, including the King house. On the bottom of the ornament is stamped 47 WEST BROADWAY, BANGOR, MAINE 1854–1856.

A tempest in a teapot brewed when Betts Bookstore unwittingly used discarded wood from the King home for mounting the ornament. As Stuart Tinker of Betts Bookstore explained, in a letter published in *The Red Letter*: "Tabitha is upset with us for selling the house ornament on the clapboard. She and Steve had the ornament commis-

sioned last year and we have purchased all of ours directly from the original supplier. The clapboards from the house were given to us and we put them to use. A total of 20 were done. Since it bothered her, we have apologized and will not make up anymore." More recently, a wooden ornament in the shape of Maine was manufactured for Betts Bookstore, with the location of Derry marked on it (Bangor, by the looks of it).

The Church of Dead Girls,
by Stephen Dobyns

SK: "Long after most other tales of murder and insanity have panted to their foregone conclusions, the suspense in this tale continues to built. *The Church of Dead Girls* is a meditation on hysteria, immensely ambitious, but Dobyns tells the tale with the calm—and fearful inevitability—of a man walking down a long hotel corridor to a room where some awful thing is waiting. Best of all, he never pulls up or turns aside—I kept reading, riveted by the plot and rooting with all my heart for Dobyns to pull it off. And he did, in a terrifying climax. I don't expect to read a more frightening novel this year. Very rich, very scary, very satisfying."

Club, 249

An informal club formed in the fifties by King, his brother, and friends, located in a shed behind the family house in Durham, where they would, according to Chesley, "play cards, read magazines, things like that."

The numbers were salvaged from an abandoned apartment building and posted on the shed.

Note: In "The Breathing Method," King would later transmute the real-world 249 Club into the fictional 249 Club, in a New York City brownstone, where old men gathered to tell tales.

Cockroachus giganticus
(South American cockroach)

During the filming of *Creepshow*, one story ("They're Creeping Up on You") required a large quantity of cockroaches. Because American supply houses charged 50¢ each, and because the cockroaches were free for the taking in caves, the production staff used this species of cockroach for the shoot. (*Bare Bones*, 1988.)

Cole, Jim

A film director whose student film, *The Last Rung on the Ladder*, won high praise from King.

Collectors Editions

A line of trade paperbacks brought out by NAL intended for new collectors: "handsome, affordable paperback editions, the perfect start to a permanent collection of works by our undisputed master of horror."

Five King novels—*Carrie*, *'Salem's Lot*, *The Shining*, *The Dead Zone*, and *Cujo*—were published beginning 1991 in uniform editions, in trade paperback, with distinctive cover designs, new introductions from brand-name writers, and a color plate showing the original hardback cover art.

The initial plan was eventually to reissue all of the books in this format, but after the first five were done, the project was abandoned, and the books were remaindered.

From a collector's point of view, the project had a number of conceptual problems: lack of uniqueness (the new introductions were nice, but not enough to compel readers to buy yet another edition of a familiar book); lack of durability (trade paperbacks aren't as well made as hardbacks); lack of intrinsic collectibility (the large runs in reprint editions made the books themselves the middle ground between the hardbacks and mass-market paperbacks); and the lack of anything personalizing the books (no books were signed by King or the authors who contributed introductions: Tabitha King for *Carrie*, Clive Barker for *'Salem's Lot*, Ken Follett for *The Shining*, Dan Simmons for *Cujo*, and Anne Rivers Siddons for *The Dead Zone*).

In short, it was a good idea poorly executed. Had NAL done its homework and consulted with book dealers on the secondary market, they would have been told that these were books for which no real market niche existed. Neither fish nor fowl, these editions were clearly not collectible in the eyes of the hard-core collectors who want signed,

limited editions, nor did the general public see them as good value for the money. King's general audience did subscribe in droves to the hardback editions of King's novels, bound in red boards, published as part of the Stephen King Library.

Collings, Michael R.

English professor at Pepperdine University who wrote a bibliography of SK, *The Work of Stephen King*.

An advocate of fantasy literature, Collings—a prolific King critic who also writes poetry, nonfiction, and fiction—is the author of numerous books on King, has contributed to books about King (notably *The Stephen King Story*, *The Stephen King Companion*, and *Stephen King: America's Best Loved Boogeyman*), has delivered papers on King at conferences, and reviews King books for *Phantasmagoria* and other King resources.

A highly respected critic in the field, Collings is considered a King expert by fans and academicians alike.

Commencement addresses

When King gave a commencement address at his alma mater, the University of Maine at Orono, in May 1987, he said that he had previously gotten 134 invitations to speak, but accepted only 6 of them, including this one. "I'm telling you how curious it is to find that so many people want a man who writes about monsters, murder and the supernatural to give them their final hail and farewell." ("Newsmakers," *Bedford Daily Mercury*, May 11, 1987.)

Constant readers

SK: "I feel a certain pressure about my writing, and I have an idea who reads my books; I am concerned with my readership. But it's kind of a combination love letter/poison-pen relationship, a sweet-and-sour thing. . . . I feel I ought to write something because people want to read something. But I don't think, 'Don't give them what they want—give them what you want.'" (Quoted in Bill Goldstein, "King of Horror," *PW*, Jan. 24, 1991.)

SK: "It was always important to me that I be read. It didn't matter that readers did not always agree—though it's very pleasant when they do—but it did matter that the book be read. After all, the art of writing is the art of communication." (Quoted in Robert H. Newall, "Novelist King Stresses Creativity," *BDN*.)

Contemporary poetry seminar

A dozen handpicked students at UMO, including Stephen King, were interviewed in 1969 by Burton Hatlen and Jim Bishop for this upper-level class. Stephen King was accepted, but, ironically, one of the other interviewees, Tabitha King, was rejected.

Jim Bishop (*Moth*, 1970): "From that seminar . . . came a half dozen or so energetic and highly individual young poets who have been rapping in the hallways, in coffee shops, in front of Stevens Hall, or wherever any two of them chance to meet, ever since, and that original group has grown this year to a dozen, sometimes as many as twenty, who meet every other Friday in an informal workshop to read their poetry, and hopefully to emerge with a better understanding of themselves, their world, and their work."

Conventions

King no longer attends conventions because he gets overwhelmed with attention.

Early in his career, King attended the science fiction, fantasy and horror conventions, enjoying what everyone else does: attending panels, meeting friends in the bar for drinks, and searching for collectibles in the Huckster's Room.

All of that changed, however, as King's fame and popularity grew exponentially, to the point where even the small conventions like the World Fantasy Con and regional cons like NECON would be overwhelmed by his presence, as fans mobbed him in hallways, in the dealer's room, and anywhere else they could find him.

At the 1982 World Fantasy Con (New Haven, Connecticut), "King spent a lot of time in his suite because he was mobbed wherever he went," reported *Locus* (January 1983), a con at which writers whom King admired were also present: Manly Wade Wellman, Frank Belknap Long, Fritz Leiber, and Joseph Payne Brennan (*Weird Tales* writers).

A year later, in *Locus*, King was quoted: "I love the conventions, but may have to give them up if this continues. They're no longer any fun."

There was even a convention *for* King fans, Horrorfest, which, if he had attended, would have been a real nightmarish situation: He would have had no privacy whatsoever.

It was nice while it lasted; too bad the fans drove him out.

Converse All-Stars

King doesn't wear designer clothes, nor does he wear designer athletic shoes—he wears ordinary red sneakers, the kind he probably wore in his youth.

Cooking

King admits he's not much of a cook. He's been known to bake bread and plain fare like "lunchtime goop"—throw everything in the pot—but that's the limit of his culinary talents.

Corgi

King's dog, Marlowe, is a Welsh corgi. In Jill Krementz's collection of photographs of writers, *The Writer's Desk*, the man and his dog are in his office. That photo was also used for the author's photo on the dust jacket flap of *Desperation*, and for a calendar, to illustrate the month of—you guessed it—October.

The Corner

Aborted novel begun in 1976. Nothing is known about its contents.

Cowan, Liebowitz & Latman, P.C.

Attorneys retained by King to represent him in his lawsuit against New Line Cinema for its misleading use of King's name in association with *The Lawnmower Man*, billed as *Stephen King's The Lawnmower Man*.

Cowboy Boogie

A bar in Anaheim, California, that was the site of the first plugged performance of the band the Rock Bottom Remainders, on May 25, 1992.

The Creature from the Black Lagoon

A 1954 black-and-white horror movie.

At age seven King saw this movie, which Leonard Wolf, in *Horror*, termed "a darling of horror film aficionados." In fact, King frequently alludes to this movie in interviews, citing that in good horror movies, you don't see the zipper on the monster's rubber suit—a reference to the Creature in this movie.

Creepshow

A graphics album published as a trade paperback by NAL as a tie-in to the film. The full-color book sported a cover by the E.C. artist Jack Kamen and interior art by Berni Wrightson.

Wrightson, on his short deadline: "My understanding of what happened is that they started work on the movie and got Jack Kamen to do the

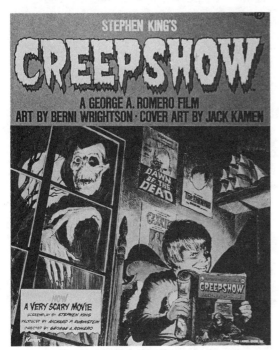

Cover to the trade paperback edition of *Creepshow*, with art by Jack Kamen, a former E.C. artist.

"Splash" page for *Creepshow*, illustrated by macabre cartoonist Berni Wrightson.

cover. That was the initial inspiration. Then there was talk of a comic book being done. But I guess the lines of communication got broken down along the way because they assumed he was going to do it. I think what happened was that very late in the game somebody called Kamen and said, 'How's the comic book coming?' And he said, 'You've got it all wrong. I'm not doing a comic book. You're going to get somebody else to do the comic book.' And that's where I came in.

"Stephen King called me about *Creepshow* and explained the situation. 'Is there any possibility that you could do the comic book?' And at the time, there was something else I had to put aside to take it on. They wanted the whole thing done in two months, but it took me four months to do it."

Creepshow (film), 1982

Creepshow was the first anthology-style film King wrote, bringing together five separate stories loosely linked with a framing device, recalling the E.C. Comics horror line from the fifties.

The problems from the audience's perspective: First, there's no advantage to produce this for the big screen, as opposed to episodes on a television series like *The Twilight Zone* or *Amazing Stories*. King had in fact been approached numerous times but turned down the opportunity to host a "New England" horror-themed show, for which the *Creepshow* stories would have been ideal. Second, inherent in the E.C. formula of storytelling, in which the bad guys get their comeuppance, the stories tend to be repetitious. You know *what* is going to happen; you just don't know *how* it will happen.

In "Father's Day," Bedelia Gratham, who killed her father on Father's Day, just before he could get his cake, gets her comeuppance at a family reunion as her father returns from the grave, croaking, "I want my cake!"

In "The Lonesome Death of Jordy Verrill," King himself plays the country bumpkin who finds a meteor on his farm and assumes he can sell it to the Department of Meteors at the local college, for $200. Unfortunately, he breaks the meteor in half, but figures he can still sell it, albeit for a little less.

After he puts it in a bucket, an alien fungus grows, enveloping the meteor and Verrill as well, who takes a shotgun to his head and wishes that, just this once, things would work out.

Note: Verrill is the last name of King's editor at Viking, Chuck Verrill.

In "The Crate," Henry Northrup, a henpecked university professor at Horlicks University, uses a ruse to get his wife, Wilma, to meet him at school at a specific stairwell, under which had been stored an ancient wooden crate found by a janitor.

The crate harbors a man-eating monster, which pulls Wilma into the box, and Henry takes the box for disposal at a local quarry.

In "Something to Tide You Over," adultery is punished, as is murder: Henry Wentworth, played by Ted Danson, and Becky Vickers, played by Gaylen Ross, return from their watery graves to exact revenge on Richard Vickers, played by Leslie Nielsen, for having murdered them, burying them alive up to their necks as the tide came in. The E.C. touch: Wentworth is videotaping their death throes, and each adulterer can watch the other die, before the water shorts out the videocameras.

In "They're Creeping Up on You," a Howard Hughes–like figure—obsessive about cleanliness, living in a sanitized high-tech fortress apart-

ment—gets his just deserts: Upson Pratt (played by E. G. Marshall) is instrumental in the suicide of a business associate who was driven to bankruptcy . . . and Pratt is headed for a fall: a bug infestation—a symbol of his own infestation of greed—invades his penthouse apartment and, in time, literally infests him as well.

The $8 million film, more than anything else, shows King's and George Romero's roots as fans who loved campy horror and wanted to serve it up to a new generation, too young ever to have seen the E.C. Comics on which it was based.

Creepshow 2 (film), 1987

A sequel to *Creepshow* (1982), this serves up a trio of stories, each introduced by The Creep, a skeletal figure, and a running animated story about Billy, who plants Venus flytraps—a touch reminiscent of Ray Bradbury's short story, "Boys! Raise Giant Mushrooms in *Your* Cellar!"

Featuring a cameo by King, in "The Hitchhiker," and his former secretary, Shirley Sonderegger, as Mrs. Cavenaugh in "Old Chief Wood'nhead," the second serving offers up a story from *Skeleton Crew*, "The Raft," and two new stories, "Old Chief Wood'nhead" and "The Hitchhiker."

In true E.C. fashion, the teenage murderers in "Old Chief Wood'nhead" get their reward: The wooden Indian in front of the store comes to life, killing both.

The other two stories are typical fare. In true King fashion, a sentient oil slick in "The Raft" attacks and kills college students who venture out on a raft in a lake in the middle of nowhere; and in "The Hitchhiker," the dead come back, again and again, to haunt an adulterous Annie Lansing (played by Lois Chiles).

A midlist King offering, this one's definitely a video flick.

Cronenberg, David

The director of *The Dead Zone*, Cronenberg, whose major successes were yet to come (notably *Scanners* and *Videodrome*), made his mark with this King adaptation, his first major studio release. Shot on a $10 million budget, *The Dead Zone* was faithful to the book. The actor Christopher Walken deserves considerable credit for his haunted interpretation of Johnny Smith.

"Crouch End"
(collected in *Nightmares & Dreamscapes*)

Originally published in 1980 in *New Tales of the Cthulhu Mythos*, an Arkham House anthology, this story has no explanatory note at the end of *Nightmares & Dreamscapes*.

Peter Straub, then living in Crouch End, London, extended a dinner invitation to Stephen and Tabitha King, who were temporarily living in England.

The Kings took the Straubs up on the dinner invitation but got lost in Crouch End . . . just like the American couple in this story, who take a wrong turn and find themselves in a Lovecraftian nightmare, complete with a cast of ungodly creatures from his pantheon, including The Goat with a Thousand Young and other Eldritch horrors.

As this story clearly demonstrates, King has an uncanny talent for picking up the texture, the unmistakable "feel" of the landscape and its people, and its lingo, as this (literally) haunting story proves.

Cujo

Hardback, 1981, 319 pages, Viking, $13.95

Dedication: "This book is for my brother, David, who held my hand crossing West Broad Street, and who taught me how to make skyhooks out of old coathangers. The trick was so damned good I just never stopped. I love you, David."

Background: King, then living temporarily in England, was hoping to pick up the local color with which to "paint" his new ghost novel, set in a haunted Victorian castle. However, he never wrote that novel. Instead, he wrote *Cujo*, a novel set in Maine that recalls *The Shining*.

In an exploration of everyday horror—the Trentons have a disintegrating marriage on their hands and a four-year-old son, the sacrificial lamb, Tad Trenton—Cujo, a two-hundred-pound Saint Bernard belonging to Brett Camber, goes rabid and attacks Tad and his mother Donna, trapped in their ailing Pinto at the Camber garage.

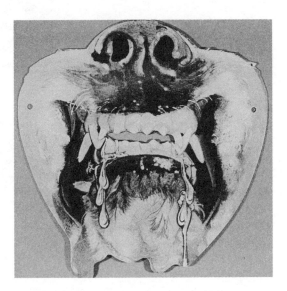

Cujo face mask, which was distributed at the ABA.

It's a battle to the end, and Cujo has the upper hand.

As Michael Collings points out, the first draft of *Cujo*, lacking the supernatural touches present in the subsequent drafts, has a distinct Bachman flavor, and for good reason: It was intended to *be* a Bachman novel. As Collings points out, the injection of Frank Dodd, the monster in the closet (a frequent King theme), and the references to Castle Rock make it clearly a King novel in "feel."

King, a firm believer that in life as in fiction bad things happen to good people, starts out the novel with the beguiling line, "Once upon a time . . ." But this is no fairy tale, it's a horror story, a naturalistic novel in which the only constant is pain, and even love is not enough to save the victims.

Cujo (film), 1983

If I had to reduce this movie to a one-liner, it'd be this: "*Cujo* is essentially *The Shining*, except more claustrophobic."

Instead of being trapped in a hotel, the protagonists are trapped in a broken-down Ford Pinto on the outskirts of Castle Rock, Maine.

The Shining is the story of a man in a disintegrating marriage, haunted by his past, with ghosts from the Overlook Hotel haunting him as well, resulting in dire consequences for his wife and son. In *Cujo*, the Trentons face a similar disintegration

Cujo (**film**) *continued*

of their marriage, but instead of being marooned in a ghostly hotel in the mountains in winter, Donna Trenton and her son, Tad, are trapped by a rabid Saint Bernard that assaults them in the yard of Joe Camber's home-garage shop.

In the novel Tad Trenton dies, but he lives in this movie.

The book was intentionally claustrophobic, and the movie is more so; the book was intentionally assaultive, and again, the movie is more of the same.

A faithful if harrowing adaptation of the book, this film earned kudos from King, who rewarded the director, Lewis Teague, with the opportunity to direct *Cat's Eye* in 1985.

Cujo guitar

Two hundred fifty copies of this guitar, inspired by the novel *Cujo*, were manufactured by Taylor Guitars of San Diego, California, using black walnut wood from a tree that was growing at the location of the 1983 filming of the movie.

Individually signed by King on a "dog tag" label, the guitar is a sound collectible, the first copy of which was presented to King.

Each guitar cost $3,498.

Cussler, Clive

A novelist specializing in deep-sea adventures featuring the character Dirk Pitt. Cited by King, in "Reading King," as a writer whom he does not care to read. According to King, there's room in the world for Cussler and himself . . . so long as King doesn't have to read him.

Note: King and Cussler share the same publisher, Simon & Schuster. Predictably, after King got a partnership deal, Cussler decided he wanted one, too, and got one for himself, for a new series of novels, "The Numa Files."

Cycle of the Werewolf

Hardback, 1983, 114 pages, Land of Enchantment, $28.50

Originally conceived as a calendar idea—one vignette per month—the idea grew in the telling until it became a short book, an evocative tale of a werewolf that afflicts Tarker's Mills, Maine.

One of King's shorter books—this edition was fleshed out for republication as *Silver Bullet*, which featured additional frontmatter and the complete text of King's script—this straightforward story of Marty Coslaw and his inevitable showdown with the werewolf is beautifully illustrated with pen-and-ink illustrations and watercolors by Bernie Wrightson, whose work here recalls his fine pen work for *Frankenstein*.

An enjoyable little tale of terror, this is one of the few times a werewolf has made a notable appearance in King's fiction.

According to Peter Schneider (*Denver Post*, April 1, 1984), King was unhappy with the pricing on the various editions from Land of Enchantment. "King was furious. He threatened to break the contract and take the matter to court if he had to. The publisher finally relented to the extent that he dropped the prices to $28.50 (trade edition), $75 (a limited, signed edition), and $175 (limited deluxe edition with original art by Wrightson)."

King also signed 350 numbered copies of the portfolio of artwork from the book.

Jeannine E. Klein (UPI, May 6, 1985): "This 128-page tale is a howling success for horror fiction connoisseurs."

Dust jacket front cover for the Land of Enchantment edition of *Cycle of the Werewolf*, with art by Berni Wrightson.

Daniloff, Nicholas

A journalist for *U.S. News and World Report* who was charged with spying by the Soviets.

Daniloff, who claimed he was set up, said he was supposed to meet a friend to exchange gifts and, as per his friend's request, brought two novels . . . by Stephen King.

Danse Macabre

Hardback, 1979, 400 pages, Everest House, $13.95

King's only nonfiction book to date, this accessible, very readable, and informative overview of the horror field in all media from the fifties through the seventies is a "must" read for any King fan or anyone with an interest in popular culture. Unlike other texts on the subject—which are either excessively fannish or tediously academic—King's long and loving look at the genre whence he came is a page-turner.

In his introduction, King states: "It's my Final Statement on the clockwork of the horror tale."

Among other gems in the book is King's oft-quoted dictum: "I recognize terror as the finest emotion and so I will try to terrorize the reader. But if I find that I cannot terrify, I will try to horrify, and if I find that I cannot horrify, I'll go for the gross-out. I'm not proud."

The *Baltimore Sun* said the book "succeeds on any number of levels, as pure horror memorabilia for longtime ghoulie groupies, as a bibliography for younger addicts weaned on King; and as an insightful noncredit course for would-be writers of the genre."

Contents

"I wrote *Danse Macabre* for a friend of mine, Bill Thompson, who edited all my early books at Doubleday. He asked me: If I were sitting in a bar room with a friend and I could say everything that I thought about horror fiction, horror movies, and what it all means—because I'm asked [those] questions time and time again—would I be interested in doing a book like that?" (*The Larry King Show*, April 10, 1986)

Darabont, Frank

Early on, Darabont directed *The Woman in the Room*, one of the few student films King cites as a favorite. Darabont went on to make a name for himself as the director of the critically acclaimed *Shawshank Redemption*. His current project: *The Green Mile*.

SK: "Frank sent me a videocassette of his film [*The Woman in the Room*], and I watched it in slack-jawed amazement. I also felt a little sting of tears. *The Woman in the Room* remains, twelve years later, on my short list of favorite film adaptations." (From "Rita Hayworth and the Darabont Redemption," the introduction to *The Shawshank Redemption: The Shooting Script*.)

Frank Darabont: "Every once in a while, if we're

lucky, somebody comes into our lives and helps it along. If this help is consistent and meaningful, that person eventually assumes Patron Saint status. In my life, though he may not have even intended it, Stephen King has become such a person." (From "Stephen King and the Darabont Redemption," the introduction to *The Shawshank Redemption: The Shooting Script*.)

The Dark Descent: Essays Defining Stephen King's Horrorscape,
edited by Tony Magistrale

Published by Greenwood Press in 1992, these 15 essays approach King from multiple perspectives, concentrating on his work up to *Misery*, all academic in approach.

Contents:
Foreword: "The King and I," by Joseph A. Citro
Acknowledgments
Stephen King Chronology

1. "Defining Stephen King's Horrorscope: An Introduction," by Tony Magistrale
2. "The Masks of the Goddess: The Unfolding of the Female Archetype in Stephen King's *Carrie*," by Greg Weller
3. "Partners in the *Danse*: Women in Stephen King's Fiction," by Mary Pharr
4. "Complex, Archetype, and Primal Fear: King's Use of Fairy Tales in *The Shining*," by Ronald T. Curran
5. "The Three Genres of *The Stand*," by Edwin F. Casebeer
6. "Some Ways of Reading *The Dead Zone*," by Michael N. Stanton
7. "Fear and Pity: Tragic Horror in King's *Pet Sematary*," by Leonard Mustazza
8. "The Mythic Journey in 'The Body,'" by Arthur W. Biddle
9. "'Everybody Pays . . . Even for Things They Didn't Do': Stephen King's Pay-out in the Bachman Novels," by James F. Smith
10. "Science, Politics, and the Epic Imagination: *The Talisman*," by Tony Magistrale
11. "A Clockwork Evil: Guilt and Conscience in 'The Monkey,'" by Gene Doty
12. "Playing the Heavy: Weight, Appetite, and

Embodiment in *Three King Novels* by Stephen King," by Bernadette Lynn Bosky
13. "Riddle Game: Stephen King's Metafictive Dialogue," by Jeanne Campbell Reesman
14. "Stephen King Reading William Faulkner: Memory, Desire, and Time in the Making of *It*," by Mary Jane Dickerson
15. "'The Face of Mr. Flip': Homophobia in the Horror of Stephen King," by Douglas Keesey
16. "Reading, Writing, and Interpreting: Stephen King's *Misery*," by Lauri Berkenkamp
A Stephen King Bibliography
Index
About the Contributors

The Dark Half

Hardback, 1989, 431 pages, Viking, $21.95
Dedication: "This book is for Shirley Sonderegger, who helps me mind my business, and for her husband, Peter."

It's an axiom in the writing profession that, when writing fiction, it's best to stay away from protagonists who are writers, because the readers can't identify with them.

It's an axiom that King has routinely ignored; more important, his choice of a writer as his protagonist has been skillfully explored in several of King's best works, such as *Misery* and *Bag of Bones*, with noteworthy results.

In *The Dark Half*, in the wake of the Bachman revelation, King explores the notion of the pen name that refuses to be killed off, literally taking on a life of its own: Thad Beaumont's alter ego, George Stark, was put to rest in a symbolic grave, but comes murderously back to life to confront him.

An evocative study of the duality of a writer's psyche in conflict, *The Dark Half* is a riveting read and, in light of the Bachmanlike allusions, sheds considerable light on King's understandable anger at what he in this novel terms a creepazoid: a persistent, invasive person who, like a rat terrier, won't let go until he's taken a large chunk of out of you and your life.

The Dark Half (film), 1993

The sparrows are flying again . . . or, rather, several thousand cutthroat finches, trained to fly on command in this effective thriller about a writer, Thad Beaumont, and his dark half, his fictional alter ego, George Stark, who comes to life and murders everyone standing between him and Beaumont.

In a very noteworthy performance, Timothy Hutton plays the dual role of Beaumont and Stark, switching between the two with consummate skill. As Beaumont, he's the loving father and best-selling writer who has deliberately buried his pen name in a mock burial; and as Stark, he's a cold-blooded killer with his own agenda.

Sometimes, as King has said, they come back . . . with disastrous consequences.

A horrific, effective movie that faithfully translates the book, *The Dark Half* is worth seeing—it's two hours of scary entertainment.

Darkshine

An aborted novel inspired by Ray Bradbury's short story "The Veldt," exploring the idea of children as psychic receptors.

The story idea wasn't wasted, however, since King recycled it for *The Shine*, later retitled *The Shining*.

"I was wondering what would happen if you had a little boy who was sort of a psychic receptor, or maybe even a psychic amplifier. And I wanted to take a little kid with his family and put them someplace, cut off, where spooky things would happen."

The Dark Tower: The Gunslinger

Hardback, 224 pages, 1984, Donald M. Grant, $20.00

Dedication: "To Ed Ferman who took a chance on these stories, one by one."

Contents:
The Gunslinger
The Way Station
The Oracle and the Mountains
The Slow Mutants
The Gunslinger and the Dark Man
Afterword

Trade paperback cover for *The Dark Tower*, with art by Michael Whelan.

Genesis: Spaghetti westerns, epic quests

Projected to be a seven-book series, this was originally serialized in the *Magazine of Fantasy and Science Fiction*.

In a striking departure from tradition, the book was issued not by King's trade publisher but by a small press in Rhode Island, Donald M. Grant, Publisher, known for its beautifully produced and illustrated books catering to the same horror aficionados that supported Arkham House.

Published in a limited edition of 500 numbered and signed copies and a trade edition of 20,000 copies, this novel went quietly out of print. However, when it showed up as a title listed in the front part of *Pet Sematary*, the novel ignited a firestorm of controversy, prompting King to authorize a second printing of 10,000 copies, hoping that would stem in part the criticism regarding the book's availability.

Predictably, the second print run sold out quickly, leaving King with a major public relations

The Dark Tower: The Gunslinger *continued*
problem on his hands: a body of faithful readers who were denied the opportunity to read the novel, since King steadfastly refused to authorize a trade edition.

The controversy prompted King to write a long essay, serialized in *Castle Rock*, "The Politics of Limited Editions."

In time, however, King changed his mind and authorized a trade edition.

The Dark Tower 2: The Drawing of the Three

Hardback, 1987, 401 pages, Donald M. Grant, $35.00

Dedication: "To Don Grant, who's taken a chance on these novels, one by one."

Illustrator: Phil Hale

Contents

Argument

Prologue: The Sailor
The Prisoner
  1. The Door
  2. Eddie Dean
  3. Contact and Landing
  4. The Tower
  5. Showdown and Shoot-Out
Shuffle
The Lady of Shadows
  1. Detta and Odetta
  2. Ringing the Changes
  3. Odetta on the Other Side
  4. Detta on the Other Side
Reshuffle
The Pusher
  1. Bitter Medicine
  2. The Honeypot
  3. Roland Takes His Medicine
  4. The Drawing
Final Shuffle
Afterword

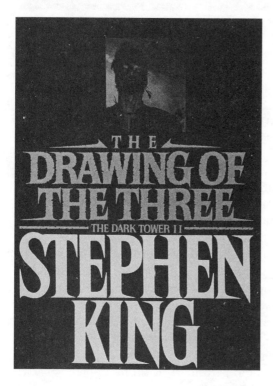

Cover to the advance reading copy of *The Dark Tower II: The Drawing of the Three*, published by NAL.

A plate from the portfolio of the Grant edition of *Dark Tower III: The Wastelands.*

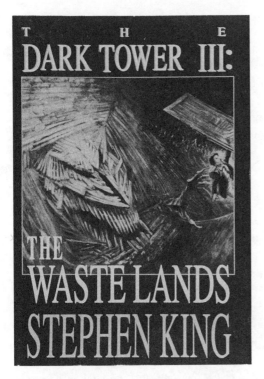

The dust jacket to the Grant edition of *The Dark Tower III: The Wastelands*.

The Dark Tower 3: The Wastelands

Hardback, 1991, 512 pages, Donald M. Grant, Publisher, $38.00

Dedication: "This third volume of the tale is gratefully dedicated to my son, Owen Philip King: Khef, ka, and ka-tet."

Contents
Argument
Book I. Jake
   1. Bear and Bone
   2. Key and Rose
   3. Door and Demon
Book II. Lud: A Heap of Broken Images
   4. Town and Ka-tet
   5. Bridge and City
   6. Riddle and Waste Lands
Author's Note

The Dark Tower 4: Wizard and Glass

Hardback, 1997, 787 pages, Donald M. Grant, $45.00

Cover to the trade paperback edition of *The Dark Tower IV: Wizard and Glass*, with a cover design similar to the newly designed *Dark Tower* volumes I through III, available in a boxed set.

Dedication: "This book is dedicated to Julie Eugley and Marsha DeFilippo. They answer the mail, and most of the mail for the last couple of years has been about Roland of Gilead—the gunslinger. Basically, Julie and Marsha nagged me back to the word processor. Julie, you nagged the most effectively, so your name comes first."

Contents
Argument
Prologue, Blaine
Part I. Riddles
Part II. Susan
Interlude—Kansas, Somewhere, Somewhen
Part III. Come, Reap
Part IV. All God's Chillun Got Shoes
Afterword

A firestorm of controversy ignited with the publication of the Grant edition. For the first time a Grant edition was made available through major chains, which bought up most of the 40,000 copies, leaving few copies for independent booksellers.

The cumulative impact of the chain stores' buy put this edition on the *New York Times* best-seller list—a first for any Grant title.

Nonetheless, sentiment among the independ-

ents could be summed up in one word: frustration. As an Oregon bookseller who wrote to King explained, "I was very distressed to discover last week that *Wizard and Glass* could be found in Portland only at Barnes and Noble . . . and would not be available for another month to the independent riff-raff on the West Coast and our loyal customers. Since I think of you as a supporter of

D Is for Dark Tower

Douglas E. Winter remarked in an interview that what he liked best about King's fiction is his ability to surprise readers with each new book.

Though King seems at times to go in writing cycles—*Gerald's Game, Dolores Claiborne*, and *Rose Madder* all explored social issues—he is by and large not predictable in terms of output.

This philosophy of giving the reader what he wants by *not* giving him what he *thinks* he wants makes reading King an ongoing pleasure. (Do you *really* want to read another haunted house novel by King? Or another small-town vampire infestation?)

A reviewer once remarked that the science fiction writer Robert A. Heinlein wore imagination like a suit of clothes, a description that fits King to a *T* as well, especially when King digresses from his patented supernatural fiction to write cross-genre fiction, providing himself a broad canvas to paint on.

Nowhere is this more evident than in King's story cycle—an epic story, in fact—called *The Dark Tower*, a work-in-progress that is clearly King at his imaginative best, with four books completed and three more to go.

The genesis of *The Dark Tower* dates back to King's college days, when he started writing the first book, using his office Underwood to type on the odd-sized lime-green paper that had mysteriously showed up at the UMO library where he worked.

In a cabin near the river that flanks the UMO campus, King began what would be his most ambitious literary project to date. He showed an early draft to his childhood friend Chris Chesley, who told him that it was the "best thing you've ever written."

The story cycle appeared not in book form but serialized in a pulp magazine, *The Magazine of Fantasy and Science Fiction*. King, no stranger to the readers of this literary zine catering to fantasy fans, published "The Gunslinger" in its October 1978 issue, followed by four more chapters.

The five chapters of *The Dark Tower* would never have seen publication if fate hadn't intervened. At a university dinner attended by the small-press publisher Donald M. Grant and Stephen King, Grant asked King if he had anything that might be suitable for publication as a Grant title.

King gave it some thought and, recalling *The Dark Tower*, said that he did indeed, and offered those stories to Grant, who published the book in 1982.

King, who had already seen himself becoming what he termed a "*Bestsellersaurus rex*," a major economic force in the book trade, felt that because this book was clearly not horror, the kind of book his readers expected, would be best published in a small run for fantasy aficionados who had previously seen it in *The Magazine of Fantasy and Science Fiction*.

Everything was jake until *The Dark Tower* was listed in the front matter of *Pet Sematary* in 1983, and the fit hit the shan: King's readers, who haunted the bookstores for each new King novel, were stunned—shocked, in fact—that they had somehow missed a King novel! How, they asked, could this have happened?

Immediately the mail deluge began from King's readers. King's publishers (including Grant), friends and professional associates of King, and King himself found themselves swamped with phone calls and letters, all asking: Where can I get a copy of *The Dark Tower*?

Booksellers were at a loss. *The Dark Tower* had never been made available to them, to the normal book distributors, and had never been advertised. So they, too, flooded Grant, King, and his publishers with requests for copies.

Even in the face of obvious demand, King felt that the book was too specialized and that his mainstream readers wouldn't want it if they knew it was a fantasy book, and was only the first book in the series. So King dug in his heels and refused to allow a trade edition sufficient to slake the demand.

King's fans were insistent, however, and King reluctantly agreed to let Grant reprint *The Dark Tower*—10,000 copies, just like the first print run, which he felt would take some of the heat off. Part of the print run was reserved especially for King correspondents who had written him to ask where they could buy it.

Predictably, those 10,000 copies went quickly, and the problem worsened. *More* readers were besieging him and his publishers for a copy of the book, and libraries that had bought the book found it vanishing mysteriously from their shelves. The patrons figured it was worth paying for its loss, since they couldn't imagine any other way to get a copy.

Finally King relented, and a trade paperback edition was released in September 1988, a facsimile reprint of the Grant edition. Its sales proved to King that, insofar as his readers were concerned, it was pointless to second-guess them.

None of this, however, sat well with King, who felt that the fans had a sense of ownership regarding the book, that they demanded its publication, that they felt it was cruel for King not to release it to the book trade.

In "The Politics of Limited Editions," serialized in two parts in *Castle Rock* (June and July 1985), King discussed his philosophy of issuing the small-run books purchased principally by the fantasy fans, making it clear that the brouhaha over *The Dark Tower* did not sit well with him; in fact, he was downright upset, and said so.

All of that is history now, and King has published three more books in the series, though not quickly enough to satisfy the fans, who continue to write him and ask, "When's the *next Dark Tower* novel coming out?"

The form of Chinese water torture inflicted by the reader on the author finally made King realize that it was in his best interest to finish the series as soon as possible, which he has promised to do, clearing the deck, so to speak, so he can concentrate on other projects without the enormous aggravation of having to respond to the plaintive cries of the fans who want the *next* book, as soon as possible.

When the next *Dark Tower* will be out nobody knows, not even King. He knows what the fans do not: That he can't *force* the book, or it'll be stillborn. In due time, when the story demands to be told, it will be told, and no sooner.

The fans will just have to wait.

As for Donald M. Grant, the man who had the vision to ask for the first book, his small press—now based in New Hampshire and ably run by Grant's partner, Robert Wiener—remains the publisher of the *Dark Tower*. They issue each new volume in hardback, sumptuously illustrated and beautifully designed, in two states: a signed, limited edition and a trade edition that has now grown to 45,000 copies; *Dark Tower IV: Wizard and Glass* sold out soon after publication.

In a way, it'll be a sad thing to see the series end. But after all, Roland deserves a break; it's been a long trek for him—and for its author, as well, who has more stories to tell . . . and miles to go before he can sleep.

Note: Because the story is not fully told, I have deliberately refrained from giving a plot synopsis of each book published to date. In a future edition of this book, after all seven are in print, a long essay will incorporate a plot summary and critical comments.

The Dark Tower 4 continued

independent bookstores, I can only hope that there is an explanation for this dire state of affairs."

Specialty booksellers were similarly frustrated in attempts to buy copies of the signed, limited edition, which were sold mostly through Grant directly to customers on his mailing list.

Dave's Rag

An amateur local newspaper, published by a teenage David King, Stephen's brother.

Its first issue was individually hand-typed, in an edition of only two copies, but subsequent issues were mimeographed. Begun in January 1959, when David King was only 13 years old and Stephen King was 11, the letter-size newspaper was a home-brewed effort, produced in the basement.

Staffers included David King (editor-in-chief and illustrator), Donald P. Flaws (sports editor), and Stephen King (reporter).

The paper cost a nickel a copy, but a subscription could be had for a dollar.

Don Hansen wrote an article in the Brunswick *Record* in its April 23, 1959, issue, about *Dave's Rag*: "3 Durham Lads Publishing Bright Hometown Newspaper." Hansen wrote: "Boasting an all paid circulation of 20 copies, the typewritten newspaper thus far has had a good reception with read-

ers. . . . Although Dave is probably the nation's youngest newspaper editor, he doubts that he will make newspapering a career."

Davis, Bette

Actress in *Hush, Hush, Sweet Charlotte* who was cited by King in a *Boston Globe Magazine* interview as being the "best screamer in the movies."

Dead White, by Alan Ryan

SK: "*Dead White* is tight and exciting and readable. A good tale."

The Dead Zone

Hardback, 1979, 426 pages, Viking, $11.95
Dedication: "This is for Owen I love you, old bear"
Contents
Part I. The Wheel of Fortune
Part II. The Laughing Tiger
Part III. Notes from the Dead Zone
Background: unknown
Johnny Smith suffers an accident and goes into a coma. When he comes out of it he realizes that he has precognitive powers, not unlike Danny Torrance's "shining." Invested with powers he doesn't understand, he tries to use his powers for good,

which leads him to a moral dilemma: choose action and change the future irrevocably, or choose inaction and watch the world take a dark turn because of one man—the presidential candidate who is not what he seems.

One of King's best novels and a personal favorite, *The Dead Zone* was written from an outline, a departure from his usual method of writing, which he admits is largely intuitive. The problem is that intuitive writing can lead to epic digressions, lack of focus, and unresolved or poorly resolved endings.

SK: "I'm very proud of that book. It says serious things about the political structure of America and how it's set up." ("Author to Sign Books," *New England Newsclip*, Sept. 14, 1980.)

The Dead Zone, (film), 1983

When adapting King's fiction to the screen, two factors help immensely: First, pick the right actor for the main role; and second, try to adapt a King novel that is filmable—less reliant on the supernatural, and more reliant on characterization.

In *The Dead Zone*, director David Cronenberg found the ideal actor for the role of Johnny Smith. Although all the performances were good—unobtrusive, the actors slipping into their roles with ease—Christopher Walken, in the lead role of Johnny Smith, is outstanding.

More than any other actor who comes to mind, Walken *looks* haunted, recalling the Patrick McGrath line, "The most haunted of all houses is the human mind." It's a look he uses to maximum effect in *The Dead Zone*, a novel King feels is a standout among his works.

Unlike many of his other novels, some of which have lackluster endings, the ending of this novel is predicated on the dilemma that Smith faces: Does he become complicit by default in the human tragedy that will result if Greg Stillson (played by Martin Sheen) becomes the next president, or does he change the course of history for the better by becoming involved, even if it means it will cost him his own life?

Foreshadowed from the beginning, the ending is not so much a matter of choice but of destiny: The wheel of fate randomly chose Smith, as it were, as the instrument of fate.

A remarkably good film that stands on its own, this masterful film adaptation, like the book, shows off King's storytelling talents.

"Dedication"
(collected in *Nightmares & Dreamscapes*)

Originally published in *Night Visions V* (1988), edited by Douglas E. Winter, this is one of three stories by King in that original anthology; "The Reploids" and "Sneakers" (also in *Nightmares & Dreamscapes*) also were in it.

"Dedication," wrote Winter in his introduction to *Night Visions V*, "melds his enthusiasm for outrage with his penchant for the ironic. A tale of witchcraft centered on the bizarre relationship between a black hotel maid and the tormented white novelist whose suite she cleans, the story was not well met with editors. The reader is thus forewarned: 'Dedication' is perhaps Stephen King's least palatable story, and is certain to prove one of his most controversial works of fiction."

To which I'll add: A black chambermaid at Le Palais, a fancy hotel in New York city, shares a long-held secret with her friend that explains the not coincidental connection between her son, who published his first novel, and the man whose hotel suite she cleaned.

De Laurentiis, Dino

The movie producer who, through his production company, was involved in adapting several of King's stories to film, though none of distinction.

Harlan Ellison: "Dino de Laurentiis is the Irwin Allen of his generation, coarse, lacking subtlety, making films of vulgar pretentiousness that personify the most venal attitudes of the industry." (From his column, "Harlan Ellison's Watching," "Part One: In Which We Scuffle Through the Embers.")

SK: "He is a man for whom the word *style* seems to have been invented; a man of poise, charm, persuasiveness, *panache*. And he is *very* fond of the grand gesture." (King's foreword to *Silver Bullet*.)

Demon Driven: Stephen King and the Art of Writing,
edited by George Beahm

Published in 1994 by GB Publishing/Ink in a limited edition of 300 numbered copies. Numbers 1 to 100 were the deluxe edition, numbered in red ink, slipcased, at $75, signed by all the contributors. Numbers 101 to 300 were the limited edition, numbered in black ink, not slipcased, at $35, signed by the editor-publisher, George Beahm.

There was no trade edition of this book published.

Contents included

"Creatures of the Night," by George Beahm

"Of Books and Reputations: The Confusing Cases of King, Koontz, and Others," by Michael R. Collings

"Stephen King Meets the Jim and Tammy Zombies," by Howard Wornom

"Stephen King: Dreamweaver—Thoughts on *Nightmares & Dreamscapes*," by Stephen J. Spignesi

"Stephen King's Main(e) Haunts," by David Lowell

"Digging Up Stories with Stephen King," by W. C. Stroby

"Demon-Driven: Stephen King and the Art of Writing," by George Beahm

De Palma, Brian

Director of *Carrie*. Originally budgeted at $1.6 million, the flick was a monster hit at the box office: $30 million domestically. Prior to *Carrie*, De Palma had paid his dues, directing *The Phantom of the Paradise*.

Following *Carrie*, De Palma directed *The Fury*, *Dressed to Kill*, and *Blow Out*, among other hit films.

Desperation

Hardback, 1996, 690 pages, Viking, $27.95
Contents
Part I. In the House of the Wolf, The House of the Scorpion

Advertising slick from NAL promoting *The Regulators* and *Desperation*, with a split cover visually tying the two books together.

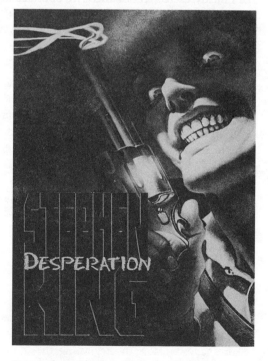

Dust jacket art by Don Maitz for the Grant edition of *Desperation*.

King on the book's simultaneous publication with *The Regulators*, by Richard Bachman: "I did it because the Voice told me to do it. Not because I thought it would sell well or because people would like it or because critics would say 'Oh wow' or even 'What a bogus marketing trick.' The Voice doesn't talk very much, so when it does you have to listen." ("Spectacular Fall Performance," *PW*, "Bookwire," August, 1996.)

PW also commented: "*Desperation* first flowered in the Nevada desert in 1991, when King was driving his daughter's car cross-country. Passing through Ruth, a small town with seemingly no inhabitants, King, 'being who I am,' immediately thought, 'They're all dead,' and then, 'Who killed them?' At that point, King says, the Voice surfaced: 'It immediately came back with: "The sheriff killed them all." And when an answer comes back that quickly, there's a book there.'" ("Spectacular Fall Performance," *PW*, August, 1997.)

A film version is in the works.

Different Seasons

Hardback, 1982, 527 pages, Viking, $16.95

Dedication: One for each novella, but not for the book itself. "Rita Hayworth and Shawshank Redemption" ("For Russ and Florence Dorr"), "Apt Pupil" ("For Elaine Koster and Herbert Schnall"), "The Body" ("For George McLeod"), "The Breathing Method" ("For Peter and Susan Straub").

Contents

In the epigraph at the front of the book, King writes, "It is the tale, not he who tells it," taken from "The Breathing Method," an idea at the center of King's perception that the story holds dominance over everything else. He expounds on this at length in an introduction to *Night Shift*. It also shows King's desire to separate the story from the storyteller, although some critics feel differently, that it is the tale *and* he who tells it, since you cannot divorce the two.

Interestingly, in an "author's note" in *Christine*, King writes: "In the world of popular song, it is as the Rolling Stones say: the singer, not the song." The epigraph, then, may simply have been restated by King to suit his own ends.

The first collection of King novellas, this is by any standard a remarkable quartet of tales. For King, who by now had built his reputation as a spook writer, this collection of original novellas was distinctly mainstream with no supernatural elements, except for "The Breathing Method."

For those who had stereotyped King as only a supernatural writer, the first three stories in this collection came as a pleasant surprise: the same man who wrote *Carrie*, *The Shining*, and *'Salem's Lot* could write a poignant story like "Rita Hayworth and Shawshank Redemption," a horrific story about the Holocaust like "Apt Pupil," and a gentle story like "The Body."

In the afterword, King states that each novella was written immediately after he completed a novel. (King's accounting of which novella followed what novel is contradicted by Douglas E. Winter in his study *Stephen King: The Art of Darkness*.)

In order of appearance (loosely organized in a four seasons motif):

"Rita Hayworth and Shawshank Redemption" could have been, in the hands of a less capable writer, a straightforward "break out of prison" story. But King's careful characterization of Andy Dufresne and especially Johnny "Red" Smith creates considerable empathy for these two men and their slow, cautious friendship set against the backdrop of a Maine prison in the late forties.

An emotional story that packs a considerable punch, this was faithfully adapted to the screen by director Frank Darabont as *The Shawshank Redemption*, a title that had movie-goers scratching their heads, especially after it was revealed that King had written it.

"Apt Pupil" is the kind of contemporary horror story that, if written by Joyce Carol Oates, would have drawn considerably more attention. The story of a very apt pupil—a California teenager, Todd Bowden—with a morbid preoccupation with the Nazi death camps, this story was in fact partially shot for a feature film some years ago, but the funding ran out and the project died . . . only to resurface in recent years, with a new cast.

Todd Bowden learns the grisly details of the death camps from a former camp commandant, Dussander, who relives his former glory and finds himself in a *danse macabre* with Bowden, as both descend into moral hell together, feeding their blood lusts by killing stray animals, and then bums from under a nearby bridge.

"The Body" is, simply, pure King. The most autobiographical work of fiction King has produced to date, this combines all of the best elements of King's fiction, evoking the world of childhood, with all its patented tics and tropes; recreating the Maine milieu, specifically Castle Rock, Maine, which he's traversed numerous times; and evoking the wistfulness that characterizes a rite-of-passage story, if done right.

With this story, King hit the high notes, and sustained them.

"The Breathing Method" is the odd story in the bunch. Ironically, it is the only story in this quartet with a supernatural element. A story within a story, "The Breathing Method," told by a doctor— a member of an old men's club that meets at a New York brownstone to tell tales—is a disquieting story about a very unusual birth

This first-rate collection of King fiction showed —as King would begin loudly to assert in the late nineties—that he wasn't just a spook writer. In fact, as Casey Stengel would say (a line King has quoted), you gotta put an asterisk by this one.

Years after this quartet's publication, King said that he knew he'd never write a quartet of stories or a collection of short fiction this good again. He may be right, but I'm hoping he's wrong. Lightning *can* strike in the same place twice.

"Writers of grue sometimes also go straight. . . . The point is, when you live in your imagination a lot of the time, it may take you anywhere—anywhere at all. The four stories in *Different Seasons* were written for love, not money, usually in be-

tween other writing projects. They have a pleasant, open-air feel, I think, even at the grimmest moments. . . . There's something about them, I hope, that says the writer was having a good time, worrying not about the storyteller but only the tale." (*Dear Walden People*, a Waldenbooks house publication.)

Different Seasons was banned by the Lanark County Board of Education in Smiths Falls, Ontario, from high school English classes, according to a *BDN* story (July 20, 1995). One trustee, Ruth Ain, remarked: "I could not even read it ["Apt Pupil"]. Mr. King is a very popular author. But does that mean that's enough to teach it in schools?" King fired back: "I know the attitude and the mindset. These people love to be little despots in their own territory. . . . Book banning is never about what's pornographic or what's not. It's always about who's got the power to . . . try and impose their view of the way the world should be on the minds of the young ones in their charge. To call my work pornographic is ridiculous and wrong."

Diforio, Robert

CEO of NAL when King was with that house.

Diforio, on King's four-book deal signed in December 1988: "We enjoy being King's publisher and we're happy that we'll be continuing that relationship." (*Castle Rock.*) The deal reportedly cost NAL an estimated $30 million to $40 million.

Diner's Club card

Travel and entertainment credit card that, in late 1979, King could not obtain because, as he put it, "I'm still considered a freelance." (Peter Costa, "Novelist Throws the Book at his Worn-out Blue Jeans," UPI, Oct. 30, 1979.)

Discovering Stephen King,
edited by Darrell Schweitzer

A Starmont House book published in 1985, this collection takes a page out of the Underwood-Miller playbook: Collect articles about King, reprinted from various sources, and dish it up to King fans, some of whom are completists that *have* to buy this.

Of this collection with pieces of varying quality and interest, editor Schweitzer says in his introduction that "the purpose of *Discovering Stephen King* is to present a more intelligent discussion of his work than you are likely to find in *The New York Times* or *Time*, a variety of explorations from informed viewpoints. The basic premise is that if you like King's work, you will be interested in reading something *about* it."

The book contains the following essays:

"What Makes Him So *Scary*?" by Ben P. Indick, in which he explores the nature of fear in King's fiction.

"Has Success Spoiled King?" by Alan Warren. He asks, "But has all this attention fundamentally altered his craft?" No, Warren explains, but King "may have to wait for the dust of critical scorn to settle before a more accurate evaluation of his work can be made."

"The Biggest Horror Fan of Them All," by Don Herron, puts forth his thesis: "I doubt that the majority of fans or even his most intelligent critics read him for Deep Meaning. Capital 'D,' capital 'M.'" Suffice it to say that the majority of fans or even the most intelligent critics won't read *this* piece by Herron for Deep Meaning. Capital D, capital M.

"King's American Gothic," by Gary William Crawford, discusses the relationship of King "to the emergence of American gothic art forms." An academic but readable discussion putting him squarely in that tradition.

"The Early Tales: King and *Startling Mystery Stories*," by Chet Williamson, looks at King's earliest professionally published fiction. An interesting piece intelligently discussing King's strengths and weaknesses as a writer.

"King and Peter Straub: Fear and Friendship," by Bernadette Bosky, delineates the nature of the friendship between the two men, drawing heavily on published texts of their meetings. A very thorough piece—86 footnotes needed to document the text—it's fascinating reading for anyone who wants to know more about the nature of literary collaboration and, specifically, the story behind *The Talisman*.

"*The Stand*: Science Fiction into Fantasy," by Michael R. Collings, is a discussion of the science fiction and fantasy elements of the first version of *The Stand*.

"King with a Twist: The E.C. Influence," by Debra Stump, discusses the connection between King's fiction and Educational Comics (E.C.), which featured horrific (in the best sense of that word) art and stories with a moral, which may be one reason why King liked them so much. Good horror fiction is always moral, and E.C. Comics always made sure the bad guys got their comeuppance.

"King and the Lovecraft Mythos," by Robert M. Price, discusses linkages between the fiction of King and H. P. Lovecraft. To my mind, King was influenced less by Ech-Pi-Ehl, as he called himself, than by more contemporary writers, like Matheson. Lovecraft's Cthulu Mythos, at the heart of his fiction, postulated cosmic gods in an uncaring universe in which man was insignificant; King's mythos postulates a world filled with horror, tempered by humanity, in which the good sometimes loses out, but more significantly, sometimes wins the battles, offering hope and redemption.

"Three by Bachman," by Don D'Ammassa, discusses common themes among *The Long Walk*, *The Running Man*, and *Thinner*.

"A Matter of Choice: King's *Cujo* and Malamud's *The Natural*," by Debra Stump, is an academic piece linking Malamud as a writer to King's fiction—King mentions him in *Danse Macabre*—and discussing *The Natural* and *Cujo* as novels in which the theme of making personal choices becomes paramount.

"Collecting King," by the book's editor, Darrell Schweitzer, is in retrospect considerably dated, in light of the current market for King collectibles, which shows no signs of abating, given the size of King's audience and the growing number of mainstream collectors buying the more esoteric editions. Thirteen years later, the proof is in the pudding: Without exception, every signed, limited edition by King has sold out, usually before publication, and King collectibles continue to be highly collectible, proving to be long-term investments. The fan who wisely bought King first editions or the more collectible limiteds—especially the *Dark Tower* books—saw his investment multiply in value considerably. No question: King remains *the* most collectible author in our time; Schweitzer notwithstanding, forget Krugerrands. They're always making more of them, but the number of truly collectible King items gets swallowed up faster by the ever-growing numbers of new King collectors who are willing to spend the bucks.

"Synopses of King's Fiction," by Sanford Z. Meschkow, with additions by Darrell Schweitzer, Michael R. Collings, and Ben Indick, offers short summaries of King's fiction.

"King: A Bibliography," by Marshall B. Tymn, covers ground that Winter covered, for the most part, in *Stephen King: The Art of Darkness*, though readers today are advised to get the Collings bibliography, *The Work of Stephen King* (1996).

Dixie Boy truck stop

Location near Wilmington, North Carolina, where King filmed *Maximum Overdrive*. During the shoot, truckers who pulled into this truck stop figuring they could get refueled never knew they were on a movie set.

"The Doctor's Case"
(collected in *Nightmares & Dreamscapes*)

Originally published as the final story in a collection of Sherlock Holmes pastiches (*The New Adventures of Sherlock Holmes*). The title "The Doctor's Case" says it all: Watson, not Holmes, solves the case, one that Holmes would have killed to solve, so to speak. A locked-room mystery in which a vindictive old man is murdered. *Why* is obvious, but *how?* Watson, the game's afoot . . .

Dodge Shadow commercial

Inspired by King's fiction, the ad clearly traded on the pop culture recognition of King's haunted car (Christine) and dog (Cujo).

"Dolan's Cadillac"
(collected in *Nightmares & Dreamscapes*)

Until its appearance in a revised version published as a limited edition by Lord John Press in 1989, it was previously available only in *Castle Rock* (issues 2 to 6), which meant that most King fans would likely not have read it at all.

A strong story in the lead-off position in *Nightmares & Dreamscapes*, it's a revenge story, pure and simple, and very well told, with the right touch of irony. Dolan, a Las Vegas hood, kills a schoolteacher after she promises to testify against him in court. Despite police assurances that she would be protected, Dolan manages to kill her with a bomb wired to the ignition of her car. With the only witness gone, Dolan thinks he's a free man, but her husband, Robinson, bides his time, laying a trap for him, one from which there will be no escape . . . except death.

Knowing that Dolan drives a reinforced Cadillac Sedan DeVille on Route 71 from Las Vegas to Los Angeles, Robinson takes a page from Poe, specifically, from "The Cask of Amontillado," in which the victim is entombed alive. Working on a highway construction crew, Robinson waits until a holiday weekend to dig a giant pit in which to trap Dolan's Cadillac.

The trap is set, and sprung, and Dolan finds himself trapped in his own car, with its bulletproof windows, and not enough room to open the doors on either side. Dolan, in short, is trapped like the rat he is, but keeps upping the ante to Robinson, if only he'll let him go.

As each spadeful of dirt hits the roof of the car, Dolan grows more desperate, more anxious, and with growing horror, realizes that there's nothing, absolutely nothing, that he can offer that Robinson will accept, short of his entombment.

The car, built to exacting specifications, and built like a fortress, becomes Dolan's coffin; and with Dolan's death, Robinson's nightmares about his deceased wife, Elizabeth, are finally put to rest.

Dolores Claiborne

Hardback, 1993, 305 pages, Viking, $23.50
Dedication: "For my mother, Ruth Pillsbury King"

Contents: Single narrative

The second of three novels that form a loose trilogy (preceded by *Gerald's Game* and followed by *Rose Madder*), this is the strongest of the three. It is a first-person narrative told by a Maine woman who has lived a hard life, and explores spouse and child abuse with a depth and poignancy that is lacking in *Gerald's Game*.

In interviews over the years, King has pointed out that there's a side to Maine that most people never see. They see Bar Harbor, the pretty coastal villages, and U.S. Route 1, festooned with restaurants and souvenir shops and other tourist traps. What they *don't* see: the unremitting pockets of poverty and the hardscrabble life that is the lot of many Mainiacs, who live a difficult, rural existence in which pain and misery are a way of life.

As this novel begins, Dolores Claiborne is at the sheriff's office, telling her side of the story. Dolores, who appears to have had a hand in the death of her employer, Vera Donovan, has to defend herself. Already marked by the suspicious death of her husband, Dolores stands to inherit the Donovan estate, if she can convince the police that she had no hand in Donovan's death.

In telling this long, sustained narrative, King delivers loud and clear a damning indictment of the uglier parts of rural Maine society, and in doing so he delivers a first-rate story.

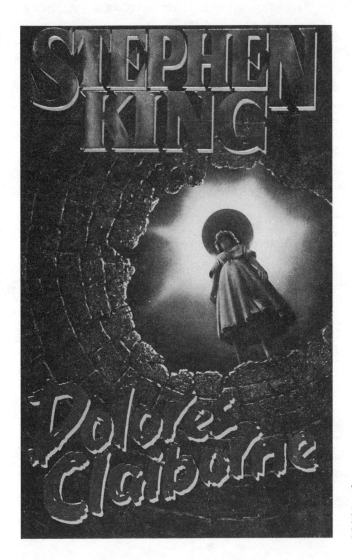

The cover to the hardcover edition of *Dolores Claiborne*, showing Dolores looking down the pit into which her husband had fallen.

Dolores Claiborne (film), 1994

If Stephen King had written nothing but stories set in Maine, devoid of the supernatural except for an occasional ghost or two, he'd be hailed as a major regional writer, and he'd be taken seriously.

King the regional writer wins over mainstream audiences with films like *Stand by Me* and *The Shawshank Redemption*. Add *Dolores Claiborne* to this list.

The film adaptation is rigorously faithful to the book, which is a grim recounting of a grim woman's hardscrabble life, which is about as far away as you can get from the usual Hollywood pap, where everything is just hunky-dory and ends on an upbeat note.

That's not how life is, and that's certainly not the life that Dolores Claiborne lived.

In an outstanding performance, Kathy Bates makes us *believe* she's Dolores. Her daughter, competently played by Jennifer Jason Leigh, is a hard-living woman, a heavy smoker and drinker who comes back to the island where she grew up to be with her mother, who is under suspicion for the murder of her admittedly no-account, no-talent, thieving, drunk husband.

This is a view of Maine that most people can't see or don't want to see—the ordinary people for whom King has considerable empathy, as far away from the tourist traps and "Vacationland" as can be imagined.

A grim but in the end uplifting movie.

Donald M. Grant, Publisher, Inc.

A small press specializing in illustrated books and catering to fantasy, science fiction, and horror fans, and notable for its publication of signed, limited editions.

Grant's claim to King fame was the publication of the *Dark Tower* novels, to date four books, all beautifully printed and bound, magnificently and imaginatively illustrated with black and white and color plates and decorations, and affordably priced. They offer the best bang for the buck among King's trade publishers. To own a Grant book is to see just how beautiful a book can be in its own right, as an art object.

Write to 19 Surrey Lane, PO Box 187, Hampton Falls, NH 03844. You can also contact them via e-mail at: grantbooks@aol.com. Or check out their Web site: http://www.nh.ultranet.com/~dmgrant

"The Dreaded X"

An essay by King on movie ratings. As the director of *Maximum Overdrive*, King, who ran up against the limits of cinema as dictated by the movie ratings board, wrote this lengthy, thought-provoking essay on what's wrong with how movies are rated in the U.S., and what he recommends as remedial measures: not worry about counting every episode of what appears to be objectionable, but hewing to the British system of rating, in which "intent and effect" are the criteria instead of "content and extent."

SK, on the "dreaded X": "I think *X* is going to be the slut on the block for ever and ever . . . but I think it can be a *useful* slut."

Drew University

A university in New Jersey that was King's first choice, but, as Winter pointed out in *The Art of Darkness*, "His family finances were insufficient to enable him to attend."

Dr. Seuss
(pen name of Theodor Seuss Giesel)

King credits two of Dr. Seuss's works as formative in his vision as a writer: *McElligot's Pool* and, more important, *The 500 Hats of Bartholomew Cubbins*.

Sarah W. Spruce: "Bartholomew cannot take his hat off to the King because he always has another under it. Bartholomew has done nothing to deserve this fate; it simply happens. And just as mysteriously stops. King noted that many of his works owe a great debt to *Bartholomew Cubbins*, starting with the ordinary and turning into the fantastic." (*Castle Rock.*)

Drugs

In college, King, like many of his contemporaries, experimented with hallucinogens. In a *Playboy* interview he said, when asked whether he smoked grass, "No, I prefer hard drugs. Or I used to, anyway; I haven't done anything heavy in years. . . . Even at the University of Maine, it was no big deal to get hold of drugs. I did a lot of LSD and peyote and mescaline, more than sixty trips in all." (*Bare Bones,* 1988.)

Dunkin' Donuts

In the early years of her marriage to Stephen, Tabitha King worked as a waitress at one of two Dunkin' Donuts in Bangor, where she quickly learned the art of scarfing up her own tips, though company policy dictated that all tips be shared.

Dunn, William

A fellow Maine resident and, like King, a former schoolteacher, Dunn optioned *Graveyard Shift,* paying $2,500 for the film rights. A location scout for *Creepshow* and location manager for *Pet Sematary,* Dunn, with King, pushed for a Maine film office.

SK, on movie options: "Anybody can make a movie out of anything of mine if they have enough money. If it's a major novel, I want to get paid major bucks." But of Dunn's option he said: "It's a short story, and it's a small company that's got interesting ideas that doesn't have much money. You pay as you go, as far as I'm concerned." (Quoted by Gary Wood, *Cinefantastique,* December 1990.)

Durham Elementary School

This school's librarian, Sherry Dolloff, wrote to King asking for a donation to buy books for the school. She hoped to get a small donation but instead got a $10,000 check with a note: "Enclosed you will find a check to buy the kids some books; get 'em some great stories."

King attended this school when he was growing up in Durham, Maine. (*BDN,* April 20, 1992.)

A beaming Bill Dunn (coproducer) at the world premiere of *Graveyard Shift* at Hoyt Cinema in Bangor, Maine.

popular writer as we've been privileged to experience in many a year. He writes a good stick. He never cheats the buyer of a King book. You may or may not feel he brought off a particular job when you get to page last, but you *never* feel you've been had. He does the one job no writer may ignore at the peril of tar and feathers, he *delivers*."

SK: "For whatever it's worth, Harlan Ellison is a great man: a fast friend, a supportive critic, a ferocious enemy of the false, maniacally funny, perhaps insecure . . . but above all else, brave and true." (Introduction to Harlan Ellison's *Stalking the Nightmare.*)

"The End of the Whole Mess"
(collected in *Nightmares & Dreamscapes*)

Originally appearing in *Omni* (October 1986), this story recalls Keyes's "Flowers for Algernon," with its first-person narration by Howard Fornoy and the use of intentional misspellings to show the effects of a home-brewed panacea, termed the "calmative" by Fornoy's genius brother, Bobby, who has decided he has had it with the violence in the world. After experimenting with bees and wasps, he invents a calamative that, when spread around the world, will put an end to the endless suffering, the bickering, the wars.

Released worldwide through a volcanic explosion, the calmative does indeed work as advertised, but with one unforeseen side effect: It produces premature senility.

As Howard—probably the last person on earth with a grip on reality, a grip that's quickly fading—types this last record of what happened, he forgives his brother. For a troubled world, it is indeed the "end of the whole mess," but not in the way that Bobby or Howard ever anticipated. After Bobby destroys the forest to save the trees, the world's population is, finally, at peace.

End-of-world novels

As examples of this genre King cites Shiel's *The Purple Cloud* and George Stewart's *Earth Abides*, which was an early influence on *The Stand*. (*Bare Bones.*)

Eads, Ashley

An angel-faced nine-year-old girl suffering from cystic fibrosis who appeared in a scene in *Thinner* through the offices of the Dream Factory in Kansas City, Missouri, which fulfills the dreams of sick children.

SK, on Ashley's having a speaking part in the film: "I think it's fantastic." (*BDN*, Sept. 14, 1995).

Easton Press

A "collectors only" book club whose Masterpieces of Science Fiction included a small run of *The Dead Zone*, bound in leather, with moiré fabric endpapers, gilded edges, and a satin ribbon. With an introduction by James Gunn and illustrated in full color by Jill Bauman, this edition was issued in a run of approximately 1,200 copies, at $39.50.

Ellison, Harlan

Prolific writer and social gadfly in whose forthcoming anthology, *Last Dangerous Visions*, King's "Squad D" will appear. The story was contributed especially for the anthology. In an interview conducted by George Beahm and Howard Wornom, Ellison said that King is "one of the most accomplished storytellers the twentieth century has produced," adding, "It is because he is as honest a

E Is for E.C. Comics

"In the old E.C. Comics, the guilty were always punished. That was the traditional American view of morality." (King, quoted in Jessie Horsting, *Stephen King at the Movies.*)

In the opening scene of *Creepshow*, an homage to the horror comics of the fifties, an enraged father snatches a Creepshow comic book out of his son's hands and symbolically throws it in the trash.

The message is clear: Comic books are the lowest form of trash literature, unfit for human consumption, and will surely pollute the minds of the youth, a message that Dr. Frederic Wertham espoused in *Seduction of the Innocent*, published in 1953 by Rinehart & Company. Its dust jacket copy said it all:

This is the most shocking book of recent years. And it should be the most influential.

Seduction of the Innocent is the complete, detailed report of the findings of famed psychiatrist Frederic Wertham on the pernicious influence of comic books on the youth of today. No parent can afford to ignore it.

You think your child is immune? Don't forget—90,000,000 comic books are read each month. You think they are mostly about floppy-eared bunnies, attractive little mice and chipmunks? Go take a look.

On the basis of wide experience and many years' research, Dr. Wertham flatly states that comic books: are an invitation to illiteracy; create an atmosphere of cruelty and deceit; stimulate unwholesome fantasies; suggest criminal or sexually abnormal ideas; create a readiness for temptation; suggest forms a delinquent impulse may take and supply details of technique.

Wertham's stamp of disapproval on four-color pulp entertainment, readily endorsed by the Senate at its subcommittee hearings, was just the ammunition parents needed. As a result, comics became "self-regulated," a polite way of saying "self-censored," and the comic book industry was irrevocably changed, not for the better.

As of October 1954, comics carried a seal of approval prominently posted on the covers, one adopted by the comics industry instead of having outsiders come in and regulate it for them. Some of the best comics of the fifties, including E.C. Comics, underwent a slow death.

What Wertham wouldn't acknowledge and parents never perceived was that the E.C. Comics line, in contrast to its competitors, was a quality line, sufficient to justify Russ Cochran's reprinting them three decades later in full color from the original art, in hardback, with illustrated slipcases. The "trash" that Wertham condemned had become four-color pop culture treasures, reprinted with the kind of attention normally reserved for prestigious art books. (King himself has a complete set in his home library.)

The E.C. line included *Weird Science*, *Weird Fantasy*, *Frontline Combat*, *Two-Fisted Tales*, *Vault of Horror*, *Tales from the Crypt*, *Haunt of Fear*, *Crime Suspense Stories*, *Shock Suspense Stories*. They were works of comic book art, well written and drawn, and above all they were moral fiction.

King has repeatedly said horror stories must have a sense of morality. It's not enough, he argues, to throw in shock effects to surprise or stun the reader into submission. The writer's job is to show the truth, and that means the bad guys get their comeuppance—the seeds of destruction lie within.

That sense of morality was the cornerstone of E.C. Comics. Despite the admittedly grue-some fare between the lurid covers—shown out of context by Wertham to a worried nation that thought, "I don't have to *read* trash to *know* it's trash"—the bad guys reaped what they sowed in an E.C. story.

Creepshow is a loving homage to those comics. Both King and George Romero (who directed the film) loved the E.C. line, and it shows. In both the film and comic book adaptation, the look and feel of the horror comics of the fifties is deliberately evoked.

The comic book adaptation is replete with direct and indirect E.C. references. The cover was drawn by Jack Kamen, an E.C. artist; the framing device of a ghoulish figure introducing each story was the technique E.C. Comics employed; the theme of just revenge is incorporated in the stories; and Bernie Wrightson, who illustrated the book, would have felt right at home in the stable of E.C. artists in the fifties, whom he studied and admired.

Is *Creepshow* great art?

No, of course not!

But it's great fun, and moral fiction, and if it doesn't terrify, it at least achieves the lowest level of horror fiction: the gross-out. If it's not educational, it certainly is entertaining.

Enterprise Incidents Presents Stephen King, edited by James Van Hise

Published in 1984 by New Media Publishing, Inc., this 58-page publication is an overview with sophomoric plot summaries, curiously illustrated. Though some art obviously draws on King's work, other pieces clearly do not.

The bulk of this publication consists of plot summaries of the novels and short fiction, though for reasons unknown, the editor has included—for visual relief, perhaps—a three-page comic strip, "Egyptian Graffiti," which has nothing to do with King. Nor is that the only oddity: The chapter "Stephen King One of a Kinds" (*sic*) consists of three paragraphs with bare-bone mentions of *Danse Macabre*, the audio dramatization of "The Mist," and *Creepshow*, the comic book tie-in.

This one is for completists only.

Esquire Register

King was nominated for inclusion in 1985. The Register honors people under forty who have made a significant contribution to their field.

"'Ever Et Raw Meat?' and Other Weird Questions"

Originally published in the *New York Times Book Review*, this essay humorously sheds light on what it's like from inside the goldfish bowl, as a pro writer examines his fan mail.

Over the years, King has determined that the questions he gets asked fall into three categories: the one-of-a-kind questions (like "Ever Et Raw Meat?"), the old standards, and the real weirdies.

Occasionally, he admits, he gets an interesting question—like whether or not he writes in the nude. In the end he asks himself, "Do I mind these questions? Yes . . . and no."

King may elaborate more on the questions his fans pose in *On Fiction*, an autobiographical retrospective look at the art and craft of fiction writing. But one thing is certain: On the evidence of letters, phone-in interviews, and public appearances, his readers are a curious lot, asking questions that range from the insightful to the plain foolish.

"The Evil that King Does"

In a letter to the editor published in the *Bangor Daily News*, Gordon R. Heath of Ellsworth, Maine, who saw *Pet Sematary*, expressed his grave concern that the movie was a "monstrosity," one that reviewers couldn't see for what it is because they were all "suffering from the emperor's clothes syndrome. They were so much in awe of King's success at the bookstore cash registers that they could see no evil in his work."

Heath contended that King made it appear "usual and normal" that the mayhem wreaked on the dead who came back to life to haunt the living would induce nightmares in children who have lost loved ones. Heath's perception was that King's movie, appealing to impressionable teenagers, "seemed to be telling [them] that it was quite acceptable behavior to pour kerosene over household furnishings and then to touch a match to it in order to get rid of any evil spirits which might lurk there. . . . [King] has done a great injustice to the public, and he should set up a fund to prevent crime in young people to counter the evil he has done."

Heath's admonition to King: "Pay up, Steve, or watch the flames of arsonists consuming the houses around you. You will know that every flame that you see was touched off by your own hand. What you did was equivalent to shouting 'Fire!' in a crowded theater."

Eviction

Shortly after Doubleday bought *Carrie*, the Kings were evicted from their double-wide trailer in Hermon, Maine.

Ewing, Bobby

In the August 30, 1988, issue of *TV Guide*, celebrities answered the question "Why did Bobby Ewing come back?" King's answer was that he's still dead. "He has been reanimated."

EW's 101 Most Influential People

Entertainment Weekly's round-up of the main players in entertainment, "our annual ranking of the folks who decide what we see, hear and read." Over the years, King has gone up and down that ranking. A sample entry: In 1991, *EW* ranked King number 63, citing *King's Golden Years, Needful Things* in hardback, *Four Past Midnight* in paperback, and two movies in production, *The Dark Half* and *King's Sleepwalkers*.

The Eyes of the Dragon

Hardback with slipcase, 1984, 314 pages, $120.00

Dedication: "This story is for my great friend Ben Straub, and for my daughter, Naomi King."

Contents: Numbered sections.

Those who think that King writes only horror would be surprised to find that this fairy tale—a tale with teeth, as King put it—is a wonderful read, one that begs for a sequel.

Set in the land of Delain, this is the story of two sons pitted against each other: Peter, the good son, imprisoned after the death of his father, King Roland; and Thomas, the son raised to the crown by the machinations of Flagg, a dark magician who poisoned the king.

The once-happy kingdom of Delain is thrown in chaos as Flagg plays Thomas like a marionette, and its only hope is Peter, who escapes from the tower in which he was wrongfully imprisoned by tying napkins together—hence the story's original title, *The Napkins*.

Peter puts things right and Delain is once again peaceful.

The background is that King's daughter, Naomi, would not read his horror stories, so he decided to write something specifically for her, a children's story, since she read and enjoyed fantasy.

Self-published in a limited edition of 1,250 copies (1,000 numbered in black, 250 numbered in red for presentation purposes), the book was designed by Michael Alpert and illustrated by Ken-

The Eyes of the Dragon *continued*
neth R. Linkhäuser the pen name of Kenny Ray Linkous.

According to Alpert, the book required over 45,000 large sheets of paper made in France, which took over four months to produce

The trade edition, published in 1987 by Viking, was different textually and visually from the Philtrum Press edition. New material was added at the suggestion of the book's editor; and the Linkhäuser illustrations were dropped in favor of David Palladini's newly commissioned pieces. The earlier illustrations are unquestionably superior.

The novel also marks the return of Randall Flagg.

Exorcism

A novel purportedly written by King under the pen name Eht Natas, "the Satan" spelled backward.

This rumor made the rounds in the wake of the Bachman disclosure, but it was clearly speculative and misinformed.

Eyeglasses

King wears glasses with Coke-bottle lenses to correct his nearsightedness.

SK on Ackerman: "He has always seen the fiction of the fantastic—the stories and the cinema—as a gateway to wonder."

Fan mail

As early as 1990 King was receiving, directly and indirectly, through his publishers, about 500 pieces of mail a week, of which 80 percent requested a response.

In his informal forewords, forenotes, and afterwords that bookend his short fiction collections, King writes in a way that seems to invite direct feedback from readers. That kind of connection from writer to reader inevitably results in mail from readers wanting to be pen pals.

Though King has been known to dash off typed postcards with brief notes, he usually sends a preprinted postcard thanking the sender and explaining that the volume of mail makes individual responses impossible. "I love the people who read my stuff, and I don't just love them because they support me. I love them because they listen. . . . There are people who write who believe that the act of putting it down on paper is enough, and I've never felt that was the end of it. I've always felt that to make it complete, it had to go out to some other person. What we're talking about is communication," King said in an interview with Recorded Books, on *The Author Talks*.

Famous Monsters of Filmland

A pulp magazine published by Forrest J. Ackerman for juvenile boys, emphasizing monster movies from the fifties. The magazine has been cited by Steven Spielberg and George Lucas as an early inspiration.

This magazine, in fact, was the first one to which King submitted a story for publication: "The Killers" was a two-page, single-spaced story that eventually saw publication in Ackerman's zine years after it had originally been submitted, after King became famous, as a piece of literary history.

F Is for Fans and Fame

Martin Myers wrote, "First you're unknown, then you write one book and you move up to obscurity."

That may be true for many writers, but it wasn't true for Stephen King, whose short novel *Carrie* heralded the arrival of a new fictional voice.

Doubleday's modest $2,500 investment soon yielded a monstrous $400,000 paperback reprint sale, with a movie to follow, directed by Brian De Palma, starring virtual unknowns like John Travolta, Sissy Spacek, Amy Irving, William Katt, and De Palma's then wife, Nancy Allen.

The film helped King reach the critical mass, bringing large numbers of moviegoers to the bookstore where they made King's third novel, *The Shining*, his first hardback best-seller. With his second novel, *'Salem's Lot*, King was still relatively obscure in the book trade, though the fantasy community had by then embraced him, recognizing one of their own who in time would go on to define the field to a larger world.

Once King became a brand-name writer with the publication of *The Shining*, the third horror book in a row, he put obscurity behind him permanently and dealt with the real-world horrors of success, as Mel Allen pointed out in a profile for *Writer's Digest*. "[He's] had his phone number changed, and the local operator tells countless people every day, 'No, I'm sorry, we are not permitted to disclose that number,' because strangers call from all parts of the country to ask for money, interviews, help in finding a publisher for the 800-page novel they've written about werewolves, or advice on how to do away with the demonic neighbor who has caused the vegetables to succumb to root rot."

The book sales were already impressive: The paperback of *'Salem's Lot* initially sold a million and went on to sell 2.25 million within a half year of publication, goosed by the film *Carrie*.

The growing number of fans who avidly collected his every book meant that the fan mail arriving via his publishers would itself be a thing of horror. Each new book brought mailbags of letters, a good number of them from readers claiming to be his number one fan.

At a certain level of sales, the incessant demands from fans are unending. Instead of working on the writing, you are working on *being a writer*, as King explained: You're answering fan mail and fending off requests for autographs (in person and by mail) and requests for public appearances, requests for charitable contributions, requests for library donations, requests for interviews, from fanzines to professional magazines, and the electronic media as well.

"Most of [the fans] are normal people, but when they're off the beam, they're way off the beam." (Quoted in John Healy, "The 'King of Horror' to Pack City Hall Tuesday Night," *Evening Express*, March 1, 1990.)

SK: "Your mother was right when she told you reading science fiction and fantasy books will make you warped. All fantasy people are warped." (This UPI quote, taken out of context from King's public address at the fifth World Fantasy Con, Oct. 15, 1979, made him appear as if he said his fans were crazy.)

Naomi King: "The press is as the press will be. The American public tends to have an appetite for knowing the private lives of people that they adore, to make themselves feel closer to these people. That's as it will be. I can't change that." (*BDN*, date unknown.)

Here are some choice selections from letters sent to King:

♦ After reading *The Shining*, a reader wrote that he wanted to read *Carrie* and *'Salem's Lot*, but had reservations: "Though I consider myself a strong person, I must think of my own mental health."

♦ Linda Z., Plymouth, Connecticut: "While reading, it is almost as if I'm right there when everything is going on."

♦ Peter C., Portland, Maine: "All I want is for someone to tell me that I'm a lousy writer who should stop wasting his time or that I have some potential and should keep trying. P.S. If there is nothing you can do, send money."

♦ Lisa B., Hickory, North Carolinia, working on a term paper and needing help from King: "Due to the fact that I live in a small town, I have been unable to find enough articles and reviews of *The Shining*. Therefore, I would appreciate it greatly if you would send me your personal analysis and any other articles and reviews you may have."

♦ Linda N., Clinton, Iowa: "My husband, who very rarely reads books, could not put it down."

♦ Paul G., Maryville, Missouri: "Do you write just as a money-making job, for literary value, or in hopes it will be sold for a television or movie screenplay?"

♦ Randee T., New Baltimore, Michigan: "It's gotten so that all it takes is the *name* Stephen King on a book and I know it will be good."

♦ Tamara J., Oceanside, California: "Pardon the phrase, but you scared the shit out of this twenty-year-old."

♦ Joyce F., a 16-year-old novelist: "I've been working (and I really mean *working*) on a novel for close to a year, and it is a lot tougher than I thought writing one would be. It's a pretty good little book but there are so many *problems*! I really need help! Sometimes I can be writing a very gory blood and guts scene that should make a person want to throw up, but when I take the scene from my mind and try to put it down on paper, it just doesn't seem scary."

♦ Shelly C., Battle Creek, Michigan: "How did you get started in the writing business? Where do you get the ideas for your books? How come all your books are about something that is possessed? Do you enjoy writing? Do you have any suggestions to a sprouting writer?"

Fan Mail, by Ronald Munson

SK: "A fantastically crafty nail-biter in the Ira Levin tradition—I loved it!"

Fans' favorite King novel

Hands down: *The Stand* in the new, improved edition. (The more, the better!)

Fantasy Annual demise

In *Fantasy Review,* Karl Edward Wagner echoed an idea he had heard before—one he didn't hold —that King's refusal to allow reprinting of stories had perhaps contributed to the demise of *Fantasy Annual,* an anthology series edited by Terry Carr.

The thinking behind it: An anthology needs brand-name writers who in effect sell the book, carrying the lesser-known or less popular writers.

King's justifiable complaint was that his name was prominently listed on virtually every anthology book cover, which put him in an uncomfortable position: "My name has been used prominently on enough covers stateside to make me feel a little bit like the come-on girl in the window of a live sex show on 42nd Street," a view he expressed in a letter to *Fantasy Review* (January 1984).

To minimize the impression that King does "whore duty for some marketing guy" (*FR,* Janu-

ary 1984), his contracts for reprinting stories specify that his name be inserted alphabetically and be set in the same typeface and size as the other contributors'.

Farris, John

A horror novelist best known for *Harrison High,* a best-selling book cited by King as an early influence.

Favorite books as a student

In *Scholastic Scope* (April 1986), King cites his favorite books when he was a college student: *I Am Legend,* by Richard Matheson; *Hot Rod,* by Henry G. Felsen; *Jude the Obscure* and *Tess of the D'Urbervilles,* by Thomas Hardy; *Lord of the Flies,* by William Golding; *The Collector,* by John Fowles; *The Grapes of Wrath,* by John Steinbeck; and *The End of the Night,* by John D. MacDonald.

Favorite crime novelist, King's

Jim Thompson, who wrote *The Killer Inside Me* (for which King wrote an introduction, for the Blood and Guts Press edition), *After Dark My Sweet, A Swell-Looking Babe, A Hell of a Woman,* and others showing seamier and psychotic slices of life.

Favorite foods

The *New York Times* reporter Bryan Miller interviewed King for the October 26, 1988, edition and noted that King ate a "monstrous steak" and commented that he "liked to make simple foods that you can work on and make well. A good beef stew, homemade bread. That kind of stuff." (*Castle Rock.*)

Favorite story

King cited "The Body," from *Different Seasons*, at a talk in Pasadena, California, in 1989.

Fear, by L. Ron Hubbard

SK: "L. Ron Hubbard's *Fear* is one of the few books in the chiller genre which actually merits employment of the overworked adjective 'classic,' as in 'This is a classic tale of creeping, surreal menace and horror.' If you're not averse to a case of the cold chills—a rather bad one—and you've never read *Fear*, I urge you to do so. Don't even wait for a dark and stormy night. This is one of the really really good ones."

Fear Itself: The Horror Fiction of Stephen King,
edited by Tim Underwood and Chuck Miller

Contents
Introduction—"Meeting Stevie," by Peter
  Straub
Foreword—"On Becoming a Brand Name," by
  Stephen King
"Beyond the Kittery Bridge: Stephen King's
  Maine," by Burton Hatlen
"Cinderella's Revenge—Twists on Fairy Tale
  and Mythic Themes in the Work of Stephen
  King," by Chelsea Quinn Yarbro
"Horror Springs in the Fiction of Stephen
  King," by Don Herron
"Horror Hits a High," by Fritz Leiber
"The Movies and Mr. King," by Bill Warren
"Stephen King: Horror and Humanity for Our
  Time," by Deborah L. Notkin
"The Grey Arena," by Charles L. Grant
"King and the Literary Tradition of Horror
  and the Supernatural," by Ben P. Indick
"The Marsten House in *'Salem's Lot*," by Alan
  Ryan
"The Night Journeys of Stephen King," by
  Douglas E. Winter
Afterword, by George A. Romero
"Stephen King: A Bibliography," by Marty
  Ketchum, J. H. Levack and Jeff Levin
Notes on the Contributors

Published by Underwood-Miller in 1982, this anthology of original essays was the first and best book about King published by Underwood-Miller. It was also the only one that King signed for its limited edition, owing to the inclusion of his essay "On Becoming a Brand Name."

Like that of *Stephen King: The Art of Darkness*, the success of *Fear Itself* proved that there was a market for books *about* King, starting a cottage industry that caters mostly to hard-core King fans.

Fears, King's

In "The Horror Writer and the Ten Bears," King lists, in descending order, his top ten fears:

10. Fear *for* someone else
 9. Fear of others (paranoia)
 8. Fear of death
 7. Fear of insects
 6. Fear of closed-in places
 5. Fear of rats
 4. Fear of snakes
 3. Fear of deformity
 2. Fear of squashy things
 1. Fear of the dark

Ferman, Ed

The founding editor of *The Magazine of Fantasy and Science Fiction*. In the Dec. 1990 King issue Ferman observed: "[W]hy have I read every word of every Stephen King novel (with the exceptions of *It*, somehow missed, and the collaborative *The Talisman*, never finished?) And further, why do I remember them all, and rather vividly. . . . They do stick in the mind, his books, like old friends, and perhaps that's part of the answer. . . . Stephen King is unique."

Fictional deaths

Stephen Spignesi obsessively catalogued every method of death in every work published by King, in, *The Shape Under the Sheet: The Complete Stephen King Encyclopedia*.

There were so many that Spignesi had to break them down by group:

1. Death from amputation(s), decapitation, or loss of bodily parts or fluids.
2. Death from being eaten (by anything, including animals and/or bugs)
3. Death from disease
4. Death by monsters
5. Drowning deaths
6. Most bizarre deaths
7. Gentlest death
8. Nonsupernatural deaths (nonspecific, but including murders and vehicular deaths)
9. Suicides

"Field of Screams"

The Little League ballpark behind King's home, so nicknamed by the local residents of Bangor. It was a gift to the city and cost $1 million. At King's suggestion it was named the Shawn Trevor Mansfield Complex, after coach Dave Mansfield's 14-year-old son, who died of cerebral palsy in 1980.

A plaque at the park's entrance states simply that the ballpark was dedicated to SHAWN TREVOR MANSFIELD AND ALL THE OTHER BOYS WHO NEVER GOT TO PLAY BASEBALL.

"The Fifth Quarter"
(collected in *Nightmares & Dreamscapes*)

Originally appearing in *Cavalier* (April 1972), this is a King rarity: his only short work of fiction published under a pen name, John Swithen. The likely reason: *Cavalier* had been publishing King's fiction, all obviously horror, so the magazine didn't want to confuse its readership with a crime story published under King's name.

Barney, an ex-con's friend, was a get-away driver for a Brink's truck robbery. His friend and three other robbers each hold a quarter of a map that, when assembled, shows the location of the buried loot. In the postrobbery bickering, the ex-con's friend is killed. The ex-con metes out justice to the remaining three, thus becoming the "fifth quarter" and securing the pieces to the map.

The Films of Stephen King,
by Michael R. Collings

Unlike the other books about King, this one, published by Starmont House in 1996, has no illustrations. (The German edition, however, is profusely illustrated with movie stills.) Even without photos, the text is outstanding; Collings does what others who have written books on King's visual adaptations have not done: compared the films to the texts on which they are based. As a result, this thought-provoking book illuminates King's fiction, instead of merely cataloguing technical data, credits, and a bare bones summary of the plot, which seems to be standard operating procedure for books of this kind.

The Films of Stephen King, by Ann Lloyd

Originally appearing in England, this book was reprinted in the U.S. by St. Martin's Press in 1993. It is very similar in content and approach to the Jessie Horsting book, *Stephen King at the Movies*, which covered King's visual adaptations chronologically, reprinting the oft-seen production stills from the movies. Unlike the Horsting book, which had original interviews with King and others involved in the films themselves, the text to this book is wholly drawn from existing texts, as far as I can tell.

For each film, a listing of credits, a synopsis, and a short discussion are provided. The sections of the book are:
Introduction
Carrie
The Shining
Creepshow
Cujo
The Dead Zone
Christine
Children of the Corn
Firestarter
Cat's Eye

Firestarter

Hardback, 1980, 428 pages, Viking, $13.95

Dedication: "In memory of Shirley Jackson, who never needed to raise her voice. *The Haunting of Hill House;* 'The Lottery'; *We have Always Lived in the Castle;* 'The Sundial'"

Contents: Individual chapters (not numbered) with text headings

Background: King has said that this book is a riff on *Carrie.* While that is true, it also has a touch of *'Salem's Lot* and *The Shining.*

Like Carrie White and Danny Torrance, Charlie McGee, the daughter of Andy McGee and Vicky Tomlinson, has a wild talent: She is pyrokinetic. An outsider by virtue of her unwanted "talent," Charlie is on the run from The Shop, a secret government agency hell-bent on finding and harnessing her power for destructive purposes.

When circumstances force Charlie to unleash her power she lays waste to everything around her, demonstrating the lethal power she possesses.

There was talk about publishing a special student edition of *Firestarter,* an idea King at first thought had merit. At an American Library Association convention in 1989, he was approached by a publisher who said, "We could go through it and we would consult with you completely, but there are a number of questions about some words and passages, and we could take these out and not hurt the story."

The problem, said an angry librarian who stalked away after King told her of the proposed edition, was that publishing such an edition was tantamount to King's endorsing censorship of his own books. She told him, "I put my job on the line to keep that book in the library the way that you wrote it and you tell me that this guy comes up and says he wants to expurgate it and you're taking him seriously."

King said he had never thought of it that way and put an end to her ire by dropping the idea of an expurgated *Firestarter* immediately.

Firestarter (film), 1984

Never have so many labored so hard for so many hours with so many dollars in the budget to produce a King film that so completely and utterly failed to ignite the audience's interest.

Boasting one of the largest budgets for King's movies to date, $15 million, the film, directed by Mark Lester, also featured what promised to be a lot of acting talent: David Keith as Andrew McGee, Heather Locklear as Vicky McGee, Martin Sheen as Captain Hollister, George C. Scott as John Rainbird, Louise Fletcher as Norma Manders, Art Carney as Irv Manders, and the child actress wunderkind of *E.T.* fame, Drew Barrymore.

Despite the dollars spent on above-the-line talent and stuntmen trained in working with fire scenes, the movie's believability boiled down to Drew Barrymore's performance.

If she could convince you that she was in fact pyrokinetic, that she was in fact an orphan on the run, overwhelmed with grief, feeling very much the outsider, then the film had a chance. But this combustible *Carrie,* with Barrymore at its center, sparked little interest.

It's a shame, really, that *Firestarter* proved to be a visual failure on the screen. There was *so* much to work with, but in the end, Barrymore's acting was, more or less, less.

Joe Bob Briggs: "Big Steve King has a new flick out called *Firestarter*. (This is only Steve's second movie in two months and the fourth or fifth one in the last year. What's wrong, big guy, you send the typewriter out for repairs?) What we got here is a little girl who when she gets mad can stare at your shirt and turn your body into Bananas Foster.... Drive-in Academy Award nominations for Drew Barrymore, the little girl, and Mark Lester, the director who never lets the plot get in the way of the special effects. Joe Bob says check it out." (*Joe Bob Goes to the Drive-in*, 1987)

Firestorm

Term NAL used to characterize four King books published in a 14-month period: *It, The Eyes of the Dragon, Misery,* and *The Tommyknockers.*

"Some critics will want to dismiss it as a grandstand act," King told *USA Today* (1985). "But most, I hope, will view it as a remarkable feat."

First Bank of New England

This bank printed the dummy checks used as limitation sheets for the limited edition of *The Regulators.* The name on the checks was Richard Bachman, whose printed address on the checks was "432 Marsten Street, Starkeville, NH 03057." "Marsten" is a reference to the Marsten house in *'Salem's Lot,* and "Starkeville" is a take-off on the name "George Stark," the pen name that comes to life in *The Dark Half.*

Each dummy check was made out to a character in one of King's stories, and the memo section listed the reason for purchase—inevitably, in-jokes. For instance, check #0007 was in the amount of $1.95 for a copy of "The Fifth Quarter," made out to John Swithen.

First printings

In the book trade, the first printing is what the publisher *expects* to print, not necessarily what he *does* print. If the sales reps can't push their allot-

ment into the stores, then the first printing is cut accordingly. Also, a large first printing gives the impression to the trade that the publisher is getting behind the book.

Reported first printings of hardback editions of King's books (*PW*, Jan. 24, 1991):

Carrie:	30,000 copies
'Salem's Lot:	20,000 copies
The Stand:	70,000 copies
The Dead Zone:	80,000 copies
Firestarter:	100,000 copies
Christine:	250,000 copies
Pet Sematary:	335,000 copies
The Talisman:	600,000 copies
It:	1,000,000 copies
Misery:	900,000 copies
The Tommyknockers:	1,200,000 copies
The Dark Half:	1,200,000 copies
Four Past Midnight:	1,200,000 copies
The Stand: The Complete and Uncut Edition:	400,000 copies

Firsts

First published story (self-published): "I Was a Teenage Graverobber," in *Comics Review.*

First professional sale: "The Glass Floor," to *Startling Mystery Stories.*

First paycheck for writing: Sportswriting for a local newspaper when he was in high school. He earned a half cent a word.

First published book, film adaptation, and theater adaptation: *Carrie.*

First best-selling book: *The Shining.*

First book inscription: On a galley proof of *Carrie*: "I love you, mom—Stephen King."

First jobs: From a press release issued by NAL: "janitor, bagger, dyer and sewer in a mill, a baseball coach, library shelver and stacker,

Firsts *continued*

industrial washroom worker, and for a while in a laundromat." King termed a lot of these jobs "shitwork."

First publication *about* Stephen King: *The Novels of Stephen King: Teacher's Manual*, by Edward J. Zagorski, from NAL (1981).

First nonfiction book by King: *Danse Macabre*.

First nonfiction book of essays about King: *Fear Itself*, published by Underwood-Miller.

First single-author book about King: Douglas E. Winter's *Stephen King: The Art of Darkness*.

First printing of *Carrie*: 30,000.

First printing of *Bag of Bones* (estimated): 1,200,000.

The 500 Hats of Bartholomew Cubbins

Children's book by Dr. Seuss, considered by King a "grim situation comedy." This book was pivotal in his storytelling, since it showed him that "sudden weirdness can happen to the most ordinary people, and for no reason at all."

Flat signing

King's term for writing only his name in his books, with no inscription.

According to informed sources, King rarely flat-signs books, preferring instead to personalize copies by inscribing them. The reason: On the secondary market, book dealers prefer signatures only, no inscriptions, since an inscription (unless it's associational) reduces the book's worth for resale purposes.

After King's *Insomnia* tour, he was distressed when numerous copies showed up immediately on the secondary market from fans who turned copies around for a fast buck. Did King *really* think that none of those copies would resurface as resold books at inflated prices? Hence, King's policy.

Flaws, Ethelyn Pillsbury and Oren

King's aunt and uncle who lived in Durham when he was growing up, less than a mile down the road.

In their attic King discovered a box of paperback novels that had been his father's, which was a turning point in his life; the compass needle pointed to true north, as he stated in *Danse Macabre*. Horror fiction, King knew, was his passion, his Great Interest.

As King wrote in *Danse Macabre*, it was "a cold day in 1959 or 1960 . . . the day I happened to come on a box of my father's books."

Flying

SK: "I hate to fly. It scares the devil out of me." (Profile by Carol Lawson, "Behind the Best Sellers," *NYTBR*, Sept. 23, 1979).

Foor, Roland

A teacher from Lilly, Pennsylvania, who was fired for showing *Carrie* to his class.

Footsteps V

A special issue of Bill Munster's zine honoring King, featuring articles about him as well as a cover illustration of him.

Forbes magazine

This business magazine publishes a list of estimated incomes of the top 40 entertainers. The unofficial list gives estimates of income for a two-year period.

For 1987 and 1988, King was rated twenty-third, with an estimated $25 million income.

For 1989 and 1990, King was rated thirty-fourth, with an estimate of $22 million.

For 1995 and 1996, King came in twelfth place, with an estimate of $71 million.

Forbidden Planet

A bookstore in London, England, where on May 14, 1983, King signed more than 500 copies of *Christine*—the store's greatest number of book sales in a single day by a single author. The three-hour signing started at 2 P.M., but the line constantly grew, so the number of waiting people never dropped below 150. King had to extend the time by a half hour to accommodate everyone. (*San Francisco Chronicle*, Aug. 1983.)

"For Owen" (collected in *Skeleton Crew*)

Poem King wrote for his second-born son, Owen.

Four Past Midnight

Hardback, 1990, 763 pages, Viking, $22.95
Dedication: One for each novella. "The Langoliers" ("This is for Joe, another white-knuckle flier"); "Secret Window, Secret Garden" ("This is for Chuck Verrill"); "The Library Policeman" ("This is for the staff and patrons of the Pasadena Public Library"); "The Sun Dog" ("This is in memory of John D. MacDonald. I miss you, old friend—and you were right about the tigers.")

Contents
Straight Up Midnight: An Introductory Note
The Langoliers
Secret Window, Secret Garden
The Library Policeman
The Sun Dog

Comparisons between this quartet of stories and *Different Seasons* are inevitable, though such comparisons are patently unfair. These are two completely different books, in subject matter, tone and treatment. This collection is what the average King reader—and certainly King's mainstream reader—would expect from the man billed as America's best-loved boogeyman: four supernatural tales, exploring four very different fears.

In "The Langoliers," what looks to be a routine red-eye flight from the West to the East Coast takes a little side trip into the "Twilight Zone": Most of the people on the plane simply disappear; only the sleeping passengers remain. One of the remaining passengers providentially happens to be an airline pilot. The plane lands in Bangor, Maine, where the band of survivors find a brave, new world fraught with terror: Langoliers, otherworldly creatures, literally race across the earth, erasing it. (The similarities between this story and "The Mist" are striking.)

In "Secret Window, Secret Garden," King explores yet another twist on his ongoing exploration of the intersection of the worlds of reality and unreality: Morton Rainey, a writer, is haunted by another man who claims Rainey has stolen his story from him—a fascinating premise, one that King pulls off.

In "The Library Policeman," what appears on the surface to be a typical King story turns out to be nothing of the sort. The bizarre library policeman is a boogeyman representing contemporary fears that haunt the characters in this story. This exploration of child abuse foreshadows *Gerald's Game*.

In "The Sun Dog," Kevin Delevan gets what he wants for his birthday, a Polaroid Sun camera. But it takes otherworldly pictures: in every picture an attacking dog is bounding toward the photographer. What happens when the dog *reaches* the photographer? To my mind this story required editing—it's too long in the telling—but it serves to prepare the reader for King's 1991 novel, *Needful Things*.

Fowler, Stephanie

King's production assistant during the filming of *Maximum Overdrive*, filmed in Wilmington, North Carolina.

Friends

In an interview in 1985 for *People* magazine, King cited Peter Straub as "a friend, and I only have about three of them."

The problem, King has said over the years, is that when he hears from people his immediate impulse is to think: "What do they want from me?" It's one of the high costs of success—people approach you not because they necessarily like you but for what you can do for them.

f-stop Fitzgerald

Photographer whose collection of photographs have been published in *Weird Angle, X-capees, Doc.u.men.tia* and *Pillars of the Almighty*, though King fans know him for his photo work in *Nightmares in the Sky*, which featured an original essay by King. His pen name is an allusion to F. Scott Fitzgerald and, of course, to the name given to aperture openings for lenses.

Fuddruckers Burgereaters Review
(May 1986)

Journal in which a fictitious letter "written" by King was published, signed "King lurking in the Shadows with pliers," in which he discussed his latest story, "The Tooth Fairy Liveth," a story about "little demons who sneak into houses at night ... extract people's teeth, leaving dimes and quarters in their place."

"Garbage Truck" controversy

In 1990 the UMO newspaper wanted to reprint the King columns ("Garbage Truck") as a separate book. After contacting King's office for permission to reprint and offering royalties, the book's editor, Steven M. Pappas, was surprised at the chilly reception. "They told me to stick it basically. They were really nasty about it."

Pappas then received a letter from King's attorney in New York, stating: "[King] feels embarrassed by these early columns and considers them juvenilia. . . . [He] has a faithful readership which expects the high caliber of literary materials customarily handwritten by him. . . . The material you want to reprint is not up to this standard."

After talking to King, Pappas knew he was in for a fight, so he retained the attorney Jeffrey Edwards, who said, "My general understanding is, if you write a column for a newspaper, it belongs to the newspaper. This looks like it will be a lot of fun."

In the end, King prevailed and the columns were not collected for the intended book or any other book. Looking at the big picture, the university surely realized that there was no value to be derived in a nasty legal battle with its most famous alumnus.

"We just don't have the kind of funds to take on protracted litigation," said *Maine Campus* newspaper editor Doug Vanderweide. "We don't want to cause him any professional discomfort. . . . I think it's best to be fair to the man, and the way to be fair to him is just to let this issue slide." (*BDN*, Dec. 6, 1990.)

Garris, Mick

Having directed *Sleepwalkers*, a ho-hum horror film based on an original King screenplay, Garris directed *The Shining*, the ABC-TV miniseries, and is currently working on King's *Desperation*.

The General Alumni Associations Career Award

Given to King at the UMO's homecoming festivities in 1981, this annual award goes to an alumnus who has enhanced the reputation of the university through distinguished career accomplishments. At 34, he was the youngest alumnus ever to receive the award.

Gerald's Game

Hardback, 1992, 332 pages, Viking, $23.50
Dedication: This book is dedicated, with love and admiration, to six good women: Margaret Spruce Morehouse, Catherine Spruce Graves,

Artwork for King's column, "Garbage Truck," in *The Maine Campus*.

Gerald's Game *continued*

Stephanie Spruce Leonard, Anne Spruce Labree, Tabitha Spruce King, Marcella Spruce

Contents: 40 numbered sections

Gerald's Game, Dolores Claiborne, and *Rose Madder* form a loose trilogy of sorts, all exploring social issues. In *Gerald's Game,* the novel is not so much about Gerald's game, a game of bondage that gets out of hand, as it is about his wife Jessie Burlingame's introspection while handcuffed to the bedposts in their summer home. As Jessie ruminates on her dilemma, on how to free herself from the confines of the cuffs, she digs deep in her memory . . . and recalls a horrific event from her past: the child molestation she suffered at her father's hands, on the day of an eclipse, a memory buried so deep that it took a traumatic episode to trigger its recall.

King fans felt that there was too much message and not enough story—too introspective. Though well written, it clearly wasn't in the first rank of King's fiction.

Gervais, Stephen

The artist who illustrated the Grant edition of *Christine.* The wraparound color cover for the book, showing a wide-angle look at Christine, and the moody black-and-white interior plates gave the book the perfect visual touch. Gervais later reprinted the art in a portfolio, sold through his small press.

Getting It On

Original title for what was later published as *Rage.*

The title was drawn from the rock and roll song by T. Rex, "Bang a Gong (Get It On)."

Geyer, Mark

The artist who created the interior art for *Rose Madder* and *The Green Mile.* Geyer's realistic pen-and-ink style was appropriate for both books, especially *The Green Mile.*

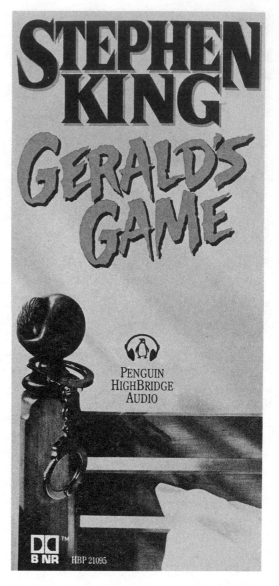

Box design for the audiotape recording of *Gerald's Game.* (Handcuffs *not* included.)

Ghost Story, by Peter Straub

One of King's favorite novels: "The terror just mounts and mounts." King's professional respect for Straub was clear early on, when Straub's publishers sent him galleys, requesting blurbs.

King's lengthy endorsements made Straub real-

ize that they had a lot in common, and a friendship ensued, resulting in an ambitious collaboration, *The Talisman.*

Cover to the reincarnated *Weird Tales*, containing the
reprint of "The Glass Floor," King's first professionally
published story.

Gifts from fans

King's fans send him everything from unwanted kitten bones to paintings. In fact, they
send him so much stuff that a special room at the
office harbors the growing collection.

Sometimes, a gift gets a place of honor, a place
on the wall in his office. A photo of a teddy bear
threatened by a knife made the cut; the caption
read, "Publish the next *Dark Tower* novel soon or
the bear gets it!" King put it up as a reminder that
his fans care about his work, and that the remaining three *Dark Tower* books still need to be
written.

Gilded Needles, by Michael McDowell

SK: "Riveting, terrifying, and just absolutely
great. To say that [it] is a great read and that it offers the deep pleasure of going along for the ride
with a novelist who is coming to the height of his
powers, is to say two thirds of it. The rest is the
simple fact that Michael McDowell must now be
regarded as the finest writer of paperback originals in America."

Glaser, Paul Michael

The director of *The Running Man* (1987), which
starred Arnold Schwarzenegger. Glaser's previous
credits included *Band of the Hand,* a thriller, and
several episodes of the TV series *Starsky and Hutch.*

"The Glass Floor " (uncollected)

King's first professionally published short story.
Submitted to Robert A. W. Lowndes, this story
earned King $35. Published in 1967 in *Startling
Mystery Stories,* this story was prefaced with a note
from its editor: "King has been sending us stories
for some time, and we returned one of them most
reluctantly, since it would be far too long before
we could use it, due to its length. But patience may
yet bring him due reward on that tale ['The Night
of the Tiger']; meanwhile, here is a chiller whose
length allowed us to get it into print much sooner."

Clearly derivative of Poe, the story nevertheless
is of professional quality—a first effort that requires no apology. For years King refused to allow
it to be reprinted, but he finally relented. He resisted the temptation to revise it—a temptation he
gave in to on numerous occasions, when reprinting other earlier work in his collections. "The Glass
Floor" fittingly saw republication in a modern-day
edition of the classic *Weird Tales* (fall 1990). Of this
fledgling effort and its modest payment, King
noted, "I've cashed many bigger ones since then,
but none gave me more satisfaction; someone had
finally paid me some real money for something I
had found in my head!"

King acknowledges that the story is a "most un-
remarkable work," but also admits that it has its

moments, and that its reprinting in *Weird Tales* may encourage budding authors who, like him, started out with nothing but imagination and a desire to tell tales.

Goden, Craig

Proprietor of a mail-order bookstore, The Time Tunnel (now defunct), that for years was a first-rate source for King collectibles.

Goldberg, Whoopi

Comedienne who published a review of *The Eyes of the Dragon* for the *Los Angeles Times Book Review*. She loved it.

The Golden Years (film), 1991

King has always wanted the luxury of telling a long story, longer than a two-part miniseries allows, and had sufficient cachet to sell CBS on the idea of a seven-part miniseries, though they wanted an anthology-type show with King as the host. Can you see it? King stepping out of the shadows, wearing his T-shirt and jeans and sneakers, as a ghostly painting materializes behind him. "Submitted for your approval," he begins. "Hey, wait a minute, that's Serling's line. Okay, let me try it *my* way. Here's a humdinger of a story, so pull up a bar stool and let me tell you what happened. It began . . ." and King fades away, as the viewer falls into the painting.

But I digress.

In *The Golden Years*, King combines several of his favorite fictional devices: the evil shop (from *Firestarter*), an experimental government lab where things go inexplicably wrong, with disastrous results ("The Mist"), and people on the lam from the authorities (*'Salem's Lot, Firestarter*).

An original story written especially for television, the miniseries would have evolved into a series, à la *The Fugitive* (a show King watched and loved as a kid) if the ratings had justified it, but the glacial pacing never caught on with the audience.

It is a touching love story of an elderly couple, that concludes with a final, poignant episode in which Harlan, who is growing younger because of a lab accident, embraces his wife, Gina, and they literally die in each other's arms.

Standout performances from Keith Szarbajka as Harlan Williams and Frances Sternhagen as Gina Williams were complemented with the performances of Felicity Huffman as Terry "Terrilynn" Spann, a sexy and feisty security agent, and Ed Lauter as General Louis Crewes, a military man with a radical change of heart. The head of the CIA experimental lab, General Crewes forsakes the mission and follows his heart and his conscience, seeking a peace of mind he's never known before—and Terrilynn as well.

Note: Of the six scripts that aired, King wrote the first four; the remaining two were written by Josef Anderson from King's story.

Jonathan Levin, CBS vice president for drama development: "We do business with him like no one else. We don't talk direct, he doesn't come down, we get mysterious faxes from his lair in Maine." (Quoted in Matt Rousch, "Stephen King Scares Up a Summer Series," *USA Today*, May 1991.)

SK: "I'd like to do the equivalent of a novel for TV. I'm real tired of dramatic TV that tells a beginning, a middle and a middle and a middle. . . . What if it's a hit—it would be like killing the golden goose. But if it's over this year, you just do a different one." (Matt Rousch, *USA Today*, May 7, 1991).

Jay Sharbutt, Associated Press: "So, yes, add 'Golden Years' to your list of summer watchables. It's fun, interesting, and well-crafted. And, unlike 'Twin Peaks,' it actually has a story line. In this day and age, that's radical, but it sure beats reruns."

Steve Warner (famous last words from CBS's vice president of special projects): "We're definitely thinking about bringing it back in the spring." (Quoted in Matt Rousch, *USA Today*, Aug. 1991).

Gonis, Jim

The director of a student film, *The Lawnmower Man*, which is faithful to the short story in a way that the film adaptation was not. Which is to say: The film adaptation was l-o-o-s-e-l-y based on the story.

Gornick, Michael

The cinematographer for *Creepshow* and a colleague of George Romero's. He did a commendable job in his directorial debut with *Creepshow 2*.

The Gothic World of Stephen King: Landscape of Nightmares, edited by Gary Hoppenstand and Ray B. Browne

Published by Bowling Green State University's Popular Press in 1987, this anthology of critical articles was clearly written for academic consumption.

Contents
Introduction
"The Horror of It All: King and the Landscape of the American Nightmare," by Gary Hoppenstand and Ray B. Browne
"Blood, Eroticism, and the Vampire in Twentieth-Century Popular Literature," by Carol A. Senf
"Of Mad Dogs and Firestarters—The Incomparable King," by Garyn G. Roberts
"Reading Between the Lines: King and Allegory," by Bernard J. Gallagher
"A Blind Date with Disaster: Adolescent Revolt in the Fiction of King," by Tom Newhouse
"Freaks: The Grotesque as Metaphor in the Works of King," by Vernon Hyles
"Viewing 'The Body': King's Portrait of the Artist as Survivor," by Leonard G. Heldreth
"King's Creation of Horror in *'Salem's Lot*: A Prolegomenon Towards a New Hermeneutic of the Gothic Novel," by James E. Hicks
"Love and Death in the American Car: King's Auto-Erotic Horror," by Linda C. Badley
"*The Dark Tower*: King's Gothic Western," by James Egan
"Taking King Seriously: Reflections on a Decade of Best-Sellers," by Samuel Schuman
"A Dream of New Life: King's *Pet Sematary* as a Variant of *Frankenstein*," by Mary Ferguson Pharr
"King's *Pet Sematary*: Hawthorne's Woods Revisited," by Tony Magistrale
"'Oz the Gweat and Tewwible' and 'The Other Side': The Theme of Death in *Pet Sematary* and *Jitterbug Perfume*," by Natalie Schroeder
Contributors

Grades, high school

In chemistry and physics, King got C's and D's, which is why he cannot write hard science fiction, preferring instead to write contemporary horror stories, a branch of fantasy.

King, who enjoyed reading hard science fiction, the kind written by Robert A. Heinlein and Joe Haldeman, tried his hand at writing science fiction stories, submitting to pulp magazines as a teenager. But all were rejected, and rightly so, on the grounds that the stories weren't scientifically plausible. (Horror requires no such plausibility;

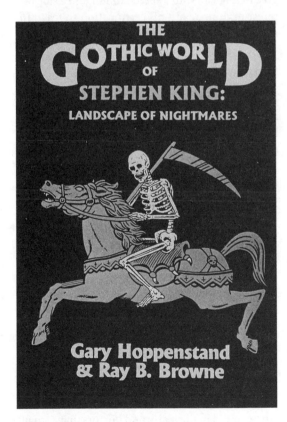

Cover to the trade paperback edition of Gary Hoppenstand and Ray Browne's book, *The Gothic World of Stephen King: Landscape of Nightmares.*

instead, simply put the characters in a situation and rely on the suspension of disbelief to carry the day . . . and the protagonists to their untimely deaths.

Graduation, college

King graduated from UMO on May 21, 1970.

Marking the occasion, King wrote in the last installment of "King's Garbage Truck" that "this boy has shown evidences of some talent, although at this point it is impossible to tell if he is just a flash in the pan or if he has real possibilities. It seems obvious that he has learned a great deal at the University of Maine at Orono, although a great deal has contributed to a lessening of idealistic fervor rather than a heightening of that characteristic."

King graduated with a bachelor of science degree in English, with a speech minor and a side interest in drama, and his certification to teach in secondary school.

"Gramma" (collected in *Skeleton Crew*)

Originally published in *Weird Book* (1984), this is one of King's most horrific stories, transmuting his real-life experiences, vividly recalled from his early years, into fiction.

As King has frequently recounted, their family moved to Pownal, Maine, where his mother, Ruth, was paid by the other members of her family to care for their ailing, elderly parents. King called it share-cropping—only in this case, it wasn't crops but these two people.

King's grandmother lived in the small living room. One day when his mother went out he was left to care for his grandmother, who quietly died. Taking a cue from a television show, King used a mirror to see if she was really dead.

Much of the story rings so true because it happened, up to the point of George's "Gramma" coming alive, of her being a witch, of her father being a Lovecraftian monster (Hastur). Its power can be found in the real-world horrors that a small child faces, magnified by imagination: His old grandmother looks to be a thing of horror; the skeletons in the closet are not a figure of speech but are real; and his greatest fear is that he doesn't want to be left alone with her, because he is justifiably afraid of her.

Gramma (film), 1987

Harlan Ellison, an exceptionally talented writer who wisely turned to scriptwriting to pay the bills so he could buy the time to write what he considers to be his more important work, imaginatively adapted "Gramma" for *The Twilight Zone* (its second incarnation on TV).

A marvelously effective adaptation, King's story is brought to life visually, *adding* to the power of the original story, which drew its strength from a real-world incident in King's life.

In this teleplay, George (aged 11) realizes his grandmother is dead. She calls out to him, and in a truly effective horrific scene, he comes to her out of a sense of duty, but with understandable reluctance, and for good reason: She literally sucks his shadow from him, his life force.

Grann, Phyllis

A book publishing executive who now heads Penguin Putnam Inc. after the merger. The bones of contention between the company's position and King's position were sufficiently insurmountable that the two parted company on *Bag of Bones*.

Grant, Donald

The founder of Donald M. Grant, Publisher, a small press catering to fantasy, science fiction, and horror fans. Inspired by Arkham House, Grant, formerly the publications director at a Rhode Island college, gained fame in the King community by publishing some of the most beautiful limited editions of King's books, notably *The Talisman* and the *Dark Tower* series.

In a phone interview with the *Denver Post*, Grant explained how the *Dark Tower* books had come to be published by his small firm instead of a large publisher: "I asked [King] if he had any material lying around that hard-core science-fiction buffs might appreciate and that I could get out a limited edition on. He said sure, there was the *Dark*

Tower stuff—which would eventually run to probably three volumes. But he insisted the first volume would have to be limited to just 10,000 trade copies, plus a signed, deluxe edition of 500. He's been putting out a lot of books lately, and he's starting to get concerned about overexposure."

Grant's small press, though well known in the fan community, was virtually unknown in the book trade at large. When a listing for *The Dark Tower* appeared in the frontmatter of *Pet Sematary*, it prompted hundreds of thousands of King fans to deluge King, Grant, booksellers, and King's trade publishers with requests for copies.

Now retired and living in Florida, Grant has left his small press to be ably run by Robert K. Wiener, who works out of his home office in New Hampshire.

"Graveyard Shift" (collected in *Night Shift*)

An effective, horrific short story that originally appeared in *Cavalier* magazine and was collected in *Night Shift*. It is the basis for the movie of the same name.

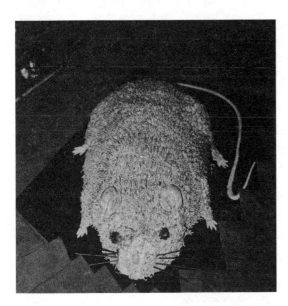

A cake in the shape of a giant rat, served at the world premiere of *The Graveyard Shift*, at Hoyt Cinema, a Bangor movie theater. King held a press conference there in the company of coproducer William Dunn and screenwriter John Esposito. (The cake was delicious.)

The story is set in Gates Falls, Maine. It's June, hotter than the hinges of hell, and over the Fourth of July weekend a group of men from the mill, under the supervision of the sadistic supervisor Warwick, go to the basement of the mill to clean it out . . . only to discover that what grew and mutated down there was best left undiscovered.

The rats that infest the mill above ground, also infest it below ground; the difference is that the rats topside are merely large and aggressive, but the subterranean ones are considerably larger and more aggressive and, living in the darkness, have become monsters of nature.

Background: King worked at a local knitting mill from 3 to 11 P.M. after high school. "It was a strange place, but I got a lot of stories from the job," he told Mel Allen ("Witches and Aspirin," *Writer's Digest*, June 1977).

"I wrote most of 'Graveyard Shift' in the office of *The Maine Campus*. I had this idea for a story: Wouldn't it be funny if these people cleaned out the basement of the mill—a job I had at one time—and found all these big rats? Wouldn't that be gross?

"Think of all the things you could do with that. So I wrote the story.

"The real impetus to write this particular story was the mill I worked in. It was a nonunion shop, and when they had vacation week, the people who had 'tenure' got a paid vacation; the rest of us also got the week off—without pay, unless you wanted to work the clean-up crew, which was going to go down in the basement.

"I worked in the bagging area. They'd blow fabric up into these huge bins and we would bag it. Between the times you were waiting for your bin to fill up, you'd throw cans at the rats, because the rats were everywhere. They were big guys, too; some of them would sit right up and beg for it like dogs, which stuck in my mind. So when I was asked to join the clean-up crew, I said, 'No, I can't do that. I'm going to beg off. You guys have a good time.'"

Graveyard Shift (film), 1990

At a press conference at Hoyt's Cinema in Bangor on opening night King said, "This movie was made by cannibals." By that he meant the princi-

Graveyard Shift (film) *continued*

pals were hungry for success, just as he was when he originally wrote the short story "Graveyard Shift," which first saw print in *Cavalier* (October 1970) and was collected in *Night Shift*.

Putting on his best face, King praised the energy of the young screenwriter, John Esposito, with whom he compared himself. King also cited the hard work that William J. Dunn, a fellow Mainiac, had put in on the film.

Because of King's efforts, *Graveyard Shift* was filmed in Maine, bringing a welcome infusion of Hollywood dollars into the coffers of the small communities that benefited from location shooting.

This story would have made a tight, suspenseful thirty-minute segment on a television show like *Night Gallery*. At 87 screen minutes it was far too long.

Graveyard Shift's oppressively dark cinematography, its dismal location (the Bachman Mills), and its subject matter (rats in the basement!) makes this film a one-time viewing.

Gray, Paul

Writer who reviewed *Different Seasons* for *Time* (Aug. 30, 1982) and found it lacking. "The only reader," he wrote, "likely to find these long tales truly frightening is an old-fashioned book lover: they are spooky examples of what can be called postliterate prose." He added that "King takes them dead seriously, and so, evidently, do his millions of readers."

The review, King commented, depressed him for weeks afterward.

"Gray Matter" (collected in *Night Shift*)

Originally published in *Cavalier* (October 1973), this odd little story recalls "The Lonesome Death of Jordy Verrill." Richie Grenadine loves his beer and usually stops by Henry's Nite-Owl for a case of brew, but after sustaining an injury on the job, he starts sending out his son instead. After drinking a bad beer, however, Grenadine changes . . . into an amorphous gray blob.

After the press conference for *Graveyard Shift* at Hoyt's Cinema in Bangor, Maine, King answered questions and signed autographs for his fans.

Great American Catalogue

In an article published in *The Register* (June 1988), King likens mail-order catalogues to chain letters, explaining that the companies rent their customers' names to other mail order companies with similar products.

The Green Mile 1: The Two Dead Girls

Mass market paperback, 1996, 92 pages, NAL/ Signet, $2.99

Contents

Foreword: A Letter

Eight numbered chapters

"I was having trouble moving that story. So when Ralph brought up the serial idea, I thought, if I agree to this, it will be like burning my bridges. I'll have to go on." (*PW*, "Bookwire: Spectacular Fall Performance," 1996.)

Elaine Koster (then executive v-p and publisher of Dutton/Signet and senior v-p, Penguin USA): "We didn't plan for *The Green Mile* to be an entryway to the fall novels, but that's what it has turned out to be." (*PW*, Bookwire, "Spectacular Fall Performance," 1996.)

The Green Mile screensaver for IBMs and compatibles atop the trade paperback reprint of the novel.

Promotional bookmark distributed in stores to push The Green Mile.

The Green Mile 2:
The Mouse on the Mile

Mass market paperback, 1996, 92 pages, NAL/Signet, $2.99
Contents
11 numbered chapters

The Green Mile 3: Coffey's Hands

Mass market paperback, 1996, 90 pages, NAL/Signet, $2.99
Contents
10 numbered chapters

The Green Mile 4:
The Bad Death of Eduard Delacroix

Mass market paperback, 1996, 90 pages, NAL/Signet, $2.99
Contents
Nine numbered chapters

The Green Mile 5: Night Journey

Mass market paperback, 1996, 90 pages, NAL/ignet, $2.99
Contents
Nine numbered chapters

Property of Lodi Memorial Library

The Green Mile 6: Coffey on the Mile

Mass market paperback, 1996, 138 pages, NAL/ Signet, $3.99

Contents

13 numbered chapters

Author's Afterword

With the death of the pulp magazines, the concept of serializing stories died.

King, who has always been troubled by the notion that the reader need simply flip to the back of the book to see how the story turns out, decided to write a serialized novel that, in effect, would hold the reader hostage until the last page. This state of misery would, he hoped, be followed by a state of happiness as the reader watched the story unfold at the pace he intended.

To NAL's credit—although you get the sense that King did some arm twisting—they agreed to put the concept to the test and publish a serialized novel: Would today's reader put up with this arrangement? In a time when consumers demand instant gratification, would they wait patiently until each new installment was published?

They would . . . and they did, resulting that year in a publishing anomaly: King had an unprecedented *eight* books on the best-seller lists: The six installments of *The Green Mile* were followed by his "twinner" novels, *Desperation,* under his own name, and *The Regulators,* under Bachman's name.

In fact, this literary experiment proved so durable that John Saul followed suit, with *The Blackstone Chronicles.* (Said King in *Entertainment Weekly:* "Saul's a pretty good writer and I hope he pulls it off.")

The story itself, set in 1932 at Cold Mountain Penitentiary in Maine, is first-rate King, the kind of story that tapped into his new, mainstream readership, likely surprised that the King of Horror could write with such poignancy.

The penitentiary's green mile is a long hallway lined with green linoleum that terminates at a juncture: Go one way and you're an inmate for life; go the other, and you're on Death Row, scheduled for execution.

The prison's latest inmate is John Coffey, a giant black man convicted of a heinous crime: raping (and in the process, killing) two young girls, both aged twelve. Coffey, you can be sure, will have to walk the green mile.

To tell you anything more about Coffey would give away too much, but suffice it to say that your hard-earned sympathy for Coffey is justified, and the story ends with an emotional punch that King delivers with sudden impact.

As this is written, Frank Darabont, set to direct the film version, is holding auditions to find an actor who can fill the large shoes of John Coffey, a role that will likely be nominated for an Academy Award. King's personal choice is Shaquille O'Neal. Clearly, Shaq looks the part, but the acting required to pull off this role is considerable—more, I think, than he can deliver.

Greene, Arthur B.

A New York lawyer who serves as King's business manager and book agent, Greene engineered King's move from New American Library to Simon & Schuster.

Because Greene is not a literary agent per se, he handled King's move in an atypical manner. Instead of handling this privately, inviting publishers to meet with his client, Greene sent out a letter in November 1997 to select publishers, inviting them to make bids on *Bag of Bones,* which had previously been seen only by NAL. King, meanwhile, was in Australia, taking a much-needed and long overdue break, during which he straddled a rented Harley and trekked across the plains from Sydney to Perth.

Green paper

According to King ("The Politics of Limited Editions," Part I), King inherited a ream of bright-green paper, which he used to write *The Dark Tower: The Gunslinger.* (King's wife-to-be, Tabitha, got a ream of bright-blue paper.) An odd size (seven by ten inches) and thick, this magical paper (as he called it) was delivered literally out of the blue: Nobody knew whence it came, but it was quickly put to good use.

Groupies

King, like any other celebrity, has had his share of overzealous fans of the opposite sex, but he wisely gives them a wide berth when on the road, because you never know when one of them might be named Annie and claim to be his number one fan.

Gumm, Dale

The winner of a *Castle Rock*-sponsored contest in which 70 subscribers wrote letters in which they used as many King references as possible.

For his efforts Gumm won a copy of the Philtrum Press edition of *The Eyes of the Dragon*.

Gumm's first paragraph: "After working the *graveyard shift* at *the plant* in *Jerusalem's Lot*, I rushed home to pick up *Carrie* and *Cujo*. I was exhausted from working the *night shift* but we jumped into *Christine* and headed for Castle Rock. We passed *Gramma* driving *Uncle Otto's truck* as we were leaving town."

GWOP

Abbreviation coined by one of King's editors, meaning "glamour world of publishing." A far cry from King's situation as a lonely writer sitting in a small room in Hermon, Maine, and staring at words on a page, the GWOP is "where we take off our Clark Kent outfit and turn into Superwriter," as he told Mel Allen of *Writer's Digest* (1977). It's the fabulous authors' lunches, the famous actors' names tossed off during lunch as possible casting choices for movies to be adapted from the fiction, etc. It is, in short, what wannabe writers *think* writing is all about: *having* written and published successfully, not writing itself.

Hackford, Taylor

Directed *Dolores Claiborne* for Castle Rock Entertainment. A first-rate film adaptation that explores the Maine locale to be revisited in *The Storm of the Century* and showcases Kathy Bates as Claiborne, a survivor type.

Hair dryer

When King heard about the paperback rights sale of *Carrie*, he wanted to mark that momentous occasion by buying something for Tabitha, so he went across the street from their apartment and, at a drugstore, bought a hair dryer for $16.95.

Hale, Phil

New England artist who illustrated *The Dark Tower II: The Drawing of the Three*. King selected Hale after seeing his work for the limited edition of *The Talisman*.

An exceptionally talented artist who shared a studio with Rick Berry, Hale depicted King's gunslinger as weather-beaten, rough around the edges, like a Clint Eastwood figure, a stark contrast to Michael Whelan's romanticized depictions.

Hale subsequently illustrated *Insomnia* for Mark V. Ziesing, a small press.

Halloween

The holiday from hell, as far as King's concerned, which he has grown to hate. Predictably, large crowds congregate at his house on West Broadway on Halloween, even if he's not there. He usually puts a small ad in the local newspaper and heads out of town for the weekend: "We're sorry, but the Kings will not be giving out trick-or-treat candy this year, but wish you all a happy and safe Halloween."

In the few cases when he's been home, he's had long lines of people lining up for treats . . . but King usually plays a trick on them! One year, he had a speaker mounted in the ground, so when the kids passed nearby, spooky sounds seemed to emanate from the ground.

Stephanie Leonard: "With each successive year, the number of visitors grew and the number of cars on West Broadway multiplied on Halloween. Local gendarmes had to hang out to direct traffic and the whole thing took on the trappings of a circus." (*Castle Rock*)

SK: "I wish you all a happy Halloween. I fucking hate it. I've turned into America's version of the Great Pumpkin. It used to be Alfred Hitchcock, but he's dead. On Halloween night, six thousand kids show up at my house in their little Freddie Krueger and Jason outfits." (At a public talk at the Santa Cruz Civic Auditorium in Santa Cruz, Calif., on Oct. 25, 1994.)

The annual Halloween ad that the Kings publish in the *Bangor Daily News* to keep the crowds down on Halloween.

Hampden Academy

Public high school in Hampden, Maine, where King taught high school English for two years, at a salary of $6,400 annually. He quit teaching to write full time after the paperback sale of *Carrie*.

Robert W. Rowe, principal: "King was a promising teacher. It was hard to catch him without a book under his arm. If he had the spare time, he'd be reading a book. But he always took the time to write. He was disciplined in his writing, consistent in sitting down and doing the work."

Brenda Willey, a former King student: "He was a good teacher who had seven classes a day and a study hall. He told us that he liked to write, and I think he wanted us to write. He was fun and had a pretty good sense of humor."

Hancock County, Maine

County where *Pet Sematary* was largely shot on location, which pumped up to $5 million into the local economy. Approximately 350 locals were hired as extras, and over 300 local vendors provided goods and services.

At King's insistence, rights to the movie were not sold until guarantees were made that it would be filmed in Maine, a case in which King's influence was put to good use, giving back to the state that he has championed.

Handwriting

King is left-handed. According to K. G. Stevens, who analyzed King's handwriting, "King loves to venture into the unknown. He can think in terms of what does not yet exist and is able to theorize accordingly. He is interested in learning the theories behind abstracts such as cameras and photography, flying, space and religion.

"He has more mental energy than physical and is always thinking. He could literally 'dream up' an idea.

"He gives of himself emotionally all day long. He is so enthusiastic that he could tire everyone out, including himself.

"Would you believe he also has a sense of humor? He does.

A sign on the grounds of the Hampden Academy in Hampden, Maine, where King taught high school English for two years.

"His signature says he is not as vulnerable to criticism as the next person because he believes in himself and feels good about himself and his work. He does not need approval from others in order to function strongly. However, he does enjoy a sincere compliment.

"He is a man of firm beliefs who works with great emotion and feeling." (*Castle Rock*)

Harley Davidson motorcycle

King is a Harley person. His hog is a 1986 Heritage Softail. It's a *man's* bike, not a sissy bike from the Far East. Harleys are made in America!

King rode his hog during a cross-country tour when promoting *Insomnia*; the bike also figures prominently in *Desperation*.

Harmony Grove Cemetery

A cemetery in Durham, Maine, transplanted to Jerusalem's Lot (*'Salem's Lot*, as the locals called it) as Harmony Hill cemetery. In King's novel *'Salem's Lot*, this cemetery is the site of unholy activity.

Harmony Grove Cemetery *continued*

Chesley recalls that this cemetery is where he and King "went . . . under the light of the late, sinking summer moon" and "ran among the old markers—Death's plain calling cards."

Hart, Gary

Former senator whose presidential bid King endorsed. King felt the youthful senator had some great ideas and traveled with Hart to campaign on his behalf.

While on the campaign trail in New Hampshire with Hart, King was asked by a reporter why he looked uneasy, and he replied, "I hate to fly. Today is the day that Buddy Holly went down. I was wondering who would get the most ink. Gary or I." (Quoted by Patrick Yack, "Superstar of Horror a Hit with Political Reporters, *Denver Post*, date unknown)

Hart was derailed by monkey business: Donna Rice was a blonde siren who was photographed on his lap. A married man, Hart's indiscretion cost him his party's nomination. Rice went on to fame and glory as a member of the right and is vocal in her moral opposition to pornography on the Internet. Hart, meanwhile, faded away into political obscurity.

Haskell, Bob

Sportswriter for the *Bangor Daily News* who lost a bet to King and, in front of the newspaper's office on Main Street, had to eat his words dressed in his skivvies—symbolic crow, actually chicken.

Haskell predicted that for the 1986 season, the Boston Red Sox, King's favorite baseball team, would be out of the running for the pennant. King, however, disagreed and backed it up with the bet.

Haskell, Gloria

In a letter to the editor (*BDN*, July 15, 1987), this Stillwater, Maine, woman complained that King used a specific cuss word excessively in *Misery*. "Let's put words like these back into the gutter where they belong and help clean up the language of this great country." (Which word? Go read the book and find out.)

Hatlen, Burton

College professor at UMO. Encouraged King's writing efforts when he was a student at the college. A King critic who has published several papers about King and his work, Hatlen introduced King at the "Reading Stephen King" symposium at the UMO campus.

Haunted, by James Herbert

SK: "*Haunted* is one of Herbert's best. Riveting, nonstop reading. . . . James Herbert is one of the best horror/suspense novelists around—if you want the you-know-what scared out of you, James Herbert will do it. . . . Herbert is one of England's best-selling novelists. *Haunted* is just the latest reason why."

Burton Hatlen—professor at UMO, a friend of the Kings, and a noted King scholar—poses in front of his home in Bangor, Maine.

Hautala, Rick

A graduate of UMO and Maine writer of horror novels, Hautala has had to write in King's long shadow cast from Bangor that eclipses other practitioners in the trade.

King has blurbed two of Hautala's novels, *Moondeath* and *Moonbog*.

Hautala: "Sure, a blurb from Steve helps sell a book, but even better, I like knowing that he's read my books and liked them. Steve's been a tremendous inspiration for me in my career because he was the first 'flesh and blood' writer I ever knew, and that gave a reality to the possibility of me getting my own work published. I don't think I would have had that if I hadn't known him before he or I got a book under contract." (Interviewed by David Lowell, *Castle Rock*.)

Hayford Park

The park behind King's home in Bangor, where he constructed a baseball diamond for the city's youths.

Headaches

King gets 'em, real head-splitters, monstrous ones. He said that his doctor calls them "stress aches."

"Head Down"
(collected in *Nightmares & Dreamscapes*)

Originally published in the *New Yorker* magazine and reprinted in an anthology of the best sportswriting for that year, this lengthy nonfiction essay is a grand slam, with the bases loaded at the bottom of the ninth.

King is in rare form with this essay, demonstrating his considerable talent for description, for capturing dialogue, and telling the story of how the Bangor West Little League team made it all the way to a state championship.

King's son Owen played first base for the team and King himself rolled up his sleeves and assisted coach David Mansfield whenever he needed a hand.

After King saw the poor condition of the baseball fields the boys played on, he dug deep and gave the city a custom-designed baseball park, named after Dave Mansfield's late son, Shawn Trevor Mansfield, at King's suggestion.

Clearly in a league of its own, King's nonfiction is unfortunately the least visible part of his literary output. All the more's the shame, since he has written over two hundred pieces, from which an excellent collection could be published.

Heart arrhythmia

King had symptoms of this condition, forcing him to change his lifestyle.

Hell House,
by Richard Matheson

SK: "May be the scariest haunted house novel ever written."

"Here There Be Tygers"
(collected in *Skeleton Crew*)

Originally published in *Ubris* (the UMO literary magazine, spring 1968), this is a good example of the kind of story King tells so well: the elments are an ordinary fear—a third-grade boy who is embarrassed at having to admit he has to go to the bathroom; his teacher, Miss Bird, who needlessly embarrasses him in front of the class; and an intrusion of the supernatural.

The boy goes to the bathroom in the basement, but balks when he sees a tiger. Another boy, Kenny Griffen, is sent down to find out what's taking so long, but he's devoured by the tiger. Finally, the no-nonsense Miss Bird becomes prey when she makes her appearance; like Griffen, she's devoured too.

In "Notes" following the main text of *Skeleton Crew*, King notes that the character of Miss Bird was based on his first-grade teacher when he was in Stratford, Connecticut.

Hermon, Maine

The city near Bangor where the Kings rented a double-wide trailer on top of a hill. After King criticized the town in *Playboy*, the town decided to cancel plans for a King Day and a King Museum, which was to be built on the original site of the double-wide trailer.

King made it clear in a letter to the editor published in the *BDN* that he could do without such honors from Hermon, for which he harbored few good memories.

Heroes for Hope: Starring the X-Men

A one-shot comic book published in 1985, as a fund-raising effort from Marvel Comics. "All proceeds from this comic book are being donated to famine relief and recovery in Africa."

King's contribution was three pages (10–12), with Berni Wrightson (penciler), Jeff Jones (inker), Tom Orzechowski (letterer), and Christie Scheele (colorist).

Herron, Don

A contributor to and editor of critical collections on King, published by Underwood-Miller. Don Herron's abrasive writing style has won him few readers in the King community.

Ian Harris (in *Castle Rock*): "He is my candidate for the most irritating, obnoxious writer that editors insist on including in essay collections about King." Harris takes Herron to task because his "deductive process consists of sarcasm, ridicule, and tiresome wit."

Which, Ian, is why they're called *critics*.

Heston, Fraser

The director of *Needful Things*, a very faithful adaptation of King's long novel brought to the screen by Castle Rock Entertainment.

Heston: "Stephen King, who has seen the footage, is very pleased with our work, which has made me extremely happy. Now that I've pleased him, I'm very confident I'll delight his fans."

Hilton Hotel

King gave a reading at this hotel in Sydney, Australia, his only public appearance during his first trip to the country. In the foyer of the hotel, a bookseller set up tables to sell King books and videotapes of the movies.

SK: "I think what I will remember about Australia is how quiet it is and how empty it is. There's no empty [in the United States] like the empty in this continent. If you stop, the silence is incredible. You feel very small, you can almost hear God breathing." (Quoted by Kendall Hill, in *The Sydney Morning Herald*, Oct. 30, 1997.)

Hinchberger, David

A King fan turned bookseller turned publisher, David specialized in selling King collectibles through his Overlook Connection, then branched out with the Overlook Connection Press to issue signed, limited editions of horror novels, including a reprint of *The Girl Next Door*, by Jack Ketchum, for which King wrote a lengthy introduction. His forthcoming book project is a signed, limited edition of *The Lost Work of King*, by pop cult chronicler Stephen J. Spignesi.

"The Hitchhiker"

An episode from *Creepshow 2* that was filmed in Bangor, Brewer, Hampden, and Dexter, in November 1986. The Bangor footage was shot at the I-95 construction site in Brewer, and on the University of Maine campus. The filming pumped an estimated $750,000 into the local economy.

King had a cameo appearance in this segment.

Hobbies

King said in an interview that his hobbies include "reading (mostly fiction), jigsaw puzzles, playing the guitar ('I'm terrible and so try to bore no one but myself'), movies."

Hoffman, Barry

The founding editor of *Gauntlet* magazine, the only serious journal discussing censorship in all its dimensions. Barry started Gauntlet Press to issue small-run, limited-edition books by fantasy greats, including Ray Bradbury, Richard Matheson, and others.

Barry published a limited edition of *Gauntlet* (issue number 2), for which King, along with other contributors, contributed and signed the limitation sheet.

Holland, Tom

Directed *The Langoliers* in 1995 for ABC television. A three-hour film that could have been cut to a tight one-hour television feature, *The Langoliers* was an ambitious effort that, in the minds of some King fans, never quite got off the ground. Holland had even less success with his subsequent directorial effort, King's *Thinner*, whose original release date in the summer was postponed, reportedly because King was unhappy with the footage. Anxious to please King, the powers that be shot new footage and finally released it later that year.

Holmes, Ted

A former professor at UMO, now retired, who encouraged King in his writing efforts as an undergraduate student.

"Home Delivery"
(collected in *Nightmares & Dreamscapes*)

Originally published in *Book of the Dead*, an anthology of zombie stories, this story, set on Little Tall Island off the coast of Maine, is quintessential King. With considerable skill and sympathy, King writes about islanders who must band together after they reluctantly believe the incredible news that zombies, arising from their coffins, are literally taking over the world to haunt the living.

It's a bad enough situation under any circumstances, but for one of the islanders, the indecisive Maddie Pace, it's a real nightmare. Pregnant by her late second husband, who died at sea during a storm, Maddie and her mother are adrift without a man to tell them what to do. Her first husband, a poor excuse of a man, died under less noble circumstances: In an abortive store robbery, his gun blew up in his face.

As the zombies literally go to town, munching on everyone from the president on down, and attempts fail to destroy Star Wormwood, the source of the infestation, the men on Little Tall Island have decided that they've had enough of this shit, so at a men-only meeting, they make plans to defend themselves from the undead that will surely rise and attack them as well.

It's hard, nasty work, killing the undead, as the men find out. Maddie also realizes the truth of that statement after her second husband, resting in Davy Jones's locker, comes back to life to haunt her. But she does her duty, just as the men did, and they put the dead to rest, finally, by all means possible.

George Romero's cult classic *Night of the Living Dead* postulates a world in which a returning spacecraft brings unwelcome cargo—space radiation that reanimates the dead, bringing them to

Retired Professor Ted Holmes (UMO), a creative writing teacher who taught King as an undergraduate.

H Is for Hollywood

Stephen King once quipped to an interviewer that whenever he went to Hollywood, he felt that he needed to bring his passport. That environment, he suggested, was so alien, it was as if he were on another world.

Though King may perceive himself as a stranger in a strange land when he leaves the East Coast for the West Coast, one thing is clear: He has had more of his books adapted to the screen than any other contemporary writer. He's also one of the few writers who is actively involved in the film community.

Though most people see him as connected to Hollywood through the film adapations, King is also active as a screenwriter, actor, producer, one-time director, and occasional member of the crews that work behind the scenes. In addition, he's been a major force in getting the Hollywood community to make films adapted from his works in Maine, deal-breaking clauses that forced Hollywood to shoot *Pet Sematary* and *Graveyard Shift* in his own backyard, instead of in Northern California.

His work on *Maximum Overdrive* earned him a Razzie Award nomination for "worst director," and his cameos are strictly for his own amusement. King's major contribution as an active participant in the film community is as a screenwriter.

King has written the screenplays for *Creepshow, Cat's Eye, Silver Bullet, Maximum Overdrive, Pet Sematary, Golden Years, Sleepwalkers, The Stand,* and *The Shining.* He doesn't list his shorter teleplays, which add up to an impressive list.

At last count (Internet Movie Database), King's fiction has been adapted to the screen or television over 50 times, a number that grows annually, since his work is frequently optioned.

Admittedly, the adaptations have ranged from those in name only—so loosely connected as to be fraudulent, as with *The Lawnmower Man*—to a handful in which fidelity is paid to the original, most recently *The Night Flier* and *Stephen King's The Shining.* Box office results have ranged from the dismal to the impressive. At this writing, *Carrie 2* is in the works.

Why, though, have so many of his stories been visually adapted? And why have the majority of them failed to please the King community?

King has given that question a lot of thought, discussing it at length in a two-part interview with Gary Wood. The unpublished interview, King said, was an opportunity to look at all of his films, to get an overview and see what worked and what didn't. It might offer a fresh perspective, he felt.

There are two principal reasons why so many of his stories have been adapted:

♦ King is a brand-name author, and although that's not necessarily a guarantee that the work in question will be adaptable to film, or that the work is worth filming, it makes selling the film to the studios much easier. Like book publishers, they'd prefer to have a known over an unknown any day.

♦ King's stories are very visual, easy to imagine, so when Hollywood looks for properties to adapt, King's stories come to mind. It's easy to "see" them as movies.

As to why so many of them fail, it's useful to look at the ones that have successfully made the transition from printed page to the screen. All are stories that at heart are about character: *Carrie, The Woman in the Room, The Dead Zone, Stand by Me, Pet Sematary, Misery, It, The Shawshank Redemption, Dolores Claiborne, The Stand, The Shining,* and *The Night Flier.*

My best guess as to the forthcoming films that will join the first rank of his visual adaptations: *Apt Pupil* and *The Green Mile*. *The Mist* and *Storm of the Century* may also be standouts.

When asked about the ingredients that make a good horror story, King cites characters as the most important element. Get the reader involved, concerned about the fate of the characters, and turn the monsters loose. It's a formula that works well both in print and on screen. The plot, King realizes, is important, but without memorable characters, there's no story, only a string of loosely connected events propelled by cardboard cut-out characters on the screen.

"Home Delivery" *continued*

life to feed on the living. King's take is similarly horrific: The dead come back to feed on the living.

King's story draws its strength from the horror of the supernatural situation, and the horror of Maddie's situation, with which she must cope.

Hooper, Tobe

The director of the television miniseries *'Salem's Lot*, Hooper—known mostly in horror film circles for *Chainsaw* and *Eaten Alive*—took on the project after it languished for two years for want of a brand-name horror director. On a very tight schedule, Hooper shot *'Salem's Lot* in 37 days, on a $4 million budget. He later went on to direct King's *The Mangler*.

Horrorfest '89

The first convention celebrating only King, it was held May 12–14, 1989, at the Stanley Hotel in Estes Park, Colorado. King was invited but declined to attend, and who can blame him? Imagine being at a convention where everyone knows your name . . .

Con organizer Ken Morgan's first King book was *The Shining*, a gift from his wife. Ken went on to collect other King books, then started receiving *Castle Rock*, a gift subscription from his wife.

Over 300 people attended, not bad, considering the costs involved in getting to a remote location high up in the Rockies. On Friday the dealer's room opened, where hucksters hucked the King fans, followed by a "get-acquainted" buffet-style dinner, though Morgan ruefully noted that the buffet was nowhere near as grand as the hotel staff had promised. Afterward, a drawing was held for books, signed by the guests of honor—writers like Michael R. Collings and Douglas E. Winter, who made names for themselves writing King criticism—followed by a talk from a hotel staffer, midnight readings, and horror movies until dawn.

On Saturday and Sunday the weather worsened and the rain turned to snow, but inside it was party time: Panels were held, a King film festival was shown, authors read from their works, and a benefit auction for Horror Writers of America (HWA) raised money to help the fledgling organization.

Ken Morgan, con chairman: "The convention attracted a wide variety of people—young and old, hip and straight-laced—from a variety of professions and regions. . . . But all of these people had one thing in common. Every single person I spoke with, member and guest alike, said the same thing—that this was beyond a shadow of a doubt the best convention they had ever gone to, an assessment with which I am in full agreement."

Horror genre

SK: "I've written twenty-five fairly long books —but I have redefined the genre of horror-writing in this country." (Quoted in Bill Goldstein, "King of Horror," *PW*, Jan. 24, 1991.)

"Horror-teria: The Beginning"

A song by the rock group Twisted Sister, on *Stay Hungry* (Atlantic Records, 1984). Dedicated "to King. Thanks for the inspiration." (*Castle Rock*, June 1985.)

Horsting, Jessie

Copublisher of *Midnight Graffiti*, Horsting did her homework to write *Stephen King at the Movies*, drawing on original interview material in her discussion of King's films and teleplays.

Hot line

To promote King's novels, NAL used toll-free hot lines with recorded information to keep the fans updated. For *The Regulators*, the hot line updated fans on how to order the signed, limited edition, available only from the publisher.

The House Next Door,
by Anne Rivers Siddons

Novel for which King wrote a three-paragraph foreword for a limited edition of the book, published by the Old New York Book Shop Press in 1993.

Noting that this book was only her second published novel, King praised it for its "horror in the sunlight" quality, which he associated with Shirley Jackson.

Note: The limited edition, at $150, failed to sell out its first printing of 450 copies. After binding 125 copies, the publisher sold the remainder of the print run, in folded and gathered sheets, to Betts Bookstore, which bound them as trade paperbacks and sold them out at $44.95 each.

"The House on Maple Street"
(collected in *Nightmares & Dreamscapes*)

There's only one illustration in *Nightmares & Dreamscapes* rendered by Chris Van Allsburg. His drawing was the visual stimulus for "The House on Maple Street." The illustration depicts a night scene of a house rising on a pillar of fire, wreathed by smoke, taking off from its foundation—a rocket house.

In the notes at the end of *Nightmares & Dreamscapes*, King explains that the art was from Allsburg's book, *The Mysteries of Harris Burdick*. One illustration in this book—of a thing under the rug—recalls Gahan Wilson's or Edward Gorey's work.

The plot: The Bradbury children hate their new stepfather, and for good reason. In his worldview, children should not be seen or heard. As for his wife, she soon learns that her place is under his thumb, just like her children. Spankings and threats are the order of the day for the kids, and intimidation is the weapon of choice against his wife.

Feeling sorry for their mother, the kids want to do something about the nightmarish situation but don't know just what to do . . . until a series of discoveries suggest a course of action that rids their family of their monstrous stepfather.

For reasons unknown, the house is literally changing, day by day. The cellar provides the answer as to why: An alien metal is growing up through the house. The wine cellar harbors a strange room which is the cockpit of an alien spacecraft, with a clock marking the seconds, counting down to zero.

Now, thinks Trent Bradbury, all he has to do is make sure that only his hated stepfather is in the house when the counter zeroes out.

Trent's stepfather is going up . . . with a bang.

Recalling *The Tommyknockers* and the first *Alien* movie (the alien cockpit), this story, with some variations, has been told by King to schoolchildren as "The Wicked Witch and the Farting Cookie." (I wish he had printed *that* story instead.)

"How to Scare a Woman to Death"

In this article in *Murderess Ink* (Workman Publishing, 1979), King discusses five ways to scare women.

Huff, Charles

A retired postmaster from Orr's Island who provided lay services at the West Durham Methodist Church, which Stephen and David King attended as youths, "Huffy" was a father figure for the King boys, who grew up without a father.

At Huff's memorial service, held at the West Durham Methodist Church, King gave the eulogy, concluding that "it has been a good thing for me to reconsider Mr. Huff, who meant so much to me as a child."

Hughes, Terence J.

A college professor who, in the *BDN* (April 13, 1982), wrote an anti-abortion op-ed piece, which prompted King to respond with his own op-ed piece, titled by the paper "The Land of Lunacy."

King wrote: "I don't believe I have ever been so distressed or disgusted by an opinion column" in the paper and went on to deconstruct Hughes's argument, which he felt confused personal opinions with facts. "It's scary to see . . . inflammatory rhetoric labeled 'facts,'" King pointed out, noting that he was particularly upset to hear it coming from a university professor, who he felt should have offered more rigorous reasoning in putting forth his argument.

Hyperbole Studios

A Seattle-based firm that develops interactive video-based games and is working on King-related projects.

"I am the Doorway"
(collected in *Night Shift*)

Originally published in *Cavalier* (March 1971), this story is a perfect example of how King is at heart a horror writer, not a science fiction writer, despite the story's science fiction trappings. A two-man spacecraft, an expedition returning from Venus, returns to Earth, crashing in the ocean. Arthur, the sole survivor, is crippled for life; five years later he discovers to his horror that his hands have metamorphosed: the itching turns to pronounced red welts that turn into eyes that peer up at him (a favorite J. K. Potter image).

Convinced that he is in fact the "doorway" for Venusians, he asks his friend Richard to come over for a look and to offer an explanation—if indeed one exists.

After the alien hands kill Richard, Arthur puts his offending hands into the fire, mutilating himself, but years later, the alien eyes reappear ... this time, on his chest.

Like *Alien*, this one's a horror story at heart.

The image of the alien eyes became the design motif for the cover of the paperback edition of *Night Shift*, in which this story was reprinted.

Id

A parody of *It* that appeared in the *New Yorker* (December 1986), this piece skillfully mimics some of King's patented writing tricks (italic type, dialogue in parentheses, etc.) to good effect.

Idea journal

King doesn't maintain one. His opinion is that if any idea isn't good enough to remember, it's not important enough *to* remember.

The Ideal, Genuine Man

A novel by Don Robertson, published by Philtrum Press in 1987, it is the only publication from Philtrum that was not written by King.

In his "forenote" to the book, King wrote that "to not publish when I have the means to do so would be an irresponsible act. . . . Don Robertson was and is one of the three writers who influenced me as a young man who was trying to 'become' a novelist (the other two being Richard Matheson and John D. MacDonald)."

Ideas, sources of

"Where do you get your ideas?" is the number one question with a bullet, and over the years King has answered it in various ways, according to Charlie Fried, who compiled a short list of some of King's responses:

"I really don't know." (October 4, 1994, in Manchester, Vermont, at the first stop on his *Insomnia* book tour.)

"I get mine in Utica, New York." (September 1986, in Virginia Beach, Virginia, at the Friends of Library public talk.)

"Utica, New York, there is a little shop there." (1988, in "Letters from Hell," a broadside published by Lord John Press.)

"Well, there's a great little bookstore on Forty-second Street in New York called Used Ideas. I go there when I run dry." (1985, in a speech given at the University of Massachusetts at Amherst.)

"I get them at 239 Center Street in Bangor, just

around the corner from the Frati Brothers Pawnshop." (1982, *Sourcebook*, in an interview conducted by Keith Bellows.)

"That's the toughest one. Usually what I say is Utica, I get my ideas in Utica. There's no satisfactory answer to that question, but you can answer it individually and say this idea came from here, this idea came from there." (1982, from King's article "On *The Shining* and Other Perpetrations.")

"I do research. I get different ideas from one source or another. You know, a lot of the phenomena, the case histories you read of psychic phenomena, things like telekinesis or telepathy or pyrokinesis. Those things fascinate me. If you read a few case histories you get a kind of feel for it. Then I'll sit down and write the book." (1983, at a public talk, "An Evening with King at the Billerica, Massachusetts, Public Library.")

"So where do the ideas—the salable ideas—come from? For myself, the answer is simple enough. They come from my nightmares. Not the nighttime variety, as a rule, but the ones that hide just beyond the doorway that separates the conscious from the unconscious." (1981, in an interview conducted by Joyce Lynch Dewes Moore.)

"When you sit down to write a book, is the idea already there? No, sometimes the idea just sort of pogos into my mind all at once." (in *Castle Rock*, vol. 1, no. 10).

"Where do you get your inspirations? It comes from nowhere, it comes from everyplace. Something just hits. For me, writing is like walking through a desert and all at once, poking up through the hardpan, I see the top of a chimney. I know there's a house under there, and I'm pretty sure I can dig it up if I want. That's how I feel. It's like the stories are already there." (April 10, 1986, on *Larry King Live*).

"Utica! No, really, I don't know. There is no way to answer that question so I just say the first thing that comes to mind. They come from every place. When people ask, 'Where do you get your ideas?,' the reason that question is so frustrating for a writer is because he knows they do come from some central source but there's no way to pinpoint that because it is somewhere deep down inside. It is some subconscious thing." (Loukia Louka, "The

Dispatch Talks with: Writer King," *Maryland Coast Dispatch*, August 8, 1986.)

If You Could See Me Now, by Peter Straub

SK: "An electrifying finish: During the last forty pages my hands were as good as nailed to the book."

"I Know What You Need"
(collected in *Night Shift*)

Originally published in *Cosmopolitan* (September 1976), this is a story about obsessive love. Elizabeth Rogan, a pretty coed, is the target of Hamner's misplaced affections. Despite misgivings expressed by her roommate, Alice, Rogan throws caution to the wind and plays into Hamner's hands; after all, he's so solicitous, so anxious to please her, to give her what she needs.

Things look too good to be true, as they always are in such situations.

After her boyfriend dies under suspicious circumstances, she hires a private detective to unearth the truth about Hamner, who uses black magic to sense her every need, allowing him to literally tailor himself to be her perfect man. But when she catches on to his covert manipulations, she confronts him and dumps him.

His childish reaction, damning her, confirms her worst nightmare: He's not the perfect gentleman at all—he's a perfect monster. "Go on then!" he shouts. "But you'll never be satisfied with any man after me! And when your looks go and men stop trying to give you anything you want, you'll wish for me! You'll think of what you threw away!"

Rogan, now a changed woman, realizes that there's a price you have to pay for everything, and in this case, the price was too high: Her affections had been bought too easily because she saw what she wanted to see, playing into the hands of a boy who gave her what she thought she needed.

Image Design

A design firm in New York that produced all the visual special effects for the television adaptation of "The Langoliers." Rick Murphy, the company's

Image Design *continued*

managing director and executive producer, commented that the creation of the Langoliers themselves was a first for television: "In the past, creatures were created by using miniatures, puppets, and stop-motion filming. This is the first time a creature like this has been generated entirely by computer. It's similar to what was done in *Jurassic Park*, but there they had data on dinosaurs to work from. We had to make it all up ourselves, based on the visions of King and director-screenwriter Tom Holland." (*BDN*, April 26, 1995.)

Imaginos

Album by Blue Oyster Cult for which King taped an introduction.

"Incredibly Gross Postcards"

A book of 24 postcards published by *Fangoria*, which included one of King as Jordy Verrill (from "The Lonesome Death of Jordy Verrill").

Independent bookstores

Bookstores that aren't affiliated with a chain. To support the independent stores, King did a coast-to-coast tour, deliberately avoiding the chains, megastores, and discount warehouses. Citing the "buy narrow, stock deep" buying mentality of the superstores, King observed, "It's not right. It's bad for diversity. It's bad for American thought when American fiction is represented only by Sidney Sheldon, Danielle Steele, Tom Clancy, and King. That's not the way it's supposed to be, and it's a dangerous philosophy."

Insomnia

Hardback, 1994, 787 pages, Viking, $27.95
Dedication: "For Tabby . . . and for Al Kooper, who knows the playing-field. No fault of mine."
Contents
Prologue: Winding the Deathwatch (I)
Part I. Little Bald Doctors
Part II. The Secret City
Part III. The Crimson King

Part IV.
Epilogue: Winding the Deathwatch (II)

King readers who were expecting him to follow up *Nightmares & Dreamscapes* with another ur-King novel were probably surprised to see *this* novel, a long, thoughtful novel that like an iceberg moves slowly but carries with it a considerable presence. Deliberate in pace, the novel introduces us to an elderly man, Ralph Roberts, who suffers a *Thinner*-like problem: He wakes up every morning a minute earlier than the day before, until he's living on a few hours of sleep—but to what end?

What appears to be a straightforward story turns out to be nothing of the sort: Reflecting elements from his recent novels that address social concerns, this one focuses on the abortion issue, at which point the narrative increases its tempo.

This sudden change is deliberate, a counterpoint to the earlier part of the novel. The pace accelerates as Roberts confronts the truth: His insomnia is intentionally caused by three creatures who have a greater purpose in mind than merely disrupting his sleep patterns: Lachesis, Clotho, and Atropos, fighting on behalf of Purpose against Random, explain their presence to him, and in so doing connect *Insomnia*'s storyline to *The Dark Tower*.

Although King has, in the past, run a common thread through two works—for instance, Randall Flagg, who makes an appearance in *The Stand* and also in *The Eyes of the Dragon*—the connection between what will happen at a public address in Roberts's town of Derry, Maine, and the world of the "docs" also stands at the center of King's fiction: The tapestry connects to the fantasy worlds of *The Eyes of the Dragon*, *Talisman*, and *The Dark Tower*.

Purpose triumphs over Random, but it's a temporary victory; things can change in ways that are unforeseen.

A complex and ambitious novel that repays a second reading—a careful reading—*Insomnia* will keep you up late at night, turning pages by its length, if not the intricate working of its theme.

Note: King suffers from insomnia, but instead of wasting his time boring himself by counting sheep, he dreams up stories. With each new bout of insomnia, he continues the story until it's completely "written."

Insomnia portfolio

A set of prints limited to 400 sets, numbered and signed by King and artist Phil Hale, published by Glimmer Graphics at $85.

Insomnia tour

To promote *Insomnia*, King set out on a coast-to-coast tour, starting out at the Northshire Bookstore in Manchester Center, Vermont. From there he stopped at Ithaca, New York; Worthington, Ohio; Lexington, Kentucky; Nashville, Tennessee; St. Louis, Missouri; Manhattan, Kansas; Colorado Springs, Colorado; Sun Valley, Idaho; and Santa Cruz, California—a 6,400-mile trip in which he rode his Harley into town, followed by a support van that hauled his Harley between cities.

On the moral grounds that the large chain stores didn't need him to help move books—they discounted so heavily that it brought in the customers by the droves—King opted to support the independents that he felt were besieged by the big boys, the ones that needed a helping hand, since they couldn't afford deep discounting. "It's more difficult for independent books stores to sell my books. . . . Independent bookstores are a dying breed," he told the *Santa Cruz Sentinel*.

After his speaking engagement and book signing in Santa Cruz, King flew back to Bangor.

Intellectual Freedom Committee of the Maine Library Association, and the Maine Educational Media Association

The association gave King an award for taking a stand against the 1986 Maine Obscenity Referendum. King received a plaque and a $500 check, which was given in his name to the library of his choice, the Old Town Public Library.

Internet

The advent of the Internet has fundamentally changed how King fans get their news, interact with other fans, and collapse the window in terms of response time for ordering King limiteds—an early-warning system, as it were, for Net surfers and those who read the postings in the "alt.books" King discussion group.

For instance, when Philtrum Press was ready to take orders for *Six Stories*, the original plan was to advertise in three specialty publications in the fantasy field. But it soon became obvious, after the word of its release was posted on the Net, that the advertising was superfluous. Instantly King collectors got the word and sent in checks to reserve copies, and in short order, the book sold out. (In fact, it was oversubscribed and checks had to be returned.) Though two postcard mailings from specialty publications boosted the subscription of *Six Stories*, the impact of the Internet had made its presence felt in the King community.

On an ironic note, premature discussions on the Net of the British limited edition of *Bag of Bones* killed that project.

Web sites from King's publishers also have helped keep his fans informed, some with interactive sites. (There's even *The Green Mile* screensaver, for IBM and compatibles only.)

See "Web sites" for recommended places to start your hunt for King pages, but be forewarned: Electronic publishing is here today and may be gone tomorrow, so it's best to periodically check in at Betts Bookstore's Web page and use their links to find the other sites, or use your search engine and type in "Stephen King," then allot an evening to scan through the hundreds of listings.

Internet posting

King is wired. He has e-mail capability, as does his wife, Tabitha, and the staffers at the office participate in SKEMERs and the Internet King discussion group.

King rarely posts, but has done so twice.

Using a Cornell University bookstore computer and its account, on October 6, 1994, King posted:

> Someone wondered if I ever get into these electronic bulletin boards. I got a peek into this one while preparing to do a speaking gig at Cornell University, in Ithaca, on October 6th, 1994. I haven't been in Colorado buying Slurpies at any 7-11s lately, but I was in Christie's in Hoosick, New York yesterday. The

new book is *Insomnia,* and that's what I'm promoting. I'm glad so many people liked Frank's version of *Shawshank,* and I hope to see many of you on my tour . . . if the Harley doesn't break down . . . or I don't break down. The question that occurs is whether or not the people reading this will believe I'm me. It really is, but if I put in something only I would know in order to prove it, everybody would know it. It's the only catch, Catch-22. In closing, the big cahunas and cahunettes here at Cornell want me to tell you that I don't have an account or an electronic postbox here. In fact, I don't really know what the fuck I'm doing. Oh, I think I *do* know how to prove I'm me. First, the next book is called *Rose Madder*—June of 1995 from Viking. Second, it will be Eddie, not Roland, who saves the party of travelers from Blaine the Mono. Joe Bob sez "Check it out." Check ya on the flip-flop, *King*

Later, in a November 21, 1996, posting King addressed the matter of the freebies that accompanied his "mirror" novels, *Desperation* and *The Regulators.* The posting was done by his publisher on his behalf, on the King discussion group on the Internet:

Gentle Readers:

It's reached my attention that there's been a fair degree of pissing and moaning about the *Wizard and Glass* booklet which comes with a dual purchase of *Desperation* and *The Regulators.* I swear to God, some of you guys could die and go to heaven and then complain that you had booked a double occupancy room, and where the hell is the sauna, anyway? The major complaints seem to be coming from people who have already bought both books. Those of you who bought the double-pack got the light, right? A freebie. So whatcha cryin' about?

The booklet was my idea, not the publisher's—a little extra for people who wanted to buy both books after supplies of the famous "Keep You Up All Night" light ran out. If you expected to get the booklet *in addition* to the light, all I can say is sorry, Cholly, but there may not be enough booklets to go around. If you bought the two books separately, because

there weren't any gift packs left (they sold faster than expected, which is how this booklet deal came up in the first place), go back to where you bought them, tell the dealer what happened, show him or her your proof of (separate) purchase, and they'll take care of you. If they get wise wicha, tell 'em Steve King said that was the deal.

If you're just jacked because you want to read the first two chapters of *Wizard and Glass,* wait until the whole thing comes out. Or put it on your T.S. [tough shit] List and give it to the chaplain. In any case, those of you who are yelling and stamping your feet, please stop. If you're old enough to read, you're old enough to behave.

Invasion, by Dean R. Koontz

A paperback novel written under the pen name Aaron Wolfe, purportedly by King in the wake of the Bachman disclosure. It is a supernatural story set in Maine.

It

Hardback, 1986, 1,142 pages, Viking, $22.95

Dedication: "This book is gratefully dedicated to my children. My mother and my wife taught me how to be a man. My children taught me how to be free. Naomi Rachel King, at fourteen; Joseph Hillstrom King, at twelve; Owen Philip King, at seven. Kids, fiction is the truth inside the lie, and the truth of this fiction is simple enough: the magic exists. S.K."

Contents

PART 1. The Shadow Before
Derry: The First Interlude
PART 2. June of 1958
Derry: The Second Interlude
PART 3. Grownups
Derry: The Third Interlude
PART 4: July of 1958
Derry: The Fourth Interlude
PART 5: The Ritual Chüd
Derry: The Last Interlude
Epilogue: Bill Denbrough Beats the Devil

In a letter to Michael Collings King explained

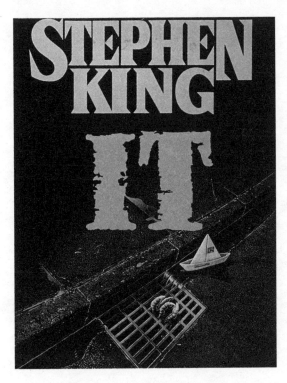

Promotional ad for the Viking edition of *It*.

that "the idea came to me in Colorado, while I was writing *The Stand*." King said that the transmission to his AMC Matador had dropped out on the street, so he had the car towed to the service station.

When it was ready to be picked up, he decided to walk to the dealership, and in a field near there, he crossed a small bridge, which made him think of the story "The Three Billy Goats Gruff," "and the whole story just bounced into my mind on a pogo-stick. Not the characters, but the split time frame, the accelerating bounces that would end with a complete breakdown which might result in a feeling of 'no-time,' all the monsters that were one monster . . . the troll under the bridge, of course."

In a second letter (March 3, 1986), King told Collings that this novel was "a final summing up of everything I've tried to say in the last twelve years on the two central subjects of my fiction." Amplifying that in *Time*, "Wouldn't it be great to bring on all the monsters one last time? Bring them all on—Dracula, Frankenstein, Jaws, the Werewolf, the Crawling Eye, Rodan, It Came from Outer Space—and call it It."

It, the television miniseries, aired on November 18 and 20, 1990. It ran four hours. It cost an estimated $11 million and it was shot in Vancouver, directed by Tommy Lee Wallace from a screenplay by Lawrence D. Cohen.

A richly complex novel and one of King's longest, at 1,138 pages, *It* is an ambitious story spanning 27 years in two time frames with seven key characters. Aptly described as a summing up by King of his exploration of children and monsters, this is his Final Word, as it were, on the territory he mined successfully for years.

It, a shape-shifting entity that transforms itself into every conceivable kind of monster, must be defeated by the seven characters to achieve closure in their lives. (Seven is a number fraught with religious significance.)

David Gates (*Newsweek*, 1986): "The exciting and absorbing parts of *It* are not the mechanical showdowns and shockeroos—and certainly not the 'ideas'—but the simple scenes in which King evokes childhood in the 1950s. If—fat chance—he ever takes a vow of poverty and tries for true literary sainthood, this intensely imagined world would be a good place to begin his pilgrimage."

Matt Rousch (*USA Today*, 1986): "With *It*, King has delivered a masterstroke—a funky, junky monster mash that celebrates an ever-young imagination."

Walter Wager (*NYTBR*, 1986): "Where did Stephen King, the most experienced prince of darkness, go wrong with *It*? Almost everywhere. . . . Mr. King has given us a semiautobiographical horror novel. The stuttering boy grew up to attend the University of Maine, where his nonintellectual and straight-ahead stories were derided as junk. So he wrote a novel to defy the snide faculty scoffers and sent it off to a New York publishing company because he liked the firm's logotype. It was Viking."

E. F. Bleiler (*Twilight Zone*, February 1987): "*It* runs to more than 550,000 words. . . . Is such length really necessary? Certainly not, from the text. A good editor would have urged King to cut the book down by a third to a half. But unfortunately, Stephen King, who is in many ways the Thomas Wolfe of our times . . . has never met the Maxwell Perkins that he needs and deserves."

It (film), 1990

It's hard to imagine this as a feature-length film, because it could not be adequately compressed into a two hour time frame. For that reason, it was a good thing that a decision was made by King and ABC to run it as a two-part miniseries: Television would give it the room to breathe—four hours.

So how successful was *It* on television?

It was a solid production with commendable performances from the cast, especially the child actors who practically stole the show in the first installment, playing the members of the Losers' Club who would band together three decades later to confront, and ultimately defeat, It.

Throughout both installments, the one constant is Pennywise the Clown, one of the many faces of It, superbly portrayed by Tim Curry.

Set in the fictional Derry, Maine—a thinly disguised Bangor—*It* is a very faithful and evocative adaptation of a major King novel, showing that the television medium isn't necessarily anathema to horror material.

Matt Rousch (*USA Today*, Nov. 16, 1990): "If *Twin Peaks* is a midnight movie for prime-time live, then Stephen King's *It* is the miniseries equivalent of those Saturday matinee shockers that merrily warped a generation before Freddie and Jason began staking their more graphic turf. . . . Accept *It* on its own popcorn-munching terms, and keep the lights on high."

Ken Tucker (*Entertainment Weekly*, Nov. 16, 1990): "*It* features a high level of ensemble acting rare for any horror film. . . . In addition to *It*'s slow pace, I found the ending a big letdown—unimaginative special effects animate the monster in its final incarnation. But the cast is terrific, Curry's cackle is chilling, and King's usual buried theme—about the pain adults inflict on children without even realizing it (It?)—is always worth pondering."

For King, *It* was "my final exam as far as supernatural horror went, like my master's thesis on everything. I'd done vampires and werewolves, now let's do it all at once, and call it by that quintessential movie-poster word 'IT.'" (*USA Today*, Nov. 16, 1990.)

Tom Shales (*Washington Post*): "Did Stephen King have an unhappy childhood, or what? If he did, no unhappy childhood ever turned so handsome a profit. . . . Whatever the intermittent shocks . . . the net effect is nil. 'It' is just one of those things."

"It Grows on You"
(collected in *Nightmares & Dreamscapes*)

Originally published in *Marshroots* (fall 1973), this is a fine example of King's regional writing.

An odd house goes up in Castle Rock, built by a rich outsider, Joe Newall, whose wife gives birth to their deformed child—a freak, an accident of nature that lives briefly, then is put out of her misery. It's a harbinger of things to come; death comes to his wife and to him as well (he hangs himself). Times change and the old-timers who remembered the house and its occupants pass on—it's been fifty years, after all—but the new owners build on to the house, and one by one they also die.

A love song, King said, to the rural life he experienced. This story, set in Castle Rock, foreshadows the destruction of the town in *Needful Things*.

Note: For its inclusion in *Nightmares & Dreamcapes*, the story was significantly rewritten.

"I Was a Teenage Grave Robber"
(uncollected)

King's first published story exclusive of his self-published work, the fanzine consisted of 12 mimeographed pages.

Its title was inspired by the fifties monster movies (*I Was a Teenage Werewolf* and *I Was a Teenager Frankenstein*); this first-person narrative was published in *Comics Review*, a fan magazine.

The story was later reprinted by Marv Wolfman in his fanzine, *Stories of Suspense*, under the title "In a Half-World of Terror."

King, unlike H. P. Lovecraft, realized that fan publication was merely a means to the end. The goal was to submit professionally, not languish in anonymous fan circles forever, which is why this is his *only* fan appearance, for which he got payment in copies, not cash.

"I Wrote King's Last Two Books: Young Re-Write Author Exposes King's True Fear!"

In what has to be the most laughable story ever published about King, on page four of the tabloid *Confidential: Secrets of the Rich and Famous* (December 1991), a "determined freelance investigative reporter, Chris Wolffe" had "unearthed the young re-write author who claims that it is his work, and not King's, that has been on sale for the last two years." Wolffe met the "re-write" author at a restaurant. The reason the "re-write" author gave was that King was suffering from writer's block.

"At last report, Wolffe was on his way up to King's home in Bangor, Maine to get to the bottom of this mystery."

A photo of King and his son Joseph, both dressed in tuxedos, ran with the article. The photo never bothers to identify his son, because the caption wants to mislead you into thinking that the young man in the photo is the alleged Viking Press staffer in the "re-write" department: "A young Viking Press staffer alleges that King's biggest fear is writer's block." (And, no, Joe King doesn't work for Viking Press in any capacity.)

The truth is out there, but it ain't gonna be found in the pages of *that* rag!

was invented by an impecunious but serendipitous scientist.

The only catch with the Jaunt technique is that it requires each traveler to be unconscious, in a deep sleep, as in Robert A. Heinlein's novel *The Door into Summer*, in which the science of the "cold sleep" has been perfected.

In the King story—unlike the Heinlein one—curiosity kills the cat, so to speak; twelve-year-old Ricky deliberately holds his breath, so after experiencing the Jaunting effect, he ages incredibly.

Regarding scientific plausibility and the interior logic of the story: The dangers of the Jaunting when one is wide awake would make it quite likely that, to prevent lawsuits, the machines would be set up so that you couldn't Jaunt unless you were undeniably unconscious—easy enough to check by monitoring brain waves.

But you don't read King for his science fiction. This one's an out-and-out horror story, which makes its horrific point just as you'd expect.

Jaspers

A "hamburger joint," as King termed it, in New York City where he told Bill Thompson the plot of *The Shine*, later retitled *The Shining*, in October 1975.

Thompson's initial reaction was lackluster; he cited the book's similarities to *Burnt Offerings*, a novel by Robert Marasco that King knew well.

"The Jaunt" (collected in *Skeleton Crew*)

According to King, in his afterword to *Skeleton Crew*, this story was originally submitted to *Omni* magazine but was rejected on the grounds that its science was too "wonky." True enough, which is what makes it ideally suited for *Twilight Zone* magazine, where it first appeared.

A horror story with science fiction trappings, this one clearly shows why the technology of *Star Trek* and its transporter beam ("Energize!") is superior to the science of Jaunting: The Oates family is teleporting from Earth to Mars. To pass the time at the Jaunt center, at New York's Port Authority Bus Terminal, Mark Oates tells his family the history of the Jaunt, a transportation breakthrough that revolutionized the world and that

Jeopardy

On November 6, 1995, King appeared on this popular trivia game show with two other celebrity guests, the actress Lynn Redgrave and the actor David Duchovny, of *X-Files* fame. This close encounter with the King showed that he was the King of trivia as well.

Though Duchovny was a strong contender—Redgrave, alas, was clearly out of her element—it came down to Final Jeopardy, and a literary question was posed: What was the store that on March 24, 1994, held a breakfast to announce the new Truman Capote literary trust?

King correctly answered Tiffany's—Capote made the store famous with his story *Breakfast at Tiffany's*—and earned $11,400 for charity.

In addition to being a good-deed doer on the show, King's encounter with the *X-Files* actor led to King's writing a script for the *The X-Files*, a show he admitted that he hadn't watched, though his kids loved it. So he started watching it and became hooked.

Note: King appeared for the second time on the show April 28, 1998.

"Jerusalem's Lot" (collected in *Night Shift*)

An epistolary tale, the only one King has written, consisting of extracts from letters discovered by James Robert Boone, an ancestor of Charles Boone. This story is an obvious homage to H. P. Lovecraft, who wrote "The Rats in the Walls." The first letter by Boone is dated October 2, 1850. The relative who unearthed this set of letters noted that "this place badly needs the services of an exterminator. There are some huge rats in the walls, by the sound."

"Jhonathan and the Witchs" *(sic)*

A short story King wrote at age nine; it was published by Workman Publishing in *First Words*, a collection of first stories by famous authors.

Job: A Comedy of Justice,
by Robert A. Heinlein

SK: "Following World War II, Robert A. Heinlein emerged as not only America's premier writer of speculative fiction, but the greatest writer of such fiction in the world. He remains today a sort of trademark for all that is finest in American imaginative fiction."

Jobs King held pre-*Carrie*

Mill worker in Lisbon Falls, Maine
Worker at an industrial laundry in Bangor
Dishwasher
Little League coach
Laborer picking potatoes for a quarter a barrel
Gas station attendant (King made $1.25 an hour, at a gas station near Brewer, Maine, where a fill-up earned you a free loaf of bread, an oil check, and a free Flintstone glass. This was his first job after college.)
High school English teacher

John Cafferty and the Beaver Brown Band

At a University of Maine concert in April 1986, this band was surprised when King came onstage, took a guitar, and played some rock and roll tunes. King would later play in a band of authors, the Rock Bottom Remainders, fulfilling a lifelong dream.

Joyride, by Jack Ketchum

SK: "There's a dark streak of American genius in this book. Read it if you dare. . . . Begins with a planned murder and explodes into a terrifyingly believable killing spree. . . . But be warned: Ketchum never flinches, never turns aside. He is, quite simply, one of the best in the business, on a par with Clive Barker, James Ellroy, and Thomas Harris. Hey, want some good advice? Don't open this book unless you intend to finish it the same night. You may be shocked, even revolted, by Jack Ketchum's hellish vision of the world, but you won't be able to dismiss or forget it."

Jury duty

King served five months of federal jury duty without being picked for a jury. He was rejected for the jury in a trial of a man accused of possessing three counterfeit $100 bills. U.S. District Judge Morton A. Brody told King and the other nonselected members of the jury pool, "I can assure you, it's not personal."

King was invited to the judge's chambers to discuss what he called his "particular problem" as to why he hadn't been selected for any jury duty. King said he was "a little bit disappointed" that he hadn't been selected. When asked whether the experience would give him any material for books, he replied that it hadn't.

Afterward King chatted with court clerks and signed autographs. (*BDN*, Aug. 11, 1982.)

"Keeping a Promise"

The name of the fund-raising campaign to raise $5.5 million for the construction of a new pediatrics unit on the eighth floor of the Grant Building, at the Eastern Maine Medical Center in Bangor.

King, who donated $750,000, was on hand for the groundbreaking and wore a suit and tie especially for the occasion. "You know that I'm serious about this," he said.

King told the *BDN* that the children, parents, and community need this facility, and also that "for the community to live and thrive and grow and be vital, it needs to give to those who can't do for themselves." (Quoted in Roxanne Moore Saucier, "EMMC Breaks Down the Roof, New Pediatrics Unit Going Up," date not known.)

Kadi, Frank

Student at UMO who shot King . . . with a camera, and got the classic photo of King in college, looking suspiciously like Charles Manson and aiming a double-barreled shotgun at the viewer. Captioned: "Study, dammit!"

Keene, Eric

Termed a "publicity seeker" by Deputy District Attorney Michael P. Roberts, Keene broke into the King home in Bangor on April 20, 1991. Keene, who pleaded guilty to the charge, broke into the house, occupied only by Tabitha King at the time, and claimed to be holding a bomb-detonating device.

Keene had no bomb, as the police discovered when they ferreted him out of the attic.

After the incident, the Kings installed video cameras at the office and house, posted signs warning trespassers off, and installed high-security devices.

The house is now closed off completely all the way around, and to preserve privacy it is partially shielded from street view with a row of hedges. (Any malevolent topiary?)

The cover to the *Maine Campus* showing Stephen King in what is described as his Charles Manson pose. (The photograph was taken by Frank Kadi.)

The King home in Bangor, Maine, with newly planted shrubbery—no topiary?—that provides some protection from prying eyes.

Kendrick, Walter

A teacher and critic who "reviewed" *Needful Things*, prompting King, in one of his few responses to a reviewer, to charge that the review was "a combination of academic arrogance, elitism and critical insularity." King termed Kendrick's piece a "jeremiad," not a review.

Ketchum, Jack

The pen name of Dallas Mayr, who writes unbelievably horrific novels, like *The Girl Next Door*.

For a limited edition of that book, published by Overlook Connection Press in 1996, King wrote a lengthy introduction in which he compared Ketchum's in-your-face fiction to Clive Barker's and Jim Thompson's, noting that Ketchum's books will never be made into Disney movies because of the subject matter and treatment. (If you read the novel, you'll see why.)

In King's introduction he stated: "Jack Ketchum is a brilliantly visceral novelist whose bleak perception of human nature is perhaps only rivaled by that of Frank Norris and Malcolm Lowry."

Key to the city

The city of Truth or Consequences, New Mexico, gave King the keys to the city on November 19, 1983, designated Stephen King Day by its mayor, Elmer Darr. King then signed books, rode in a convertible to the Damsite Restaurant, where he was the guest of honor at a barbecue luncheon sponsored by the Chamiza Cowbelles, then gave a talk to 800 people at the city's middle school.

Key to the city *continued*

In the evening, he attended a reception in his honor at the Geronimo Springs Museum, followed by a book signing at which he signed so many books that his writing hand cramped up, making it impossible to sign for the hundreds of readers who were still waiting to get his distinctive signature on his books they brought.

"The Killer"

Two-page short story (typed single-spaced) that King submitted to Forrest Ackerman's magazine, *Famous Monsters of Filmland*, under the name Steve King when he was a teenager.

Although it was not published at the time of submission, it finally appeared in print in the magazine *after* King became a brand name.

Kimball, Michael

The author of *Firewater Pond*, which King had a hand in getting published.

Kimball sent *Wind in the Pines* (the book's original title) to King, hoping the novel would catch his attention. It did—King proclaimed it his "favorite new book read in 1984." King passed it on to his wife, who also liked it, and then sent it to Howard Morhaim, an agent who had once shared office space with King's then agent, Kirby McCauley. Morhaim in turn sent it to Alan Williams at Putnam, which had published King's *Skeleton Crew*.

King doesn't have the time to read unpublished manuscripts and act as literary agent, as Stephanie Leonard pointed out in *Castle Rock*, when she recounted this book's circuitous route to publication: "I foresee an even larger flood of manuscripts turning up in Stephen's mail, but I must warn aspiring writers it is *extremely* unusual for him to find time to read any of them, and they are simply returned with a note saying just that. He sympathizes with how difficult it can be to get unpublished work read by anyone, but he doesn't want to turn into a literary agent rather than a writer!"

"King: An Alumnus in Profile"

This profile produced by the University of Maine at Orono's Public Information Office and WABI-TV was the first videotaped profile to be aired on him.

King, Ben E.

Musician whose poignant song "Stand by Me" provided the title for Rob Reiner's adaptation of "The Body."

David Hinchberger: "King has certainly boosted Ben E. King's career, even though King wasn't the person who selected the song for the movie. I think we owe a great deal to these wonderful Kings for a great movie." (*Castle Rock.*)

King, David

King's only sibling, David, was adopted by the Kings as a newborn. He published *Dave's Rag*, an individually typed, then mimeographed, community newspaper to which King was a contributor.

Dave returned the favor by contributing technical data Stephen needed for "Dolan's Cadillac."

To find out what Stephen King thinks of his older brother, see the notes for "Dolan's Cadillac" at the end of *Nightmares & Dreamscapes*, or check out the dedication to *Cujo*.

An evangelical Christian ("We are of the group that believes the Bible is the total and factual and complete word of God," he told Stephen Spignesi in *Shape*), David King currently lives in New Hampshire.

King, Donald

Stephen King's father was born in Peru, Indiana, as Donald Spansky. He later went by the name of Donald Pollack and finally changed his name legally to Donald King. A merchant mariner, after the war he married Nellie Ruth Pillsbury.

Abandoning his family when Stephen King was two, Donald King seemingly walked out into a twilight zone, since he has never been seen or heard of since his abrupt departure in 1949.

He left the house for a pack of cigarettes and never returned.

King's memories of his father are understandably faded by time, but he recalled in *Danse Macabre* that his father was of "average height, handsome in a 1940s sort of way, a bit podgy, bespectacled."

Donald King was an aspiring writer who submitted stories to the pulp magazines of his time but never was published. "None of the stories sold and none survives," King wrote in *Danse Macabre*.

King, Joseph

Son of Stephen and Tabitha King.

Born June 4, 1972, Joseph King has followed in his parents' footsteps, reportedly having submitted a novel for publication under a pen name.

King, Naomi

The only daughter of Stephen and Tabitha King. Like her two brothers, she's been in the public eye by default, witnessing the intrusive behavior of what the King family calls the "graphers" (autograph seekers), and enduring the inane questions people pose to her because of her famous parents.

She currently runs her own business in Maine.

King, Owen

The second-born son of Stephen and Tabitha King. Played on the Bangor West team that won the state championship, where he played relief pitcher.

King, Ruth

King's mother, who single-handedly raised Stephen and David King after her husband, Donald King, took a walk out of the front door and never looked back, abandoning the family.

Ruth King lived long enough to read *Carrie*—she got one of the first proof copies—but not long enough to see King publish the book in its trade edition, which launched his career.

Born Ruth Pillsbury (nicknamed "Ruthie Pill"

in high school), she was known for her talents in public speaking and drama.

From her high school yearbook: "It's no use to try to tell what Ruth can do, for she does so many things so well, even to broadcasting over Station WHDH. Her 57 varieties of faces make her a bright spot in dull weather. Ruth's ability in public speaking has won distinction for her in numerous plays and honor for the school in every contest she has entered."

Her obituary was published in the December 19, 1973, issue of *The Lewiston (Maine) Daily Sun*:

> DURHAM—Mrs. Ruth P. King, 60, a resident of Methodist Corner, died Tuesday at the home of her son in Mexico. She was born in Scarborough, Feb. 3, 1913, the daughter of Guy H. and Nellie Fogg Pillsbury. She was educated in schools of Scarborough and the New England Conservatory of Boston, Mass. She was a retired worker from the housekeeping department at the Pineland Hospital. She was a member of the First Congregational Church of Durham. Surviving are two sons, David V. of Mexico and Stephen E. of North Windham; three sisters, Mrs. Mary Donahue, Durham, Mrs. Lois Storey, Scituate, Mass., and Mrs. Ethelyn P. Flaws, Durham.

SK: "As children, we need to have our dreams encouraged and nurtured. My mother did that for me." (Spoken at the dedication of an arts and music center at Milton Academy.)

King, Tabitha

Wife of Stephen King, novelist, philanthropist.

In a profile by Kathryn Shattuck (*PW*, Feb. 10, 1997), Tabitha King observed, "When people think of a Maine novelist, they think of my husband." King's long shadow reaches across much of New England, but especially Maine, overshadowing all the other novelists.

There are similarities in their writing careers: Both are strongly identified as regional writers, both have carved out their own fictional towns (Stephen's Castle Rock, Tabitha's Nodd's Ridge), and both have principally published novels. But there the comparisons end: Stephen's books are best-sellers, whereas Tabitha's books—for which sales figures are unavailable—are critical successes, solid midlist titles that have a smaller but just as devoted audience.

In addition to a self-published book, *Playing Like a Girl*, about UMO basketball star Cindy Blodgett, Tabitha King's books include:

Small World, 1981

Caretakers, 1983

The Trap, 1985

Pearl, 1985

One on One, 1993

The Book of Reuben, 1994

Survivor, 1997

Douglas E. Winter: "There is an aspect of her work in which she is a very strong regional writer, and I say that in a complimentary sense. We're talking about Faulkner, O'Connor, or a Steinbeck. There is regional power in her books. In other words, part of the power of her fiction is its setting, its people. It is a peculiar kind of people who live within that peculiar kind of setting. Now, on the other hand, I don't think that limits her powers, as it does some regional writers. I think that she's also very capable of communicating the peculiarities of that region to outsiders like me. I've read, for example, some other Maine writers who make the society so alien that essentially it *becomes* an alien society, and you don't feel that you understand that much about it."

Harlan Ellison: "There is a quality of kindness in [Tabitha King's work] that is missing from Stephen's work. There are a number of women writers I read specifically because there is a quality of humanity, a kindness in their work. Tabby's stuff is quite different from Stephen's, and in some ways is far more mature."

King bookmark

Published by the ALA, the bookmark has a photograph of King on the front (taken by Tabitha King) and on the back lists his novels through 1992 and also lists 10 novels that he says represent "everything in the genre that is fine."

Tabitha King gives a talk at Bookmarc, a bookstore in Bangor, Maine.

Kingdom of Fear: The World of Stephen King,

edited by Tim Underwood and Chuck Miller

An anthology originally published in 1986 containing 17 essays of varying quality about King.

King's "The Horror Writer and the Ten Bears," a reprint of an article that originally appeared in *Writer's Digest* in 1973, functions as the book's foreword.

That article deals with selling to men's magazines, so it's awkward when billed as a foreword. On the whole, though, this is a good collection. In fact, this is among the best of the collections on King published by Underwood-Miller.

The book's strength has to do with the quality of the individual contributions. Predictably, some of the offerings seem slight—notably, the two pieces by the book's editors.

The book contains the following:

Foreword: "The Horror Writer and the Ten Bears," by King. Good discussion on the nature of fears—King's ten bears—but the advice on writing markets for short fiction is woefully outdated.

"King's Horror Has a Healing Power," by Andrew M. Greeley. A very short piece, two pages, emphasizing that despite the naturalism in King's stories, they also offer "tiny smidgens of hope, but hope, like goodness and love, needs only to exist to finally win."

"Monsters in Our Midst," by Robert Bloch. A delightful personal look at King as a "fellow monster" by a practitioner of dark fantasy, one of the giants of the genre.

"A Girl Named Carrie," by Bill Thompson. The only instance in which King's editor provides a "story behind the story" look at King and *Carrie*, setting the record straight.

"Welcome to Room 217," by Ramsey Campbell. A loving tribute to King from one of Britain's best practitioners of the modern horror tale.

"Thanks to the Crypt-Keeper," by Whitley Strieber. An appreciation of King with lots of personal anecdotes and fascinating observations from one of the writers way, *way* out there.

"Fantasy as Commodity and Myth," by Leslie Fiedler. An accessible discussion of where fantasy and horror intersect, and King's role in his chosen field.

"Surviving the Ride," by Clive Barker. The young Turk of terror writes of King's strengths as a writer. An illuminating piece.

"Two selections from 'Harlan Ellison's Watching,'" by Harlan Ellison. Ellison dissects King's failed movie adaptations, explaining that the failure is not with the writer but with the presence of too many cooks spoiling the broth.

"The Unexpected and the Inevitable," by Michael McDowell. An accomplished writer of suspense fiction, McDowell praises King's writing, in particular, his writing rhythm.

"The Good Fabric: Of Night Shifts and Skeleton Crews," by William F. Nolan. The author of *Logan's Run* contributes summaries of the stories in *Night Shift* and *Skeleton Crew*.

"The Life and Death of Richard Bachman: King's Doppelganger," by Stephen P. Brown. A blow-by-blow description of how Brown's diligent efforts revealed Richard Bachman to be King in disguise.

"King: The Good, the Bad and the Academic," by Don Herron. Herron, who edited a wonderful collection of essays on Robert E. Howard, *Dark Barbarian*, praises King with faint damns and damns him with faint praise. Taking King to task in a section titled "The Bad," he concludes the essay with a section on "The Good," and praises "Apt Pupil" because King "takes the material which seems most uniquely his own, and makes *literature* out of it."

"King Goes to the Movies," by Chuck Miller. A movie-by-movie look at King's film adaptations, reiterating common knowledge.

"King as a Writer for Children," by Ben P. Indick. An illuminating discussion of King's so-called children's books, *The Eyes of the Dragon* and *The Talisman*, in the context of children's literature.

"The Mind's a Monkey: Character and Psychology in King's Recent Fiction," by Bernadette Lynn Bosky. A lengthy, thoughtful piece discussing one of the cornerstones of King's strengths as a writer, his ability to build a character from the inside out, emphasizing fictionally rounded characters. An academic discussion but very readable.

"King's Characters: The Main(e) Heat," by Thomas F. Monteleone. A good follow-up piece after Bosky's, emphasizing King's strengths in inventing memorable characters.

"The Skull Beneath the Skin," by Tim Underwood. A very general piece talking about King's fiction, running quickly through his canon. Underwood's thesis: "King is so contemporary and fashionable in his concerns, his work probably won't last." I disagree. First, King is a storyteller, and those guys have a tendency to last, no matter how topical or contemporary the work. Second, in King's more mainstream fiction, notably his short fiction or regional fiction, he more than holds his own.

King Kon '97

A small convention held in Chicago, Illinois, July 25–27, 1997, at a hotel in the Lincoln Park section of the town. Activities: Friday, a reception and a pajama party for "King movie night"; Saturday, a trip to the Chicago zoo and Navy pier, dinner at a local restaurant, a costume party (dressed as your favorite King character), and a midnight tour of graveyards; Sunday, breakfast, a social gathering, and a farewell brunch.

The King Newsletter

Intended as a replacement to *Castle Rock*, this unofficial newsletter, published by Kerry Kernaghan, folded after a handful of issues. A letter-size zine, its purpose was "to provide King fans with information on King books (both trade and limited editions), short stories, articles, and films. We also alert subscribers to books and articles written about King."

King's Crypt

Short-lived fanzine about King, edited by Tom Simon and Bill Geoghegan in Alexandria, Virginia, published in 1985.

King's dictum

From "Blue Air Compressor," an intrusive authorial comment: "Rule one for all writers is that the teller is not worth a tin tinker's fart when compared to the listener." King's expansion (from *Different Seasons*): "It is the tale, not he who tells it."

"King's Garbage Truck"

The informal, infrequent column that King wrote when he was at UMO.

Of King's work habits one staffer observed: "King was always late. We would be pulling our hair out at deadline. With five minutes or so to go, Steve would come in and sit down at the typewriter and produce two flawless pages of copy. He carries stories in his head the way most people carry change in their pockets."

King's list of ten scariest movies

This list was published in *TV Guide* on October 30, 1982:

1. *Night of the Living Dead*
2. *An American Werewolf in London*
3. *Invasion of the Body Snatchers*
4. *The Thing*
5. *The Shining* ("Stanley Kubrick's film only mildly resembles my novel. . . .")
6. *Rabid*
7. *Wolfen*
8. *Dead of the Night*
9. *The Fog*
10. *The Toolbox Murders*

"King's Ten Favorite Horror Books or Short Stories"

From *The Books of Lists #3*, compiled by Amy Wallace, Irving Wallace, and David Wallechinsky:

Ghost Story, by Peter Straub
Dracula, by Bram Stoker
The Haunting of Hill House, by Shirley Jackson
Dr. Jekyll and Mr. Hyde, by Robert Louis Stevenson
Burnt Offerings, by Robert Marasco
"Casting the Runes," by M. R. James
"Two Bottles of Relish," by Lord Dunsany
"The Great God Pan," by Arthur Machen
"The Upper Berth," by F. Marion Crawford
"The Colour Out of Space," by H. P. Lovecraft

"King's *The Stand*: A Portfolio by Berni Wrightson"

Glimmer Graphics published the black-and-white pen-and-ink illustrations from *The Stand* in two editions; a regular edition of 12 prints in an illustrated envelope for $20, and a numbered edition of 1,200 copies signed by the artist at $40. (King declined to sign.)

Kostner, Elaine

Former publisher of Dutton and NAL, who in 1972 joined NAL as its vice president and editor-in-chief. During her stint she shepherded King's career at the house, but after NAL lost *Bag of Bones* and its star author, she resigned to start a literary agency.

Kubrick, Stanley

A celebrated, controversial film director whose interpretation of *The Shining*, depending on your mind-set, proved to be either the ultimate horror film or (if you're a King fan) a major disappointment.

Kubrick promoted the movie as "a masterpiece of modern horror," and his avowed aim was to produce *the* ultimate horror flick, just as *2001: A*

Space Odyssey was *the* ultimate space flick.

Kubrick: "There's something inherently wrong with the human personality. There's an evil side to it. One of the things that horror stories can do is to show us the archetypes of the unconscious: We can see the dark side without having to confront it directly."

"There's hubris and then there's Kubris." (Calvin Ahlgren, "King of Horror Finds Directing Unnerving," *San Francisco Chronicle*, 1986.)

cessful in this effort, perhaps a new aspect of King's creative imagination will be illuminated, or maybe my readers will view King's work in a different context after discovering what I have to say about him. . . . If there is a core liability to Winter's approach, however, it is that he must often sacrifice analyses of unity and depth in favor of tracing the broad sweep of King's prolific canon. On at least one level of being, then, my book seeks to fill this gap by deliberately restricting its scope to the major themes and recurring patterns found in King's fiction."

Lambert, Mary

Director of *Pet Sematary*, as well as *Siesta* and several television commercials and music videos. Lambert worked within constraints dictated by King: She had to use his script and had to shoot the film in Maine.

SK: "Mary Lambert did a good job. She went in and she didn't flinch. In a way, that's a pretty good complement to the way that I work. My idea is to go in there and hit as you can. Mary understood that." (Interview with Gary Wood, *Cinefantastique*.)

"Land of Confusion"

A rock video by Genesis, with puppets of famous figures, including King, wearing a white baseball jacket with red trim.

Landscape of Fear: Stephen King's American Gothic,
by Tony Magistrale

Published by Bowling Green State University's Popular Press in 1988, this thoughtful academic look is intended to fill a hole left by Winter in *Stephen King: The Art of Darkness*: "I offer this book as a vehicle for understanding and appreciating his fiction even more. If I have been suc-

The cover to the trade paperback edition of Tony Magistrale's *Landscape of Fear: Stephen King's American Gothic*.

"The Langoliers"

(collected in *Four Past Midnight*)

Dedication: "This is for Joe [King], another white-knuckle flyer."

Though there's no requirement for a writer to tell the story *behind* the story, doing so accomplishes two things: First, it instantly connects the writer to the reader, as if he's being addressed directly. Done skillfully, as Harlan Ellison and Stephen King have done in the introductions to their books, it puts the reader at ease and removes some of the mysteries surrounding the writing trade. Second, it goes a long way toward answering that age-old question all writers are posed: Where do you get your ideas?

In this case, King admits that an image arrested his attention: a frightened woman in an airliner, with her hand covering a wall crack in its fuselage. (The image was so strong, King wrote, that he caught the scent of her perfume, L'Envoi.)

King also notes that the story has a "feel" similar to that of "The Mist," a quintessential King story that has escaped film adaptation because its three film options were dropped, though special effects technology with computer-generated imagery can now make the monsters convincing. If Spielberg can make you believe dinosaurs are alive in *Jurassic Park*, the monsters in "The Mist" can also be recreated convincingly, byte by byte, pixel by pixel.

As for "The Langoliers," it's set mostly at the Bangor International Airport, where a cast of characters bands together to discover why they are in a world that's fundamentally changed. In a world in which matches won't light and guns don't fire as they should, the central question that must be answered is: How can they get back to where they started? How can they get back to the real world, instead of *this* world that's being erased by the Langoliers?

It's a story perfectly suited for *The Twilight Zone*; you can see Rod Serling stepping out of the darkness to introduce it.

The Langoliers (film), 1995

If you ever fly into Bangor International Airport—on a puddle jumper, most likely—you can say to yourself that you've been on a movie location, for "The Langoliers" was filmed there.

An unnerving story in print, the Langoliers played out beautifully in the mind's eye, but less so when on the small screen: rolling balls that race across the land, literally erasing the earth.

To my mind, this would have been fine as an hour-long installment on *Amazing Stories*, *Night Gallery* or *The Twilight Zone*, but it clearly didn't merit treatment at this extended length.

It's watchable but not one of the best television adaptations.

Larson, Gary

Cartoonist of "The Far Side."

King wrote an introduction to his collection, *The Far Side Gallery II*. Returning the favor, Larson drew a cartoon about King: "King's Ant Farm" (published on May 21, 1987).

"The Last Rung on the Ladder"

(collected in *Night Shift*)

Published for the first time in *Night Shift*, this story, like the others in the collection, is an excursion into horror, but with a difference: This is not supernatural horror, but everyday horror—the kind King handles effectively, showing his ability to write mainstream.

Clearly sentimental, it's the story of a relationship between a brother and sister symbolized by a childhood incident the two experienced in a barn: Larry had laid down hay, so when the last rung on the ladder broke, it broke Katrina's fall. But that was when they were young . . . But in time, they grew up on wildly divergent paths: Katrina suffered a bad marriage and later turned to prostitution, while Larry had become a busy corporate lawyer, too busy to be there for his little sister.

Though Katrina writes a letter that finally catches up with him as he moves across the country, he unfortunately does not catch up with her in time to save her life: She takes a swan dive off a high-rise in Los Angeles.

In his introduction to this collection, John D. MacDonald wrote, "One of the most resonant and affecting stories in this book is 'The Last Rung on the Ladder.' A gem. Nary a rustle nor breath of other worlds in it."

It showed a different side of King's writing talent, one that proved, as MacDonald predicted, that King was not "going to restrict himself to his present field of interest."

LaVerdiere's

Drugstore in downtown Bangor, Maine.

When King got a call that *Carrie* had sold for $400,000, of which he would get half, he was so overcome that he had to mark the occasion. As he tells it, "I slid to the floor. It was absurd. I went out to LaVerdiere's and bought my wife a hair dryer. When she came home and I gave it to her she said, 'We can't afford this,' and I told her we could. She cried. That was great."

"The Lawnmower Man"
(collected in *Night Shift*)

This very strange story originally appeared in *Cavalier* (May 1975). It's mid-July, Harold Parkette's lawn is overgrown, and he finally decides to do something about it. He calls Pastoral Greenery and Outdoor Services to send someone out to cut his lawn.

The service sends out a most peculiar man who's not troubled by the thick carpet of grass. In fact, the man says, "The taller, the better. Healthy

soil, that's what you got there, by Circe. That's what I always say."

The lawnmower man starts up his aged, red mower and, stripping naked, crawls behind the mower to eat the freshly cut grass.

After watching the lawnmower swerve lifelike to kill a mole, which is eagerly gobbled up by the lawnmower man, Parkette faints.

The lawnmower man in fact is no ordinary man, nor is he a nut; he's an emissary serving Pan, the Greek god of pastures. And when, in fright, Parkette calls the police to file a complaint report, the "sacrifice" the lawnmower man mentioned earlier turns out to be the hapless Harold Parkette.

The story was also adapted for the comic book *Bizarre Adventures* (October 1981).

Lawsuits

King has sued on one occasion only: the misuse of his name in connection with the film version of *The Lawnmower Man*, but he's been on the receiving end of nuisance lawsuits, which is typical for any wealthy celebrity.

One woman, whose case never went to court, claimed that King has spied on her and stole story ideas, for which she wanted all the profits from *Misery*.

In another case, a man claimed that King stole the idea of a haunted car from his unsolicited screenplay, which he had submitted to one of the companies with which King had done business. (Considering the number of studios involved in making his films, that kind of tenuous connection is inevitable.) But the man could never prove his case.

In any event, lawsuits are a way of life for King, who retains a law firm to protect his interests.

"The Ledge" (collected in *Night Shift*)

Originally appeared in *Penthouse* (July 1976). Tennis pro Norris has fallen in love with Marcia, whose husband, Cressner, is a crime overlord. Cressner wants to force Norris to walk the plank, so to speak—to negotiate a five-inch-wide ledge around Cressner's penthouse apartment, over 40 stories up, at night. He has planted heroin in Norris's car, which will be removed only if Norris agrees to the wager. All it'd take is a phone call to the police, and they'd discover the drugs and arrest Norris, sending him up the river.

Norris reluctantly agrees, determined to exact revenge.

After a harrowing circumnavigation of the building—which Cressner never believed Norris could do—Norris foolishly believes he's going to get the promised $20,000 and Marcia on his own terms.

He gets Marcia, but not in the way he imagined: She's at the city morgue. Enraged, Norris overpowers Cressner and forces him out on the ledge to walk the walk: Even if Cressner makes it, which is doubtful, Norris will welch on his bet. (To my mind, there are echoes of "Dolan's Cadillac" in this story.)

Legends: The Book of Fantasy,
edited by Robert Silverberg, $27.95, Fall 1998

This anthology of original stories contains an original "Gunslinger" novella, "The Little Sisters of Eluria." (It is not an excerpt from a forthcoming Dark Tower novel.)

Leonard, Brett

Director of *Stephen King's The Lawnmower Man*, a film that has no linkage to the story "The Lawnmower Man" except in name. It is, however, an entertaining movie in its own right.

Leonard, Elmore

SK: "After finishing *Glitz*, I went out to the bookstore at my local mall and bought everything by Elmore Leonard I could find—the stuff I didn't already own, that is." (From a review of *Glitz*, "What Went Down When Magyk Went Up," *NYTBR*.)

Note: Elmore Leonard figures prominently in *Bag of Bones*.

Leonard, Stephanie

King's sister-in-law, first secretary, and editor-publisher of *Castle Rock*. Stephanie ran the roost but in due time she turned the reins over to Shirley Sonderegger, who was hired on a temporary basis but stayed on until 1997.

Working initially out of King's home office, Leonard and the other staffers later moved to a rented office building on the outskirts of Bangor, which allowed the Kings to shift all the business activities and meetings where they belonged—out of the personal residence.

Lester, Mark

The director of *Firestarter*. Lester, whose previous credits included low-budget films like *Roller Boogie, Truck Stop Women*, and *Gold of the Amazon Women*, found himself with a formidable task: handling a big budget with big-name stars, on a set that required difficult shoots, including handling fires.

Shot at Dino De Laurentiis's studio in Wilmington, North Carolina, *Firestarter* was subjected to criticisms by King, who felt that the film was a big letdown. (Reminiscent of the Kubrick-King brouhaha, Lester and King engaged in a war of words in *Cinefantastique*.)

Lester went on to show his directoral talents in *Commando*, starring Arnold Schwarzenegger.

"Letters from Hell"

A broadside published by Lord John Press (Northridge, Calif.), with the full text of an article by King originally published in the *New York Times*, "Ever Et Raw Meat?" A numbered edition of 500 copies signed by King, the broadside is 20 by 25 inches, designed and printed by letterpress by Patrick Reagh, using three colors, on heavyweight Arches paper. Available only by mail order, $125.

Levin, Barry R.

A book dealer specializing in fantasy and science fiction collectibles, who heads a company called Barry R. Levin Science Fiction and Fantasy Literature.

He is the premier dealer of the rare, the obscure, and the one-of-a-kind item. Levin collab-

Levin, Barry R. *continued*

orated with Beahm on a price guide to King collectibles that appeared in the 1989 edition of *The Stephen King Companion*.

Lewiston, Maine

A larger town near Durham, Maine, where a teenage King saw movies at the (now closed) Ritz Theater.

"The Library Policeman"

(collected in *Four Past Midnight*)

Dedication: "This is for the staff and patrons of the Pasadena Public Library."

At a public talk in Pasadena, California, King explained the genesis of this story: His son Owen was reluctant to use the local library to check out books because of his fear of the library police—the boogeyman that plagued all children with overactive imaginations. Owen explained that he wanted his father to use his own library card to check out the books. (Let Daddy contend with the library police!)

So King began writing this story, thinking it'd be a lark, but realizing—as he pointed out in his introduction to the story in *Four Past Midnight*—that the childhood fear of the tall, faceless library police who would come and get you if you didn't return the books on time drew its strength from a deeper, darker fear, which is what King so skillfully explores in this story.

Lightfoot, Steve

A King harasser from Berkeley, California, who at a book signing in Santa Cruz, California, where King made his final stop during his 1994 *Insomnia* tour, carried a sign that read KING IS A MURDERER. IT'S TRUE OR HE'D SUE.

Lightfoot was arrested at the bookstore—he had violated the restraining order that had been put on him—and was put in jail with a $10,000 bond. He greeted King at the bookstore by yelling out, "King eats meat. He's a murderer!" On his van's side: KING SHOT JOHN LENNON. GOVT. MEDIA PUSHING LOOK-ALIKE; CHAPMAN.

This wasn't the first time Lightfoot had been on King's case: Two years earlier, in Bangor, Lightfoot had been served notice by the police to stay away from the King family and their employees, home, and office.

The police had also gotten complaints that he had been harassing customers in front of Betts Bookstore, where he had parked his van, handing out a typewritten thesis expounding on his conspiracy theory that King, not Mark David Chapman, was the real killer of John Lennon. ("The Kings are strongly concerned about the welfare of this person. They are very much concerned that people may take matters into their own hands. The Kings don't want to see that happen," said a security representative of the Kings.)

"I just want to say that this guy's been doing this for 10 years. . . . I hate it, of course. This is what he wants. We live in a society where this sort of publicity is a drug. . . . One of the things that hurts most, this guy lumps me with Reagan and Nixon." (*BDN*, June 27, 1992.)

Linkous, Kenny Ray

A talented artist who was hired by King to illustrate the Philtrum Press edition of *The Eyes of the Dragon*, Linkous published under the pen name of Kenneth R. Linkhäuser to preserve his anonymity. Later, as he began illustrating other books—*War of Words: The Censorship Debate*, *Stephen King: Man and Artist*, and *The Stephen King Story*—he used his real name.

Lisbon High School

High school in Lisbon Falls, Maine, that King attended. Lisbon is generally believed to be *a* model, if not *the* model, for Castle Rock, Maine.

"The Lists That Matter"

King aired these lists of his favorite raves and rants on his AM radio station, WZON.

There were plans to syndicate these on radio stations nationwide, but those plans never materialized. Some of the topics: a listing of the best things by age (at 7, an ice cream cone; at 70, to still be alive and working); King's favorite movies; the ten worst movies ever made; and personal fears.

Lists That *Really* Matter

The Association of American Publishers published its list for 1986 of the best-selling horror paperbacks, on which Stephen was clearly the king: He had four out of the ten, including *Night Shift*, *The Stand*, *Thinner*, and number one on the list, *Pet Sematary*.

Literary criticism

In "Books" (*Adelina*, June 1980), King expressed the thought that as far as literary criticism was concerned, if the critics disagreed on a specific literary work, it was merely opinion, but if they agreed, it was an informed opinion and likely had some truth to it—a viewpoint put forth by King's writing teacher in college, Ted Holmes, whom he characterized as a "wise teacher and a fine short story writer" in *Adelina*.

Literary Guild and *The Talisman*

In a radical departure for King, the book club rights to *The Talisman* were not sold.

The Literary Guild offered $400,000, an offer rejected by Kirby McCauley, who wanted $700,000, the price King set. The difference in amount, and King's opinion about the role of book clubs, killed the deal.

A late autumn day on the grounds of Lisbon High School in Lisbon Falls, Maine, where King attended high school.

"A book club edition is essentially a remainder before publication rather than after. Once your books sell a certain number of copies, you become important as an instrument to bring in future members. Book clubs are an integral part of the industry. I'm not out to bust them. But I think the climate that spawned clubs has changed radically." (*San Francisco Chronicle*, January 1985.)

McCauley: "Originally, their purpose was to expand the market by mail-order sales. But in this day of chains and discounts, I believe the clubs are a competitive element." (Quoted in Paul Nathan, "Rights," *PW*, Nov. 23, 1984.)

Literary muse

King harbors no romantic notions of what a muse looks like or does. As he told *Time* magazine (Oct. 6, 1986), "People think the muse is a literary character, some cute little pudgy devil who floats around the head of the creative person sprinkling fairy dust. Well, mine's a guy with a flat-top in coveralls who looks like Jack Webb and says, 'All right, you son of a bitch, time to get to work.'"

Literary posterity

In *Conversations with Anne Rice*, she shared with Michael Riley an anecdote regarding King and the literary scene that underscored the misperceptions of King as a literary figure. Riley commented, "I've referred to the American literary scene, but that's probably a misleading term, or at least one that oversimplifies. The literary scene is made up of not just the publishing houses that determine what gets published, but what the reviewers are saying. It's also the bookstores that decide what they'll carry, and what's actually bought in those bookstores. Even film rights are a part of it."

Anne Rice replied:

What's being published and bought is John Grisham and Danielle Steele, overwhelmingly. This may not strike you as relevant, but let me tell you a story. A couple of years ago a woman calling herself "a better fiction writer" wrote a letter to PEN, the writers' organization, saying that she and the other "better fiction writers" were depressed and upset by the fact that everywhere they went they saw Stephen King, Danielle Steele, Tom Clancy, and a few other big megasellers, and they felt that they, the writers of better fiction, were being pushed out. Well, this is a common cry. It comes up year after year. This "better fiction writer" defined herself as somebody who doesn't write detective fiction, fantasy, horror, romance, or just about anything else. [*Laughter*] What that person basically was arguing for was being allotted some space, almost like being subsidized. The argument is that "better fiction writers" should be subsidized, whether they sell or not. That's a popular idea in academia, that if somebody has worked very hard on his thesis and done a good job, he should be awarded a master's degree and if possible a job. But, you see, that doesn't work in the American book world. Novels are not published simply because somebody has worked hard and done an acceptable job. Those who are rewarded are those who make an impact, and that's all there is to it. If you talk to these "better fiction writers," who write largely American realism, you'll find they feel they're a martyred group, that because of what they've put into it, and because of their intentions and their hard work, they should have earned some recognition, and that there's something radically wrong with a world that gives that recognition to Stephen King instead. That's bullshit in the arts! That wasn't true two thousand years ago, it wasn't ever true in the arts, and it never will be. Whether you took five days or twenty years to write a book doesn't make a damn bit of difference. It's whether the book grabs people by the throat. That's what's going to be rewarded. I wanted to write a response to the letter. PEN called up and invited me to, but I just couldn't get my thoughts together about it. This troubled me for years. Stephen King did write a response, and he went way out on a limb saying, "Who says you're a better fiction writer, what makes your fiction better?" It was a big controversy. But, in a way, that original letter was outrageously arrogant.

Many novels are published in America with the belief that a particular new voice should be heard because the dues have been paid and it's time to publish that kind of novel, but it's often a terrible disservice to these writers because their works are never truly published. They rarely get more than a few thousand copies, and a few book review copies, and perhaps a mention in *Publishers Weekly*. Maybe a review in the *New York Times* if they're very, very fortunate. And those people go off aggrieved, believing we're nothing but a nation of crude thrill-seeking monsters who have relegated them to the back shelf. Their arguments do imply that they should have a government subsidy.

Over the years, King's has joked that he's not making room on his shelves for a National Book Award, and that he doesn't think he'll "ever be remembered as a literary giant." (*Bare Bones.*) But the simple truth is that King *has* achieved recognition from the literary establishment: "The Man in the Black Suit" was a first-place winner in an *O. Henry* collection of best short fiction of the year, and Joyce Carol Oates, the first lady of American fiction, introduced him as a serious and important writer when he delivered an address at Princeton University.

If any comparisons need be made, the truth is this: In many ways, King writes in the same vein, with the same seriousness of intent, as did Shirley Jackson; the difference was that Jackson's husband, Stanley Edgar Hyman, was well regarded in critical circles, and that insulated her from some of the more harsh criticism.

It doesn't help King that his public persona, that of an everyday Joe—informal, joking, and hamming it up for the cameras—is so at odds with his writing persona. King, who doesn't take himself seriously but takes his work very seriously, is erroneously perceived as the Jordy Verrill of American literature, and his work is, according to his more harsh critics, meteor shit.

Harlan Ellison: "Stephen King is neither Marcel Proust nor is he Salman Rushdie, to take the current icon. King is one of the most accomplished storytellers the twentieth century has produced. As a consequence, his strengths are in the storytelling area, and his weaknesses are in more specific areas. For instance, I can't think of any King novels with the possible exception of maybe *It* or the two *Dark*

Tower books that could not have been told just as well as a novella. This is to me the main flaw in Stephen's work. There is very little complexity in his ideas. They are all ideas that have been done ad infinitum in the fantasy and horror genres." (*The Stephen King Companion*, 1989.)

SK: "I'd like to win the National Book Award, the Pulitzer Prize, the Nobel Prize, I'd like to have someone write a *New York Times Book Review* piece that says, 'Hey, wait a minute, guys, we made a mistake—this guy is one of the great writers of the 20th century.' But it's not going to happen, for two reasons. One is I'm not the greatest writer of the 20th century, and the other is that once you sell a certain number of books, the people who think about 'literature' stop thinking about you and assume that any writer who is popular across a wide spectrum has nothing to say." King wants to "build a bridge between wide popularity and a critical acceptance." (Quoted in a profile by Bill Goldstein, "King of Horror," *PW*, Jan. 24, 1991.)

Burton Hatlen: "On the one hand, there have been a lot of people who are regarded as major writers who were very popular—Mark Twain, Charles Dickens, William Shakespeare. I think that there's another issue here, and that is that Steve's work really in some ways grows out of a conscious critique of that cultural split itself, and his critique of it is that what the split does is automatically write off everything that's on the popular culture side as mere commodity, trash, a contribution to the debased tastes of an illiterate mob. . . . We have a massive rethinking of the whole issue of canonicity and canonization; Steve's work is one of the forces that has initiated this rethinking of that issue." (*Stephen King's America.*)

Douglas E. Winter: "I tend to think, from what I've read of the negative criticisms of Steve's work, that most of it is based on his popularity and the fact that he's a personality now, as well as a writer, and not on an understanding of either his fiction or horror fiction. On the other hand, there are some negative critiques that I've seen that are entirely fair and honorable, that you shouldn't ascribe to ill motivations but to someone's critical or aesthetic perspective being a little bit different. And sometimes I find myself agreeing with those people." (*The Stephen King Companion*, 1989.)

"Living with the Bogeyman"

An article for *Murderess Ink* (Workman Publishing, 1979), in which Tabitha King discusses the difference between the fantasy of what King's readers perceive him to be (a bogeyman) and the reality of what he really is (an ordinary-looking man). Never reprinted, this piece shows a side of King that most people will never see: the family man, the husband, the man behind the fright mask.

Lloyd Elliot Lecturers

In the fall semester of 1986, Stephen and Tabitha King were named Lloyd Elliot Lecturers at UMO, for which he presented a public talk on November 6 at the Maine Center for Performing Arts, followed by a reception. Also, during this period, UMO's English department scheduled a retrospective of films based on King's books, screened in the Hauck Auditorium.

Tabitha King gave her lecture in Neville Hall on October 29, followed by a reception. She also spoke to students in English classes.

According to Sarah W. Spruce, writing in *Castle Rock*, the King films were shown over a five-day period. Burton Hatlen presented a paper on King ("King and the American Dream: Alienation, Competition, and Community in *Rage* and *The Long Walk*"). Tabitha King's planned talk on "The New Prudery" was jettisoned in favor of reading her own poetry.

Lobsterland

A restaurant near Bangor where Tabitha worked operating the lobster press.

SK: "Whatever the customers didn't eat, the legs and all, was sent there and squeezed to make the next day's lobster salad or lobster roll. She's not too big on lobster, either." (Quoted in Bryan Miller, "Writer Eats Steak Before It Eats Him," *NYT*, Oct. 26, 1988.)

Long Lake, Bridgton

Town in the Cumberland region of Maine, west of Sebago Lake, where the Kings owned a house. The location formed the backdrop for one of King's most popular stories, "The Mist."

Long Lake *continued*

In August 1997, the house came on the market, offered at $450,000. Maine Star Realty Inc., which handled the sale, pointed out its most salable feature in its headline: KING WROTE HERE! The copy read, "The sun shines all day on these 2.65 private acres at 'The Ledges.' The 250 feet of waterfront includes beach and deep water with a separate cover. The daylight Ranch has 5 bedrooms, 2 1/2 baths, fireplace, full basement [King's home office]/garage and separate 3-car garage with unfinished apartment above."

The Long Walk,

by Stephen King, writing as
Richard Bachman

Mass-market paperback, 1979, 245 pages, NAL/Signet, $1.95

Dedication: "This is for Jim Bishop and Burt Hatlen and Ted Holmes."

Contents: 18 chapters

Background: Unknown

An admittedly bleak novel by Richard Bachman that is set in the near future, *The Long Walk* foreshadows a later Bachman book, *The Running Man.* Both use a story of attrition to advance the plot in a measured way.

The Long Walk is the story of 100 boys who start at the northernmost point of U.S. Route 1, at Fort Kent, Maine, and walk south until only one walker —Ray Garrity, the focal point of the book—remains. The others are picked off one by one as the clock ticks down, minute by minute, as in *The Running Man.*

Like *Rage, The Long Walk* is principally a study in psychological horror. There are no supernatural boogeymen—only those found in real life.

Written while King was in college, this grim story of the future drew its inspiration from the walkathons endorsed by President John F. Kennedy in the sixties, In 1962 he urged the public to take up the activity. "I would encourage every American to walk as often as possible. It's more than healthy; it's fun." It certainly isn't fun for the characters in this novel.

"I thought of it while hitchhiking home from college one night when I was a freshman," King wrote in a letter to Dr. Michael Collings.

King approached Burton Hatlen at UMO for a reading. Years later Hatlen observed, "I brought it home and laid it on the dining room table. My ex-wife picked it up and started reading it and couldn't stop. That was also my experience. The narrative grabbed you and carried you forward. That was what was most striking about *The Long Walk*—King had a fully developed sense of narrative and pace. It was there already. It was quite amazing to see that."

In addition to Hatlen, Ted Holmes, Jim Bishop, and Carroll Terrell also read the work.

Terrell's observations, published in *Stephen King: Man and Artist*, were revealing. Initially he thought the book presented technical problems, that the design of the book itself "made the action repetitive." He added: "I am conscious now that I thought *The Long Walk* was a first novel. But I should have known that it could have been no such thing: No one could have written such a balanced and designed book without a lot of practice; not just aimless practice, but conscious and designed practice."

The book failed to win a first-novel competition, demoralizing the fledgling author. "I was too crushed to show that book to any publisher in New York," King later wrote in the essay "On Becoming a Brand Name."

The book was finally published as a mass-market paperback original by NAL.

Lord John Press

The small press of Herb Yellin, which produces beautiful broadsides whose type is set on letterpress, and beautiful books as well. Publications include *Dolan's Cadillac* and a broadside, "Letters from Hell," in which King discusses the mail he gets from fans.

The Lord of the Flies, by William Golding

According to Stephanie Leonard, King "is often asked what book affected him most when he was young and this is the book he always names."

The Lord of the Rings, by J. R. R. Tolkien

Epic fantasy trilogy by the British philologist and professor that was a blueprint for *The Stand*.

SK: "That was intended. It's not something I ever mention unless somebody brings it up because it didn't succeed anywhere near as well as Tolkien succeeds, mostly because I thought that I'd try to make Middle Earth the United States after the plague. One of the things that provided the impetus was that I said in the book, 'After the plague, there's magic.' The best review I've had on the book said that Stu Redman is an American Frodo who sits around the gas station with his fellow hobbits and finally goes on a quest."

Love Lessons

A hoax novel that backfired on all parties concerned. Intended to test the drawing power of *Fantasy Review* advertising, this porn novel published by "Pinetree Press," written by "John Wilson," was attributed to King. According to *Fantasy Review*, it was written at "the same time he was selling short stories to men's magazines. . . . According to Pinetree Press, based in Georgia, there are four other erotic novels that King wrote, which they plan to publish if there is sufficient demand."

After reading the hoax review, King lit a fire under the magazine, as reported by in the *San Francisco Chronicle* (Aug. 1985):

> The review resulted in a stern letter from King's lawyer to *Fantasy Review*, noting that "the statements in said article . . . are inaccurate, highly libelous and of great damage to Mr. King." The letter further demanded an immediate retraction, a written apology to King, and continued, warning that despite such steps, King reserved the right "to sue for equitable relief and/or damages, including general, special and punitive damages. We are reserving the right to bring suit at any time hereafter."

Neil Barron, in a form letter, wrote that he had gotten 16 replies, including 7 with checks, which he had returned. Wrote Barron, "Bob Collins did not know that the review was pseudonymous or that the book was mythical, although perhaps plausible given the recent disclosure of King's Bachman pseudonym. . . . I hope you aren't too annoyed by this *jeu d'esprit* and regard it as little more than an April Fool's joke."

King also sent a letter to *Twilight Zone* (October 1985) to set the record straight, clearly stating that he had never "published a so-called porno novel under any name. In 1969, when I was an impoverished college student . . . I actually *did* try to write a porno novel. About forty pages in, while writing a scene in which gorgeous twin sisters are making love in a birdbath, I collapsed in shrieks of laughter and banished the project into the oilstove."

The hoax novel was the misguided brainchild of merry prankster Charles Platt, who had interviewed King for *Dream Makers 2*.

Lovecraft, H. P.

A New England writer of the supernatural whose work in the pulp magazine *Weird Tales* influenced a generation of postwar writers.

A dour, lantern-jawed writer who lived most of his life in Providence, Rhode Island, HPL's cosmic views of horror, of alien races from faraway planets, his baroque writing style and literary style showed King the power of evoking the New England atmosphere in writing horror stories. Unlike HPL, however, King did not spend a lifetime in amateur publishing, which is one reason why HPL lived in genteel poverty, but King went on to commercial success.

Chris Chesley: "What Steve learned from Lovecraft was the possibility of taking the New England atmosphere and using that as a springboard. Lovecraft showed him a milieu that was definitely New England horror. Dracula could be moved to Durham, basically.

"He didn't keep on reading Lovecraft, but in terms of his development, he took that European kind of horror and set it on this continent."

"L.T.'s Theory of Pets"
(collected in *Six Stories*)

A short story that made its first appearance in print in *Six Stories*.

"Luckey Quarter"
(collected in *Six Stories*)

Originally published in *USA Weekend* as part of their series of summer stories, this story came about after King saw a tip envelope in his hotel room when traveling through Nevada.

"The Ludlum Attraction"

In a humorous, biting review of Robert Ludlum's *The Parsifal Mosaic*, King takes Ludlum to task for writing a book without worrying about such "minor things as language, plot, character development, style, tone, mood, and coherence."

The review, written in the form of a letter from Reed "Vested Tweed Reed" Smalley of Smalley, Halle, and Polly to Mr. Theodore "Glen Plaid Tad" Smoot of Smoot, Hoot, Doot, and Froot.

King cares little for Ludlum's writing, but instead of descending into vituperation, as some of his own critics have done, he demolished it with gentle humor.

"Lunch at the Gotham Café"
(collected in *Six Stories*)

Originally published in *Dark Love*, this story won a Bram Stoker Award for short fiction.

McCauley, Kirby

King's second literary agent, whom he met at a literary party in 1976 in New York. McCauley, who then represented several writers in the science fiction and fantasy field, wrote: "I partly saw his success growing. I saw that he was going to get bigger and bigger. But . . . I can't say I foresaw Steve King being the literary phenomenon of the last half of the twentieth century."

After that party, King and McCauley corresponded. After McCauley sold several short stories to markets that King was unable to crack, McCauley became King's literary agent in 1977.

Major accomplishment on King's behalf: engineering the move from Doubleday to New American Library.

In its September 1988 issue, *Castle Rock* confirmed McCauley's departure: "A recent article in *Fantasy Newsletter* mentioned a shake-up at the Kirby McCauley agency. It is true that King is no longer represented by Kirby McCauley, as the article implied. At this time he has not signed with any other representatives."

King finally decided not to sign another literary agent, preferring to put all of his eggs in one basket and have his longtime lawyer and financial manager, Arthur B. Greene, represent him in all financial matters.

McCauley was profiled in *Success* magazine (April 1987).

McCauley: "By the time I met Steve, I had made it over the hump as a literary agent. I was earning a modest income, but I was by no means big time. But I did represent a number of minor, prestigious writers in the science fiction and fantasy field. Steve and Tabby, quite frankly, took a chance. It put me in a whole different league. Not just income, but now that of a major agent." (*Castle Rock*, May 1986.)

MacDonald, John D.

A formative influence on King as a writer, MacDonald—a popular novelist, best known for his Travis McGee books—wrote an introduction to *Night Shift*, observing that "Stephen King is a far, far better writer at thirty than I was at thirty, or at forty." Citing the importance of "Story. Story. Dammit, story!" above all else, MacDonald notes that although King currently writes horror stories, "Stephen King is not going to restrict himself to his present field of intense interest." Citing "The Last Rung on the Ladder" as "A gem" and indicative of the promise of King as a *non* horror writer, MacDonald notes, "Insofar as story is concerned, and pleasure is concerned, there are not enough Stephen Kings to go around."

MacDonald added that he knew "of a dozen demons hiding in the bushes where his path leads, and even if I had a way to warn him, it would do no good. He whips them or they whip him." (Years later, in the dedication of "The Sun Dog" to the late MacDonald, King writes, "I miss you, old friend—and you were right about the tigers." I think King meant "demons," but the message is clear: King's gone through the gauntlet and survived on his own.)

McDonald's

Hamburger chain that produces what Harlan Ellison terms "toadburgers." King, however, loves them—or used to. In an unpublished manuscript, "Your Kind of Place," he talks about the company's founder, Ray Kroc, and states, "I love McDonald's; I am hopeless."

McLeod, George

The restaurateur in Bucksport, Maine, who told King about a story that was making the rounds: A dog that had been struck by a train, and its remains were still on the railroad track. King said that he was going to write a story about it but never did. But he used the kernel of the idea, changing the dog to a boy, and writing "The Body," which he dedicated to McLeod.

McLoughlin, Tom

The director of *Sometimes They Come Back*. Previous credits included *Friday the 13th*, *Jason Lives*, and *Date with an Angel*, starring Emmanuelle Beart.

Tom McLoughlin, talking about his generation, which included Stephen King, George Lucas, and

The cover to the special Stephen King issue of *Fantasy & Science Fiction*.

Steven Spielberg: "We were all shaped by the same influences. So I can see where King is coming from. And I can appreciate King's genius for reinterpreting and drawing on those common influences."

Macular degeneration

A condition with which King is afflicted whose symptoms include blurry or fuzzy vision, straight lines appearing wavy, and a dark area appearing in the center of vision. There is currently no known cure for this disease, which can cause irreversible blindness.

The Magazine of Fantasy and Science Fiction

The most literary pulp magazine in the field, to which King as a budding writer submitted stories.

In due time, King broke through, but readers remember him best for the serialized installments of *The Gunslinger*, which made their first appearances in print in this magazine.

For its December 1990 issue, King was the cover subject—an honor bestowed on only a handful of other writers, including Isaac Asimov, Ray Bradbury, and Harlan Ellison.

Maine Commission for Women

Tabitha King addressed this organization on June 14, 1989.

Maine General Hospital

King was born on September 21, 1947, at this hospital in Portland, Maine. A postcard shows the building to be spooky-looking, appropriate for the birthplace of America's best-loved boogeyman.

Maine State Library

King gave a talk on October 26, 1979, at the Maine Street Library, as part of the library's annual Meet the Author program. Approximately 400 people showed up to listen to him read from *Danse Macabre*. Commented librarian Sharon

Hanley, "We've never had this much of a crowd."

Ironically, a power failure struck at the time King gave his reading, but emergency lighting ensured the show would go on.

Maine State Police

In the hardback edition of *The Dark Half*, King needed to use the phone number of the Maine State Police, but instead of using a fictitious one (with a 555 prefix, as is used in films and TV), he published the real one, causing curious fans to call the number to see if it was real. "When I came to that part of the book, I thought, 'Well, I'm using the Maine State Police in Orono, I'll use the right number,'" King said. "I got out the phone book and there it was in bold type." (Quoted in Renee Ordway, "King's New Book Rings Phones at Police Barracks," *BDN*, Nov. 21, 1989.)

Maine writers

In "The Voices of Maine," in *Down East* magazine, King observed that when he was young, the only Maine writer he could cite was Kenneth Roberts, but the new Maine writers include "Carolyn Chute, Martin Dibner, Michael Kimball, Margaret Dickson, Rick Hautala, Janwillen van de Wetering, and Bill Kotzwinkle."

"The Mangler" (collected in *Night Shift*)

Originally published in *Cavalier* (December 1972), this disturbingly effective story, drawn from King's personal experience as a laundry worker at a Bangor industrial laundry, is a trial cut for *Maximum Overdrive*: A virgin high school girl accidentally cuts her hand on an electric speed ironer and folder . . . and the machine becomes possessed. The investigating police officer, John Hunton, decides to call a friend, an English professor, who joins him at the laundry to perform an exorcism. His friend fails, becoming victim to the malevolent machine with a mind of its own. As Hunton watches in terror, the machine literally uproots itself, stalking off, in search of human prey.

The Mangler (film), 1995

King, who has recycled his life experiences into fiction in the most imaginable ways, drew on his background as a laundry worker to write "The Mangler," a short story that, unfortunately, made the leap from printed page to silver screen. Starring Robert Englund (Freddie's back!), this film adaptation reinforces my notion that, when it comes to badly adapted King fiction to the screen, nothing exceeds like excess.

In this film, there's an excess of everything—mostly blood and gore, since they are implicit in the title. Unfortunately, what's left out is a solid dose of entertainment.

Taking a clip out of *Maximum Overdrive*, not only does an industrial-strength laundry presser become sentient and go amok, but so does a refrigerator!

Like the seemingly endless *Children of the Corn* films, this one occupies the lowest rung on the ladder.

"The Man in the Black Suit"
(collected in *Six Stories*)

One of King's best short stories, this story was originally published in the *New Yorker* magazine, and was reprinted in *Prize Stories 1996: The O. Henry Awards*, edited by William Abrahams. Abrahams said of the stories in this collection: "For the 1996 volume I have chosen twenty stories from among the approximately one thousand that were eligible. . . . The winnowing and sifting procedure reduced the number of plausible candidates dramatically. Perhaps one hundred stories remained to be reread and reconsidered. Then, another winnowing—and several worthy stories were reluctantly let go. Ultimately, I settled on the final twenty, making a collection about which I am prepared to say: This is one of the very best."

And in 1996, the best of the best, according to Abrahams, was "The Man in the Black Suit," by Stephen King.

In his note on the story, King wrote that it "comes from a long New England tradition of stories which dealt with meeting the devil in the

"The Man in the Black Suit" *continued*

woods. . . . Sometimes he's known as Scratch, sometimes as the Old Fella, sometimes as the Man in the Black Suit, but he always comes out of the woods—the uncharted regions—to test the human soul."

In this case, the soul tested is that of a young boy, who encounters the devil on a fishing trip, when he ventures farther than he should.

A typical King story in terms of structure—a first-person narrator recounting his boyhood years when growing up in rural Maine—this one is in the first rank of his fiction.

It's a powerful story with a considerable emotional punch—especially the carefully limned relationship between the boy and his mother, who the devil tells him has died of a bee sting. This story is prime evil and prime King as well.

Mansfield, Dave

Little League coach of the Bangor West team that went to the Maine championship in 1989. That year, Mansfield was voted amateur coach of the year by the Maine division of the United States Baseball Federation.

Manuel, Richard

A real estate broker from St. Paul, Minnesota, who is a friend of Kirby McCauley's. His photo was used as the author's photo for *Thinner*. (Funny. He doesn't look anything like King.)

"The Man Who Loved Flowers"
(collected in *Night Shift*)

Originally published in *Gallery* (August 1977), this short but effective story, set in New York City in 1963, is not what it seems. It *seems* to be a story about a young man in love who buys flowers for his girlfriend, Norma, but as I said, things are not what they seem: Norma's been dead for a decade, so why is he accosting strange women on the street, giving them flowers, and calling *them* Norma?

Indeed an excursion into horror. As the book cover states, this is the kind of horror story that hammers its point home: Everyone loves a lover, but you can't be taken in by mere appearances.

"The Man Who Would Not Shake Hands"
(collected in *Skeleton Crew*)

Originally appearing in *Shadows 4* (1982), this story takes the reader to a poker club in a brownstone in New York City, at 249B East Thirty-fifth Street. Here George Gregson tells the others that he "once saw a man murdered right in this room . . . although no juror would have convicted the killer. Yet, at the end of the business, he convicted himself—and served as his own executioner!"

The story he tells dates back to 1919. They are lacking a fifth for a poker game, and so a newcomer to the club, Henry Brower, joins in. Curiously, Brower refuses to shake hands with anyone, citing an old habit he picked up during a two-year trade mission while stationed in Bombay. But you had to hand it to Brower, who proved himself to be a whiz at cards, winning the not inconsiderable pot.

After the win, Jason Davidson, in a spontaneous gesture of fellowship, reaches out to shake Brower's hands, which causes him to scream, then bolt inexplicably out into the street.

As it turns out, Brower, under a curse afflicted upon him when in Bombay, cannot shake the hand of any living thing without killing it—a point hammered home when Davidson, a healthy man of twenty-two who had shaken Brower's hand, is inexplicably found dead of a heart attack.

By the time Gregson tracks down the Man Who Would Not Shake Hands, he's too late: Henry Brower has committed suicide, by a most unusual method—shaking hands with himself.

The Many Facets of Stephen King,
by Michael Collings

Published by Starmont House in 1985, this book urges "readers to approach King from multiple directions, just as he approaches his craft from multiple directions."

Contents

Foreword

Marriage

January 2, 1971. Stephen and Tabitha were married in Old Town, Maine. Clergyman John M. Anderson performed the ceremony. King took the day off from the laundry but was docked pay.

Marshall, John

Known as Mighty John Marshall, he was WZON's program director in the mid-eighties and designed the WZON "creep shirt," which sports a one-color logo and King's signature. It is available by mail order only, in small, medium, large, and extra large, in light blue, gray, light yellow, lavender, lime green, or pink.

A later design, with art by Dom Pelliccio, showed a skeleton's head with the call sign WZON forming its mouth, an antenna protruding from the top, and a tuning knob on its side.

"Mars is Heaven" radio dramatization

At age four, King heard this dramatization of Ray Bradbury's story from *The Martian Chronicles*; it scared him so badly that he couldn't sleep in his own bed, so he took refuge under his brother's bed.

This may explain in part King's affection for radio dramatizations, for the oral tradition of storytelling, and for the power that good horror fiction can wield.

"This memory is interesting because it is not a memory of literature—one thing the memory says is that I did not come face to face with fantasy by way of print. . . . It was rather a technological medium." (*Danse Macabre.*)

Matheson, Richard

A writer who was a key influence on King's writing; Matheson's novels showed King that it was possible to write horror set in suburbia.

Matheson is best known for his novels, notably *I Am Legend* and *Hell House*, and television work for *The Twilight Zone*, and his literary influence on King is obvious.

Richard Matheson: "I gather, from what King has said himself, that reading my work—in particular, *I Am Legend*—indicated to him that horror need not be (indeed, in my point of view, should not be) confined to crypts and ancient cellars. When Lovecraft was writing, that sort of thing was in vogue. These are modern times. The approach to horror must accommodate these times." (*The Shape Under the Sheet.*)

SK: "I liked a guy named Richard Matheson. I think that he was the first guy that I ever read as a teenager, who seemed to be doing something that Lovecraft wasn't doing. It wasn't Eastern Europe, it was like the horror could be in the 7-Eleven store down the block, or it could be, you know just up the street something terrible could be going on. Even in a G.I. Bill–type ranch, a development near a college—they could be there as well. And to me, as a kid, that was a revelation. That was extremely exciting. He was putting the horror in places that I could relate to." ("Horror Panel I and II, with King, Ira Levin, Peter Straub, and George Romero," *The Dick Cavett Show*, air dates Oct. 30 and 31, 1980.)

Maximum Overdrive (film), 1986

In numerous interviews King points out that he views his fiction apart from the film adaptations—the two, he stresses, are separate entities, and you shouldn't confuse them. A bad film adaptation doesn't change the fact that its source is a printed book, which remains unchanged. In short, King is philosophical about the movie-making process, because he considers himself a writer whose primacy of vision can be found only in the stories themselves.

Still, King has taken a lot of flak from interviewers, who have noted his distaste for many of the adaptations.

In defense of those who tried and failed—including King—one simple truth must be acknowledged: the time and effort and expense required to script, produce, direct, edit, promote, and distribute a major motion picture is almost beyond the telling, as Frank Darabont (director of *The Shawshank Redemption*) explained in *The Shooting Script*. In other words, nobody deliberately sets out to make a bad film.

In the case of *Maximum Overdrive*, King decided that he'd try his hand at directing, an opportunity movie stars get, but one that writers almost never get . . . unless your name is Stephen King.

King's goal was to translate himself to the screen by writing a script based on one of his short stories. His hope was that his direct involvement would translate to a visual adaptation faithful to the original, retaining the distinct Stephen King flavor that his readers savor in his prose.

Unfortunately, King did not succeed.

A great deal of his failure was in picking a devilishly difficult story to adapt, "Trucks," a story that plays well in the mind's eye but not on the screen. The story, from *Night Shift*, explores a world in which trucks run amok, brought to life, no longer serving man but being served *by* humans who are drones that exist only to build them, fuel them, maintain them.

In the film version, a rogue comet's tail passes over Earth, and that's the explanation—such as it is—for the trucks on the loose. (That premise is absurd enough to cause the scientists at the Jet Propulsion Laboratory to break out in peals of laughter, which is unfortunately what the moviegoers did when they saw the final version. They laughed *at*, not *with*, the film.)

With a head-banging soundtrack by AC/DC, one of King's favorite bands, the movie is aurally assaultive. A little classical music might have been more appropriate in places; perhaps a balletic piece as the trucks synchronize their movements, converging on the truck stop with its inhabitants making their stand. Instead, visually and musically the movie runs at full-tilt boogie, and the suspension of disbelief is never achieved. More damning, the trucks don't seem alive, animated, but in fact are seen to be what they are: mechanically controlled devices manipulated by behind-the-scene operators.

Regardless of the merits (or demerits) of the film, one thing is clear: King at least deserves credit for attempting to direct one of his own works of fiction. If nothing else, it gave him an appreciation of how difficult it is to make a first-rate film. Even a moron movie like this was, truth be told, hard work. King got up early, worked hard all day on the set, went back to the house, watched the dailies (filmed footage), then spent his evening writing a novel until he was exhausted. He came to resemble the hapless humans in *Maximum Overdrive*, driven on by sheer will to survive.

I would have liked to see King try his hand at "The Body," which was carefully, lovingly adapted to the screen as *Stand by Me* by Rob Reiner, who did a masterful job. It's a story that is King to the core, so how might he have handled that one?

As to whether King will direct again, who can say? For now, at least, he's leaving the films to the film community and concentrating on what he does best—writing stories, and more stories. After all, there are *always* more tales.

SK on his movie: "I think most of you knew the movie was a critical and financial flop. The curse of expectation wasn't the only reason . . . but it was certainly one of them." (from "A Postscript to 'Overdrive,'" *Castle Rock*).

"Listen, this movie is about having a good time at the movies, and that's *all* it's about. Believe me, it's not *My Dinner with André*. And little Stevie is not rehearsing his Academy Award speech for *this* baby." ("Full Throttle with Stephen King," *New Times*, 1986.)

"When you write a novel, you are the cinematographer, the star, the special-effects crew, everything. You are in total control. Making a film, you have eighty people standing around, waiting for the sun to come out. . . . Now *that* is a primitive way to create. For the record, I don't think the picture is going to review badly. If I'm wrong, I'm wrong, but I was right about the Red Sox and I'm usually right about these things." (*New Times*, 1986.)

Merchandising

King has vigorously resisted merchandising himself and his work, so there has been no official fan club, no official trinkets and other gimcracks bearing his name, face, or product endorsements, for the most part.

The exception: a hilarious send-up of himself for the American Express Card. Other than that, nothing.

But imagine the possibilities: Cujo pet food, "Year of Fear" calendars (only two to date; a third was given out freely as promotions to booksellers), Christine car decals, and fan clubs, complete with annual tours to Bangor, Maine. (The Kings are particularly sensitive to the possibilities of the merchandising of their Bangor home.)

The merchandising monster is enough to make any horror-meister quake in fear.

In contrast, consider what Anne Rice hawks through her official, 100-page Web site (*http:// www.annerice.com*): T-shirts (seven designs, including one of a magnetic resonance image scan of her brain), posters, wine labels, burgundy ($35 a bottle), and postcards.

Personally, I would have bought several copies of a bumper sticker with a quote about King using all of his fingers on his Wang word processor.

Methodist

King's faith, though he admits to being a "fallen-away Methodist." His wife is Catholic.

Methodist Corners

The part of Durham, Maine, where the Kings grew up, so named because of the proximity of West Durham Methodist Church to a local crossroad.

Mid-Life Confidential, or From Acid to Anti-acid

This was the original title for what was subsequently published as *Mid-Life Confidential: The Rock Bottom Remainders* and, ironically, was remaindered in hardback. (King sold Viking on the idea of the book.) The book contains original essays by the band members, illustrated with photos by Tabitha King.

An indispensable account of the best literary garage band in the country, this is required reading for baby boomers who wish that, for one day, they too could live their fantasies and be rock stars like the Beatles or Bruce Springsteen.

Mike's Taxi of Lisbon

This taxi service ferried King and others to school. The taxi itself was a converted hearse.

One of the other riders was a strange girl who was the model for Carrie.

For a profile of Brian Hall, who grew up with King, Jeff Pert wrote: "Durham couldn't afford a school bus for only a few kids, so they hired Mike's Taxi of Lisbon. Mike had an old limousine, and he'd haul the handful of Durham kids to school in that. Hall says one of the regular riders was one of two girls on whom King based the protagonist of Carrie. When the limo arrived, there was a rush to get the best seat. You didn't want to ride all the way to Lisbon with Carrie on your lap."

Milton Academy, Milton, Massachusetts

A prep school attended by the Kings' three children.

King attended a dedication in his mother's honor of the theater portion of an arts and music center, which bears her name. Ruth King was a talented musician who played the organ and the piano.

The Elizabethan theater was built from the royalties from *The Dark Tower*, an amount in the "low millions" said one insider, according to the *Boston Globe*.

Misery

Hardback, 1987, 310 pages, Viking, $18.95
Dedication: "This is for Stephanie and Jim Leonard, who know why. Boy, do they."
Contents
I. Annie
II. Misery
III. Paul
IV. Goddess
Note: As a young boy, King cited John Fowles's *The Collector* as one of his favorite novels. *The Collector*'s plot (from the back cover of the Dell paperback edition): "The setting is a lonely cottage in the English countryside. The characters are a brutal, tormented man and the beautiful, aristocratic young woman whom he has taken captive. The story is the struggle of two wills, two ways of being, two paths of desire—a story that mounts to the most shattering climax in modern fiction."

For a good explication of the novel, read Tabitha King's "Co-Miser-a-ting with King" (*Castle Rock*, August 1987), in which she wrote, "*Misery* is not the first novel to examine the relationship between writer and reader, or between celebrity and fan, but its exploration of the worst aspects of the celebrity-fan connection is obvious and real."

According to King, in a letter to Michael Collings (Aug. 3, 1985), he said that if the Bachman pen name had not been uncovered, he would have published this as a Bachman book.

Misery explores the intertwined creator-reader relationship taken to the extreme, amplified by a fan's obsessive nature. In *Misery*, the best-selling writer Paul Sheldon deliberately kills off Misery Chastain, a romantic heroine whom he's forced to revive in a sequel, *Misery's Return*, to satisfy the demands of his self-proclaimed "number one fan," Annie Wilkes, who cannot and will not accept the fictional death of her favorite literary character.

In exchange for nursing Sheldon back to health from his car accident, Annie Wilkes wants him to bring Chastain back to life.

He does so, realizing his life depends on staying in Wilkes's good graces, and plots the novel while plotting his escape.

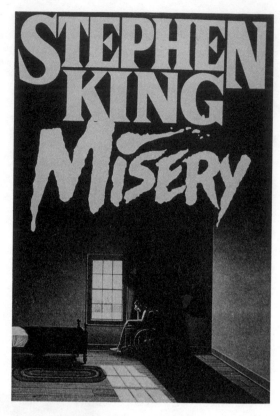

Dust jacket for the Viking edition of *Misery*.

Misery is a riveting read, a psychological study in conflict that underscores the fears of every creative person of the audience *demanding* more of the same, to the exclusion of anything new or different. *Misery* is a cautionary tale for creators and fans alike, drawing its considerable power from King's own experiences with his fans (as opposed to the more sane reader), including one who broke into his house and another who approached him in New York, then went on to murder John Lennon.

"It's pretty accurate in terms of emotional feeling. I sometimes don't know what people want. . . . People really like what I do, or at least some people do, but some of them are quite crackers. I have not met Annie Wilkes yet, but I've met all sorts of people who call themselves my 'number one fan' and, boy, some of these guys don't have six cans in a six-pack."

Misery (film), 1990

The movie poster says it all: "Paul Sheldon used to write for a living. Now, he's writing to stay alive."

Rob Reiner hit a home run in 1986 with *Stand by Me*, and he swatted another one out of the park with this masterful adaptation from one of King's most horrific novels.

Aptly cast with Kathy Bates as number one fan Annie Wilkes and James Caan as her favorite writer, Paul Sheldon, *Misery* is a psychological study in terror. Like that of *The Shining*, the setting is deliberately claustrophobic: Colorado, where Sheldon's car spins out of control up in the mountains, but he's saved from certain death by a former nurse, Annie Wilkes.

She nurses him back to health so he can bring back from the dead her favorite heroine, Misery Chastain, in a novel that would bear her dedication, *Misery's Return*. It's the least he can do for her, since she saved his life.

In an award-winning performance, Kathy Bates brings Wilkes to life—a terrible figure with a haunted past, holding and held by the writer whom she providentially found and brought back to her farmhouse. For his part, James Caan as Paul Sheldon, gives an outstanding performance as a writer tormented by Wilkes.

Reiner found the story hitting close to home; he commented that it meant a lot to him because, as a creative person, he's always torn between the need to create new work that breaks fresh ground

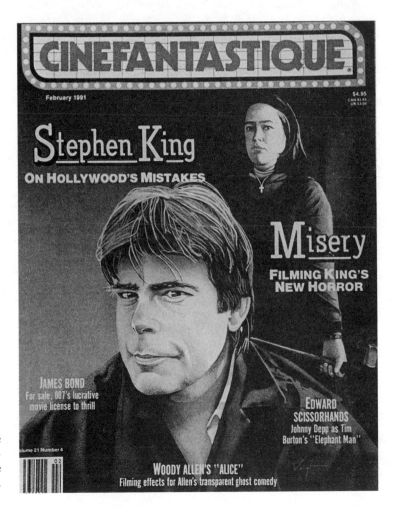

Cover to the film magazine *Cinefantastique*, which included a lengthy review of the film version of *Misery*.

instead of repeating himself, even if the latter means financial or critical success. But the fans with their ravenous appetites don't necessarily want more rarified fare; they usually want more of the same.

Reiner and King know full well the horrors of being typed. King, in fact, is just now starting to get beyond the label of "boogeyman," though he will never completely escape it. *Misery* explores that theme without flinching.

A first-rate film that works from first frame to last.

Rob Reiner: "The thing that drew me to the film was not that it was a suspense thriller genre. That's not what I was interested in doing next. What I was drawn to was the theme of it, the artist's dilemma of attaining a certain success doing something, and the fear of breaking away from that in an attempt to grow and change, the fear that you'll lose your audience." (Quoted by Malcolm L. Johnson, "Director Tamed 'Misery,'" *The Hartford Courant*, 1990.)

Mike Clark (*USA Today*, 1990): "Though *Pet Sematary* and *Graveyard Shift* have inspired countless moviegoer moratoriums on Stephen King adaptations, non-fans might consider giving *Misery* a shot. . . . The original novel has a huge following—not just by read-them-all fans but by dabblers who otherwise have no use for King's oeuvre."

Owen Gleiberman (*Entertainment Weekly*, Nov. 30, 1990): "After years of churning out *Misery* novels, Paul realizes that on some level he did it to himself. He got the fan he deserved."

Abdul Alhazred, author of *The Necronomicon*: "A spooky flick!"

"The Mist"

(collected in *Skeleton Crew*)

If you'd never read a King story but wanted me to recommend just one, it'd be a tough call, because I can think of many short stories, novellas, and novels that are worth recommending. But if forced to pick just one, I'd pick "The Mist" because it's prime King. Written for inclusion in Kirby McCauley's *Dark Forces*, an original anthology following his successful *Frights* anthology, "The Mist" grew in its telling. What was originally a short story eventually grew in length to become a short novel of around 50,000 words. It was so good, in fact, that it was the leadoff story in the anthology and, years later, was the leadoff story in King's own *Skeleton Crew* as well.

In "The Mist," King's classic formula works to perfection: Take ordinary people, put them in an extraordinary situation, and watch the thin veneers of civilization get peeled off layer by layer, until their true natures emerge. In some, it brings out the best, in others, the worst, and in others, a simple inability to accept what is happening.

In "The Mist," a freakish summer storm afflicts western Maine. It's the middle of July and the storm of the decade heralds its coming.

The day after the storm, as David Drayton, his son Billy, and his neighbor Brent Norton head into town to the local Federal Foods supermarket, a strange mist rolls in . . . bringing with it unimaginable monsters—accidents of nature, the locals contend, created by the top-secret Arrowhead Project run by the U.S. Army.

Now under siege by monsters—giant insects, mutated creatures, and other radiation-infected monstrosities—the customers of the Federal Foods supermarket fight a war on another front: reason gives way to unreason, and the customers must choose among the three camps: Drayton's group, representing rationality and the voice of reason; Mrs. Carmody's group, representing irrationality and the voice of unreason; and Norton's group, who choose not to believe what's happening at all, and in so choosing their own fates as they walk out of the supermarket and into the mist to their inevitable deaths.

The story ends on an indeterminate note: Drayton, his son, and two women from his group make it to Drayton's Scout vehicle. They stop at a Howard Johnson's restaurant, and he writes down what's happened to date on a HoJo napkin and wonders what life now holds for them in this brave, new post-Mist world.

The unique feel of this story will be recreated visually in *The Storm of the Century*, a miniseries written by King especially for television.

"The Mist"
(audio dramatization)

If ever there was a quintessential King story, this one is it. And if ever there was a King story ideally suited for dramatization, again, this one is it.

The dramatization, available on CD, chrome audiocassette, and regular audiocassette, is best experienced with headphones on, which gives you the eerie feeling of being in the story.

As *PW* (July 3, 1987) put it: "The slithering, creeping activity going on inside the deadly black cloud is simulated vividly in this frighteningly real and unreal 3-D production, which lets conversation among characters, special effects, and eerie music—rather than endless narration—do the work of scaring us. Chockfull of sounds you don't want to know from, this is easily the most successful of the 3-D sound productions mentioned here [in these reviews of audiotapes]."

"The Mist" (software)

Mindscape brings you the software game that promises to put you in control of the nightmarish situation: "Your commands control the action. Those you confront along the way react to your every move.... The setting is a quiet New England town. Or is it? Because when a mysterious mist descends upon it, anything can happen."

Momilies

A book of homilies by mothers, compiled by Michele Slung and published by Ballantine Books in 1985. It is notable for the inclusion of several momilies from King's mother, Ruth King, who was fond of them: "You'll never be hung for your beauty"; "You need that like a hen needs a flag"; "People have more fun than just about anything, except horses—and they can't"; "He's no better than you—we all stand up naked inside our

clothes"; "Keep all string a' drawing." (*Castle Rock*, June 1985.)

Mondale-Ferraro ticket

Stephen and Tabitha King paid for the following ad in the hometown newspaper (Nov. 5, 1984), in which they stated their reasons for supporting the Mondale-Ferraro ticket:

$2,500,000

That's what my wife and I have paid in State and Federal taxes since Ronald Reagan took office. No one likes taxes, and yet most of us cough up—because we love our country and want to repay the almost unpayable debt we owe her. We have been dismayed by the things our tax dollars have bought in the last four years. Included in the bill:

The invasion of a small Caribbean country. A military build-up in Central America. CIA assassination manuals. An American presence in Lebanon that made widows ... but nothing else. The continuing accumulation of nuclear weapons which only madmen would ever dare use.

Our tax dollars aren't ending the threat of acid rain. They're not going to human service agencies which save the lives of the old, the poor, and the battered. Not enough is going to improve schools or find energy alternatives or a road to a more peaceful world.

We don't mind paying, but we're ashamed of what we're paying for. We believe America is strong enough to offer its own people and the people of the world a helping hand instead of a loaded gun.

On November 6th, we'll be voting for Walter Mondale and Geraldine Ferraro. We urge you to join us. (Stephen and Tabitha King. Paid for by Tabitha and Stephen King.)

Money

King, on life between Hampden (where he lived in a rented double-wide trailer) and Bridgton (where he bought a house, with a Cadillac in the

Money *continued*

driveway, after the paperback rights to *Carrie* were sold): "We don't have to worry about money anymore." (*BDN*, Feb. 12, 1977.)

Arthur B. Greene: "All of his years are very lucrative, he has a very substantial income." (AP, "King Earns Frightening Sums of Cash," *Portsmouth Herald*, Dec. 24, 1990.)

To a writing class: "Money is important to me, however, only as it gives me time to write." (Quoted in Robert H. Newall, "Novelist King Stresses Creativity," *BDN*.)

"The Monkey" (collected in *Skeleton Crew*)

First published in *Gallery* magazine (Nov. 1980), this story foreshadows "Chinga," an *X-Files* episode that King wrote, in which an evil doll comes to life and exerts its unholy influence. In this story, though, it's a monkey doll with cymbals, which can wind itself up and clap—but this leads to an accidental death.

When Hal Shelburn realizes the monkey's evil nature, he gets a bag, puts rocks in it, and puts the monkey in the bag, thinking to sink it to the bottom of a lake. The monkey, though, isn't so easy to kill. As Shelburn hears the cymbals beating, his rowboat literally starts tearing itself apart, and he's forced to swim for his life.

Not long afterward, a short story appears in the local paper, *The Bridgton News*. In Betsy Moriarty's "Mystery of the Dead Fish," she writes that the Fish and Game authorities are mystified by the hundreds of dead fish found floating belly-up, mostly around Hunter's Point . . . which was where Shelburn threw the grinning monkey overboard.

The plot touches on King's real life. The characters in this story, two boys, have been abandoned by their father, a merchant mariner, just like David and Stephen King by their father, Donald. In the story, a back closet is the repository of the past, their only link to their father, who left navigational charts and books, binoculars, and souvenirs from ports of call. (In real life, the attic of Evelyn and Oren Flaws was Donald King's repository.)

Also, the last name of the reporter who writes about the "Mystery of the Dead Fish" shares, not coincidentally, the name of Sherlock Holmes's arch nemesis, Professor Moriarty! (King, a big Sherlock Holmes fan, would go on to write a Holmes pastiche, "The Doctor's Case," collected in *Nightmares & Dreamscapes*.)

After reading this story, it's not likely you'll look at those little grinning monkeys in the same light, just as you're not likely to look at clowns in the same light after reading *It*.

The Moral Voyages of Stephen King,
by Anthony Magistrale

This Starmont House book, published in 1989, had as its purpose "to continue the advance of [the] emerging corpus of critical labors by presenting a still more focused approach. I have deliberately narrowed my scope to an examination of several of [King's] paramount literary themes and philosophical concerns."

Contents

"Morning Deliveries (Milkman #1)"
(collected in *Skeleton Crew*)

Part of an aborted novel, *Milkman*, this is the surreal story of Spike Milligan, a deliveryman for Cramers Dairy, who makes his appointed rounds on Culver Street, at dawn ... but he spikes the deliveries with acid gel, cyanide, belladonna, and continues on his route. Nope, nothing wrong here. (Harlan Ellison wrote a similar story in which a deliveryman made his deadly rounds in the morning.)

Mother's Day, 1973

The day that King's life permanently changed—for the better. On this day King got a phone call from Doubleday that paperback rights to *Carrie* had sold for $400,000, of which King would get half.

For days afterward King brooded about the possibility that he had misheard the dollar amount and that the amount was only $40,000.

This unexpected windfall allowed King to quit teaching and begin his career as a full-time writer.

Motorcycle helmet laws

In an op-ed piece for the *BDN* (Oct. 16, 1991), King, an avid motorcyclist, said that he feels motorcyclists should wear helmets, including him; and that he would be wearing one in the next year, not only because he's older now and his reflexes are slower, but "the major deal is that forty-four is just too old to behave in such a consistently stupid way."

"The Moving Finger"
(collected in *Nightmares & Dreamscapes*)

This is a surreal story originally published in the special Stephen King issue of *F&SF* (Dec. 1990): Howard and Violet Mitla (a CPA and a dental assistant) live in an apartment in Queens, New York, where Howard notices an unwelcome visitor—a finger protruding from the sink in his bathroom. At first he thinks he's hallucinating, but as the finger points out, it's no hallucination, so Howard's got to *do* something. After all, he can't have a *finger* sticking up out of his sink, shocking his wife, can he? And what would the neighbors think? Feh!

Mount Hope Cemetery

A cemetery in Bangor used during the filming of *Pet Sematary*. The cemetery is the second-oldest garden cemetery in the country and is listed on the National Register of Historic Places.

King had a cameo in the movie, as the preacher presiding over the service for Gage Creed.

"Mrs. Todd's Shortcut"
(collected in *Skeleton Crew*)

Originally published in *Redbook* in 1984, this is the story of Worth Todd's first wife, Ophelia, who disappeared in 1973. Mad for shortcuts, Ophelia raced down country roads in her two-seater champagne-colored Mercedes in the endless pursuit of saving time, chasing the moon away like the mythological goddess Diana ... She chances on a road that's actually a wrinkle in time, offering a shortcut. She not only saves time but in fact turns *back* the hands of time—she becomes younger. She's not the only one who becomes younger, though. The caretaker of the Todds' summer home, Homer Buckland, tells a friend in Castle Rock that he's headed out to Vermont, but leaves no forwarding address. He wants to make a "clean break" and does so riding off with Ophelia, "the beautiful girl who leaned over to open his door ... she looked like a girl of no more than sixteen," the narrator says.

Ophelia and Homer have found their way out of the real world where time marches relentlessly on, the world the narrator prefers because he knows "Castle Rock like the back of my hand and I could never leave it for no shortcuts where the roads may go."

Muller, Frank

A prolific narrator who has since 1979 read over 100 books for Recorded Books and read all of the unabridged readings of King's works for that company. His personal favorite: "The Body" from *Dif-*

Muller *continued*

ferent Seasons. He also read all four *Dark Tower* novels, *Different Seasons, The Green Mile,* and selected stories from *Nightmares & Dreamscapes.*

Muller's baritone voice is capable of tremendous range and depth and brings a mellifluous quality to King's written work. A sharp contrast to King's tenor voice, Muller's voice is admittedly easier to listen to on an unabridged recording than King's, but it's not the Master's Voice, complete with the Maine accent, the way the author intended.

SK on Muller: "I feel very small sitting next to the master here. This is tough. It's like the understudy—get in there and dance your balls off, boy." (*The Author Talks,* Recorded Books.)

Mune Spinners

The rock and roll band King belonged to briefly in high school. King admits he was no great shakes as a rhythm guitarist then, but has worked himself up to garage-band quality after jamming with the Rock Bottom Remainders.

"My Pretty Pony"
(collected in *Nightmares & Dreamscapes*)

King explained in the notes to the story in *Nightmares & Dreamscapes* that this was first published in an "overproduced" edition initially, a $2,200 limited edition, followed by a $50 reprint edition by Knopf.

An extract from an aborted novel by Richard Bachman (*My Pretty Pony*), this gentle story is a discussion on the nature of time, explained by a grandfather to his grandson, Clive Banning. Time, his grandfather explains, typically controls people, but in knowing how to stable the horse, so to speak, you control time.

Clive hears but doesn't understand, and in his frustration he says that much to his grandfather, who explains that *knowing* it, taking it to heart, is more important than understanding it.

"My Say"

An op-ed column by King in *Publishers Weekly* (Dec. 20, 1985).

In response to a "My Say" column (November 15, 1985), in which Ron Busch talked about the problems of paperback book publishing, King wrote that he and other baby boomers no longer wait for the paperback reprints because they don't *have* to wait: They have become affluent enough to buy books in hardback, a far cry from life up through the college years, when King was so poor that he can remember buying only one hardback.

Noting that paperback book publishers had been reaping the harvest for years, he said it was now time for them to "plant and cultivate as well."

Mystery Weekends

Sponsored by the Mohonk Mountain House in the Catskills, this annual event requires a three-night stay during which a designated guest is the leader and guides the other guests in solving a mystery.

King attended two weekends on March 13–16 and March 20–23, 1985.

The theme for both weekends was Transylvania Station.

A report about those weekends appeared in *Castle Rock* (May 1986), written by Naomi King.

National Book Award

A prestigious literary award that King states he'll never win, and one for which he's not making space on his shelf. At one National Book Award banquet, King, in the company of John Grisham and others, bought a table so they could sit upfront to tweak the noses, so to speak, of the other attendees, who put on literary airs along with their tuxes that night, looking down critically and literarily at the popular novelists, who, like King and Grisham, sell millions of copies of their books.

Naturalism

A literary term meaning "a more deliberate kind of realism in novels, stories, and plays, usually involving a view of human beings as passive victims of natural forces and social environment. . . . Novelists and storytellers associated with naturalism include . . . Theodore Dreiser and Frank Norris in the United States." (*The Concise Oxford Dictionary of Literary Terms,* 1990.)

King subscribes to this worldview, though in his fiction, people are not necessarily passive, but they must contend not only with real-world forces but with supernatural ones, as well.

As for King: He never truckles—he tells the truth.

Nebel

An unauthorized translation of "The Mist" published in Germany as a 248-page book with dustjacket and slipcase. The print run was 500 copies, signed by the artist. It was seized by U.S. Customs as copies arrived stateside, but some copies did get through and, predictably, became instant collector's items. King bootlegs are always collectible, especially since they are so rare.

Needful Things

Hardback, 1991, 690 pages, Viking, $24.95

Dedication: "This is for Chris Lavin, who doesn't have all the answers—just the ones that matter."

Contents

Part I. Grand Opening Celebration

Part II. The Sale of the Century

Part III. Everything Must Go

Castle Rock, King's Yoknapatawpha County, had by King's own admission become too comfortable a fictional milieu, requiring drastic action on his part: he would have to burn his bridges, so to speak, behind him. Castle Rock had to go, not with a whimper but with a bang—and what a hell of a bang!

King begins this richly complex novel informally: he tells the reader, "You've been here before. Sure you have. Sure. I never forget a face."

King then points out what's going on in Castle Rock, making sure you are properly oriented before he gets into the main story.

Recalling *'Salem's Lot,* the outsider that comes to plague the town is not so much a devastator as an instigator; the hand of the outsider puts things in motion, as seemingly innocuous events have, in the end, disastrous consequences.

The outsider is a beguiling proprietor, Leland Gaunt, of Needful Things, located on Main Street. His first customer—that is to say, victim—is Brian Rusk, who buys a baseball card inscribed by Sandy Koufax, for a bargain price of eighty-five cents. Sometimes, though, you get more than you bargained for . . . and in this case, the diabolical interest he'll have to pay is more than he wanted to pay, just as the other innocents in the town find themselves slowly drawn into acts of self-destruction.

Leland Gaunt is no friendly proprietor but Old Scratch himself, who has come to Castle Rock not to save it but to destroy it. Hell, let the townsfolk destroy themselves, he thinks. All they need is a nudge in the wrong direction, which he gladly offers.

Needful Things (film), 1993

In King's fiction, the outsider is inevitably the instigator of trouble, and in *Needful Things,* as in *'Salem's Lot,* the outsider is the catalyst that brings out the devil, so to speak, in the townsfolk.

In this case, the townsfolk live in King's quintessential small town, Castle Rock, and speaking of the devil, it's Lucifer himself who comes to town, setting up shop—a front, actually—for his nefarious plan: to set neighbor against neighbor, in an inversion of the biblical admonition of turning cheeks. In short order, the storm that's brewing breaks with hellish fury over this hapless town.

Leland Gaunt is played by Max von Sydow, who in 1965 played Jesus in *The Greatest Story Ever Told.* Portraying an urbane, witty older man with charming ways—think Hannibal Lecter from *The Silence of the Lambs*—Von Sydow's interpretation, at King's suggestion, was more beguiling than bedeviling.

Faithful to King's long novel, *Needful Things* shows clearly the too-high price that people pay for the things they want to own . . . and the things that own them.

Note: Two and four-hour versions aired on the television network TNT.

Negotiations for *Bag of Bones*

After a faux pas of the kind he rarely commits, King had the good sense to publicly acknowledge the awkward manner in which he engineered his move from NAL to Scribner through his lawyer-

A promotional three-by-five-inch color postcard that heralded the arrival of *Needful Things.* (The postcard shows Castle Rock's Main Street.)

agent Arthur B. Greene. In a *New York Post* story (Nov. 9, 1997), King admitted that asking $17 million up-front and announcing his desire to leave NAL created a backlash. As King discovered, the media had a field day, relishing the details of what looked to be a messy divorce, with comments from the book trade on King's demands, mixed reviews of *Bag of Bones,* and speculations galore. What should have been a stealth move under cover of darkness looked like a Chinese fire drill.

Insofar as his departure from NAL was concerned, the straw that broke the camel's back was the integration of Putnam with NAL, which pushed him out of the catbird seat and into the backseat; Tom Clancy, with his recent $100 million book deal, was the king of the hill—not King.

King, who has said before that he has no great love for the publishing industry per se, commented that "Putnam brought in a very potent list. Tom Clancy. Dick Francis. I'm only speculating here, but I think I was just not that important anymore to them. It was either that or an inept negotiator."

It's not likely that King was any less valued at NAL, now in bed with G. P. Putnam, nor is King an inept negotiator; the truth was somewhere in the middle. But King's perception of the situation was unshakable: "I got the feeling from them, 'If you want to go, go.' That hurt."

NAL did get a first look at *Bag of Bones*, but it was no guarantee that they would come to terms with King on its purchase; instead, it appears they came to blows over its price. In the end, *Bag of Bones* was not a needful thing for NAL. (Truth be told, King has in the past signed multiple book deals with NAL, but after his last contract expired, no new contract was signed, so he was in effect a free agent with *Bag of Bones*.)

NAL put on its best face during what was obviously a tense and politically embarrassing time, as the details of the negotiations made news nationwide, but in the end, they did what Doubleday had done years earlier: They unintentionally alienated King, who, so to speak, took a walk down publisher's row to find himself a new home. (If NAL had offered a partnership deal, would that have satisfied King? Maybe, but there's more to this matter than we are ever likely to know. At this point,

NAL and King are keeping mum, preferring to get on with life and leave the past behind.)

It was enough of a royal pain that King left, taking with him *Bag of Bones*, a short story collection, and a nonfiction book on writing. (As for his backlist, it's likely that he will take them to his new publisher, who can reissue them under the Pocket Books imprint, its mass market paperback line.)

"Asking for a big advance was a bad mistake," King told the *Post.* "I'd self-publish before I do this again."

Now *there's* a real Stephen King horror story for his publisher!

New Franklin Laundry

An industrial laundry in Bangor, Maine.

After graduating from college, King took a job at the laundry, earning $1.60 an hour, $60 a week. But even after he got a teaching position, the pay was so low that in the summer between his first and second year, he went back to the laundry to work full time, and supplemented his income with free-lance writing.

But the experience did not go to waste: King used the laundry as the background for "The Mangler" (*Night Shift*) and for two fragments of an aborted novel, "Morning Deliveries" (Milkman #1) and "Big Wheels: A Tale of the Laundry Game" (Milkman #2).

New Haven, Connecticut

The site of the 1983 World Fantasy Convention, which King attended.

This city, wrote King, has "all the charm of a rat-infested cellar in a James Herbert novel." (From "You Are Here Because You Want the Real Thing," a profile of Clive Barker.)

New York literary establishment

"There is a writing sort of mythos that centers around New York. You hear stories about these great writers gathering at the round table or down in Greenwich Village. Writers are very congenial people and one of the reasons they are congenial is because they are also lazy bastards. The more they talk, the less they have to write." ("The Dispatch Talks with: Writer Stephen King," *Maryland Coast Dispatch*, Aug. 8, 1986.)

"The Night Flier"
(collected in *Nightmares & Dreamscapes*)

Originally published in Douglas E. Winter's anthology *Prime Evil*, "Night Flier" is prime King. Eschewing Anne Rice–type vampires—urbane, sophisticated, stylishly sexy in their own way, superhuman creatures that contemplate the mysteries of life and death—King hews close to the bone: Dracula is the model, just as it was for *'Salem's Lot*, and King's bloodsucking vampire is a hellish creature with utterly no remorse.

Berni Wrightson, who has illustrated several of King's works, explains his disgust for vampires, one that King shares: "Pfui! All we are to them is dinner . . . filthy, bloodsucking devils. . . . Crawling up through the cold, wet mud every night, hunting, clawing back down to a moldy, rotting box before sunrise. God, it's horrible. Nobody *wants* to be a vampire!"

In this story, the vampire doesn't stay in the usual coffin by day; the cargo hold of his Cessna 337 serves as his daytime abode. At night he feeds, landing at small airports up and down the Eastern Seaboard, and flying off before the authorities can find him.

Richard Dees, who made an appearance in *The Dead Zone* as the tabloid reporter-photographer pestering Johnny Smith for a story, is in search of a "killer" story, and decides he's found it in the so-called night flier, thought to be a nocturnal serial killer—human but inhumane. But, as Dees finds out, the night flier is indeed a vampire.

Vampires of course can't be seen, or photographed. Dees wanders through an airport strewn with bodies; revolted, he rushes to the bathroom to vomit, where he sees bright-red liquid splashing against the bone-white urinal. He's found the night flier . . . pissing blood.

The vampire confronts Dees, who realizes that he's bitten off more than he can chew. He surrenders his camera to the vampire, who unspools the film, destroying the only photographic proof of the night flier's plane and its unusual luggage hold. As the authorities arrive, Dees watches as the night flier takes off in search of new prey, and Dees prays that he won't have another interview with the vampire.

The police see the carnage, see Dees, throw him up against the wall, and arrest him. They got the wrong man . . . or thing, in this case.

A horrific story adapted, with some plot changes, into an effective film that aired on HBO, "Night Flier" is vintage King—fresh burgundy in an old bottle.

Night Flier (film), 1997

Original HBO movie starring Miguel Ferrer in the role of reporter Richard Dees, this adaptation ranks with the best of King's film adaptations.

Nightlight

In a 1983 profile piece by Paul Grosswiler of the *BDN,* King admitted that he keeps a night-light on, not for his kids but for himself. "I always sleep with the light on. I don't sleep with a light on right in the room. That would be bush league. I leave the bathroom light on and leave the door open a little bit. The real reason is because it keeps the monsters away."

On another note: To promote the dual publication of *Desperation* and *The Regulators,* the publishers shrink-wrapped both books with a "stay up and read all night" night-light, which proved so popular that they sold out in a few months, necessitating a second premium to satisfy the fans. The second time around, NAL offered a *real* premium: an advance copy of the first few chapters from the fourth *Dark Tower* novel—an idea credited to King, not NAL. (*That,* and not a night-light, would have been the ideal premium all along.)

Nightmares & Dreamscapes

Hardback, 1993, 816 pages, Viking, $27.50
Dedication: "In Memory of Thomas Williams, 1926–1991: poet, novelist, and great American storyteller."

Contents

Comparisons of this collection and its predecessor, *Skeleton Crew*, are inevitable. Like those in *Skeleton Crew*, these pieces appeared originally in diverse publications. This time around, it was *Cavalier* magazine, *Omni* magazine, *Castle Rock* newsletter and other fan publications, the *New Yorker* (the only nonfiction piece in the book), and the usual anthologies: *Prime Evil, Night Visions V, Book of the Dead*, etc.

But there the similarities end.

Unlike *Skeleton Crew*, opening with one of King's most memorable stories ("The Mist") and closing with one of his most moving stories ("The Reach"), *Nightmares & Dreamscapes* opens with an entertaining, little-seen novella, "Dolan's Cadillac" and closes with a coda, a story told *to* King, "The Beggar and the Diamond."

"Head Down," the last King piece in *Nightmares and Dreamscapes*, is considered by King to be his best work of nonfiction. Originally published in the *New Yorker* and reprinted in *The Best American Sports Writing, 1991* (edited by David Halberstam), the piece is King's recounting of a Little League team in Bangor that goes on to win the state championship. (King's son Owen played on the team.)

Frankly, it's a wonder that King even writes short stories. There's no money in it for him, as there is in novels, but he'd likely tell you that writing a short story, a good one, is its own reward. Unlike novels, which don't impose length restrictions, a novella or short story requires concision, forcing the writer to cut to the bone.

In King's case, the necessity to tell his story economically is good discipline, and makes for a better story as well. *The Tommyknockers* suffered from writer's sprawl, but "The Mist" is as tight as the cover on a snare drum.

As for the inclusion of "Head Down," his first work of nonfiction in any of his collections, it's a strong piece and certainly should have been reprinted in one of his collections. In fact, considering the body of nonfiction he's written, a collection of just nonfiction pieces is long overdue.

Regardless of whether or not he assembles a nonfiction collection, he's already made plans to publish a fourth collection of short fiction, which I feel may be published in 1999.

Nightmares in the Sky: Gargoyles and Grotesques

Hardback, 1988, no pagination, Viking Studio Books, $24.95

Dedication: None

Contents

Essay by King, accompanied by photographs (in black and white and color) by f-stop Fitzgerald.

According to David Streitfeld of the *Washington Post*, Viking optimistically printed 250,000 copies but saw 150,000 copies returned, "proof that King's name is not, after all, absolutely guaranteed magic." That's true . . . but not true: King's name is guaranteed magic for any book he publishes of his *own* work, but to expect his name alone to carry the day for a coffee-table book of photos is expecting the impossible. King's contribution is an

Cover to the photo essay *Nightmares in the Sky*, which featured an original introduction by Stephen King.

Nightmares in the Sky continued

illuminating essay written especially for this book, which would have made a nice little chapbook, or a piece in a King book collection like *Nightmares & Dreamscapes*, but in this instance, King fans, who would have been interested not in the photos but in the King contribution, felt that $24.95 was more than they wanted to pay for a single essay by King. The majority of his fans passed on this one, waiting for the next King book, which was *My Pretty Pony* ($50), a short story published in an edition of 15,000 copies, which sold out quickly, followed by King's next novel, *The Dark Half*, priced at a reasonable $21.95.

Night Shift

Hardback, 1989, 336 pages, Doubleday, $8.95
Dedication: Ruth King
Contents
Introduction by John D. MacDonald
Foreword by King
Jerusalem's Lot
Graveyard Shift
Night Surf
I Am the Doorway
The Mangler
The Boogeyman
Gray Matter
Battleground
Trucks

Sometimes They Come Back
Strawberry Spring
The Ledge
The Lawnmower Man
Quitters, Inc.
I Know What You Need
Children of the Corn
The Last Rung on the Ladder
The Man Who Loved Flowers
One for the Road
The Woman in the Room

All stories except five were originally published in *Cavalier* magazine, and all except the epistolary story, "Jerusalem's Lot," have been optioned for visual adaptations, though not all options have been exercised.

The original title of this book was *Night Moves*, from the Bob Seger song of the same name. (Perhaps the title was changed to eliminate confusion?) It is a good collection that shows King's strengths at writing short fiction, though he often has been criticized for verbosity in his novels.

To my mind, the strongest pieces in the book are the mainstream stories, the ones with no supernatural elements. "The Last Rung on the Ladder" and "The Woman in the Room" demonstrate what MacDonald asserted in his introduction: "One of the most resonant and affecting stories in this book is 'The Last Rung on the Ladder.' A gem. Nary a rustle nor breath of other worlds in it."

King does an excellent job in his foreword in setting the stage for the stories that follow, giving the reader a behind-the-scenes look. This became King's practice for short fiction collections—a practice that Harlan Ellison instituted years ago.

This book also signaled the end of King's relationship with Doubleday; the next book went to Viking. Because of contractual obligations, King would later publish *Pet Sematary* and *The Stand: The Complete and Uncut Edition* with Doubleday.

Bottom line: A remarkably strong collection that collects otherwise impossible-to-find short stories.

Note: At one time, NBC had planned to put on a *Night Shift* miniseries, but its censors board, Standards and Practices, made the project difficult, if not impossible. Said King, "I thought it was pretty tame, but that's the way it goes." (Quoted in Paul R. Gagne, *Cinefantastique* 10.)

"Night Surf" (collected in *Night Shift*)

Originally published in *Ubris* (Fall 1968), this apocalyptic mood piece about teenagers wandering a Maine beach foreshadowed *The Stand*. A virulent flu virus, called A6, has wiped out most of mankind . . . Only pockets of people are left, wondering what happens next.

Nixon, Richard

The reason Stephen King no longer votes the Republican ticket. Stephen, as his wife gleefully points out, believed Nixon when he said that he'd get the U.S. out of Vietnam.

"Nona"
(collected in *Skeleton Crew*)

The key to this story, originally published in *Shadows* (1978), is its reference to John Keats and Percy Shelley, specifically, to a poem by Keats, "La belle dame sans merci" ("The Lovely Lady Without Pity"). An annotation in *The Norton Anthology of English Literature* indicates that the Keats poem, a "story of a mortal destroyed by his love for a supernatural femme fatale, has been told repeatedly in myth, fairy tale, and ballad, but never so hauntingly." More recently, in Eric Kimball's poem "Lady Ice," illustrated by Thomas Canty, this haunting theme is reinterpreted, including the lines "I was more dead than alive," which are the exact words the fictional narrator in the King story uses to describe his bewitched state.

Nona is a waitress in a dead-end job at a roadside café frequented by truckers; her knight in shining armor, so to speak, is a college dropout. Taken in by her dark, disarming beauty, he's smitten with her, hopelessly hooked—she's his femme fatale.

But her dark beauty conceals her equally dark nature: After they hitch a ride, Nona, the unnatural born killer, urges her partner to kill the driver. He does so, then they steal the car and, in Charles Starkweather fashion, continue their killing spree, all the way to Castle Rock.

They reach a cemetery in Castle Rock, where he finds his mother, long dead: As for Nona, she's no

Nona *continued*

longer the dark-haired beauty, but in fact a rat-woman, with beady, dark eyes, coarse hair, and a hunched body.

The police arrive but Nona is gone, and he writes his story. From his prison cell he confesses that he still loves Nona, or what he thinks was Nona, and that their "true love will never die."

Norbert X. Dowd Award

In February 1992, at an awards banquet sponsored by the Greater Bangor Chamber of Commerce, Stephen and Tabitha King were awarded the Norbert X. Dowd Award for community service. The presenter remarked: "No two people can be credited for doing more for their community than the Kings. They have given of their time, effort and resources to various organizations throughout the area and have always made time in their busy schedules to give of themselves to the community."

Tim Sample, a Maine humorist, said of the Kings, "In a decade when selfishness was an icon, the 1980s, Stephen and Tabitha made generosity a hallmark."

A dinner ticket cost $30, a table of eight, $225. ("Kings Presented Award for Service To Community," Carroll Astbury, *BDN*, Jan. 25, 1992.)

Norris, Frank

American writer of naturalist fiction.

In *The Octopus*, Norris writes: "Should I fear? What should I fear? I did not truckle. I told them the truth."

King has quoted those lines innumerable times in interviews and articles, because it's at the core of his perception as a writer with a moral vision.

SK: "Good fiction is always the truth inside the lie; for fiction to be otherwise is to be immoral, and immoral fiction is always bad fiction. The writer of good fiction must never truckle, as Frank Norris never did." ("You Are Here Because You Want the Real Thing.")

Northeast COMBAT

Consumer group in Bangor that received $11,000, the proceeds from the world premiere of *Firestarter* in Bangor. *People* reported that at the black-tie party, many guests showed up in sweaters and jeans, prompting one attendee, Dr. Doug Cowan, to observe, "Anyone in Bangor who's wearing a sport coat *is* in black tie." (*People*, May 28, 1984.)

Now You See It . . ., by Richard Matheson

SK: "The author who influenced me the most as a writer was Richard Matheson. . . . [This story is] one of his strongest efforts. We're all a lot richer to have Richard Matheson among us."

On Fiction, which is a book about writing stories. It is also a book about my own past, and that feels very risky to me." (AOL's "The Book Review.")

Overlook Connection

David Hinchberger's mail-order book company was established to cater principally to King fans (hence the name, Overlook), but it soon branched out to cover all horror writers. Issuing catalogues infrequently, Hinchberger expanded operations to include a small press, Overlook Connection Press, which issued, among other titles, a signed limited edition of *The Girl Next Door,* by Jack Ketchum, with an introduction by King.

Address: The Overlook Connection, P.O. Box 526, Woodstock, GA 30188.

David Hinchberger: "After reading a Stephen King issue of *The Twilight Zone,* I discovered that there was a lot more work by King that was uncollected, rare and virtually unheard of. I then discovered and subscribed to *Castle Rock,* the Stephen King newsletter. In *Castle Rock* there was all this talk of *The Plant* and all these other odd stories I'd never heard of. So I started getting mail-order book catalogs. . . . So here I had all this stuff, and I put out a little catalog—just a little Xerox jobbie. I look at it now and it's just amazing how far we've come. . . . So, from that point, I started selling just Stephen King items." (Quoted by Barry Hoffman, *Cemetery Dance,* winter 1990.)

Over the Edge,
by Jonathan Kellerman

SK: "Jonathan Kellerman's third Alex Delaware novel is also his best. . . . As a result, a great many people who have so far not been lucky enough to meet Alex are going to make a wonderful reading discovery. . . . Kellerman has reinvented the private-eye story, and maybe just in time. . . . *Over the Edge* is a compulsive page turner . . . startling . . . filled with insight . . . charged with suspense. . . . If you've a weak stomach, enter Alex's world carefully, but do enter—this one is simply too good to miss."

"One for the Road"
(collected in *Night Shift*)

Chances are good that you never have run across this story, unless you were in Maine and read a lot of magazines, since this originally appeared in *Maine* magazine (March–April 1997).

A coda to *'Salem's Lot,* this story makes it clear that the vampires are still alive in that town, having survived its burning: A frantic man bursts into Tookey's Bar in Falmouth, Maine, near Jerusalem's Lot. His car went off the road. He's just walked six miles through the blizzard to get help, leaving his wife and daughter in the car, but by the time he gets back to the car, he discovers to his horror that they are not dead—they're undead.

"One Hundred Most Important People in Science Fiction/Fantasy"

In the hundredth issue of *Starlog* magazine, the top 100 VIPs in the field were celebrated, including King.

On Fiction

King's forthcoming book, not yet scheduled for publication, on the art and craft of writing fiction, of which he said, "My next big risk is a book called

Oxford University Press

King judged a short story contest for this publisher, a promotion for *The Oxford Book of English Ghost Stories*. It had to be an English ghost story of 2,000 words. First prize: an original work of art by Edward Gorey.

The winner was Sloan Harper of Mendenhall, Pennsylvania, whose story "Tabitha" won high praise from King: "The use of a ghost cat is refreshing, the English background is handled with unobtrusive ease, the writer does not attempt to surprise us with those things we already surmise, and instead of an O. Henry 'snapper' at the end, we are given a subtle but clearly intended frisson and a lingering question: Do we know everything that happened? I thought it was a fine story, and my compliments to its creator." (*Castle Rock.*)

as "a masterful study in character and suspense, but it was quiet, deliberately claustrophobic and it proved a tough sell within the house. I'd asked Stephen—for by now we were on a first-name basis—for changes which he willingly and promptly made, but even so I couldn't glean sufficient support and reluctantly returned it."

"Paranoid: A Chant"
(collected in *Skeleton Crew*)

A poem published for the first time in this collection.

Parish, Robert

A Boston Celtic whose jersey has been retired.

In 1992, Robert Parish, a King fan, received an unexpected gift: an inscribed copy of *'Salem's Lot*

The imaginative cover for the trade edition of *The Eyes of the Dragon*, with embossing to simulate the scales of a dragon. (The cover was printed in green.)

Palladini, David

The illustrator for the Viking Press edition of *The Eyes of the Dragon*.

To my mind his pencil-and-ink artwork on Bienfang velour paper lacks the charm and grace of the illustrations by Linkous in the Philtrum Press edition.

The final count: 21 interior illustrations and two different designs for the dust jacket.

Note: This book has the distinction of being the first *trade* book of King's to be illustrated.

Pall Malls

The cigarettes King preferred when he was smoking two packs a day regularly. He has since quit, for health reasons. (King, in "The Neighborhood of the Beast," *Mid-Life Confidential*.)

The Parallax View, by Loren Singer

King checked out this novel from the Bangor Public Library and, noting the name of its editor, decided to send *Getting It On* (which would eventually be published as *Rage*) to Doubleday, to the editor cited in the acknowledgments of *The Parallax View*. However, that editor had left the house and asked that *The Parallax View* be cared for in-house by William G. Thompson, who received the *Getting It On* manuscript, which he described

Parish *continued*

from Jeremy Kane of Ellsworth, Maine, a young boy whose life-threatening illness and mounting medical bills got press coverage. As a result, through the offices of Skip Chappelle, the basketball coach at the University of Maine, Parish arranged for Kane to attend a Boston Celtics game, to see his hero, Robert Parish. The boy not only saw the game but met with Parish and others.

Reading in the Celtics yearbook that Parish was a King fan, the Kanes wanted to thank Parish and called up King, who inscribed a copy to Parish "on behalf of Jeremy Kane." King also signed *The Shining* to Jeremy, "with best wishes . . . and shine on!"

Parks, Elton

One of 78 winners in a United Airlines–sponsored marathon for frequent flyers. Elton Parks passed his time during flights by reading King novels.

Pasadena, California

King gave a talk on April 26, 1989, at the Pasadena Library in California.

"Patented tics and tropes"

Some King trademarks, as identified and labeled by Stefan Kanfer in "King of Horror," a *Time* magazine (Oct. 6, 1986) profile:
The Beautiful Losers
The Validated Nightmare
The Disgusting Colloquialism
The Brand-Name Maneuver
The Burlesque Locution
The Fancy Juxtaposition
The Self-Defeating Jape
The Unconscionable Length

Pavia, Mark

Director of *The Night Flier* for Home Box Office, based on the short story by King. Pavia turned in a first-rate effort—an eerie, haunting and suspenseful film that does justice to one of King's most unusual twists to the vampire legend.

Payday candy bar

Catching King in a gaffe in the original edition of *The Stand*—Harold Lauder leaves a chocolate fingerprint after eating a Payday candy bar—readers sent King Paydays. King subsequently changed the reference from Payday to Milky Way, a very chocolaty candy bar, but it was changed back when Paydays were subsequently made with chocolate.

People, Places, and Things—Volume I

Self-published short story collection by King and Chris Chesley, under the name of Triad Publishing Company, in 1960 (second printing in 1963). Eighteen pages.

One copy is known to exist, which King discovered among his papers in 1985, when he was preparing to move from Bridgton to Bangor.

Like *The Star Invaders*, this is a one-of-a-kind King collectible, and will never be reprinted: eighteen stories, of which King contributed eight, Chesley nine, and one a collaboration; this was published in an edition of less than a dozen copies.

This is the earliest surviving example of King's juvenilia.

The "Forward" (foreword) reads:

People, Places, and Things is an Extraordinary book. It is a book for people who would enjoy being pleasantly thrilled for a few moments.

For example: take Chris Chesley's blood-curdling story, GONE. The last moments of a person left alone in an atomic-doomed world.

Let Steve King's I'M FALLING transport you into a world of dreams.

But if you have no imagination, stop right here. This book is not for you.

If you have an imagination, let it run free.

We warn you . . . the next time you lie in bed and hear an unreasonable creak or thump, you can try to explain it away . . . but try Steve King's and Chris Chesley's explanation: People, places and Things.

Stories by King
Hotel at the End of the Road
I've Got to Get Away!
The Dimension Warp
The Thing at the Bottom of the Well

The Stranger
I'm Falling
The Cursed Expedition
The Other Side of the Fog
Stories by Chesley
Genius, 3
Top Forty, News, Weather, and Sports
Bloody Child
Reward
A Most Unusual Thing
Gone
They've Come
Scared
Curiousity [sic] Kills the Cat
King and Chesley Collaboration
Never Look Behind You

Pepsi-Cola Bottling Company

In conjunction with WZON, Pepsi offered a lucky listener the opportunity to appear in a King movie. The lucky stiff who won merely had to submit a photograph of him- or herself, or someone else, with a Pepsi product in the photo, or the words "Pepsi" prominently visible, to be eligible for this rare chance to go Hollywood.

The winner was a five-year-old girl, Mandy Brigalli of Brewer, Maine, who under the rules of the contest could not appear in the movie, because she was under sixteen years of age. So her father, Walter Brigalli, appeared in the movie *Maximum Overdrive*.

Personal appearances (selected)

YMCA dinner at the Samoset Resort in Rockport, Maine, February 3, 1987.

Friends of André Dubus Literary Series at the Grand Ballroom of the Charles Hotel at Harvard Square in Boston, on March 1, 1987, with John Irving.

Boston University on April 1, 1987.

Commencement address at UMO, to the 169th graduating class, May 9, 1987, at which he and Tabitha King were awarded honorary Doctor of Humane Letters degrees. King's theme: "Education . . . is meant to prepare you for the best days of your life." UMO President Dale Lick com-

mented, "We're delighted that King agreed to speak at our commencement. He was our students' number one choice. It is significant because he's a graduate and an international literary figure. It's a special treat for us to have a person of that caliber come back and be a part of our commencement ceremony." (*BDN*, Jan. 23, 1987.)

Personal faith

According to Stephen King, Tabitha is a "fallen-away Catholic" and "I'm a fallen-away Methodist." (*Bare Bones.*)

Pet Sematary

Hardback, 1983, 374 pages, Doubleday, $15.95
Dedication: "For Kirby McCauley"
Contents
Part I. The Pet Sematary
Part II. The Micmac Burying Ground
Part III. Oz the Gweat and Tewwible

King had accepted a one-year teaching position at his alma mater, UMO, and moved to Orrington, where he rented a two-story house. Unfortunately, Smucky, the family cat, was killed on the major road near the house, which had claimed so many pet victims that the neighborhood children designated a wooded area up on a hill as a "pets sematary," marked by a crude, hand-painted sign.

Smucky was buried there. Shortly thereafter, as King crossed the street, he began thinking about what would happen if Smucky came back to life. The idea took hold and he asked himself: What if a child had been killed and came back to life? With "The Monkey's Paw" in mind, King wrote the answer to his self-posed question, exploring a parent's worst nightmare: the death of a child.

After completing the book, King put it with his other trunk novels.

One of King's truly horrifying novels, *Pet Sematary* attained legendary status as a novel too scary for even Stephen King to publish, which of course put pressure on him to publish it, to see why the boogeyman from Bangor felt the novel was so frightening that it scared even him.

Still, King thought it was a "nasty" book and had no intention of publishing it, but fate inter-

Pet Sematary continued

vened in the form of a Doubleday contract, one that withheld his royalties by virtue of a monthly payout that would, in King's lifetime, still not reach a 100 percent payout. To terminate it, conditions set by the IRS had to be met.

The conditions were dutifully met by all parties, and King fans finally got a book that was was never intended to be published. It is one of his best books, a cautionary tale about Louis Creed and his irrevocable decision to take his dead son, Gage, who had been run over by a truck, to the Micmac Indian burial grounds, which would bring him back. But at what cost?

This is an unremittingly bleak book, one of King's few books not illuminated with both light and darkness, but it's clearly one of his best.

SK: "In trying to cope with these things, the book ceased being a novel to me, and became instead a gloomy exercise, like an endless marathon run. It never left my mind; it never ceased to trouble me. I was trying to teach school, and the boy was always there, the funeral home was always there, the mortician's room was always there. And when I finished, I put the book in a drawer." (*BDN*, Oct. 12, 1988.)

Cover to the British edition of *Pet Sematary*.

Pet Sematary (film), 1989

This film occupies a warm spot in King's heart, for two reasons: It is based on a screenplay he wrote—the first time he'd adapted one of his own novels to the screen; and at his insistence it was filmed in Maine, giving a much-needed boost to the Maine Film Commission, established in 1987, then a fledgling organization looking to pump Hollywood dollars into small, local communities that could use the infusion of cash from what's considered a "clean" industry.

On the shooting of the film: "Maine is a beautiful state, so why shouldn't it get the movie business? We could have shot *Cujo* or *On Golden Pond* here, but they've got a place in northern California they call Little England, which is used for shooting New England scenes." (Inteview with Davie Bright, in *Castle Rock*.)

The novel was considered by King to be too horrible to publish, and this movie, directed by Mary Lambert, had to reflect that . . . and it did. The result: a gruesome film, appropriate fare for gore hounds who like in-your-face horror undiluted by niceties.

The movie's horrific premise: What if you could bring your loved ones back to life? Would you do it? And what would it be like? Would they be the same, or would they be changed in some way?

Solid, competent performances all the way around from the cast, but Fred Gwynne, as the Mainiac Jud Crandall, was a masterful casting call. Let's face it: *The Munsters* was fun, but his role as Herman Munster didn't stretch his considerable acting ability, as this film did.

This haunting and horrific film bears repeat viewing, if it is your kind of grisly fare.

Bon appétit.

Matt Rousch (*USA Today*, 1990): "It makes sense that Stephen King's cameo in *Pet Sematary* . . . is as a preacher. He might as well be reading the last rites on his hopes of making it—critically, anyway—as a screenwriter. . . . If *Pet Sematary* could have boasted more authentic details in telling its devastating story, it might have been a classic instead of just another pet peeve."

Fred Gwynne: "*Pet Sematary* is the first script written by King. I think it could be his best film. I was afraid it would be turned into some sort of slasher film for teens in editing, but I was pleasantly surprised. It's much more of a morality tale, which makes it stronger." (Quoted by columnist Marilyn Beck.)

Irv Slifkin: "I like the film a lot. Many of the reviews were negative. That's a good sign in a horror picture. It shows that you did something right. It means that you certainly offended somebody." (Knight-Ridder Newspapers.)

Phantasmagoria

An unofficial zine edited and published by George Beahm. Technically a quarterly publication, in truth it's irregularly published, since publication depends on the availability of news.

Originally intended as a supplement to his books on King from Andrews McMeel Publishing, the zine started out as a letter-size newsletter but evolved with issue number four into its current format: a 32- to 48-page zine with glossy covers. The seventh issue was published in spring 1998.

With the subscription come postcard alerts, sent out by first class, to inform subscribers of the imminent release of signed limited edition books by King that typically sell out long before publication, requiring early warning.

Subscription rates vary. In the U.S. the zine is sent out bulk rate or first class. Canadian subscribers get their copies by first class. All others get it via airmail.

The editor/publisher can be reached at *Phan-*

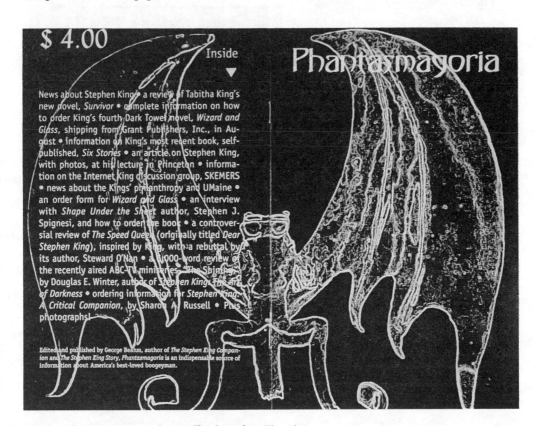

Cover to *Phantasmagoria* 6, the unofficial Stephen King zine.

tasmagoria, P.O. Box 3602, Williamsburg, VA 23187. E-mail at: *GeoBeahm@aol.com*

Stanley Wiater: "Presently the only regular newsletter devoted to all things Stephen King. Published and edited by George Beahm, one of the world's leading authorities on King, the amount of material which appears in successive issues is fast evolving this already comprehensive publication into a full-fledged magazine." (*Dark Thoughts on Writing, 1997.*)

P Is for Philtrum Press

Philtrum Press—unlike other, similar-seeming companies—is unique in several ways. First, it is well financed. Second, its publications are first-rate, beautifully designed by Michael Alpert, set in metal type, printed on beautiful stock. Third, it's not necessarily a money-making venture. Fourth, the company exists to publish anything its author/owner wishes to publish . . . and its owner is Stephen King.

I can't think of any other brand-name author who runs his own small press, but King does, which allows him the opportunity to publish, knowing that he will sell out anything under his own name, and not have to advertise to guarantee the sell-out.

Case in point: Philtrum's most recent offering was a trade paperback, *Six Stories*, published in spring 1997 in an edition of 1,100 copies (900 numbered copies for sale, with 200 reserved for the press). The original plan was to advertise in specialty publications, but it proved to be unnecessary. The word got out on the Internet—copies available on a first come, first served basis, for $80 plus shipping—and two zine publishers catering to the horror field (*The Red Letter* and *Phantasmagoria*) sent postcard alerts. In short order the 900 copies sold out *before* publication.

The limited edition, signed by King, was beautifully designed by Michael Alpert, publisher of Theodore Press/Sarah Books, and printed by the Stinehour Press. Currently the book goes for $400, but it was not issued with a slipcase or traycase, which is what its purchasers wanted, so Betts Bookstore matched the cloth used for the book and commissioned an Oregon firm to design and manufacture slipcases and traycases.

In a "forenote" to *The Ideal, Genuine Man*, a novel by Don Robertson, King readily admits that his staff of five—plus maybe a temp to help pack books—is not big time, and that is his intent. "We are, in other words, a very humble storefront in a world dominated by a few great glassy shopping malls."

Of Robertson's novel he said, "Publishing this book is no thank-you note, but a simple necessity. To not publish when I have to means to do so would be an irresponsible act."

If King had chosen instead to publish another collection of short fiction, or to collect the previously published installments of *The Plant* in one book, all copies would have sold out immediately.

King doesn't need to beat the drum for his own books, but Robertson could use a helping hand.

In addition to a signed, limited edition, the book had two trade printings, distributed to the book trade by the Putnam Publishing Group. (The second print run was eventually remaindered.)

The only other book Philtrum has published, a sumptuous edition of *The Eyes of the Dragon,* was published in 1984 in an edition of 1,250 copies (1,000 numbered in black ink, 250 in red ink, each signed by King). This oversized book was sold by a lottery administered by Stephanie Leonard, who placed three full-page ads in specialty publications. This proved more than sufficient to sell out the entire print run before publication, even at that stage in King's career.

The book would have sold out even if its production values had been modest, but King spared no expense. The project, designed to break even, required that for every one copy given away, four would have to be sold at $120. (Despite unfounded bitching by Jack L. Chalker, a writer who previously published books for the fantasy field under his Mirage Press, no other criticisms were ever voiced about this book, nor should they have been: King gave his fans a book of beauty, magnificently printed and bound, and imaginatively illustrated by Kenny Ray Linkous.)

To get to the heart of Philtrum Press, you have to read and see the first three publications: chapbooks, of a novel in progress, *The Plant*, with installments published in 1982, 1983, and 1985, given to family and friends on the Kings' Christmas list. The novel remains unfinished, nor is it likely King will ever finish it, which is a pity. Harlan Ellison, who's on the list, tantalized King fans by saying, "Those of us who have been privileged to read the first couple of sections of *The Plant*... perceive a talent of uncommon dimensions."

"It's sort of an epistolary novel in progress," King told Larry King on *The Larry King Show*. "A couple of years ago, I got to thinking about Christmas cards and how mass-produced they were. It didn't seem like a sincere, personal thing. So I thought, well, I'll do this little book ... and send it out to friends."

The "little book" is the story of an unpublished horror writer, Carlos Detweiler, who submits his novel, *True Tales of Demon Infestation*, to John Kenton, an editor at Zenith Books. But the lifelike photos of demon rituals and human sacrifice prompt Kenton to contact the police, who search in vain for Detweiler, who then sends Kenton a letter, stating that a plant will be sent. But not just any ordinary plant.

Ellison is quite right to state that those who got the work-in-progress were privileged, because a complete set now costs $5,000 or more—well beyond the reach of any but the most ardent, and well-heeled, King collector.

After hearing complaints that people had sold them on the secondary market, King said that he doesn't care what they do; the books were gifts and the recipients could do with them what they wanted. Undoubtedly the resale value meant that any recipient who needed quick cash for an emergency could raise the money by selling the books, made possible by the fact that King's stature on the secondary market has made him the most collectible author in our time.

Besides King, the one other person instrumental in creating the distinctive look and feel of Philtrum's publications is Michael Alpert. He has insured that each project received the kind of attention that is increasingly rare these days. Typography, layout, design, production values, materials used, and printer coordination—all bear witness to Alpert's refined taste, sense of aesthetics, and attention to detail.

As for what Philtrum may publish in the future: Who knows? This small press, though admittedly a giant in the collectibles market, does not to my knowledge maintain a mailing list. Still, it may not hurt to be asked to be put on a mailing list.

You can write to Philtrum Press, or its publisher, Stephen King, at P.O. Box 1186, Bangor, ME 04402-2286.

Phoenix, Arizona

In the company of Erma Bombeck, Arthur Hailey, Mary Higgins Clark, and Raquel Welch, King attended a benefit dinner for the Kidney Foundation in this city in the winter of 1984.

Pillsbury, Guy

King's grandfather on his mother's side.

He and his wife, Nellie Fogg Pillsbury, were the reason King's mother moved back to Durham with her family: to take care of her ailing and aged parents.

Pillsbury, Nellie Fogg

King's grandmother on his mother's side. (*See* PILLSBURY, GUY.)

Pinto

A miserable excuse for an automobile—it needs a fix or repair daily—made by Ford. It's no accident that in *Cujo*, when the plot required a car that broke down and needed extensive repairs, King chose a Pinto, not a Mercedes.

On a personal note: After *Carrie* sold, the Kings bought their first, new car—a blue Pinto.

The Pit and the Pendulum

An American International film by Roger Corman, released in 1961, based on the story by Edgar Allan Poe.

An inspiration for King, who wrote a novelization of the film and sold copies at school.

Christopher Chesley: "This was not a takeoff on the story. King had seen the film and in effect novelized that movie. We ran off copies and sold them in school for a dime or a quarter, but the teachers made us stop doing that."

The Plant, Part I

Saddle-stitched chapbook with covers, Philtrum Press, 1982, privately distributed to 200 people on the Kings' Christmas list.

Genesis: King wanted to send out Christmas greetings that were more personalized than the usual name-imprinted card, and so decided to start his own small press to issue this novel-in-progress. Designed by Michael Alpert, this chapbook was issued in a numbered and signed edition only, with each copy inscribed to its recipient.

SK: "*The Plant* is like all of my other novels in one respect. I thought I knew where I was going when I started. Now certain characters—like the mad general—have suddenly stepped forward.

"It's unlike the others in another respect. I pick it up in June, work on it for a month or so, and put it down for a year. There seems to be no problem with this, as there usually is with a novel where I feel under pressure to finish. Another thing: I write *The Plant* longhand in first draft. I haven't done that since I was a kid. It's extremely trying but rewarding as well—that's hard to explain, but it seems more intimate that way.

"*The Plant* is a present. If I gave someone a coffee-maker and they sold it at a yard sale, it wouldn't bother me. If they want to sell *The Plant*, fine. It's theirs. They can tear out the pages and use 'em for toilet paper, if that's what they feel like doing. For the record, I've never seen an inscribed copy for sale. Some that are sold may be printers' overruns." (*Castle Rock*.)

The Plant, Part II

Saddle-stitched chapbook with covers, Philtrum Press, 1983, privately distributed to 200 people on the Kings' Christmas list.

The Plant, Part III

The third and final installment of what was generally acknowledged as a first-rate King novel-in-progress. Saddle-stitched chapbook with covers, Philtrum Press, 1985, privately distributed to 200 people on the Kings' Christmas list, plus 26 lettered copies.

The work died prematurely after he had viewed the remake of *The Little Shop of Horrors* and saw the duplication, at which point he lost interest in telling the rest of the story.

Playing for Thrills, by Wang Shuo

SK: "*Playing for Thrills* is perhaps the most brilliantly entertaining 'hardboiled' novel of the nineties . . . and maybe of the eighties, as well. It constitutes a genre by itself—call it China *noir*—and offers guilty pleasures beyond any most readers will encounter in a bound set of Kinsey Milhones or Lucas Davenports. Just what the hell is this, anyway? Jack Kerouac unbound? I don't think so. If you can imagine Raymond Chandler crossed with Bruce Lee (or maybe Richard Brautigan crossed with John Woo), that gives you the flavor . . . but you have to experience this in order to really get it. Most ultimately cool."

Plymouth Fury

A 1958 Plymouth Fury was used as the fictional character in *Christine*. King chose it over other cars from that era because he felt it was a humdrum car for its time—nothing special. Note: The dust-jacket photo for *Christine* shows him sitting on a 1957 Plymouth Savoy, which he thought was a 1958 Plymouth Fury.

Politics

King voted for Goldwater in 1964, Nixon in 1968 (because King believed Nixon when he said that if elected, he'd get the troops out of Vietnam), and McGovern in 1972.

He went on record as passionately opposing Ronald Reagan, which is why he was actively involved in the Gary Hart bid.

"Popsy"
(collected in *Nightmares & Dreamscapes*)

Originally published in *Masques II,* this story, says King in his afterword to *Nightmares & Dreamscapes*, is connected to "The Night Flier."

Sheridan is a compulsive gambler and, unfortunately for him, is not very good at it. After losing a small fortune, Sheridan faces bodily harm, for the thugs that come to collect make it clear that either he ponies up the dough or they're going to start breaking his limbs. Desperate, he re-luctantly takes their offer to kidnap children and give them to Mr. Wizard, a big Turk, to work off the debt.

At the mall he sees a lost boy and befriends him, but it's clear that this boy is unusual. Instead of asking for his father, he asks for his "Popsy." And when the lost boy realizes he's been abducted, he fights like the devil, with almost superhuman strength for such a little kid.

The boy cautions Sheridan that he would be sorry for what he had done. The boy is ignored by Sheridan, until he hears a large thump on the top of his van. It's Popsy, a vampire, who has come to rescue his grandson.

Before Popsy slices Sheridan open so he and his grandson can drink the blood, Popsy explains that he was at the mall to get the little boy some Teenage Mutant Ninja Turtles figurines, because all the kids wanted them.

"You should have left him alone," Popsy tells Sheridan. "You should have left *us* alone," he finishes, and Sheridan, the hunter, becomes the trapped, helpless prey.

Popular literature and culture

A course King taught in college.

Ostensibly taught by Graham Adams, this course was in fact taught by King—the only time an undergraduate taught a course at UM.

The course had its genesis at a departmental meeting between the faculty and students. As Burton Hatlen explained, "I remember a meeting in which the students and faculty got together to talk about the curriculum of the English department. Several people have a memory of Steve standing up at this meeting and denouncing the department because he had never been able to read a Shirley Jackson novel in any of the courses he had taken.

"He criticized the curriculum and insisted on the value and importance of popular culture and mass culture, and people listened to him. It was an important moment. King wanted to conduct a special seminar on popular American fiction, which produced a crisis—here was an undergraduate proposing to teach a course."

Portland City Hall

On March 6, 1990, King gave a public talk at the Portland City Hall auditorium to an estimated 2,300 fans as part of the Portland Public Library's centennial celebration. It was originally scheduled at a smaller site, but the public demand required moving it to accommodate the crowd.

"People want to know why I do this, why I write such gross stuff. I like to tell them I have the heart of a small boy—and I keep it in a jar on my desk. . . . Actually, it's because I'm a sadistic, twisted son of a bitch and I love it!" (Quoted in John Lovell, "King Horrifies His Audience," *Portland Press Herald*, March 7, 1990.)

Potter, J. K.

Artist and photographer, based in New Orleans, who illustrated the Scream Press edition of *Skeleton Crew*.

J. K. Potter's sensibilities as an artist-photographer are such that King feels him to be a kindred spirit, and no wonder: Both attempt to delineate horrific images—King with words, Potter with photographs.

Potter's work—imaginative, fiendishly shocking images—is not the product of a computer using Photoshop and an electronic palette and drawing table. Potter relies on the "old-fashioned darkroom techniques of multiple printing, multiple exposure, and solarization for producing my images," he explained in "Some Notes on Technique" in *Neurotica*, his second collection of photos from the Overlook Press.

As with the work of all good photographers with a strong vision, a description pales by comparison to seeing the work. This is certainly the case with Potter's fevered dreams—or, more accurately, nightmares. Though some are representational—an illustration for "The Mist" comes to mind in which supermarket patrons stare up in horror at a pterodactyl flapping its leathery wings—most are a synthesis of various techniques, with the means justifying the end: a horrific image for Ramsey Campbell's *The Influence*, in which a lanky creature with the face of a baby doll lurches through an empty bus toward the viewer. Or an illustration for Ray Garton's *The New Neighbor*, in which a close-up of a human eye is centered in the photo, with a profile shot of a woman's leg. (The visual overlap of the eye's tear duct and the leg produce an unintentionally erotic image.)

Potter's best work is evocative and disturbing, as if he's gone to hell with a Nikon to take snapshots

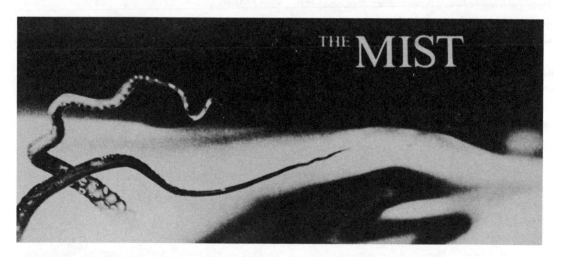

Chapter head illustration by J.K. Potter for "The Mist" in the Scream Press edition of *Skeleton Crew*. (Potter's evocative photo/artwork was used throughout the book, with rectangular heads for each story. In large part because of Potter's art, that edition of *Skeleton Crew* is considered to be one of the most beautiful King limiteds published to date.)

and returned with nightmarish scenes that depict horror in a way that illustration itself cannot.

J. K. Potter, on *Skeleton Crew:* "I was apprehensive about doing it, but it turned out that King is so American I could shoot backgrounds at the Safeway. It was a neighborhood book for me. I wanted the illustrations to be as accessible as the prose and as entertaining. Of course there are some grisly illustrations in it. I did try to gross the guy [King] out, but it didn't work." (*Locus,* January 1986.)

SK: "Many of Potter's images actually assault the eye, and of course this is the artist's intention." (King's introduction to *Horripilations: The Art of J. K. Potter.*)

A Prayer for Owen Meany, by John Irving

SK: "Extraordinary, so original, and so enriching. . . . A rare creation in the somehow exhausted work of late twentieth-century fiction. . . . Readers will come to the end feeling sorry to leave [this] richly textured and carefully wrought world."

Prematurely announced books *about* King

Over the years, authors or publishers have announced books that were not published for one reason or another. A short list includes the following:

In the Darkest Night: A Student's Guide to Stephen King, by Tim Murphy. A bibliography intended especially for students, this book was originally scheduled for publication in 1990 by Starmont House, Inc. It's not likely that this book, even updated, would see publication, since Collings's definitive *The Work of Stephen King* is in print, albeit difficult to obtain from its publisher, Borgo Press.

Infinite Explorations: Art and Artifice in Stephen King's "It," "Misery," and "The Tommyknockers," by Michael R. Collings. A scholarly examination of King's more recent novels, this book was originally slated for publication in 1990 from Starmont House, Inc.

The Stephen King Bibliography, by Douglas E. Winter. Originally scheduled to be published by Donald M. Grant, Publisher, this expansion of the bibliography in Winter's *Stephen King: The Art of Darkness*, went on the back burner as Winter took on other writing commitments, complicated by a hard-disk crash in his personal computer that proved to be a setback. Because Collings's bibliography is in print, it's not likely that Winter's will see print. Winter's book would have had annotations by Stephen King, which would have made for an illuminating bibliography.

Dirty Laundry: The Annotated, Illustrated Stephen King Laundry List, by George Beahm. Originally scheduled for publication as a small press, limited edition pamphlet, after *The Stephen King Companion* proved to be a success, Beahm, using receipts from the Blue Ribbon laundry where King had his shirts starched and his pants pressed, researched the various cleaning solvents, detergents, and kinds of garments that were used to clean King's jeans and T-shirts. However, the project died after the carefully compiled notes were destroyed in the wash at a laundromat when an attendant, C. White, threw them in with her blood-soaked clothes. The problem worsened when the laundromat's manager verbally abused Beahm, saying that he had no right to write about King's dirty laundry. Distraught by his experience, Beahm decided to come clean, so to speak, and reluctantly abandoned the project.

Princeton University

King gave a lecture here on April 16, 1997, at Helm Auditorium. He was introduced by Joyce Carol Oates, a Princeton professor and writer, who noted, "There are: Stephen King the individual, Stephen King the literary and cultural phenomenon, and Stephen King the writer." She noted that he has sold over 200 million books in the U.S., and 50 million overseas.

Joyce Carol Oates: "Like all great writers of gothic horror, King is both a storyteller and an inventor of startling images and metaphors, which linger long in the memory and would seem to

Princeton University *continued*

spring from a collective, unconscious and thoroughly domestic American soil. . . . His fellow writers admire him for his commitment to the craft of fiction and the generosity of his involvement in the literary community."

Privacy

King has little. Because of the crazies that come to Bangor—it's always the out-of-towners, King says, that give them trouble—the Kings have had to implement security measures to keep the real nuts at bay. The hope was that when they moved to Bangor, people would respect their privacy, so they had no fence around the property initially. In time, however, people did come up to the house and ring the doorbell, although a small sign posted near the doorbell stated that both Stephen and Tabitha King were writers who worked at home and could not be disturbed. The sign dissuaded most people but over the years the property has by necessity become more protected, even to the point of now featuring dense sheltering shrubbery.

Although their home in Bangor is now well known, their office on the outskirts of Bangor affords some privacy, though it, too, has security measures in place. When they really want to get away from it all, they go to their home in Center Lovell, Maine, whose location remains a well-kept secret, as it should be.

Prize money

King won $69.81 in a collegiate English department contest at UMO.

Productivity

"I'm not a fast writer, but I stick to it. I write fifteen hundred words a day, and the stuff just piles up. It's a constant secretion. I have the feeling that if I stop, I won't be able to do it again." (Profile by Carol Lawson, "Behind the Best-sellers," in *NYTBR*, Sept. 23, 1979.)

"Profound influences"

SK: "Lovecraft. Raymond Chandler (and, at second hand, Ross MacDonald and Robert Parker). Dorothy Sayers, who wrote the clearest, most lucid prose of our century. Peter Straub. And Ellison."

Psycho II, by Robert Bloch

SK: "Perhaps the finest psychological horror writer working today . . . and never in finer form."

a traveling salesman, reluctantly gives Bryan Adams a ride, but it turns out to be a one-way ride for the hitchhiker who makes the big mistake of trying to rip off "Bill the Label Dude," as Adam disparagingly calls his good samaritan, who is saved by an oversized, wind-up chattery teeth that comes alive and attaches itself in a death grip not on his Adam's apple but on another, more sensitive, part of his anatomy south of the border, so to speak.

Narrated by Christopher Lloyd, this pairing of Barker and King works because it gives both stories the room to breathe, to develop. It shows that the material can effectively be done on television, which leads to the question: Why even bother to do an anthology-style film for the big screen?

Queenie

King's dog when he was a young boy. (See the photo section in *Stephen King: The Art of Darkness*.)

Questions most asked about King

In the October 1985 issue of *Castle Rock*, Stephanie Leonard discussed the most frequently asked questions posed by fans. Of the fifteen, most had to do with how to obtain rare King books and stories, though others were more general: How do you pronounce King's name? Is his house haunted? Does King have any pen names other than Bachman or Swithen? Will there be a sequel to *'Salem's Lot*? When did King begin writing? Where does King get his ideas?

Quicksilver Highway (film), 1997

Ever since his arrival in the U.S., Clive Barker has been teamed up with Stephen King in a Barker-is-prince, King-is-king comparison: Clive Barker is the new dark prince of horror, though Stephen is still the King! That sort of nonsense is usually employed by television interviewers who have never bothered to read either man's fiction.

The film's first half is an adaptation of Clive Barker's "The Body Politic," followed by a bizarre King story, "Chattery Teeth." At Scooter's Grocery & Roadside Zoo in nowhere, Nevada, Bill Hogan,

Cover to a *Fangoria* compilation of interviews featuring Stephen King and Clive Barker, respectively billed as the Masters of the Dark: Stephen, still the King, and Clive, the crown prince.

"Quitters, Inc."
(collected in *Night Shift*)

This story could only have been written by a person who smokes, as King used to. Addicted to cigarettes, the protagonist is trying to kick the habit but can't until a friend recommends Quitters, Inc., a company that guarantees results. In fact, it's so successful that all of its new clients are word-of-mouth customers. (An astonishing 98 percent of its clients *do* quit the habit, so they must be doing something right—right?)

Wrong.

Quitters, Inc., uses negative reinforcement, sufficiently strong, to force the issue. Smoking becomes a secondary concern and, like the others who successfully quit smoking, Richard Morrison realizes that sometimes the price you have to pay for your addiction, and its cure, is more than you ever wanted to pay. The story was adapted for the film *Cat's Eye*.

"The Raft" (collected in *Skeleton Crew*)

There is an interesting story behind this story, originally submitted to *Adam* magazine as "The Float." King has never seen a copy of the story in *Adam* magazine which paid supposedly on publication. King got the check but never a copy of the story . . . and to this day, no copy has surfaced, which leads me to conclude that King was paid in error, or the story was bought but never published.

The story's a corker, though, and made an interesting, if predictable, installment of *Creepshow 2*.

Four students from Horlicks University in Pittsburgh drive in Deke's Camaro to Cascade Lake, where they swim out to a raft in the middle of the lake. Once there, they come under attack from what appears to be a floating oil slick. It kills three students one by one until only Randy is left, marooned on the lake, with nothing but the sound of the loons in the forest to keep him company, as the thing patiently waits.

Rage

Mass-market paperback, 1977, 224 pages, NAL, $1.50
Dedication: "For Susan Artz and WGT"
Main character: Charlie Dekker, student
Contents: 35 short chapters

Background: Inspired in part by *Lord of the Flies* by William Golding

Written when King was in high school and completed during his first year in college at UMO, *Rage* was published to an indifferent world since this fledgling novel was published under King's pen name, Richard Bachman. An exploration of teenage rage and frustration, this novel, like some other early King stories, probes the thin line between sanity and insanity.

A claustrophobic study of Charlie Dekker, a high school student who goes postal. (The novel was subsequently adapted as a stage play.) Dekker kills one of his teachers and holds a high school class hostage as the students chime in, venting their frustrations.

On September 18, 1989, in McKee, Kentucky, a high school senior with two revolvers and a shotgun held a class of 11 students hostage for nine hours, eventually surrendering to the police.

In a Belgian TV interview that aired in the late eighties, King explained: "I can't take responsibility for the lunatics of the world. My responsibility as an artist is to tell only the truth. If that truth involves violent behavior as the result of a situation, then I must tell that truth."

The similarities to the novel were too many to dismiss; in fact, the police combed the novel for clues on how to deal with this situation.

Observed King, quoted in his hometown newspaper after the incident: "If they didn't do it one way, they would do it another way. Crazy is crazy."

More recently, King has expressed great concern and regret that the book was published, undoubtedly because unstable students use it as a blueprint for their own hostage-taking scenarios.

Rage (the play)

Rage made its stage debut on March 30, 1989.
Pearl Productions, a production company owned by the novelist Robert B. Parker and his wife, Joan, put on *Rage* after their son, Daniel Parker, wanted his father to ask King for material. King declined but offered to sell rights to one of his stories, and sold them stage rights for $1.

Daniel Parker told his father, "The first person we thought of—sorry, Dad—was King."

Rage (the play) *continued*

According to *Castle Rock*, the company "invested an unheard-of $25,000 to $30,000 for seven performances by an unknown troupe at a small theater. The bulk of the budget went to actors' salaries during seven weeks of rehearsal."

Maine writer David Lowell reported that the performance was put on by the Road Ensemble, and that the Parkers' son, Dan, played the lead character, Charlie Dekker. Commented Lowell: "I sure hope this play goes far; it's out*rage*ously good!"

"Rainy Season"
(collected in *Nightmares & Dreamscapes*)

Published in *Midnight Graffiti*, a semipro zine, this is the story King credits with having ended one of the few writing blocks he's suffered. King knew the zine's editors, Jim Van Hise and Jessie Horsting, both of whom had written books about him, would fall on it with loud cries of joy . . . and they did, giving it the cover position, which predictably boosted the zine's subscription base.

"Rainy Season" is the kind of story King calls a "peculiar town" tale, and for good reason.

Maine is Vacationland, or so it says on the state's license plate, so John and Elise Graham plan to spend the summer in Willow, Maine, where not much of anything happens . . . but it's the rainy season, a rare meteorological event that occurs on June 17 every seven years. But the warning—a rain of frogs—is ignored. It always is . . .

The Grahams call it a night and stay at a farmhouse, the Hempstead Place, joking about the rain of toads. The local yokels, they think, are a little touched in the heads.

But as the rain begins, so does the ominous thumping, as toads strike the roof.

These are not your ordinary, garden-variety toads, but malevolent toads with razor-sharp teeth that attack the Grahams, this year's sacrificial lambs, who futilely seek refuge in the house's cellar.

When morning breaks, the sun comes out, evaporating the water and the toads. And although the Grahams are dead, the world is right again, since the rainy season is over.

Razzies

Awards given out the night before the Oscars for the worst of the previous year's offerings, instituted by John Wilson. The Golden Raspberry Award went to King in 1986 as worst director for *Maximum Overdrive*.

"The Reach" (collected in *Skeleton Crew*)

Originally published as "Do the Dead Sing?" in *Yankee* magazine (1981), its original title was restored by King for inclusion as the last story in *Skeleton Crew*.

The Reach is the body of water between the mainland and Goat Island, on which Stella Flanders lives. The oldest inhabitant of Goat Island, she's never needed nor wanted to cross The Reach. As she puts it, everything she needs is on the island, so the mainland can stay beyond her reach.

But late in life, having survived her husband, who died of cancer, and virtually all of her other loved ones, she decides it's time to cross The Reach when it freezes over, and during a blizzard she sets off to finally cross it. Her body is riddled with terminal cancer, and she knows it's now or never. It's time, finally, to go to the other side.

The ghosts from her past beckon her on, including that of her late husband, Bill, who offers up his distinctive cap after the one she's wearing blows off in a storm, a white-out so severe that visibility is nearly nil.

Bill tells her that he's not alone—"It's all of us." They sing to her ("The wind seems to sing with almost human voices"), and the next day, after the storm has passed, they find Stella Flanders frozen to death after a four-mile walk across The Reach.

But it doesn't explain to her family how she came to be wearing her late husband's distinctive, unmistakable cap that hadn't been seen in years.

Reading fix

King is a compulsive reader. In college he was often seen on campus with a paperback sticking out of his back pocket. Around town, while waiting in line, he's often seen with his nose in a book (a good way to keep people from asking for autographs). You get the sense that, if there's nothing else to read, he'd read the text of the cereal boxes during breakfast. (He's also been known to read while taking a leak.)

Reading Stephen King

A conference held on October 11–12, 1996, at the University of Maine at Orono on issues of censorship, student choice, and the place of popular literature in the canon.

This was the first symposium exclusively focused on King: considering the place of his work in the canon of books that are required reading in colleges and high schools, exploring issues of censorship in public schools, and promoting the need for adolescent readers to be able to choose books in school reading programs.

King gave the keynote address and attended the banquet, with dishes named after his literary creations: Hot Nadine Cross Buns, A New Yorker Field of Greens Salad, Annie Wilkes's Chicken Fricassee, Salem's Lotsa Pasta, and Roadkill Ratatouille.

On the theme of "King's Work and Popular Literature in the Canon," the contributions included:

"Before and After the Fall: The Passage from Childhood to Adulthood in King's *It*," Burton Hatlen, University of Maine

"Raising the Dead: Teaching Theory through Non-Canonical Texts," Miriam Heddy Pollock, New York University, New York

"Morality in the Horror Fiction of King," James Anderson, Johnson and Wales University, Warwick, Rhode Island

"Randall Flagg: The Master and the Other," Felicia Beckman, University of Missouri, Columbia, Missouri

"Receiving King: Perceptions and Responses by Students and Teachers," Michael R. Collings, Pepperdine University, Thousand Oaks, California

"Absent Without Leave: King's *Stand*," Stephen Glickman, University of Colorado, Boulder, Colorado

"Using the Low-Brow to Teach the High-Brow: Teaching Literature with Popular Culture," Lisa-Anne Culp, University of Arizona, Tucson, Arizona

"Teaching King as Rhetoric and the (Unknown) Student Body," Jeffrey Hoogeveen, University of Rhode Island, Kingston, Rhode Island

"Screams and Whispers: Redemption Through Friendship in Selected Works of King," Sandy Brawders, Center for Adult Learning, University of Maine

On "Censorship," the contributions included:

"Anatomy of a Book Censorship," Members of the Mt. Abram High School English Department, Strong, Maine

"How Patrick Buchanan Would Read King," Ed Ingebretsen, Georgetown University, Washington, D.C.

"A Combustible Combination: A Thematic Unit on Censorship and Composition," Mary Segall, Quinnipiac College, Hamden, Connecticut

"Censorship and the Purpose of Education," Danielle Mahlum, University of Wyoming, Laramie, Wyoming

"One Book Can Hurt You . . . But a Thousand Can't," Janet Allen, University of Central Florida, Orlando, Florida

"Covert Censorship," Ruth Farrar, Bridgewater State College, Bridgewater, Massachusetts.

"Censorship in the Electronic Age," Gail Garthwait, Asa Adams Elementary School (Orono, Maine), and a panel of library media specialists

On "Student Choice and Classroom Practice," the contributions included:

"When *It* Comes to the Classroom," Ruth Hubbard, Lewis and Clark College, and Kim Campbell, Riverdale High School, Portland, Oregon

"King's Work and the At-Risk Student: The Broad-Based Appeal of a Canon Basher," John Skretta, Northeast High School, Lincoln, Nebraska

"Killing the King and Facing Medusa," Brian Edmiston, University of Wisconsin, Madison, Wisconsin

Reading Stephen King: Issues of Censorship, Student Choice, and Popular Literature, a collection of the proceedings, 246 pages, was published at $19.95 in trade paperback by the National Council of Teachers of English. Edited by Brenda Miller, Jeffrey D. Wilhelm, and Kelly Chandler.

Some comments from attendees and presenters:

Pollock: "He's one of the best. Reading him is not discontinuous with traditional canonical horror works. . . . There's the worship factor that makes me uncomfortable about talking to him. I think I would become incoherent if I tried to say anything." (*BDN*, Oct. 1996.)

Unidentified girl who accidentally ran into King at the conference: "Oh, my god! There's King!"

Unidentified man at the banquet: "He's an amazing guy, really. I mean, I don't know him but you see him at the movies or at the baseball field. He's just one of the crowd."

Burton Hatlen: "It has to do with this position he occupies between mass culture and high culture. How many people would write a novel like King does and include all these epigraphs from literature? He's a key mediating figure between mass culture and traditional culture. That split between high and mass culture can be debilitating. We can't just have high culture. But if all we have is a media culture, then we're impoverished. He has allowed us another possibility: to get these two perspectives into dialogue."

Real-world influences

According to Stephen Spignesi in *Shape*, King's influences include: "fifties television, B horror movies, E.C. Comics, a single-parent upbringing, small-town living, the sixties, and Chesterfields."

"The Reaper's Image"

King's second professional sale, which earned him $35. It appeared in *Startling Mystery Stories* (spring 1969).

A haunted mirror harboring the Grim Reaper catches the attention of a skeptical John Spangler, who stares at the dark spot in the mirror. A caretaker cautiously observes, knowing that Spangler—like the others who stared at the dark spot—will never return.

Red Dragon, by Thomas Harris

SK: "The best popular novel to be published in America since *The Godfather*."

The Red Letter

A defunct fan publication that covers the horror field, with an emphasis on King, Anne Rice, Clive Barker, Peter Straub, and other big-name writers. Greg Hotchkiss's digest-sized zine was chatty, informative and unabashedly home-brewed.

It was published irregularly, when sufficient news justified publication, and may be revived at some future date, according to its editor-publisher.

The editor can be reached at *The Red Letter,* P.O.

Box 352, Miamisburg, OH 45343. E-mail: *lestat@ erinet.com*

Redrum

"Murder" spelled backward. A leitmotif in the novel *The Shining*, and an arresting visual leitmotif in both film versions of the novel.

The Regulators

Hardback, 1996, 466 pages and a 9-page fictional letter, Dutton, $24.95

Written by Richard Bachman, *The Regulators* is similar in plot and setting to "The Shotgunners," an unpublished screenplay by King written for Sam Peckinpah.

SK: "I had been toying with this idea called *The Regulators* because I had a sticker on my printer that said that. Then one day I pulled up in my driveway after going to the market and the Voice said, 'Do *The Regulators* and do it as a Bachman book and use the characters from *Desperation* but let them be who they're going to be in this story.' Of course, the first thing I say when the Voice speaks up is 'Bachman is dead,' but the guy just laughs." (*PW*, "Spectacular Fall Performance," Aug. 5, 1997.)

The limited edition of 500 copies, numbered and signed by King, was published by Dutton in September 1996. Of the 500 copies, 100 were allocated to book dealers, and the balance was sold by phone only. Fans called the Bachman hotline, 1-888-4BACHMAN, for updates on the day when orders would be taken, at $325 a copy.

Reign of Fear: Fiction and Film of Stephen King, edited by Don Herron

This is a collection of articles about King published in 1988. I'm tempted to say, as one reviewer did, that this is the sort of thing you'll like if you like this sort of thing, but the simple truth is that it's yet another grab-bag collection of pieces about King.

Herron contributed "The Summation." The collection would have been much stronger if any effort had been made to organize this material, which includes introductions made at conventions, book reviews, academic essays, personal opinion pieces, etc.

In the King community, some fans, including readers of *Castle Rock,* think that Herron is not the person who should be writing so much about King, much less editing books about him, since their perception is that his mind-set about King's work handicaps him, preventing a fair assessment. They assert—quite rightly, I think—that the tone of Herron's nonfiction about King is off-putting.

What, then, does Herron have to say about himself and King? In "The Summation," Herron writes: "Until 1986 I had some hope that King might do something better than his best and generally better than his worst, or else *why* write about him?"

Well, as Herron is obviously aware, writing about King has become, as Herron himself notes in the beginning of his piece, "fairly lucrative for part-time work," admitting that he's "been a published King critic for about as long as anyone else regularly punching the clock in this cottage industry, longer than most."

After everything is said and done, Herron's assessment of King is: "In my opinion, if King keeps writing at a reasonable professional rate . . . then he will end up in a position highly comparable to that of the late John D. MacDonald."

In my opinion, it's too early to make critical assessments about a writer who has a good 25 years' worth of productivity ahead of him, so unlike Herron, I won't presume to pass judgment.

Herron, however, puts his cards on the table. "That's my call," he states flatly. "Welcome to it." And then he quotes from a John D. MacDonald novel: "You have put your finger on the artistic conundrum we all struggle with. How, in these days of intensive communication on all levels, can you tell talent from bullshit? Everybody is as good, and as bad, as anybody wants to think they are."

Those, in a nutshell, are my misgivings about Herron as a critic writing about King. (Note to Herron: You can tell talent from bullshit by knowing the difference, as a writer, between opinion and *informed* opinion.)

The book contains the following essays:

"Interview" with King, conducted by Jo Fletcher.

"Foreword," by Dennis Etchison, a thoughtful piece discussing the connection King has with his readers—his ability to touch his readers in a memorable way.

"Digging *It*: Introduction," by Whoopi Goldberg, extolling the virtues of *It*.

"King of the Comics? Introduction," by Marv Wolfman, discussing his connection with King. Wolfman, a comic book writer, has the distinction of being the first person to publish King fiction (excluding King's self-published material, of course).

"In Providence: Introduction," Frank Belknap Long, in which a member of the Lovecraft circle praises the next generation, specifically King, with whom Long shared guest-of-honor status at the Fifth World Fantasy Con in Providence, Rhode Island, on October 12–14, 1979.

"King and the American Dream: Alienation, Competition, and Community in *Rage* and *The Long Walk*," by Burton Hatlen; a perceptive piece by one of the best King critics who also taught him in college.

"When Company Drops In," by Charles Willeford, a few thoughts on *Misery*.

"The Cycles (Tricycles and Hogs) of Horror," by J. N. Williamson, a personal assessment from another practitioner in the genre, discussing himself, King and his readers.

"The Glass-Eyed Dragon," by L. Sprague de Camp, a look at fantasy as a genre and *The Eyes of the Dragon*, showcasing King's dry wit.

"The Big Producer," by Thomas Tessier, who discusses the pitfalls and pratfalls of big-producing fictioneers—quantity over quality—and recommends that King slow down, take his time, and place quality over quantity.

"The King and His Minions: Thoughts of a *Twilight Zone* Reviewer," by Thomas M. Disch, in which he takes King to task for his perceived shortcomings as a writer, equating King's fiction with a "fictional Levittown"—rows of houses, competently built, depressingly similar.

"Snowbound in the Overlook Hotel," by Guy N. Smith, an enthusiastic piece about King's fiction from a general point of view.

"By Crouch End, in the Isles," by Peter Tremayne, a British writer who discusses the influences—mostly commercial—successful American writers, especially King, have had on their British counterparts, who he feels should go back to the roots of English horror, emphasizing its literary quality.

"Reach Out and Touch Some Things: Blurbs and King," by Stanley Wiater, discussing the one- and two-sentence raves King has written for other writers, usually at the behest of publishers, but sometimes provided on his own initiative.

"The Movies and Mr. King: Part II," by Bill Warren, a general piece discussing King at the movies.

"Come Out Here and Take Your Medicine!: King and Drugs," by Ben P. Indick, R.Ph., an esoteric discussion of drugs in King's fiction, by a pharmacist.

"Horror Without Limits: Looking into *The Mist*," by Dennis Rickard, a discussion of "The Mist," which he considers to be King's quintessential work.

"Fear and the Future: King as Science Fiction Writer," by Darrell Schweitzer, discussing King not as a horror writer but a science fiction writer. (This is an odd piece, since science fiction is a minor part of what King writes, and even some of those stories are really horror stories with science fiction trappings.)

"The Summation," by Don Herron, who says, in a long essay, "I do not see any particularly lasting power in King's works."

Rein, Michelle L.

The founder of SKEMERs, a King discussion group on the Internet.

She edits the daily SKEMERs electronic zine, which goes out to hundreds of King fans worldwide.

Begun in November 1995, this group, Stephen King Electronic Mailers, has proved to be the most active of King fan groups.

In August 1997, over 100 SKEMERs descended on Bangor to do the King Thing at its annual gathering, to see his main haunts, to enjoy the town's spooky sights. (The group met again on July 24–26, 1998.)

Michelle's e-mail: *Skemers@aol.com*

Reiner, Rob

A film director whose careful selection of King material—notably *Stand by Me* (adapted from "The Body") and *Misery*—have put him at the head of the list of directors who have successfully adapted King to film while preserving the flavor of King's distinctive prose.

Rob Reiner: "King is a good writer. He pens wonderfully complex characters and great dialogue. Yet when people adapt his books into movies, they tend to . . . just concentrate on the horror and the supernatural—all the things that seem to be the most overtly commercial. It's a grave mistake because they lose many levels of his work by doing the obvious." (Reiner interviewed by Alan Jones, for *Starburst* magazine, April 1991.)

Rejections (stories)

By King's count he had collected nearly sixty rejection slips before the sale to *Startling Mystery Stories* was made. (*Bare Bones.*)

Residences

1947: Born in Portland, Maine.

1949–58: Lived with relatives in Fort Wayne, Indiana; Stratford, Connecticut; also visited his mother's relatives in Massachusetts and Maine.

1958: Moved to Durham, Maine.

1966–70: Lived on campus at UMO, then off-campus at a cabin near the river, and in an apartment in Orono, Maine.

1971–73: Lived in Hermon, Maine.

1973: Moved to Bangor, Maine, to a second-story walk-up apartment; after the paperback rights to *Carrie* sold, moved to North Windham, Maine.

1974: Moved temporarily to Boulder, Colorado, to write a new novel with a non-Maine setting.

1975: Moved to Bridgton, Maine, where he bought a house near the lake.

1977: Temporarily moved to England, for a planned one-year stay; rented a house in Mourlands. Stayed only three months, then headed back to Maine, moving to Center Lovell, where the Kings bought a house. (It would later be designated their summer home.)

Residences *continued*

1978: Moved temporarily to Orrington, Maine, where he commuted to UMO for a one-year teaching stint.

1980: Bought a 23-room house on West Broadway, in the historic district of Bangor, and began renovations. (This is the Kings' winter home.)

A Return to 'Salem's Lot
(film), 1987

Though there are (at last count) four books about King and the movies, none acknowledge this gobbler: a King movie in name only, since the rights to the original, *'Salem's Lot*, allowed a sequel.

The result: This stake-in-the-heart cinematic excuse, trading largely on King's good name, in a vain attempt to draw an audience.

Thankfully, this turkey never saw film release in the theaters, but in its video incarnation it comes back to life again and again.

This one deserves the kiss of death.

"The Revenge of Lard Ass Hogan"

Originally published in *The Maine Review* (July 1975), this story was incorporated into "The Body" as a story by Gordon Lachance. As a story of a teen's revenge it recalls *Carrie*. David "Lard Ass" Hogan is a 240-pound target of abuse. Nobody respects him, but he gets his revenge: At the Great Gretna Pie-Eat of 1960, Hogan deliberately downs castor oil before the event, at which he consumes blueberry pie after blueberry pie while thinking of the most disgusting imagery possible, like gopher guts, causing him to upchuck on a spectator, setting off a chain reaction. (It's puke city, folks!)

Lard Ass Hogan finally gets his revenge.

Reviewers and big books

In "Books," a column he wrote for *Adelina* (November 1980), King takes reviewers to task for failing to give lengthy novels a fair reading. "Many critics," he wrote, "seem to take a novel of more than 400 pages as a personal affront."

Rexer, Ray

The editor-publisher of a *Castle Rock* parody, *Castle Schlock*. The late Rexer was well known and well liked in the King community for his infectious sense of humor, which was clearly obvious in the few issues of the not-for-profit *Castle Shlock* that he published.

Rhythm guitar

When he was in high school, King played rhythm guitar in a rock and roll band.

"Rita Hayworth and Shawshank Redemption"
(collected in *Different Seasons*)

Dedication: "For Russ and Florence Dorr."

King employs three distinct storytelling modes: the supernatural story, for which he's best known; the nonsupernatural story, typically set in Maine, for which he's undeservedly less known (except to savvy moviegoers); and a combination of the two, drawing on the strengths of each voice, as in "The Man in the Black Suit," which won an O. Henry Award in 1996.

Like "The Body" and *Misery* (both decidedly nonsupernatural stories by King, and very mainstream in appeal), "Rita Hayworth and Shawshank Redemption" is prime King in a nonsupernatural mode. The combination of the first-person narrative, a very intimate reading experience, and the down-to-earth, lemme-tell-you-a-story mode of the engaging narrator, nicknamed Red, pulls you into the story very quickly: Red wants to tell you about a new inmate, Andy Dufresne, the "Even-Steven Killer," as the Portland *Sun* called him—a banker in the outside world who joins the rest of the poor bastards at Shawshank Prison, long before prison reform guaranteed prisoners any rights. In those days, when you went to prison, you walked the line or left the prison feet first in a long wooden box.

"Red" befriends Dufresne, obtaining a large wall poster of screen actress Rita Hayworth, which Dufresne puts up in his cell. Rita's presence, while undoubtedly providing much-needed eye relief, covers the escape tunnel Dufresne has laboriously excavated with a small rock hammer, secured by Red.

The cast of engaging characters is considerable, from the sadistic warden on the take (and headed for a fall, orchestrated by Dufresne) to Brooks Hatlen (named after Burton Hatlen, one of King's UMO professors), who runs the prison library. A typical King touch: painting little cameos of the secondary characters that flesh out the story.

The result is a story about friendship between two men, both of whom go over the wall, as it were: Dufresne, who actually goes *under* the wall, burrowing his way out; and Red, who, after years of rejections, gets a pardon, which he never expected to get.

Acting on specific instructions left by Dufresne, Red finds a small box containing money, enough so that he can join Dufresne far away from the forbidding Maine landscape in a small Mexican town, Zihautanejo, about a hundred miles northwest of Acapulco, where the two finally reunite.

Ritz Theater

A movie theater in Lewiston, Maine, where King saw Saturday matinees as a child.

King, then 12, was large for his age, six feet, two inches. This presented a recurring problem every time he went to buy a ticket: They wanted to charge him the adult price, until he showed his birth certificate to prove otherwise.

River Oaks Bookstore

In Houston, Texas, the site of a joint book signing on January 29, 1988, where King and Don Robertson promoted the Philtrum Press edition of *The Ideal, Genuine Man*. According to a fan, William R. Wilson, by the time he had "arrived at the store the line was already working its way past a number of storefronts and was starting to head toward the end of the block." (Total count: 700 fans stood in line.)

Wilson, who got his copy of *The Ideal, Genuine Man* signed, was starstruck. "Then I was standing before him and my mind blanked out all my ques-

tions. . . . The bookstore clerk took two pictures of me and Mr. King while he was signing my book, and after shaking his hand and meeting Mr. Robertson, I started down the stairs. . . . It is still hard to believe." (*Castle Rock.*)

The Riverdriver's Cookbook

A fundraiser, this was published in Bangor in 1988 and sold for $5. It contains his recipe for "Lunchtime Goop." Bon appétit.

Rivers, Joan

Comedienne who published a line of cards in 1983, one of which read: "Please write! *Carrie* had more friends than I do."

Roadwork

Mass-market paperback, Signet, 1981, $2.25
Dedication: "In memory of Charlotte Littlefield / Proverbs 31:10–28"
Contents
Part I. November
Part II. December
Part III. January
Epilogue
Genesis: The oil shortage of 1974, as indicated on the book's cover: "A novel of the first energy crisis."

Barton George Dawes takes a stand against the encroachment of the government, which is building a new superhighway right through where his house stands.

Like the other early Bachman novels, this one is a psychological study of a person under stress, to see how he reacts. Unlike Charlie Dekker (*Rage*), Dawes refuses to succumb and takes a stand against the government.

Roadwork

Speaking out against a transportation referendum that supported widening the Maine Turnpike, King recorded a 60-second commercial that aired on radio stations in the state. (Associated Press, Oct. 1991.)

R Is for Rock Bottom Remainders

This band plays music as well as Metallica writes novels.

—Dave Barry

STEPHEN KING RULES!
If the publisher of this book printed that line in large type, with blood-red ink, with die-cut embossing, it would put in perspective the impact that King had on his fellow band members, the media, and the audience when he turned off his word processor and turned on an amplifier to which he hooked up an electric guitar, changing from best-selling writer to celebrity rock-and-roller.

For most writers, the fantasy is to be famous, to make a lot of money, to write the books you've always wanted to write, to be a popular and critical success—and King's had all of that, though the latter is still in contention. The fantasy, for most writers, is to be the *next* Stephen King.

So what, then, is King's fantasy?

One was to perform in a rock and roll band—a taste of which he had gotten as one of the Mune Spinners, a high school band. He later performed his one-man guitar fests at a coffeehouse when he was in college. He appeared on a real stage in April 1986, when he made an impromptu appearance at a UMO concert with John Cafferty and the Beaver Brown Band. When he took to the stage, they handed him a guitar, and he did his thing.

The opportunity to live the fantasy came when Kathi Kamen Goldmark, a San Francisco-based media escort, thought the American Booksellers Association convention would be the perfect place for brand-name authors to get together, kick out the slats, and raise money for charity by performing as a rock and roll band. The bottom line, she knew, was that the spectacle of the writers in a band was enough to draw media attention and an uncritical audience. It was a win-win situation for everyone: The prospective band members welcomed the opportunity to get away from their lives as writers, the media loved the new angle, the ABA thought it was the perfect tie-in, and the charities knew that the concert would be a sellout.

The motley crew:

♦ *Dave* (His Mind May Be Full of Boogers and Dog Poop, But His Heart Is Full of Love) *Barry*; guitar and vocals.

♦ *Tad* (Just a Tad Tooooo Bad) *Bartimus*; Remainderette vocals.

♦ *Michael* (Whoever Heard of a Man Named) *Doris*; percussion.

♦ *Robert* (But Then I Forgot It All in Grade School) *Fulghum*; mandocello, guitar, and vocals.

♦ *Kathi* (the Queen of the Book Tour) *Goldmark*; band mother and Remainderette vocals.

♦ *Matt* (Happy Families Are All Alike) *Groening*; critics' chorus.

♦ *Stephen* (and Still the) *King*; guitar and vocals.

♦ *Barbara* (She May Be the Answer to Stephen) *Kingsolver*; keyboard and vocals.

♦ *Al* (He May Be a Mother-You-Know-What, but We All Call Him Dad) *Kooper*; keyboard and guitar.

♦ *Greil* (Elvis Is Dead in My Book) *Marcus*; critics chorus.

♦ *Dave* (I'll Say "Fuck the Police" If I Want to) *Marsh*; critics' chorus.

♦ *Ridley* (He Do Know Diddly) *Pearson*; bass and vocals.

♦ *Joel* (If You Rearrange His Name It Spells Nelvis) *Selvin*; critics' chorus.

♦ *Amy* (If You Can't Stand the Heat, Get Out of My Kitchen) *Tan*; Remainderette vocals.

The band was originally called just the "Remainders." That name was already taken by another group, so the name was amplified to the Rock Bottom Remainders. Now, *there's* a name!

Even before the two-performance concert, on May 25, 1992, at the Cowboy Boogie, a small bar in Anaheim, California, Stephen King was very active, suggesting the addition to the repertoire of one of his favorite songs, "Teen Angel," which became his trademark song.

On May 25, the Rock Bottom Remainders made their first public appearance, at the Disneyland Hotel in Anaheim, where Oren Teicher of the ABA sponsored an evening of activities themed to censorship issues. Garrison Keillor was the host for the evening.

To see a group of authors actually singing instead of doing something more typically associated with them, like signing books, was in itself a sight for sore eyes. (The sore ears would come later.)

But the Rock Bottom Remainders could not stay for the entire evening's events, because they had a prior engagement, a performance at the Cowboy Boogie, about ten blocks away. The line outside the Cowboy Boogie, snaking around its front and sides, was composed of book people who had ponied up good money to see their favorite writers out of their element, pounding guitars instead of word processor keyboards. The demand for tickets to see and hear the band, scheduled to appear in only two performances, was so great that even at the last minute, desperate fans were offering up to $100 for a $10 ticket!

Inside, a table had been set up where band memorabilia was sold, raising more money for the designated local charities. The hot items were autographed T-shirts with a cartoon portrait of the band that sold for $15; autographed photos of the band sold well too.

Designed to hold around a thousand people, the Cowboy Boogie filled up fast. As soon as the spotlights lit the stage up and the members of the band walked out, introduced in NBA fashion, the cheers went up.

For the next two, maybe three, hours, the Cowboy Boogie rocked. The music was LOUD and NOT TOO BAD, though the videotape recorded by BMG sounded just awful, giving the impression that the band couldn't sing or play. In fact, the atmosphere was so infectious that after the first few songs, even those who showed up by themselves went to find a partner to cut up the rug, so to speak.

Dim lights, lots of booze, megawatt amplified music, and some of the biggest names in the book biz up-front and center, with stage lights playing them. Man, it was a night to remember!

Everyone assumed it was a one-shot gig after that night, but King had the idea that it'd be fun to actually go on tour and perform, like any other rock and roll band.

For a bunch of middle-aged writers who dreaded the prospect of going back to their lonely lives sitting in a room, staring at blank paper in the typewriter or at a computer screen, the idea had considerable merit.

In a nine-page book proposal to Viking, King suggested that to fund the tour, the band members contribute individual recollections of the tour, to be collected in *Mid-Life Confidential, or From Acid to Anti-acid.*

The book proposal was accepted—now, really, wasn't the sale of that book to King's publisher a foregone conclusion?—and the tour was arranged: eight gigs from Rhode Island to Miami in the last two weeks of May 1993.

The book would later be retitled *Mid-Life Confidential: The Rock Bottom Remainders Tour America with Three Chords and an Attitude.*

The principal difference between playing for the book crowd at Anaheim and hitting the road was that in the real world, the expectations would be higher.

From all accounts, nobody was disappointed.

Predictably, though, Stephen's king-sized presence made an impact. Within the band itself, Tad Bartimus, in her essay for *Mid-Life Confidential*, observed: "In this all-author band, Stephen King was at the top of our ziggurat by virtue of writing and selling the most books."

Outside of the band, the media dogged the best-selling, brand-name writers. In other words, the media wanted to interview the "real authors," as a perky reporter from *Entertainment Tonight* termed them.

"Where's Stephen King?" was a frequent cry, one echoed by the fans who showed up with *The Stand* in hand, wanting King's autograph. As Joel Selvin put it in *Mid-Life Confidential*: "All along the way, our fellow members of the press evidenced zero interest in the Critics' Chorus. Dave Barry, yes. Amy Tan, maybe. But as long as Steve King was available, everybody was happy. 'Stephen King, Others Killed in Crash' went the joke on the tour bus."

The media probably never noticed that Tabitha King was present, too. The designated tour photographer, she was, as any photographer should be, an observer and recorder, but not a participant on the stage. Behind the scenes, she was very active, though, buying fun gifts and silly props for the band members.

For Stephen King, the tour was a way to turn back the clock by rocking around it. Like King, Dave Barry realized that the tour was a way to break the mold and try something new, which is not necessarily a bad thing when you're middle-aged and, presumably, set in your ways, as he observed. "When you get to be in your forties, headed directly toward (can this *be*?) your fifties, you tend not to do stuff like this—make new friends, go out and have wild adventures, risk making a fool out of yourself. . . . It was worth doing."

To which you can almost hear King say: "Amen, brother!"

For King's part, it was an opportunity to sing some of his favorite songs, his trademark "Teen Angel" and "Stand by Me," followed closely by "Susie-Q," "Who Do You Love," "Last Kiss," and "Endless Sleep." It was an opportunity for him to get back to the basics, to stretch himself, to break from the writing routine.

It was a blast to the past.

Dave Barry (from *Mid-Life Confidential*): "We also got to know each other better, and got to share our ideas about the craft of writing. For example, on our first lunch break, Stephen King, whom I had never met, walked up to me, leaned down to put his face about an inch from mine, and said, in a booming maniacal voice, 'SO, DAVE BARRY, WHERE DO YOU GET YOUR IDEAS?' Stephen was making a little writer's joke. He *hates* this question. Like most writers, he has been asked this question nine hundred squintillion times."

Dianne Donovan (*Chicago Tribune*): "Were they any good, these rock 'n' roll wannabees who gamely camped their way through a generous sampling of '60s singles? Well, they probably sang better than most rock musicians can write, and with a good deal more enthusiasm. Bolstered by three 'real' musicians, ear-splitting amplification and a wildly supportive crowd of more than a thousand booksellers and publishing types, the Rock Bottoms put on a good show. Stephen King dominated center stage with his almost preternatural sex appeal, matching chords with [Ridley] Pearson and [Dave] Barry, who apparently hasn't changed a bit since 1965."

SK: "I usually play chords on a word processor, which is a very private thing. It was great. It was a lot of fun. . . . If nothing else, at least I've improved my guitar skills." (*BDN*, May 28, 1992.)

Entertainment Tonight hostess to Tad Bartimus: "Where's Dave Barry? Where's King or Tan? Where are the real authors?"

Dave Barry (in his column, titled "The Great Literary Band: If You Can't Play It Well, Play It Loud"): "Recently I played lead guitar in a rock band, and the rhythm guitarist was—not that I wish to drop names—Stephen King."

When asked by a writer for Waldenbooks's in-store newsletter, "Is there any career—other than writing or movie making—that you'd like to pursue?" King replied, "Yes. I'd like to play rock and roll. I play an adequate rhythm guitar but I'm not very versatile. So I guess I'll stay with writing. I kind of like it." But it's the typewriter that really matters. "Although I'm not much of a musician, I've been playing boogie on a typewriter ever since," he told the *Boston Globe* (1992).

Romero, George

A Pittsburgh-based movie director best known for his *Dead* trilogy: *Night of the Living Dead*, *Dawn of the Dead*, and *Day of the Dead*.

Romero has worked with King on several projects. In addition to directing *Creepshow* and adapting "The Raft" for *Creepshow 2*, he was involved in three other King film projects, *Pet Sematary*, and *It*, and *The Stand*, before directing *The Dark Half* in 1990.

Romero, on *The Dark Half*: "I had always wanted to adapt one of Stephen's novels. I enjoyed the challenge, because it's always difficult to compress an ambitious book into a manageable script. And because I know him so well, I was especially concerned to make sure that Stephen's voice as a writer could still be heard in the movie."

Room 217

The number of the infamous room cited in *The Shining*, which is assumed to be the same room number that King had when he stayed at the Stanley Hotel in Estes Park, Colorado. According to Stephanie Leonard, "I find from talking to Stephen that he just made the number up, and wasn't sure in which room he actually stayed."

Room 203, Gannett Hall

The room King shared with another freshman in his first year at UMO.

King wrote about his first-year experience in "The Garbage Truck," for the school newspaper: "There I was, all alone in Room 203 of Gannett Hall, clean-shaven, neatly dressed, and as green as apples in August. . . . I was quite sure my roommate would turn out to be some kind of a freako, or even worse, hopelessly more With It than I. I propped my girl's picture on my desk where I could look at it in the dismal days ahead, and wondered where the bathroom was."

Rose Madder

Hardback, 1995, 420 pages, Viking, $25.95
Dedication: "This book is for Joan Marks."
Contents
Prologue: Sinister Kisses
  I. One Drop of Blood
  II. The Kindness of Strangers
  III. Providence
  IV. The Manta Ray
  V. Crickets
  VI. The Temple of the Bull

Preceded by *Gerald's Game* and *Dolores Claiborne, Rose Madder* completes a loose trilogy and is in fact a trial cut on *Desperation.* In both, an officer of the law, a policeman whose sworn duty is to protect and serve the public, is the villain. In this novel, Rosie Daniels lights out for the territories after silently suffering fourteen years in an abusive marriage with her husband, Norman Daniels, a policeman, who is in hot pursuit.

A stranger in a strange city, she is befriended by Bill Steiner and begins to put back the pieces of her life, but Norman Daniels, intent on shattering her life again, closes in . . . which is when she escapes into a painting she finds in a junk store, transforming herself from Rosie Daniels into Rose Madder.

To promote the book, the publisher printed 10,000 sets of galleys, a record number for any King book in recent memory. Unfortunately, it did not goose sales, and the novel failed to make number one on the critical *New York Times* best-seller list. This contributed to *Entertainment Weekly*'s ranking King eighty-fifth on its annual list of 101 most power people in the entertainment industry. The previous year, King had been number 47.

This clearly was not the kind of novel King fans wanted, and the sales reflected it. (When was the last time a King novel *didn't* make number one on the best-seller lists?)

The *Rose Madder* publicity hot line was: 704-808-TIMES.

W. David Atwood (senior writer, Book of the Month Club): "The opening scene of King's new novel is one of the most harrowing ever written, *anywhere.* You will find yourself turning away more than once, as some of us here did when we received an early manuscript. It is hard to watch, stomach-churning in the way of those live-surgery shows you come across while flipping through the channels."

When asked what the novel was about at a book signing in Santa Cruz, California, King replied: "I can give you a sneak preview and tell you what it's about. It's *about* . . . 450 pages long." (King's a funny man.)

"Rose Red"

A screenplay King sold to Steven Spielberg about a haunted house. (Despite the word "rose" in both titles, "Rose Red" has nothing to do with *Rose Madder.*)

"Ross Thomas Stirs the Pot"

A book review by King (*Washington Post,* "Book World," Oct. 16, 1983) in which he praises Ross Thomas's *Missionary Stew,* making the comparison that the only writer that could be "classed" with Thomas is Donald Westlake.

Royal Shakespeare Company

Famed British repertory theater company that staged a production of *Carrie,* which opened in London before heading to Broadway, where it received a critical and financial drubbing.

Of the performances in England, Richard Mills wrote: "I wouldn't wish to give anybody the impression that I ever found the show less than enjoyable. The whole thing was very entertaining, but it was not a horror story anymore. Rather, it has been homogenized to gain greater credibility for family audiences. In so doing, I have to say it has had the opposite effect on plot credibility." (*Castle Rock.*)

Craig Goden (*Castle Rock*): "Seven or eight million dollars later, after a brief run in England, *Carrie* the musical tragedy hit Broadway where it scorched through sixteen previews and five official performances before the New York critics stamped it out like a brushfire in a state park."

For the record, Stephen and Tabitha King attended the first Broadway performance and enjoyed it.

The play opened on May 12, 1988, and closed three days later.

Rules of Prey, by John Sandford

SK: "Sleek and nasty.... I loved every minute of it."

Runaround Pond

A lake in Durham, Maine, where King and his childhood friends used to swim. The scene with the leeches in "The Body," visually brought to life in *Stand by Me*, was inspired by a real-life incident when a youthful King and Chesley, not knowing any better, went swimming in Runaround Pond and stayed close to the shore, not realizing that was where the leeches lay waiting in ambush.

Subsequently, newcomers would be brought to the lake, in what appeared to be an act of friendship, and urged to stay close to the shore, while those in the know swam out to deeper waters to avoid the leeches, where they awaited the inevitable screams of the boys who discovered they were victims of King and Chesley's favorite prank.

Boys will be boys . . .

The Running Man

Mass-market paperback, 1982, Signet, $2.50
Dedication: None
Contents: Countdown chapters, from "Minus 100 and COUNTING . . ." to "000"

It is the year 2025, and Big Business, not Big Brother, is in control of the country. Ben Richards, like Jack Torrance in *The Shining*, is a desperate man: He can't provide for his family and is forced to make a drastic decision, to appear as a contestant in a game show in which he's pursued by trained killers, gladiators that relish the hunt, with the masses watching their every move on television.

Ironically, the money that the network sends him is not his source of salvation, as he hoped, but his damnation: Thieves in search of the money kill his family, but he decides to fulfill the contract and becomes a running man, giving the masses what they want, but in the end getting what he wants—winning the running game and taking a toll on the network's headquarters.

About the book: Written over a weekend when

Runaround Pond in Durham, Maine, where King and Chesley grew up. (Runaround Pond figures prominently in "The Body"—remember the leech scene?)

King was teaching school, the book was submitted to Thompson at Doubleday, who rejected it—the third rejection in a row after *Getting It On* and *Blaze*. King then submitted it to Donald A. Wolheim at Ace Books, who returned it within three weeks with a short note: "We are not interested in science fiction which deals with negative utopias."

The Running Man (film), 1987

The first but certainly not the last film to be made from a Richard Bachman novel, *The Running Man* is great fun—a roller-coaster ride, especially if you divorce it from the Bachman book of the same name.

Set in the future, the film version of *The Running Man* is a riff on "The Most Dangerous Game," with game show contestants being hunted by stalkers. But the game, like everything else in this dystopia, is rigged: The game-show host, superbly played by the real-world game-show host Richard Dawson (*Family Feud*) in a frame-up sends a cop, Ben Richards (played by Arnold Schwarzenegger), on what the Dawson character expects to be a one-way journey. After a dizzying ride on a jet sled that launches Richards from the stage of the game show into a real-world maze in which television monitors track his progress—and that of the stalkers coming after him—the film becomes mostly a vehicle for Arnold ("I'll be back!") Schwarzenegger, who in his action films has come to be typecast in *Terminator*-type roles.

King has wisely disassociated himself from this action flick based on his novel, for it's clearly not the book King wrote. For the millions of Schwarzenegger fans, however, this movie is fun fare.

Russell, Bobby

Known as "Mr Trivia" at WZON, he was the station's midday personality who frequently featured contests and promotions using King as source material, for questions and prizes as well. One such promotion, centered around *Thinner*, offered as first prize the signed, limited edition by Philtrum Press of *The Eyes of the Dragon*, which was won by Al Chebba, who correctly answered a "Wicked Super Trivia" question.

Ryden, Mark

The artist who illustrated the covers of *Desperation* and *The Regulators*.

"Salami writer"

King's characterization of himself as a writer. In a note for his photo in Jill Kvementz's author's photobook, *The Writer's Desk*, he observed: "I try to write salami, but salami is salami. You can't sell it as caviar." (Predictably, when King's photo for this book was used for a 1998 calendar, it was teamed up with October.)

'Salem's Lot

Hardback, 1975, 405 pages, Doubleday, $8.95
Dedication: "For Naomi Rachel King '...promises to keep.'"
Main character: Ben Mears, writer; secondary: Susan Norton
Contents
Prologue
Part I. The Marsten House
Part II. The Emperor of Ice Cream
Part III. The Deserted Village
Epilogue
Inspiration: Bram Stoker's *Dracula*, Grace Metalious's *Peyton Place*, and rural Maine—especially Durham, Maine

A contraction for Jerusalem's Lot, *'Salem's Lot* is the story of the writer Ben Mears, who returns to his hometown to write a new novel, never realizing that a vampire has come to haunt the town and is feeding on its inhabitants. Meanwhile, the vampire's familiar, Straker, heralds his master's presence, beguiling townsfolk and taking up residence at the abandoned Marsten House.

An imaginative, uniquely American riff on *Dracula*—which has held its own for over a century—*'Salem's Lot* is a deep, rich and evocative novel. In fact, it's a quantum leap forward, in scope, in imagination, and in its evocation of small-town Maine. *'Salem's Lot* is justifiably a favorite of horror writers, of King's fans, and reportedly of King's as well.

A serious treatment of vampirism, *'Salem's Lot* has wielded a hypnotic power over King fans since its publication, which unfortunately is not the case with the made-for-TV adaptation, the first in a long string of disappointing visual treatments that in time diluted the effect of King's horror films in the film community. Compare *'Salem's Lot* with the story "One for the Road," in *Night Shift*.

Leonard Wolf (*Dracula: The Connoisseur's Guide*): "Some of the scenes in *'Salem's Lot* are candid replays of those in *Dracula*. . . . King's borrowing from Stoker is respectful, but his remake

The dust jacket to the Doubleday edition of *'Salem's Lot*. (Doubleday originally intended to create a set of King books following the design style shown here. That idea was later scrapped in favor of a photo-realistic set of covers, still in use.)

'Salem's Lot continued

of the scene is uniquely his own. That Sears Roebuck hammer [when Ben Mears and Father Callahan discover Susan Norton in the Marsten House and have to drive a stake through her heart] is as masterful as Stoker's coal-breaking hammer in Holmwood's hands."

Frank Carner (*Presumpscot*, student publication of the University of Maine at Portland-Gorham): "*'Salem's Lot* by Stephen King would certainly not find itself reviewed here if King were not a UMO graduate and if the story were not set here in Maine. . . . I hope, however, that King, having lined his pockets from the present book and *Carrie*, will turn his attention to more serious subjects and write a novel about Maine life that will lead us to a better understanding of ourselves and to a surer hold on our culture. . . . Let the next book be the one we review because it demands our attention for itself."

'Salem's Lot, TV adaptations

In *Hollywood Gothic*, David J. Skal pointed out that "*Dracula* has been a hallmark of the motion picture from the early days of German expressionism. The character has been depicted in film more times than almost any fictional being, with the single possible exception of Sherlock Holmes, and has so pervaded the world of communications and advertising that it is no longer necessary to read the novel or see one of its film adaptations to be thoroughly acquainted with the Count and his exploits. . . . For quite some time now, *Dracula* has been the perennial blockbuster attraction."

Walking in Bram Stoker's footsteps with *'Salem's Lot*, King, in light of the numerous campy versions of *Dracula* ("I vant to suck your blood!") in print and on film, had to play it straight: He had to take the vampire as a character seriously, and he did.

Despite concerns—including King's—that the television medium itself would prevent the book from being adapted faithfully, *'Salem's Lot* was remarkably faithful to the book. Although TV's censorship advisory board, Standards and Practices, did impose creative restrictions on the violence and gore, *'Salem's Lot* works best as a film when it is not focused on those elements. Instead, its

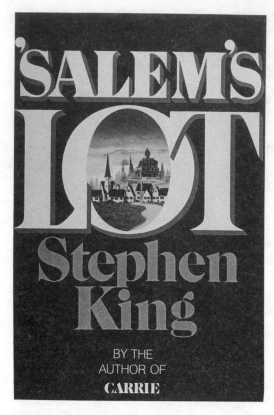

Dust jacket to Doubleday's first edition of *'Salem's Lot*. (Note: The publisher mentioned *Carrie* on the cover because King was then an unknown writer.)

proper focus should be the evil within and without: the townsfolk and the stranger from out of the town (a frequent King motif).

Although several versions were produced—the original television miniseries that aired on November 17 and 24, 1979; a television movie; a European release; and a home video—the better versions tend to be longer: The story is rich and complex and requires time for its telling. Clearly, if shoehorned into a two-hour feature film, the story would have suffered. This explains why the home video version is the least successful of the bunch.

The first King novel to be adapted to television, *'Salem's Lot* showed that, despite the medium's inherent problems—the adherence to the networks' Standards and Practices, and the interruptive nature of commercials—using it instead of film for telling King's longer, more complex stories simply made good sense: What you sacrifice in creative control, you can sometimes make up if the story has enough time to be told . . . and the story, after all, is paramount.

Clearly not for gore hounds—the horror fans who enjoy a more visceral, graphic approach—'Salem's Lot underscored the need to handle the subject matter carefully, to treat it seriously, with the result that this was the first in a string of successful television adaptations.

Sanford Street

After the paperback rights to *Carrie* were sold, the Kings moved from Hermon, Maine, to a second-story walk up on Sanford Street in Bangor, Maine.

"Say 'No' to the Enforcers"

Essay on censorship, published in the *Maine Sunday Telegram* (June 1, 1986), in which King talks about the chilling effect of censorship that he witnessed in North Carolina when filming *Maximum Overdrive*.

The occasion for the piece was that Rev. Jasper Wyman had recently spoken to the Bangor Kiwanis Club, espousing his viewpoint that pornographers were peddling their unsavory trade behind the protection of the First Amendment.

King urged everyone to say no on June 10, when the anticensorship referendum was to go up for a public vote. It was defeated by an overwhelming margin.

"Scariest book experience"

King cites *Lord of the Flies,* by William Golding. (*Entertainment Weekly*, Oct. 15, 1991.)

"Scariest movies I ever saw"

King cites *Night of the Living Dead* and *Dementia-13*. (*Entertainment Weekly*, Oct. 25, 1991.)

Scars, by Richard Christian Matheson

SK: "The stories vary somewhat in execution and effect—a rather too-elegant way of saying that some are better than others. This is to be ex-

pected; Richard Christian Matheson is still a young man and still maturing as a writer. But these stories do mark him as a writer to watch; they mark him as a writer to enjoy now."

Screenplays

Published Screenplays
Creepshow (Warner Brothers, 1982)
Cat's Eye (MGM/United Artists, 1985)
Silver Bullet (Paramount/North Carolina Film Corporation, 1985)
Maximum Overdrive (North Carolina Film Corporation, 1986)
Pet Sematary (Paramount, 1989)
Golden Years (CBS, 1991)
Sleepwalkers (Columbia Pictures, 1992)
The Stand (ABC, 1994)
The Shining (ABC, 1997)
Some Unpublished Screenplays
Battleground
Children of the Corn
Cujo
The Dead Zone
Night Shift
The Shotgunners (for the late director Sam Peckinpah)
Something Wicked This Way Comes (based on Ray Bradbury's novel of the same name)
In the Works
Storm of the Century and *Desperation*

Sebec Lake

A lake in Maine where, when King was 23, he nearly drowned by swimming out too far. (Noted by King in his essay, "The Neighborhood of the Beast," *Mid-Life Confidential.*)

The Second Stephen King Quiz Book,
by Stephen Spignesi

A mass-market paperback from Signet ($3.99), this book is the second in the series. Spignesi hopes to do a third volume, incorporating the first two books, now out of print.

Quiz Book continued

Contents

"Secret Window, Secret Garden"

(collected in *Four Past Midnight*)

Dedication: "This is for Chuck Verrill." Verrill was King's editor at Viking.

In this story, writer Morton Rainey is accused of plagiarism by John Shooter, who shows up at Rainey's house to confront him and reclaim his story.

Serialized novel

Taking a page out of Charles Dickens's book, King wrote a novel in six parts, *The Green Mile*.

King, who once observed his mother flipping to the back of a book to see how it ended, decided that writing a novel in such a fashion would give him the upper hand: The reader would have to wait until he was ready to reveal the final cards.

In the foreword to *The Green Mile*, King explained: "In a story which is published in installments, the writer gains an ascendancy over the reader which he or she cannot otherwise enjoy: Simply put, Constant Reader, you cannot flip ahead and see how matters turned out."

Shadowland, by Peter Straub

SK: "I thought it was creepy from page one! I loved it."

Shadow Prey, by John Sandford

SK: "A big, scary, suspenseful read."

The Shawshank Redemption (film), 1994

Because of the connection between King's books and their film adaptations, the tendency is to use King's original titles, unless there's a compelling reason not to: Possibly concerned about stereotyping, the director of King's "The Body" (which sounds like a horror film, especially if it comes from the Boogeyman from Bangor) wisely retitled it *Stand by Me*, which went on to critical and financial success.

In this case, we have a first-rate King adaptation, a terrific movie, but with a title that says nothing to the average moviegoer. Even though they truncated the title from the original, "Rita Hayworth and the Shawshank Redemption," it still didn't ring any bells . . . or cash registers, when the film debuted.

By the time it went to video the film had surged in popularity, since the reviews and word-of-mouth had finally caught up with the unfortunately titled film.

What *should* it have been titled? Hard to say, but it clearly *shouldn't* have been titled *The Shawshank Redemption*. What's a "shawshank," anyway? (It's a prison in Maine, but who'd have thought that?)

Never mind.

The film, directed by Frank Darabont, is one of the best adaptations to be made from a work by King.

At heart, all of King's stories deal, first, with ordinary people caught up in extraordinary circumstances, which usually means the injection of a supernatural element. But when King drops the supernatural element and concentrates on developing character, on evoking the Maine terrain, and on fashioning each major and minor character with care and individual attention, the result is noteworthy.

Nominated for seven Academy Awards, including Best Picture, *The Shawshank Redemption* boasted standout performances by Tim Robbins (as Andy Dufresne), Morgan Freeman (as Ellis Boyd "Red" Redding), and Bob Gunton (as Warden Norton). You could easily list another dozen roles of minor characters so carefully delineated that they stand out in the mind's eye. There's even an in-joke for King fans—a character named Brooks Hatlen, named after Burton Hatlen—but mostly this is serious stuff: a hard look at prison life in the late forties, when prisoners enjoyed damned few rights.

This is a first-rate movie from a first-rate story.

Now, if you want to have fun with those who poke fun at King, rent the video and watch their slack-jawed faces when you reveal that *Stephen King* wrote it.

After that, I guarantee you they'll go to see Darabont's forthcoming adaptation of *The Green Mile*, the next prison movie based on King's fiction.

The Shine

The original title of *The Shining*. It was dropped because a "shine" was a pejorative term used during the fifties for a black person; King had been unaware of the slang usage.

After the publication of *The Shining*, similarly titled horror novels began appearing. King said, "I won't mention any by name. But I see a lot of books that must have been inspired by some of the stuff I'm doing. For one thing, those 'horror' novels that have gerund endings are just everywhere: *The Piercing, The Burning, The Searing*—the *this*-ing and the *that*-ing."

The Piercing, by Yvonne McManus, clearly owed a lot to King's *The Shining*. "A masterpiece of modern horror in the tradition of King's *Carrie*. . . . Bridgewater was such a lovely place to live, a quiet place where nothing ever happened . . . until little Emma Winthrop invented a playmate named Abigail . . . until Abigail taught Emma how to make strange things happen with her mind . . . until Emma learned how to move objects, arrest heartbeats and create grisly fires . . . until blood flowed like water and people began to die."

Oh, *puh-lease*!

McManus missed the point: *Carrie* didn't sell because of the horror, the telekinesis; it sold because the character was well drawn, sympathetic and believably motivated.

The Shining

Hardback, 1977, 447 pages, Doubleday, $8.95

Dedication: "This is for Joe Hill King, who shines on."

Main character: Jack Torrance, writer; also, his wife, Wendy, and his son, Danny

Inspiration: The Stanley Hotel in Estes Park, Colorado; *The Haunting of Hill House,* by Shirley Jackson; *Burnt Offerings,* by Robert Marasco; and the desire to write a novel as a five-act play

"The shining" refers to Danny Torrance's ability to see glimpses of the future, a precognitive gift shared by Dick Halloran, a hotel employee who gives the Torrances a tour of the hotel before he leaves for Florida. He returns when Danny calls to him to bring him back to confront Jack Torrance, who has been driven to insanity.

In the original edition the book lacked the prologue and epilogue proper, though the prologue

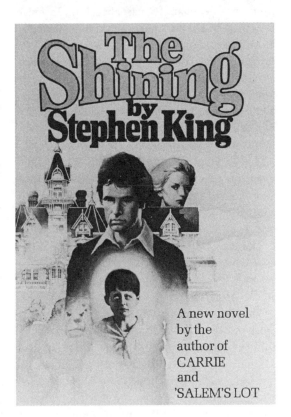

Dust jacket to Doubleday's first edition of *The Shining*. (Note: King was still relatively unknown, requiring the publisher to mention both *Carrie* and *'Salem's Lot* to goose the reader's memory.)

The Shining *continued*

was subsequently published in the King issue of *Whispers* and, in truncated form, in *TV Guide* as well, though the epilogue was never published as a separate piece. It was, however, published as part of the novel proper, in a later edition.

A study of mental disintegration and madness, *The Shining* is the story of an ex-teacher and former alcoholic, Jack Torrance, who gets one last chance to make good, to prove himself as the man of the family, the breadwinner: He takes a job as the winter caretaker for a resort hotel in the Colorado mountains, the Overlook, with only his wife and son as company. As cabin fever sets in, Jack Torrance, who is in a very suggestible state, is haunted by his past, haunted by the hotel's past, and haunted by his present, with fears of inadequacy compounded by his inability to write, which further reinforces his growing fears.

As he loses his grip on reality, as the demons from the hotel's haunted past affect him, Torrance goes mad and, finally, goes on a killing rampage.

A timeless horror story of wife abuse and of a modern marriage splitting apart at the seams, *The Shining* is also a classic horror story, exquisitely told, that showcases King's storytelling abilities and imagination in what is now acknowledged to be one of his best novels.

It is the only King novel to be adapted visually twice—by Stanley Kubrick, for a film, and by King himself for a made-for-TV miniseries. The adaptations stand in their own right as imaginative, if controversial, versions of a classic King tale well told.

The genesis of the novel is that when the Kings were living in Boulder, Colorado, they wanted to get away for a weekend. Locals recommended the Stanley Hotel in Estes Park.

The Kings arrived at the Stanley Hotel on October 30, 1974, just as it was closing down for the winter, but the manager let the Kings stay. As Stephen King made his way through the empty, cavernous halls of the hotel to his room, he went into the bathroom and saw the claw-foot tub and asked himself, "What if somebody died here? At that moment, I knew that I had a book."

Michael D. Harmon (*Maine Sunday Telegram,* March 27, 1977): "I fear that a vast potential audience—which normally does not care for novels of the horror genre—is going to pass *The Shining* by because they were turned off by *Carrie*'s buckets-of-blood approach and the vampiric fantasy of *'Salem's Lot*. If they do, they're going to miss a novel that, while flawed, contains real insights into pathologic personalities. As a psychological study, the novel approaches the status of real literature, the insightful study of humans and the inner worlds in which they are sometimes trapped."

SK: "*The Shining* . . . cost roughly $24 to produce as a novel—costs of paper, typewriter ribbons, and postage." (Quoted in "Special Make-Up Effects and the Writer," *Grande Illusions*, 1983.)

The Shining (King's film version), 1997

When you've become successful—meaning you have enough clout, you have the power—you can go back and correct what you consider were creative mistakes made by others, and by yourself as well.

King felt that Kubrick's version of *The Shining* was clearly one such mistake. Typically, King is charitable before and while a film is making the rounds, not wanting to sabotage its box-office potential. The gloves come off after the film has made the first-run theaters; then King speaks his mind, usually to the embarrassment of those involved in the production, if they're on the receiving end.

When King has an opinion about one of his film adaptations, you'll hear about it over and over in the media if he's unhappy.

Firestarter comes to mind: King's postfilm comments never sat well with its director, Mark Lester, who took umbrage at King's pointed barbs. Firing back in *Cinefantastique*, Lester dumped on King in print, who in turn dumped *back* on Lester, saying that neither were really at fault—let's lay this one on the doorstep of Dino De Laurentiis!

Sometimes, discretion is the better part of valor.

In this case, King's postfilm comments—aired at full volume, in numerous interviews—got back to Stanley Kubrick, who never showed any indication that he had heard, much less been affected by, King's criticisms, until the crucial time came when King went to ask permission for the right to

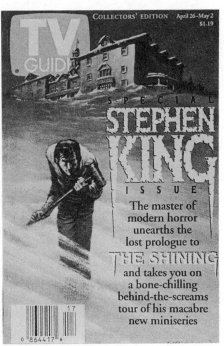

Twin *TV Guide* covers for the week of April 26–May 2, 1997, during which *The Shining* miniseries aired on ABC. (The Tom Hanks cover was sent to subscribers; the Berni Wrightson cover collectors' edition was on newsstands and at bookstores.)

do a remake from Kubrick, who had to give his approval.

What goes around comes around: When the opportunity presented itself to remake *The Shining*, one major roadblock cropped up—Stanley Kubrick set as a condition King's silence regarding the original version. Without that agreement, King could have put it on his tough-shit list and given it to his chaplain, as the plans for the remake went back into the fabled Trunk of Never Made Projects.

But King agreed, Kubrick gave his permission, and King got his chance to remake *The Shining*, not as a feature film but as a television miniseries for ABC.

The second time around was the charm, as they say. King wrote the script, worked as an executive producer, and even made a cameo appearance as the leader of the Gage Creed Band!

The result: *The Shining* as King intended, with former *Wings* star Steven Weber as Jack Torrance, Rebecca De Mornay as his wife, Wendy, and an endearing child actor, Courtland Mead, as their son, Danny.

Ostensibly the story of a haunted hotel, *The Shining*—as clearly seen in this version—is also the story of a marriage haunted by ghosts from Jack's past.

Steven Weber as Jack Torrance was a last-minute choice, but an outstanding one: His interpretation of the character renders him sympathetic, a far cry from what is considered to be an over-the-top interpretation of Torrance by Jack Nicholson in the original version.

Rebecca De Mornay was also outstanding as the loving, concerned wife, acting with a naturalness that was never evident in the performance of Shelley Duvall. When Weber attacks her with the mallet, pounding the hell out of her as she screams and pulls into a fetal position, you feel each blow.

For my money, though, Courtland Mead stole the show. As Danny Torrance, he's utterly believable and endearing, and you empathize with his dilemma: He sees the ghosts from the Overlook,

The Shining (King's film version) *continued*
and he knows there's evil, and he's a helpless victim in all of this. Keep your eye on him—he's *good!*

A first-rate adaptation and, for my money, the preferred version of *The Shining*—not because King had such an obvious hand in it, but because it's simply better than the Kubrick version.

Rebecca De Mornay: "[King] is one of the few men of his word in Hollywood. He told me, 'I want you in my next thing.' I said, 'Yeah, sure.' But eighteen months later, he called and said I was the one he wanted for *The Shining*." (Quoted in James Brady, "In Step with Rebecca De Mornay," *Parade*, April 27, 1997.)

SK, making good on an old promise: "I'd like to remake *The Shining* someday, maybe even direct it myself if anybody will give me enough rope to hang myself with." (interview in *Playboy*, June 1983.)

The Shining (Kubrick's film version), 1980

In King circles, it has become fashionable—almost an article of faith—to say that if you're a true fan, you hate Stanley Kubrick's *The Shining*, preferring the King-scripted version that aired on ABC in 1997. Truth be told, there's room for *both* in the King universe, though it's an uneasy truce.

Clearly, Kubrick took on a considerable challenge in trying to film King's psychologically rich, multilayered novel, using the classic "haunted house" motif and setting it high up in the Colorado mountains in a hotel that, like its new caretaker, Jack Torrance, has a haunted past . . . and a damned future.

Over the years, King's observations about Kubrick's version have run the gamut from mild appreciation to outright condemnation. Much of King's criticism focuses on the casting calls. Scatman Crothers as the prescient Dick Hallorann is marvelous; and Danny Lloyd as Danny Torrance is passable. Shelley Duvall, as Wendy Torrance, was clearly miscast . . . and then we come to Jack Nicholson as Jack Torrance.

In Hollywood, the prime directive is that you need a brand-name actor to "carry" the film, preferably someone who has recently had a big hit. So when various actors were suggested, Nicholson's name stood out. He was coming off of the critically and financially successful *One Flew over the Cuckoo's Nest*; his portrayal of R. P. McMurphy was a favorite with moviegoers and Nicholson fans.

Cast as Jack Torrance, a former schoolteacher and recovering alcoholic who gets one final chance to redeem himself, to prove to his family, society, and himself that he can escape the ghosts from his past, Nicholson starts out innocuously, but he slides from normality to madness in a rapid descent, as the hotel's past haunts him and calls up the ghosts that haunt his own past as well.

You never get the sense that Nicholson is slowly driven to madness; instead, you get the distinct impression that he was mad to begin with, and it wouldn't take much to push him over the edge—a point that King voiced in numerous interviews over the years.

As for Kubrick's film, it is in the end more his movie than King's book. Kubrick's unmistakable imprint—the choice of eerie, classical music; the gorgeous set designs and cinematography—makes it worth seeing as a film that stands on its own merits, but its principal demerit is that it's not Stephen King's *The Shining*. King himself would correct the situation. Agreeing not to make any more public pronouncements—denouncements, actually—on the Kubrick version, King wrote a script for a new version that aired on TV in 1997 that could rightly be termed, and was properly billed, *Stephen King's The Shining*.

The Shorter Works of Stephen King,
edited by Michael Collings and
David Engebretson

Published by Starmont House in 1985, this is a collaborative effort between Collings and one of his then students.

Eschewing simple plot summaries, Collings and Engebretson also offer "critical approaches to each story, identifying themes, symbols, and relationships between the story and the rest of King's work."

Foreword
List of Abbreviations
Chronology

Silver Bullet

Trade paperback, 1985, 255 pages, Signet, $9.95
Dedication: "In memory of Davis Grubb, and all the voices of Glory."
Contents
Foreword [first appearance]
Cycle of the Werewolf [complete text]
Silver Bullet [complete text of screenplay]
Given a choice between *Cycle of the Werewolf* and this book, King fans would be wise to choose this one, for two reasons: First, it contains a new foreword by King, which gives a detailed history of the making of this project, from calendar to book to film; and, second, it contains King's original screenplay for the film version.

Visually enhanced by Berni Wrightson's art and stills from *Silver Bullet*, this same-titled book is a welcome enhancement of the original book.

Silver Bullet (film), 1985

Director Daniel Attias's first effort, this film is a run-of-the-mill adaptation of a short King novel set in Tarker's Mill, Maine, afflicted by a werewolf that haunts the town.

The problem in filming a werewolf movie is that, unless the werewolf is believable and scary, as in Jack Nicholson's portrayal in *Wolf*, the result can be laughable. Werewolves—like mummies, vampires, zombies, Frankenstein monsters, and other creatures of the night—are integral to this film, but they fail to convince us to suspend our disbelief.

The standout performance is from the child actress Megan Follows in her role as Jane Coslaw. Gary Busey as Uncle Red and Corey Haim as Marty Coslaw turn in credible performances, but they can't carry the movie by themselves.

The result: yet another average King film—not as bad as *Children of the Corn*, but nowhere near the first rank of films like *Carrie* or *The Shawshank Redemption*.

Simonson, Walter

The artist who collaborated on a 21-page comic book adaptation of "The Lawnmower Man" with King for *Bizarre Adventures*.

Six Stories

Trade paperback, 1997, 197 pages, Philtrum Press, $80.00
Dedication: None
Contents
Lunch at the Gotham Café
L.T.'s Theory of Pets
Luckey Quarter
Autopsy Room Four
Blind Willie
The Man in the Black Suit
Originally *Six Stories* was to include "Everything's Eventual," but it was cut because of its length and was subsequently published in *The Magazine of Fantasy and Science Fiction*. The six stories in the collection are from various publications.

It was published in a minuscule print run of 1,200 copies, of which copies 1–900 were offered for sale, limit one per customer, and 200 were retained by the press for private distribution. They were numbered and signed by King. The planned advertising in specialty publications never materialized, since the need for it was eliminated by the news spreading on the Internet, in King discussion groups and in the SKEMERs group, and from two postcard mailings from *Phantasmagoria* and *The Red Letter*.

Designed by Michael Alpert, the book is as beautiful a trade paperback as you could want; however, King collectors would have gladly paid more if the book had been issued in hardback, to ensure its durability.

"The Man in the Black Suit" is a standout story

that was originally published in the *New Yorker* magazine and was reprinted in *Prize Stories 1996: The O. Henry Awards.* A quintessential King story, it contains the best of his fictional trademarks: the Maine milieu, a family relationship, and the intrusion of the devil at an unexpected moment.

King fans who missed out on this limited edition will see the stories eventually. At a Q&A session after a talk at Princeton University in April 1997, King said that the stories would eventually appear in a trade edition.

As for the lucky ones who got a copy of this edition, its value is now $400 . . . and climbing.

Skeleton Crew

Hardback, 1985, 512 pages, Putnam, $18.95
Dedication: "This book is for Arthur and Joyce Greene"
Contents
Introduction
The Mist
Here There Be Tygers
The Monkey
Cain Rose Up
Mrs. Todd's Shortcut
The Jaunt
The Wedding Gig
Paranoid: A Chant
The Raft
Word Processor of the Gods
The Man Who Would Not Shake Hands
Beachworld
The Reaper's Image
Nona
For Owen
Survivor Type
Uncle Otto's Truck
Morning Deliveries (Milkman #1)
Big Wheels: A Tale of the Laundry Game (Milkman #2)
Gramma
The Ballad of the Flexible Bullet
The Reach
Notes

Although *Night Shift* is a memorable collection, this second collection is by far more ambitious, showing King's range of talents in a way that *Night Shift* does not. From "The Mist" to "The Reach"— the former a quintessential King story, the latter an indisputable high-water mark for King—this is a first-rate collection. It brings together short and long works of fiction and showcases little-seen works that appeared in magazines, anthologies, or specialty publications—the kinds of places that King's mainstream reader would likely have missed.

A mature collection that justifiably made the best-seller list, this big book is a good place for any budding King fan to start, since its literary range literally has something for everyone.

The edition of choice is the 1985 Scream Press edition—a nightmarish project for publisher Jeff Conner, who didn't know what he had gotten into when he signed on to produce the signed, limited edition.

Jeff Conner, on his Scream Press edition:

It was a King-sized headache because I was unprepared for the intense political nature that a project like that quickly takes on. My intent was to simply make the best book I could, and really show the collectors that they hadn't been getting as much bang for the buck as they should have in the past. On the first point I think I pretty much succeeded, and on the latter I succeeded myself into near bankruptcy. (My business went down over 45 percent the year it came out, thanks to my own stupidity in underpricing the book, creating a money drain that I'm just now recovering from. I won't make this mistake with our Anne Rice project.) . . . I feel the finished book speaks for itself and we received many letters saying that the two-year wait was well worth it. I think that King could and should do more special projects of his new novels and collections, and that they do not necessarily have to all be signed in order to qualify as a limited edition. The great thing about being able to sell out a high-priced edition is that it gives one unusual manufacturing and design capabilities, ones that normal editions' budgets can never touch. Specialty publishers who simply copy the trade edition and slap on a signature sheet are ripping off King's fans and

I'm a SKEMER and I DON'T have to explain myself!

Logo for the SKEMERs (Stephen King Electronic Mailers) group.

King himself; for a writer of his stature he has been incredibly ill-served by the specialty press in this regard. He could easily have really cool editions of his work, with reasonable prices and enough copies for all who cared, and still not really compete with his New York publishers. This could really raise the level of the small press field and help educate his audience as to just what fine-edition publishing is all about. With the current explosion of new presses starting up, I do not see a corresponding increase in quality, just higher prices and more questionable "special" editions; none of which helps the field, the fans or the writers.

It appears that the King project was Conner's *Titanic:* It sank his small press. Unfortunately, the Rice project sank as well, although Conner tried to keep it afloat by advertising the book and taking subscriptions at $125 a copy. (Unfortunately, subscribers—myself included—saw neither book nor refund, and the preferred textual edition of Rice's classic vampire novel will likely never see print.)

The original plan was to issue an unexpurgated edition of *Interview with the Vampire*, with illustrations by Jeffrey Jones. It would have been a dream book project and, if published, could have saved Scream Press, but Conner never published, angering those who ordered (and paid) in advance, and the ambitious but underfunded small press quietly folded.

Too bad Conner didn't have a financial angel to finance his dreams, because he clearly knew how to put together a nice-looking book for the money, as *Skeleton Crew* clearly showed.

Michael Collings: "Taken as a whole, *Skeleton Crew* is well worth waiting for, and well worth the price for anyone interested in King. The author's apparatus surrounding the stories, coupled with the two poems, suggest even further King's interests and abilities. As an anthology, *Skeleton Crew* seems more even in quality than *Night Shift*, verbally less excessive than portions of *Different Seasons*. Strongly recommended." (*Fantasy Review*, June 1985.)

SKEMERs

Internet-based King discussion group. Abbreviation for: Stephen King Electronic Mailers. *See also* REIN, MICHELLE.

Skin

An acronym for "Stephen King Information Network," this informal, letter-size newsletter by Lori Zuccaro was a true fan's publication, done for fun but clearly not for profit.

It originally began as an on-line venture, then grew into a printed newsletter. Its first print issue was published on May 1994, and titled *Skin 1.1.* Wrote Zuccaro: "Skin . . . began in April 1994 on a computer on-line system called America Online. One night I sat down and typed a message on one of the bulletin boards dedicated to King. I asked for people to e-mail me regarding any news or comments they have regarding King. I then promised to summarize the responses on a monthly basis. That was the beginning of, what I didn't know at the time, a King newsletter."

Skin continued

In time, *Skin* folded due to the increasing demands it placed on its editor-publisher, who needed time to devote to personal and professional matters.

"Slade" (uncollected)

A hilarious send-up of the Western genre, published in eight installments in *The Maine Campus* from June 11 to August 6, 1970. Slade is a gunslinger in the grand tradition of Robert E. Howard's Breckinridge Elkins stories.

A trial cut on *The Gunslinger*, "Slade" is a rare peek at a little-known side of King: his talent for humorous fiction.

The story begins, "It was almost dark when Slade rode into Dead Steer Springs. He was tall in the saddle, a grim-faced man dressed all in black. Even the handles of his two sinister .45s, which rode low on his hips, were black."

Riding a black stallion named Stokeley, Slade is in mourning for Miss Polly Peachtree of Paduka, who he believes to be his True Love, "who passed tragically from this vale of tears when a flaming Montgolfier balloon crashed into the Peachtree barn while Polly was milking the cows."

But Slade doesn't have time to wallow in self-misery; he becomes embroiled in a land dispute between the evil Sam Columbine, whose henchman is Hunchback Fred Agnew, and the lovely Sandra Dawson.

Dawson is kidnapped by Columbine, as Slade goes off in hot pursuit. And, in the best traditions of the West, he duels Columbine . . . but it's a Pyrrhic victory for Slade: Sandra Dawson is in fact Polly Peachtree, suffering from amnesia, and *her* true love is not Slade . . . but Columbine!

Disgusted, Slade perforates them both and rides off into the sunset on his trusty steed.

Though this would be a welcome, and different, addition to any King collection, it will never be issued because King considers it juvenilia and has steadfastly refused all attempts to bring it back into print, to the point of having his lawyer write a litigious letter when *The Maine Campus* considered reprinting it, along with King's nonfiction columns, in a book for fund-raising purposes.

"Sleazy Orono, Maine, apartment"

King's assessment of his first living quarters after college. It was here that he began writing the first few pages of "The Gunslinger," which Chris Chesley read and raved about.

Sleepwalkers (film), 1992

Sleepwalkers marks the first time King wrote an original script for a stand-alone feature-length film. Unfortunately, it's pretty standard summer fare for a horror film—hardly "the scariest Stephen King film ever made! Sexy, sleek and horrifyingly scary," as one critic enthused.

The sleepwalkers, the last of a dying breed, are virtually immortal, shape changers that are not only psychic vampires but literal ones: By drinking the blood of young virgin girls, they absorb the purity, the virtue of the girls, and are thus nourished with the girls' life force.

Charles Brady, who appears to be a young, handsome high-schooler, is really nothing of the sort. In fact, he's always on the prowl for virgin girls, not so much for himself as for his mother.

Despite their considerable powers, the sleepwalkers fear only cats, their ancestral enemies.

The Brady duo—not enough left of the family to call them a bunch—are obviously not human, but manage to integrate themselves into the small, local communities until a rash of killings draws attention to them.

Now in Travis, Indiana, the two sleepwalkers are again on the prowl. This time, Charles wins the attention of a beautiful young girl, Tanya, who successfully fights him off after he shape-shifts from human to monster during a seduction scene. She runs, calls the police, and the local sheriff shows up, but it's his cat, Clovis, that recognizes its old nemesis and attacks, severely damaging Charles.

Mother then goes off to abduct Tanya, to rejuvenate her sickly son, as cats congregate around their house.

In typical King fashion—viz. *The Shining* and *Firestarter* and *Carrie*—there's a conflagration, and the Brady house is engulfed by flames that consume the house and its hellish inhabitants as well.

The idea for this story came to King after his son, Joseph, became enamored with the popcorn girl at the local cinema, the kind of all-American beauty that King portrays in this film.

Susan Wloszczyna (*USA Today*, 1992): "One can understand why horror honcho Stephen King was tired of screenwriting hacks turning his mega-selling stories into multiplex sludge. After all, as *Sleepwalkers* amply demonstrates, ol' Cujo Breath [King] can come up with his own lousy script, thank you."

Small presses, fantasy field

Small presses in the fantasy field that have published King's limited editions are:

Donald M. Grant, Publisher, Inc.
Land of Enchantment
Lord John Press
Mark V. Ziesling
Phantasia Press
Philtrum Press
Scream Press

"Sneakers"

(collected in *Nightmares & Dreamscapes*)

Originally published in *Night Visions 5*, this story shows that King has no fear of exploring the ultimate fictional taboo: a haunted *toilet stall*.

John Tell notices a pair of dirty old white sneakers under a toilet stall; each time he goes into the bathroom, he notices the sneakers are still there, festooned with dead insects (mostly flies). He thinks he's going nuts, but after getting the facts from his coworkers who confirm the killing of a drug-delivery boy, he realizes it's the ghost of that boy, and finally steps back in the bathroom, opens the stall, and confronts the ghost.

Douglas E. Winter acknowledges that he may possibly be responsible for putting the idea into King's head. In his introduction to *Night Visions 5*, Winter, who at the time was editing *Prime Evil*, said that there was a "dearth of original stories about haunted houses," to which King promptly responded, "Oh, yeah? What about a haunted *shit*house?"

Only King could have pulled this one off.

"Sometimes They Come Back"

(collected in *Night Shift*)

Originally published in *Cavalier* (March 1974). Jim Norman, a teacher, is haunted by nightmares caused by the murder of his brother 16 years ago by three teenage JD's. But the nightmare turns real when three of his students die, only to be replaced by apparitions of the three teenage boys from his past, who have come to haunt him. After they kill his wife, Jim must finally reconcile himself with the past. He calls on his dead brother's spirit to help him achieve closure.

Sometimes They Come Back (film), 1991

A made-for-TV movie, this Dino De Laurentiis film was made after the closing of De Laurentiis's Wilmington, North Carolina, studio and was intended to air principally in theaters overseas.

Based on the short story of the same name in *Night Shift*, this is standard fare for King adaptations: competent but not inspiring.

The plot: Jim Norman returns to his home town of Stratford, Connecticut, where he takes a teaching position, but he's haunted by his past: his 11-year-old brother, Wayne, was murdered by three teenagers in a railroad tunnel. Jim ran away, and the trio was killed by an oncoming train.

Now they reappear as new students in his class, replacing his favorite students, who have been killed under mysterious circumstances. The new students are the ghosts of the three boys killed years ago, and they want revenge—closure for their deaths.

In a final confrontation in an abandoned railroad tunnel, Jim Norman confronts the ghosts. This time, he doesn't run but fights, and is assisted by the spirit of his dead brother.

This time, the ghosts are put to rest; they are run over again—by a ghost train.

Note: This is the bare-bones plot of *It*, which would explore the theme of closure, reconciling with the past to put it behind oneself forever.

Matt Rousch (*USA Today*): "The concept is a knockout variation on an old King theme: the decent man returning to his hometown, dredging up

Sometimes They Come Back (film) *continued*
a haunted past of childhood trauma lying in wait to resurface at the worst possible times. . . . Ultimately, *Sometimes They Come Back* chokes on its hokeyness. But in its own modest way, it tells a fairly good campfire story."

Sometimes They Come Back . . . Again
(film), 1996

Let's see: In the first version, Jim Norman returns home and must exorcise the ghosts from his past—three teenage boys who, as ghosts, come into his life to haunt him, to force him to confront their encounter from the past that cost them their lives and the life of Norman's brother.

In this sequel, Jon Porter returns home to the funeral of his mother, but he's haunted from the past: Malevolent demons that killed his sister have come into his life again, this time to claim the body and soul of his daughter.

Sometimes . . . they shouldn't come back.

Sonderegger, Shirley

King's main secretary from November 1983 to about 1997.

Imagine the kind of response King would have gotten if he had placed a classified ad in the "wanted" section of his hometown newspaper, stating: "Secretary wanted for world's best-selling author. Good pay, good benefits. Phone for an interview."

He would have been swamped!

As with a lot of jobs, it's not who you know but who knows *you*. In this case, Stephanie Leonard knew Sonderegger, who was then working at a local bank.

The temporary job turned permanent, and for many years Sonderegger was King's majordomo.

Asked what it took to be King's secretary, Sonderegger replied: "Emotional fortitude and a sense of the ridiculous!" (*The Shape Under the Sheet.*)

Sonderegger, who had a cameo appearance in *Creepshow 2*, coshared the book dedication for *The Dark Half.*

Sonderegger, on what King is reading, when asked by the media: "He's not reading. He's busy writing what everybody else is reading." (Quoted by Rick Levasseur, *BDN*, Oct. 24, 1986.)

"Sorry, Right Number"
(collected in *Nightmares & Dreamscapes*)

Instead of writing a story based on the teleplay, King publishes the teleplay itself in this collection, which makes for an interesting reading experience: mostly dialogue with minimal stage directions, just enough to orient the reader.

Katie Weiderman's husband is a horror novelist who will have a fatal heart attack. While on the phone with her sister, she picks up the other line and, hearing a woman's distraught voice at the other end, figures it must be someone in the family; the voice, after all, is so very familiar, though she can't put her finger on it.

In short order she calls everyone in her family, but none of them made that frantic call—not even her sister Dawn, whose phone is off the hook, precipitating a quick trip in the family car to check up on her. But she's fine, too. Strange . . . She figured it must have been a wrong number . . .

Katie goes to bed, and early in the morning discovers her husband's side of the bed is empty. Concerned, she goes to his study, where her worst fears are realized: He's dead of a heart attack.

It's now five years later. She has remarried, and on a late-night TV program her late husband's movie, *Ghost Kiss*, is on. It brings back painful memories, and her grief triggers "a kind of telephonic time travel": She realizes that the distraught but eerily familiar voice she had heard years ago was in fact her own voice, calling from the future to warn her of her first husband's imminent heart attack.

It wasn't a wrong number, after all; in fact, it was the *right* number . . . but Katie never realized it until it was too late. Note: Because you hear your own voice through bone conduction, it sounds different when you hear it from another source, like a recording, so Katie understandably had difficulty in recognizing her own voice.

Sorry, Right Number (film), 1987

A second offering for *Tales from the Darkside*, this original teleplay is a time-travel story. See previous entry.

Special Collections

This room in the Fogler Library at UMO houses, among other rarities, the bulk of King's early work in manuscript form, galleys, and foundry proofs.

In the summer of 1974, Eric Flower, then the head of Special Collections, suggested to King that the *Carrie* manuscript be deposited in the collection. In November of 1975, when Flower followed up and asked if King had collected the materials as promised, he subsequently gathered together the early work and deposited it.

The holdings are considerable, especially for King scholars who want to look at the early formative years, but according to one King scholar, permission to access the King material now requires writing a letter to King, a new policy instituted by King's office that went into effect in early 1998. The scholar expressed the opinion that if access to the collection is controlled by King and not the university, then it should be housed in a private building funded by King and not public funds from the university.

To date, the collection includes materials relating to *Carrie*, *The Stand*, *Night Shift*, *The Dead Zone*, *The Shining*, *Jerusalem's Lot*, manuscripts of short stories and unpublished essays, unpublished novels (*Blaze*, *Sword in the Darkness*), the first draft of *'Salem's Lot* (titled *Second Coming*), *Firestarter*, *Cujo*, *Pet Sematary*, *Christine*, *Skeleton Crew*, *The Talisman*, and juvenilia (*The Aftermath*).

Specialty dealers on Grant's policy on the limited edition of *The Talisman*

More than anything else, the law of supply and demand forced Donald M. Grant to not sell the limited edition of *The Talisman* to specialty booksellers.

Booksellers in the fantasy field responded with an open letter sent to the media, clarifying their position that they should have had the opportunity to buy the book at a discount, citing that other publishers who have issued limited editions of King books did offer discounts, though often at a short discount of 20 percent instead of the normal 40 percent that the limited should have been priced at so it could be resold to dealers at a profit; that it prevents the dealers from selling the book to their key customers, undermining the dealer-customer relationship; that the dealers supported Grant on his other book projects, some of which were not fast sellers, and that this relationship was no longer reciprocal; and that the matter of investor speculator was a reflection of the marketplace, not the greed of dealers.

The letter was signed by the major book dealers in the field: Martin Last, Richard Spelman, Chuck Miller, Robert Weinberg, Phyllis Weinberg, and L. W. Currey.

Spielberg, Steven

Noted film director for whom Universal Pictures, in the mid-eighties, was interested in buying rights to *The Talisman* as a Spielberg project. To date the project has not materialized.

Spignesi, Stephen J.

Nonfiction writer specializing in popular culture.

Like Ray Bradbury, Spignesi doesn't like to fly—or to travel far from his home office in New Haven, Connecticut, where he produces a torrent of words.

A graduate of the University of New Haven, Spignesi made a name for himself as a pop culture chronicler with the publication of *Mayberry, My Hometown* (1987, Pierian Press), an encyclopedia of *The Andy Griffith Show*, containing an A-to-Z encyclopedic listing (4,000 entries) of the people, places, and things related to the show, supplemented by interviews, essays, and photos. It was produced with the cooperation and consent of Viacom, which owns the rights to the show, and the show's principal actors.

Spignesi followed up *Mayberry, My Hometown* with *The Shape Under the Sheet: The Complete King Encyclopedia*, which proved to be the biggest

—in size and weight—book on King yet. It was published in 1991 by Popular Culture, Ink, in an $80 trade hardback edition, 780 pages, 8.75 by 11.25 inches. This King-sized tome is for the King addict only.

This book is actually two books in one: principally a concordance to the fiction, with 18,000 entries, and a lot of companion-style material (profiles, interviews, articles) and photographs.

No matter how you look at it, the book is impressive: 750,000 words, weighing in at several pounds!

That book was the last one about him to be authorized by King, who as a matter of policy now refuses to participate in such projects.

Spignesi has since published two more books about King, both mass-market paperbacks from NAL/Signet. *The Stephen King Quiz Book* in 1990 and *The Second Stephen King Quiz Book* in 1991 are excellent appetizers to his encyclopedia, *The Shape Under the Sheet*, the main dish.

For those with a literary appetite for rare desserts, Spignesi's extensive (and exhaustive) look at the little-seen King material is the full treatment. A trade hardback by Spignesi from Citadel Press, to be published in the fall of 1998, *The Lost Work of King: A Guide to Unpublished Manuscripts, Story Fragments, Alternative Versions, and Oddities* is a must-read for die-hard King fans.

Springer Cabins

After graduating from college, King lived near the Stillwater River in one of these cabins near UMO.

Springsteen, Bruce

A favorite rock and roll musician of King's.

When Springsteen released a five-record set, *Bruce Springsteen & the E Street Band Live/1975–85*, King was photographed in line at a Boston record store, along with other fans, awaiting entry in order to purchase the set. Spotted in line, King commented: "I got some other stuff to do, but this is the most important piece of business, man."

My favorite King-Springsteen story: The two were at a restaurant when a young girl approached their table. Springsteen, assuming she wanted his autograph, unlimbered his pen as she said, "You're Stephen King! I've read all your books!" (The Boss may rule on the stage, but Stephen is the boss—and still the king!—of the bookstores and best-seller lists, bet your fur!)

Springsteen made an unannounced appearance on stage and played with the Rock Bottom Remainders.

Spruce, Christopher

King's brother-in-law, Chris Spruce, wore two hats simultaneously: manager of WZON and editor-publisher of *Castle Rock*. (He is currently station manager for King's WZON and WKIT, a rock station.)

At the WZON radio station, editor/publisher Chris Spruce takes a rare break and reads an issue of *Castle Rock*.

Sputnik I

Man-made satellite, 184 pounds, 22 inches in diameter, launched into space by the Russians.

On October 4, 1957, when King was ten years old, he realized that the Americans weren't going to be the first in space, after all. Mars may be heaven in Bradbury's fictional world, but in the real world, the skies were owned by the commies!

In "King's Garbage Truck," a free-wheeling opinion column King wrote for his college newspaper, he looked back on that moment of surprise: "Americans were always first—we had been with the telephone, the electric light, the airplane—surely the Russians, who played dirty, could not have beaten us into space! It was degrading, it was frightening . . . it was downright embarrassing."

Note: This account varies considerably from the more dramatic story King tells in *Danse Macabre*, in which he's at a theater, watching *Earth Versus the Flying Saucers*, and the houselights are brought up and the theater's manager takes center stage and announces that the Russians had just launched Sputnik, the first man-made satellite.

The Stand

Hardback, 1978, 823 pages, Doubleday, $12.95
Dedication: "For my wife Tabitha: This dark chest of wonders."
Contents
Book 1. Captain Trips, June 16–July 4, 1985
Book 2. On the Border, July 5–September 6, 1985
Book 3. The Stand, September 7, 1985–January 10, 1986
Inspiration: *The Lord of the Rings*, by J. R. R. Tolkien; *Earth Abides*, by George Stewart; "Night Surf," short story by King in *Night Shift*; a chemical-biological spill in Utah reported on the radio; and an electronic evangelist in Colorado preaching about a generational plague

The Stand was not the novel King had originally written, which was 250,000 words longer. But under edict from Doubleday, King reluctantly made cuts, allowing the firm to decrease the production costs and thereby lower the cover price.

The Stand is in the first rank of King's novels, a novel with scope that postulates a classic good vs. evil battle.

After Captain Trips, a flulike virus against which there is no defense, takes its deadly toll on humanity, the survivors form two camps: the good folk side with Mother Abigail; the bad folk side with Randall Flagg, one of King's greatest fictional creations.

After rallying their forces, the two sides do battle in Las Vegas, the stronghold of Flagg and his minions.

The Stand: The Complete and Uncut Edition

Hardback, 1990, 1,153 pages, Doubleday, $24.95
Dedication: "For Tabby, this dark chest of wonders."
Contents
A Preface in Two Parts
The Circle Opens [78 numbered chapters]
The Circle Closes
According to Peter Schneider, only 200 advance reader's copies were printed, of which 20 went to King, 5 to his agent, 125 to the publicity department, and 1 to each sales rep; the balance went for miscellaneous distribution. The trade edition, which shipped on April 23, 1990, had a first print run of 400,000 copies.

Differences between the previously published version and this one are as follows:

♦ 150,000 words (500 pages) were reinstated by King.
♦ The book's setting was updated from 1980 to 1990.
♦ A new beginning has been added.
♦ A new ending has been added.
♦ New characters appear; previous characterizations are deepened.
♦ A dozen pen-and-ink illustrations by Berni Wrightson were done especially for this edition, paid for by King, not the publisher.
♦ King wrote a two-part preface especially for this edition.

Pat Labrutto, Doubleday editor: "It is very much more apparent that he is doing *The Book of*

Revelations here . . . and there is one scene that offends *me!* It's been years since I've been offended." (*Castle Rock.*)

King's longest and most ambitious novel to date, this is *the* fan favorite, though King has said repeatedly that it's not his favorite; *The Dead Zone* and *'Salem's Lot* make up that short list. A richly complex novel, an American *Lord of the Rings*, this quest story is accessible in a way that *The Dark Tower* is not; that is to say, *The Stand* is more in keeping with what King fans like and expect.

No simple synopsis can do justice to this engaging, highly entertaining, and moral fable about good vs. evil that manifests so many of King's strengths as a writer: his ability to sustain a long story; his ability to write convincing characters, from the major ones like Mother Abigail and Randall Flagg to the minor ones, each distinctively drawn and fully realized; his ability to paint a large canvas, detailed in every way; and most of all, his ability to immerse the readers in the story—and engage in holding their attention for 1,153 pages.

King has always maintained that a good horror novel draws its strength from its moral stance and that without that foundation it is simply shock fiction relying on the print equivalent of special effects: blood and gore. In *The Stand*, morality is at its heart: After a plague destroys most of the world's population, survivors in the U.S. must start over, rebuilding society, choosing between the forces of good, embodied by Mother Abigail, and the forces of evil, embodied by King's quintessential villain, Randall Flagg.

The persistent virus, nicknamed Captain Trips (after the late Grateful Dead band member, Jerry Garcia), is as idiosyncratic as it is deadly: Why have these people escaped its fatal effects? What makes them immune from its toxicity?

In "The Mist," the government's tampering with the forces of nature produces a plague of monsters that runs unchecked. *The Stand* amplifies on that theme: A biological or chemical bug escapes from a biochemical lab and runs its deadly course, starting with the doomed (and damned) Campion family, who manage to escape from the secret facility, carrying with them the virus that, domino like, will ripple through the population in a modern-day Black Death.

In a new two-part preface written especially for this book, King patiently explains that he has not rewritten the story but has expanded it, a key concern, since the core story so cherished by King's fans is best left untouched. But *more* of the *same* story is another matter: King fans now have their favorite book with the preferred text, just as King originally conceived it, instead of a truncated version that Doubleday publisher Sam Vaughan felt was justified because the cost savings would help sales. (Imagine how Tolkien would have felt if his publishers had said, "Well, J.R.R., the book's too long! There are too many words! Tell you what: Go through and cut 15 percent out, and we'll save enough to cut the price a buck or two—the marketing guys know what the market will bear.") When telling an epic story, the author needs all the room he can get, without the publisher second-guessing what's best in the name of economy.

The Stand (film), 1994

One of the best-loved literary epics, *The Lord of the Rings*, is generally considered to be unfilmable. That book, its advocates say, is best left unfilmed. The mind's eye, they contend, is the only way to "see" the movie—a truth borne out from seeing lackluster adaptations, including an ambitious failure, Ralph Bakshi's version. To my mind, Tim Kirk's interpretation of Middle Earth is the closest to how I envision Middle Earth, and until a full-length film is done by him (or artists working under his direction), I can't imagine even *wanting* to see anyone else tackle the classic Tolkien trilogy.

Similarly, *The Stand*—heavily influenced by *The Lord of the Rings*—was considered to be unfilmable. In fact, because it's *the* fan favorite among King's books, his fans have beseeched him, in print, over the years, *not* to allow it to be filmed, for fear that their favorite book will be poorly adapted.

Over the years talk inevitably centered around producing *The Stand* as a movie, but among other difficulties one proved insurmountable: The scope of the novel, one of King's longest, made it impossible to come up with a shootable script, though King gave it his best shot.

In the end, film plans were shelved, but the idea still appealed, and in due time the decision was made to produce it not as a feature-length film but as a television miniseries.

On hearing the news, King's fans took a stand for or against. Even reassurances that King was involved did little to assuage the concerns of the doomsayers, who pointed to *Maximum Overdrive* and other King-scripted films as evidence that the

decision would be a mistake of titanic proportions. The feelings of most of King's fans, however, fell between nervous expectation and outright happiness.

As befitted the scope of the book, the miniseries was ambitious in scale. With the largest number of actors ever to appear in a King film, and the largest number of on-location shots, *The Stand* was told in four parts: The Plague, The Dreams, The Betrayal, and The Stand. *The Stand* ran six hours on videotape, and it met, even exceeded, the fans' expectations.

Adapted for television by King, who also made cameo appearances, *The Stand* proved to be a masterful adaptation of the epic tale.

One minor flaw: In the book as well as in the movie, the Hand of God literally makes an appearance. To my taste, a deus ex machina is an authorial cop-out. King, who by his own admission is an intuitive writer, does not outline his novels as Clive Barker does. The disadvantage in not outlining is that the payoff, the ending, may suffer if not sufficiently foreshadowed, a problem that plagued some of King's other book endings, in which towns simply burned up.

I would have preferred a stronger, more believable ending, but you get what you get, and with *The Stand*, we got, as the *Hollywood Reporter* termed it, "king-size chills and thrills."

It's a first-class ride, in King's amusement park of hellish delights.

Mass market paperback tie-in edition of *The Stand*, published prior to the release of the ABC-TV miniseries. (Actors Gary Sinese and Molly Ringwald are on the cover.)

Stand by Me (film), 1986

To be fair to the directors who have tackled the formidable challenge of adapting King to the screen, the bottom line is that the film—regardless of its budget, its brand-name actors, and its marketing staff—must rely heavily on the source material: the better the story, the greater the likelihood for success in adapting the work itself.

This explains why the middle-ground of King's film adaptations is occupied by what I'd term "video" movies: not necessarily worth the cost of a movie ticket, but okay for a video rental, preferably on a night when they're running specials, like a two-for-one.

Prior to *Stand by Me*, among the feature-length films only *Carrie* and *The Dead Zone* were standouts. The rest—*Creepshow, Cujo, Children of the Corn, Firestarter, Silver Bullet,* and *Cat's Eye*—were enough, one after the other, to cause film critics to joke about the "Stephen King movie of the month," since he was clearly overexposed in theaters, and everyone was getting weary of seeing King's name in connection with yet another overhyped, sometimes big-budget film that failed to draw critical acclaim and, in some cases, the crowds that were thought to be guaranteed by attaching King's name to the project.

On the surface, *Stand by Me*—based on a novella, "The Body," from *Different Seasons*—seems to be an unlikely candidate for residing in the first rank of King films. For one thing, the title suggests the supernatural, but there's nothing of that sort in this film, so the title had to be changed. For another, the story itself—a quiet, elegiac piece about a rite of passage for four boys, a story that King admits is the most autobiographical among his works—is clearly not the kind of story associated with him. Finally, the film was released in September, well after the summer crowds—the teenagers—headed back to school.

Mindful of the possible negative fallout of attaching King's name to the project in a visible manner, distributors quietly released *Stand by Me* to a handful of theaters in the bigger cities, with King's name buried in the credits. The film was deliberately not titled *Stephen King's Stand by Me.*

Stand by Me turned out to be a sleeper, and moviegoers stood by the film, giving it invaluable word-of-mouth fueled by positive reviews. When the film opened in over 700 theaters nationwide, it earned $46 million in domestic gross before year's end.

Stand by Me, directed by Rob Reiner, proved to be a critical and financial success, in stark contrast to the midlist King movies that sprocketed through the summer theaters.

After the drubbing King had gotten earlier in the year for his other films, he probably let out a big sigh of relief as this film made its way into the hearts of millions of moviegoers, many of whom had never read a King novel and would not be caught dead watching one of his movies, because they don't "like that scary stuff."

Once it was clear that the film had cleared the hurdles, and once the moviegoers got over their shock that this was a King film—in fact, an ur–Stephen King story—the word slowly spread: Go see this film! And by the way, it's by Stephen King!

A masterful film, it hits all the notes on the mark: unblemished, perfectly cast, perfectly scored, and beautifully filmed. This one's a keeper, a film to be watched again and again as King takes us back to his teenage years, as we experience our own past and go into the future—a rite of passage as much for us as it is for the four boys from Castle Rock who, in the fifties, make a trek to see a dead body. In the process, they go from an age of innocence to a world of experience.

The cast deserves special commendation: Wil Wheaton as Gordie Lachance, Richard Dreyfuss as the adult Gordie Lachance, River Phoenix as Chris Chambers, modeled in part on King's childhood friend Chris Chesley, Corey Feldman as Teddy Duchamp, Jerry O'Connell as Vern Tessio, and Kiefer Sutherland as Ace Merrill.

About the film and its fidelity to the story, King told the interviewer Bill Warren of *Fangoria*: "I think they like the voice. The voice can't be filmed, but at the same time, it can be. Rob Reiner's proved that twice, particularly with *Stand by Me*. You would freak—or maybe you wouldn't—if you knew how many people walk up to me on the street and say, 'Steve, I love your movies.' These people have no idea I do anything *but* movies, so for every person who read 'The Body,' probably fifteen people saw *Stand by Me*. I still get royalty checks on that film, big ones! The voice is there, but the only people who are really tapping into the voice are people who read, and they're a small part of the overall population."

SK: "There's a lot of stuff in 'The Body' that's just simply history that's been tarted up a little bit." (*Writers Dreaming*, ed. Naomi Epel.)

S Is for the Stanley Hotel

Some of the most beautiful
resort hotels in the world
are located in Colorado, but
the hotel in these pages
is based on none of them.
The Overlook and the people
associated with it
exist wholly within the author's imagination.

—*The Shining*

(*Redrum, redrum . . .*)

King's fictional hotel, the Overlook, is set high in the mountains of Colorado, not unlike the Stanley Hotel in Estes Park, Colorado.

Like the Overlook, the Stanley Hotel has a colorful past and has a connection to King: Not only was the King remake of *The Shining* filmed at the Stanley Hotel, but the hotel now capitalizes on the connection.

In the wake of its publicity created by the King remake, the Stanley Hotel underwent a $4 million renovation by Clarus Public Relations, Inc. The company, based in Annapolis, Maryland, purchased the Stanley in 1995 and completely renovated the guest rooms, made structural improvements, and added modern convention facilities and a museum. According to General Manager Ron Vlasic: "we will again make the Stanley one of the finest hotels in the West while also serving as a proud historic gateway to Rocky Mountain National Park."

(*Redrum, redrum . . .*)

But what of the Stanley's past? A brief history from the packet of information it provides to guests:

The grand opening of the Stanley Hotel took place in 1909. Construction had begun in 1906 under the direction of the owner, F. O. Stanley, one of the truly fascinating figures in American history.

Freelan O. Stanley and his brother, Francis E. Stanley, were identical twins. Raised in Newton, Massachusetts, they were industrialists and creative inventors who built their first Stanley Steamer automobile in 1897. F. O. Stanley was also an architectural designer, teacher, and student of political science. He and his brother patented a Dry Plate machine in 1886 and made photographic plates. In 1904, he sold his patents to George Eastman of Eastman Kodak, reportedly for $565,000.

In 1903, upon the recommendations of his doctors, F. O. Stanley moved to Colorado. He settled in Denver, but soon explored the countryside. He fell in love with Estes Park, a town nestled in an alpine mountain bowl at 7,500 feet, the Colorado Rockies towering around it. The site offered pleasant mountain weather, exceptional recreational opportunities and spectacular vistas. F. O. Stanley saw the potential for a luxury resort hotel situated in this magnificent environment.

F. O. Stanley and a partner purchased 6,400 acres in 1905 from an Irish lord, the Earl of Dunraven. The present site of the Stanley was included in this transaction. With an initial investment of $500,000 he designed and began construction of the hotel in 1906. Materials and supplies were transported 22 miles by horse teams up roads constructed for this project. Upon its opening in 1909, the Stanley was reported by the news media to rival anything of its size in the world. (Mr. Stanley also built a Concert Hall, stables and a replica 33-room hotel, the Manor House.)

Guests were transported to the Stanley in redesigned Stanley Steamer twelve-passenger "mountain wagons." This fleet of steam-driven vehicles would greet the guests as they descended from the train. (The Colorado and Southern Railroad brought them to Loveland; the Burlington deposited its passengers in Lyons.) They would then begin their slow ascent up the mountain roads through canyons, such as the Big Thompson, to the Hotel.

Guests were greeted in the vast and impressive lobby with its grand staircase. They were taken to their rooms in a mirrored, ornate brass elevator which was hydraulically run. Each guest room was color-coordinated to the then–red and yellow exterior of the Stanley—a color scheme patterned after European mountain resorts. Rooms were furnished with the finest furniture of the period, including four-poster and brass beds.

F. O. Stanley also built a nine-hole golf course on the hotel grounds to augment the 18-hole country club course (the first golf course and clubhouse built in Estes Park was completed in 1875 by the Earl of Dunraven).

There were various entertainments nightly for the guests—bowling, billiards, musicales, putting contests on the lobby carpeting, dinner-dances in the charming dining room, and evenings of musical and theatrical productions. A well-equipped livery stable catered to those with equestrian tastes, while those with "horseless carriages" were served in a complete automobile garage.

With Denver only 65 miles away, the hotel began to host such famous personages as the "Unsinkable" Molly Brown, John Philip Sousa, and Theodore Roosevelt, to name but a few. (In recent times, Stephen King stayed for some time at the hotel, drawing on its turn-of-the century ambience for his book, *The Shining*.)

In 1977, sixty-eight years after F. O. Stanley opened the doors of this "grand hotel" to the public, the state of Colorado unanimously nominated the Stanley to the National Register of Historic Places.

On May 26, 1977, the Stanley Hotel was entered into the National Register of Historic Places "in recognition of this property's significant contribution to the heritage of the state of Colorado."

Note: The hotel offers a special lodging package: "*The Shining:* Enjoy an evening at the hotel that inspired Stephen King to write *The Shining*. Deluxe accommodations for two feature a *Shining* keepsake, two bottles of *Shining* beer, dinner for two with two cocktails."

The Star Invaders (uncollected)

An early example of King's self-published juvenilia.

Published in June 1964 by Triad and Gaslight Books under the "AA Gaslight Book" imprint, this mimeographed 17-page "book" told in two parts totaling less than 3,000 words, owes much to the tenor of the times—the science fiction films of the fifties, with malevolent monsters from deep space coming to Earth to wreak havoc.

In Part I, Jerry Hiken, tortured by the Star Invaders, is forced to reveal the location of Jed Pierce, the man who invented the Counter Weapon. In Part II, the Star Invaders attack as Pierce defends the Earth, destroying alien ship after ship with the Counter Weapon, narrowly avoiding a catastrophic meltdown of the atomic-pile powered weapon.

Earth is no longer defenseless against the aliens!

Starkweather, Charles

A mass murderer who in the fifties haunted the Midwest and killed nine or ten people.

An ambivalent King collected a scrapbook about Starkweather, trying to divine the nature of true evil.

Starkweather may have been in part a model for George Stark in *The Dark Half*, and is the basis for the The Kid, a character in *The Stand*.

Starmont House

Founded by Ted Dikty, this now defunct small press issued several books about King, beginning with Douglas E. Winter's *The Reader's Guide to Stephen King*. Winter felt that an expanded version would be better suited for publication with a larger publisher, and took the revised version, *Stephen King: The Art of Darkness*, to NAL.

Dikty, who cited Winter's *Reader's Guide to Stephen King* as its best-selling title published by his firm to date, announced an ambitious program of 14 books about King, of which 10 were published:

Discovering Stephen King, edited by Darrell Schweitzer

Stephen King as Richard Bachman, by Michael R. Collings

The Shorter Works of Stephen King, by Michael R. Collings and David Engebretson

The Many Facets of Stephen King, by Michael R. Collings

The Films of Stephen King, by Michael R. Collings

The Stephen King Phenomenon, by Michael R. Collings

The Annotated Guide to Stephen King, by Michael R. Collings

The Unseen King, by Tyson Blue

The Moral Voyages of Stephen King, by Anthony Magistrale

The Shining *Reader*, edited by Anthony Magistrale

The following four were announced as "in production," but an understandably long delay ensued after Ted Dikty's death. His daughter took over the reins and ran the company, but she was unable to get these books completed, leaving them orphaned: *In the Darkness of Night: The Student's Guide to Stephen King*, by Tim Murphy; *The Stephen King Short Story Concordance*, by Chris Thomson; *Observations from the Terminator*, by Tyson Blue; and *King's America*, by Jonathan Davis (subsequently published by Bowling Green State University Popular Press in 1994).

Stationery

When King's office staff was working in his home on West Broadway, King used business stationery that showed a row of Victorian homes at the top of the sheet, with his street address in script underneath; no phone number.

Steele, Terry

A blacksmith who designed the wrought-iron fence that surrounds the King home in Bangor, Maine.

Terry Steele: "The commission took a year-and-a-half to finish—270 lineal feet of hand-forged fence, weighing 11,000 pounds, punctuated by two gates composed of spiders, webs, goat heads, and winged bats." The bat imagery, Steele told George Beahm in an interview, was inspired by Batman, the comic book character summoned by the bat symbol that flashed in the sky when activated by Commissioner Gordon.

Stephen King

Clothing store in London, with a fire-starting marketing device: a matchbook, in black with gold letters. Spooky! (*Castle Rock.*)

Stephen King: America's Best-Loved Boogeyman, by George Beahm

Published in 1998 by Andrews McMeel, this biography updates King's life and career through early 1998.

Stephen King,
by Amy and Marjorie Keyishian

Published by Chelsea House Publishers in 1996, this is a short biography for King's younger readers, with an introduction by Leeza Gibbons, of *Entertainment Tonight* fame.

Reprinting numerous photos that previously appeared in the 1989 edition of *The Stephen King Companion*, this book's selection of photos is a mixed bag: stock photos, stock studio stills from King movies, or previously published photos of King from various sources, for the most part.

Textually, there is very little new information, since the authors draw heavily on existing texts for quotes and facts.

Sporting what has to be the ugliest cover illustration for any book about King ever published, the book does an adequate if uninspiring job of providing an overview to very young, or new, King readers.

Contents

Introduction, "A Reflection of Ourselves," by
    Leeza Gibbons

The creature that stands eternally vigilant, looking in three directions, from its vantage point atop a corner of the wrought iron fence that surrounds the King residence in Bangor.

Cover to a biography by the Keyishians.

Stephen King, by Douglas E. Winter

This 128-page book was published by Starmont House in 1982 as number 16 in its "Starmont Reader's Guide" series (Roger C. Schlobin, series editor). This is a trial cut for Winter's *Stephen King: The Art of Darkness.*

Stephen King: Man and Artist,
by Carroll F. Terrell

This book, published by Northern Lights (in Orono, Maine), was written by a UMO college professor who taught King. Published in 1990, and revised for its reissue in 1991, it is a rarity among books about King: a look at SK's student years by someone in a position to have seen first-hand his growth as a writer during a formative period in his life.

Carroll F. Terrell's book is a fascinating discussion of King's fiction in classical terms and of the King canon; it is an insightful look at King as a writer and a college student from a unique perspective.

Michael Collings noted, "*Stephen King: Man and Artist* provides an invaluable next step in the critical transformation of our assumptions about King, elevating him from mere *shockmeister* to acknowledged voice of an age. Terrell is to be congratulated as much for his courage in accepting such a task and for the wealth of knowledge and perception he marshals in fulfilling it."

Stephen King: Master of Horror,
by Anne Saidman

Published in 1992 by Lerner Publications, this book has the distinction of being the only book on King so far written specifically for a juvenile audience. The book is short (53 pages) and heavy with photos, some of which appeared earlier in *The Stephen King Companion* (1989 edition).

This book is a breezy overview to King's life as a best-selling author, covered in six short chapters (it is not indexed, nor are quotations cited).

1. Reading and Writing
2. One After Another
3. Firestarter
4. More Horror
5. Too Many Books
6. Moving On

Stephen King: The Art of Darkness,
by Douglas E. Winter

Originally published in 1984 as a trade hardback from NAL Books, this book is *the* seminal work, and proper starting point, for any King fan or scholar, because Winter had access to King, giving the book a depth that many of the books that inevitably followed lacked.

Published in three editions—a trade paperback and mass-market paperback followed the hardback, both updated and revised because of the

Art of Darkness continued

Bachman revelation—this book remains one of the most readable texts on King. It is academic yet accessible, fannish but very professional.

Winter's infectious enthusiasm was to a great degree responsible for launching the dozens of books on King that followed. (My paperback copy of his book, scribbled over with notes, with annotations, and updates, has been my faithful companion since 1989, my road map to things King that keeps me pointed toward true north.)

In his foreword, Winter made it clear that his book is "an intermingling of biography, literary analysis, and unabashed enthusiasm" for King's work and the man himself.

You won't find a critical word in the book, but as Winter has repeatedly, and wearily, pointed out to interviewers, to find fault with the fiction or the work was not his intent; he leaves that to others. His book is a celebration: Come on in and join the party!

Obviously, the book needs updating, and I hope Winter finally finds the time to do so, because even with the dozens of books now available on King, Winter was there first with the best book.

The cover to the trade paperback of the British edition of *Stephen King: The Art of Darkness*, by Douglas E. Winter.

Contents

Foreword

Chronology

Keith Neilson: "*Stephen King: The Art of Darkness* is a fine critical overview of the most interesting writer active in America today. Anyone concerned with the current state of American culture *must* read King. And the necessary starting point for all future critical examinations of King's work and career will be Winter's book." (*Fantasy Review*, March 1985.)

Fantasy Review, 1984: "Douglas Winter's new book is simply a MUST for any fan of the 'Master of the Macabre.' . . . The book is extremely well written, offering deep insights into King the man and King the novelist. No collection of King's works will be complete without this book on the shelf beside them. (As I finish this up, I'm suddenly wondering why a 'King Society' or 'King Fan Club' hasn't been started yet.)"

Bare Bones, SK: "Douglas Winter's done a book called *The Art of Darkness*, published in hardcover by New American Library. I sometimes wish it had been a different publisher because I think that would lend it more legitimacy. There are cracks made in the publishing industry—my wife publishes there too—about the 'Stephen King Publishing Company.' We'd like to get away from that, but Doug's done a good job. He's a wonderful writer. We'll just wait and see whether or not the word gets out and it's taken seriously or not."

Stephen King: The First Decade, "Carrie" to "Pet Sematary,"
by Joseph Reino

Published in 1988 by Twayne Publishers, this is a scholarly but accessible look at King's work up to *Pet Sematary*.

Contents
About the Author
Preface
Chronology
Chapter One: Cinderella Hero/Cinderella Heroine
Chapter Two: The Dracula Myth: Shadow and Substance
Chapter Three: Strange Powers of Dangerous Potential
Chapter Four: One Touch of Horror Makes the Whole World Kin
Chapter Five: Two Terror Tales of a Town
Chapter Six: Impossible Cars and Improbable Cats
Chapter Seven: *Night Shift*: Harbinger of Bad News
Chapter Eight: Fantasies of Summer and Fall
Chapter Nine: Metaphor as Mask for Terror: A Final Estimate

Stephen King: The Second Decade— "Danse Macabre" to "The Dark Half,"
by Tony Magistrale

Published in 1992 by Twayne Publishers, this continues the series up to 1989.

Stephen King and Clive Barker: The Illustrated Guide to the Masters of the Macabre, by James Van Hise

Published in 1990 by Pioneer Books, this two-for-one book is a so-so overview adding little to what has already been published. For completists only.

The King portion includes the following:
The Man and the Writer [an overview to his career]
The King Interview [conducted by Stanley Wiater, portions of this interview previously appeared in *Bare Bones*]
The Long Form: Novels
The Bachman Books
The Short Form: Short Stories
The Short Form: Uncollected
Nonfiction: Danse Macabre
Media Mayhem: Film and Television

The Stephen King Archives

Argus Designs of Fort Collins, Colorado, embarked on an ambitious project to scrupulously catalogue King's books. "The King Archives are a complete description of U.S. first edition and specialty edition King publications. Its contributors include private collectors, bookstores nationwide and the publishers themselves. They are loaded with information including, but not limited to, appearance, publication date and information helpful for identification of first edition books by King."

The plan was to publish this information in loose sheets, allowing the buyer to add new sheets as needed.

The archives would include 53 separate listings, from the trade edition of *Carrie* to the trade edition of The *Tommyknockers*. The cost, with binder, was $37.50; without the binder, $17.50.

The original publication date was June 15, 1995, but the project, despite a good-faith effort on the part of its compiler, Shaun Nauman, never came to fruition.

Stephen King as Richard Bachman,
by Michael R. Collings

Published in 1985 by Starmont House, this book, though admittedly dated, is the best discussion of Bachman's books to appear in print under one set of covers.

More than simply a book-by-book look, Collings provides the background for the book by discussing the history of Bachman, then discusses the books in literary terms, then goes book by book through the canon (up to *Thinner*), ending with speculations on King's various pen names and an appendix with synopses of the books in question.

Contents
Chapter I: A History for Richard Bachman
Chapter II: Genre, Theme, and Image in
    Richard Bachman
Chapter III: *Rage*
Chapter IV: *The Long Walk*
Chapter V: *Roadwork*
Chapter VI: *Thinner*
Chapter VIII: Speculations
Appendix: The Bachman Novels—Synopses
List of Works Cited
Index

In a letter to Michael Collings, dated August 3, 1985, King acknowledged receipt of this book and a typescript of *The Shorter Works*, and wrote that he was "a little frightened to be taken so seriously."

Stephen King at the Movies,
by Jessie Horsting

Published in 1986 by Starlog (distributed by NAL under its Signet imprint), this is one of the better books on the subject, since Horsting takes the time to interview principals—including King. The magazine format has enough room to show off the photos to their best advantage. The book includes an introduction, "Who Is This Guy Stephen King?—And Why Do They Make All Those Movies?" and sections discussing the movies and the TV and short films.

The Movies (in chronological order)
Carrie
The Shining
Creepshow
The Dead Zone
Christine
Cujo
Firestarter
Children of the Corn
Cat's Eye
Silver Bullet
Maximum Overdrive
Stand by Me

TV and Short Films

Salem's Lot
The Word Processor of the Gods
Gramma
Night Shift
"Why the Children Don't Look Like Their
    Parents," by Harlan Ellison
Film Credits
Films on Video

Stephen King Collectibles: A Price Guide, by George Beahm

An illustrated price guide of King collectibles—notably the first editions and the signed, limited editions of his books—to be self-published by Beahm in late 1998 by his small press, GB Ink.

The Stephen King Companion,
edited by George Beahm

Published by Andrews McMeel in two editions, these companion-style books included interviews, reviews, profiles, and photos about all facets of King's life. In short, they were intended to be resource guides, reference works and above all else accessible books for King fans who wanted to know more about King but didn't know where to look.

The 1989 edition included three major sections and appendices:
Part I. The Real World of Stephen King
Part II. The Unreal World of Stephen King
Part III. A Look at the Books
The Appendices

1. Books in Print
2. Books about King
3. Filmography and Videography
4. Audiocassettes
5. Book Collectibles: A Price Guide by George Beahm with Barry R. Levin
6. Resources

Backmatter included an afterword, about the editor, and a continuation of the copyright page.

For the 1995 edition, about 80 percent of the original edition was discarded. The major difference between the two editions is that the new one is divided into three sections: "The Real World of Stephen King," "The Unreal World of Stephen King," and a "Chronological Look at the Books," by Michael R. Collings.

Stephen King Fan Club

None exists—no official one, anyway. King, wrote Stephanie Leonard in the first issue of *Castle Rock*, is "not comfortable with" the idea. (I was tempted, as a insider's joke, to give its address as Castle Rock, Maine, but somebody would actually send mail, get it returned, and then I'd likely hear about it.)

Stephen King Goes to Hollywood,
by Jeff Conner

A book packaged by Tim Underwood and Chuck Miller for NAL's Plume imprint, this book, written by Jeff Conner of Scream Press fame, was published at $9.95 in 1987 and covered movies from *Carrie* to *Stand by Me*.

The book suffers from its oft-seen reprints of the production stills from the films, which have appeared elsewhere in numerous other publications and books about King. Also, the text is principally a discussion of the movie-making process, instead of an illuminating discussion of the films themselves. The film credits also are available elsewhere.

In this case, it appears that NAL wanted a book discussing King's films, Underwood-Miller was glad to put it together, and Conner was happy to write it. In short, a book developed as product.

Jeff Conner: "I enjoyed writing the book as it gave me a chance to put my own spin on why so many good books are turned into so many bad, and unprofitable, movies over and over again. It's not often you get paid for the chance to mouth off in public. I haven't heard what King's response to it was, if any, though it got a so-so review by Stephanie Leonard. . . . Some other small magazine called it insightful and amusing, which I greatly appreciated." (Letter to George Beahm, Nov. 9, 1988.)

Stephen King Library

King's gargantuan output, coupled with his popularity, makes him one of the few authors for whom a book club has built an entire division. Via television ads and print ads, the Book of the Month Club offers a uniform set of King books for collectors, each book handsomely bound in red boards, called the Stephen King Library.

In truth, the trade editions from his publishers,

You are invited to join the new **STEPHEN KING LIBRARY** R.S.V.P.

Teaser ad for the Stephen King Library.

the first editions, are the most collectible editions, as are the signed, limited editions; the reprinted book club editions are virtually worthless from a collector's point of view, but for those who are more interested in a uniformly bound set of books by King, this book club set is the only source.

The Stephen King Library editions are available only by mail order, direct from Book of the Month Club.

According to the fact sheet provided by American List Counsel, Inc., the club has approximately 90,000 members, of which 66 percent are female, with an average age of 30 and an average household income of $36,000. The "marketing insight" offered: "The loyalty these buyers show to King translates into loyalty for all mail order companies they buy from. When you sign up a King book-buyer, you've got a lifetime of response ahead. They particularly respond to continuities and clubs and men's and women's specialty catalogs." Eight companies paid $85 per 1,000 names to rent the club's list; they wanted to scare up some sales. The companies: two publishing operations—Bantam and Agatha Christie—and mail-order companies—Websters Unified, Columbia House, Gevalia Kaffe, Harriet Carter, Newfield Publications, and Wireless.

The Stephen King Phenomenon,
by Michael R. Collings

Published by Starmont House in 1987, this is a broad-based look at King not so much as a writer but a phenomenon in the book trade.

Advertising piece for the Stephen King Library. (King is characteristically dressed in his lightweight jacket, jeans, and Converse sneakers.)

The Stephen King Quiz Book,
by Stephen Spignesi

A mass-market paperback from Signet ($3.95), this book was compiled by the indefatigable Spignesi: 1,510 questions arranged in 107 quizzes are guaranteed to make you think, if you don't know the answer offhand. (Don't ask me how I fared; I've already apologized to Spignesi for my apparent lack of knowledge of things King.)

Ever the cheerleader, Spignesi says: "I think it says a lot about the work of King that we as readers would care so much about his tales that we'd want to take quizzes testing our knowledge of the minutiae of the Kingdom. The work of King is im-

portant to us: It takes us away, it entertains, it educates, but most important—!!!IT SCARES US!!!"

Only the truly dedicated Kingaholic need apply pencil to paper to answer these questions, but if you can, go to the head of the class.

I. The Life and Times of King
II. "Page One" [the frontmatter in his books]
III. The Novels
IV. The Shorter Collected Works
V. The Shorter Uncollected Works
VI. The Bachman Books
VII. The *Dark Tower* Books
VIII. The *Creepshow* Quizzes
IX. The Later Short Stories
X. Miscellaneous Quizzes

Cover to the trade paperback edition of Michael R. Collings's *Stephen King Phenomenon*, published by Starmont House, with artwork by Stephen Fabian.

Cover to the mass market paperback edition of the first *Stephen King Quiz Book*, compiled by the indefatigable Stephen J. Spignesi. (He followed it up with a second King quiz book, again published by NAL.)

Stephen King's America,
by Jonathan P. Davis

Published in 1994 by Bowling Green State University Popular Press, this is a discussion of King's fiction in the context of American terrain.

The book's main value: the inclusion of four interviews with Tony Magistrale, Carroll Terrell, Burton Hatlen, and Gary Hoppenstand.

Contents
Foreword
Part I. Stephen King and the Horror Genre
Introduction
Part II. Stephen King's America
Traversing King's American Terrain
1. The Struggle for Personal Morality in America
2. Childhood and Rites of Passage
3. Technology: America's Sweetheart
4. Caught in the Machine of American Capitalism
5. Autonomy versus Societal Conformity in America
6. Survival in a Despairing World
Epilogue: The End of the Journey
Part III. The Interviews
Author's Note
1. Tony Magistrale, University of Vermont
2. Carroll Terrell, University of Maine at Orono
3. Burton Hatlen, University of Maine at Orono
4. Gary Hoppenstand, Michigan State University
Works Cited
Index

Stephen King Scream Test Contest

Sponsored by *Fangoria* magazine (#56, 1986), the contest required you answer 15 questions to be in the drawing to win prizes. The grand prize was an autographed copy of the script for *Maximum Overdrive*, the second prize was a *Maximum Overdrive* movie poster, and third prize was the Starlog/NAL book by Jeff Conner, *Stephen King Goes to Hollywood*.

Stephen King's Creepshow

Trade paperback, 1982, not paginated, Plume, $6.95
Contents
"Father's Day"
"Lonesome Death of Jordy Verrill"
"Crate"
"Something to Tide You Over"
"They're Creeping Up on You"

The official tie-in to the movie *Creepshow*, this full color collection of comic book stories is a wistful look back at the horror comics—notably, E.C. Comics—of the fifties, with artwork by Berni Wrightson (with Michelle Wrightson), and cover art by the E.C. artist Jack Kamen.

None of these are major stories, nor are they intended to be. They *are*, however, intended to be entertaining (in a dark, comic way) in their own right.

Stephen King's Danse Macabre

Hardback, 1981, 400 pages, Everest House, $13.95
Dedication: "It's easy enough—perhaps too easy—to memorialize the dead. The book is for six great writers of the macabre who are still alive. Robert Bloch, Jorge Luis Borges, Ray Bradbury, Frank Belknap Long, Donald Wandrei, Manly Wade Wellman. Enter, Stranger, at your Riske: Here there be Tygers."
Contents
Forenote
I, October 4, 1957, and an Invitation to Dance
II, Tales of the Hook
III, Tales of the Tarot
IV, An Annoying Autobiographical Pause
V, Radio and the Set of Reality
VI, The Modern American Horror Movie—Text and Subtext
VII, The Horror Movie as Junk Food
VIII, The Glass Teat, or This Monster Was Brought to You by Gainesburgers
IX, Horror Fiction
X, The Last Waltz—Horror and Morality, Horror and Magic
Afterword
Appendix 1. The Films

Appendix 2. The Books
Index

As King tells it in his forenote, this book was written at the suggestion of Bill Thompson, formerly of Doubleday, then at Everest House. (He has since changed houses.) The result: A fascinating overview of the field since the fifties.

To my mind, King is an outstanding tour guide for several reasons: He knows the horror field and loves it like a fan, which is why he loved to go to conventions, just like everyone else. His down-to-earth writing style is ideally suited for a survey of the field, since it's a welcome break from the kind of incomprehensible academic writing that typically characterizes such overviews. And finally, he writes about it so entertainingly, you want to rush out and read the books he's recommended, and see the movies he's cited. In other words, like any good teacher, he is excited by the subject material and shares that enthusiasm with the audience.

King's only nonfiction book to date, *Danse Macabre*, is an informal but informative overview of the field from the fifties to the present and covers movies, television, and books. An ideal introduction for new King fans who want to see how influential the horror field has been to his body of work, *Danse Macabre* is required reading.

SK on literary criticism: "[David Madden's] got a critical magazine called *Tough Guys* for which he writes these critical, very literary pieces, and he asked me if I would contribute a piece on [James] Cain. I told him, yeah, I would, but I never have. Mostly because that literary, sort of stuffy style kind of bums me out." (*Bare Bones*.)

Stephen King's The Lawnmower Man

In "Hollywood Happenings" King initially said of the movie, "I think it's pretty good" but quickly added, "I hate it that New Line's got my name plastered all over the place. It's the biggest rip-off that you could imagine because there's nothing of me in there. It just makes me furious. . . . The guy turns out to be this big, fat slob of a guy, who looks nothing like [the film's star] Jeff Fahey. There's also nothing about computers and virtual reality in my story, which seems to be all that the movie is about." (*Daily Press*, March 20, 1992.)

The difference between "The Lawnmower Man" as a short story optioned as a film property and *Stephen King's The Lawnmower Man* is significant enough so that King subsequently sued New Line Cinema. They had bought the rights to the story and contended that the rights included the use of his name in connection with the film.

Citing false attribution—the movie had only the most tenuous connection to the story, by virtue of a single scene—King sued and won, but even after that victory, New Line Cinema continued to stir the soup.

From the *Hollywood Reporter*, March 30, 1994:

In a landmark decision, New York federal judge Constance Baker Motley has held New Line Cinema in contempt of a court decree handed down in May, which, among other things, required the company to remove King's name from all advertising, promotional materials and videocassette packaging relating to New Line's *The Lawnmower Man*.

According to King's lawyers Paul Levinson and Peter Herbert, the case represents the first time a court has found a major film company liable for "the misleading and deceptive use" of an author's name in conjunction with the advertising and promotion of a film and has required that the company remove from the marketplace all forms of advertising, promotion and packaging carrying the plaintiff's name.

Referring to the "perverse and striking dissimilarity of the two works," King had brought suit against New Line and Allied Vision, Ltd., in May 1992, alleging that use of his name in connection with the film adaptation of his short story of the same title amounted to false attribution of authorship.

King was granted a preliminary injunction in July, but that decision was reversed.

With settlement of the dispute in May, New Line and Allied Vision paid King $3.4 million and agreed to the entry of a court order that prohibited all further use of King's name and further required the immediate distribution of corrective stickers or new videocassette packages.

However, in Friday's decision the U.S. Dis-

Lawnmower Man *continued*

trict Court, Southern District of New York, found that New Line's executives filed false affidavits attesting to compliance with the court's order.

The court has directed New Line to cure its contempt within 10 days or be penalized $10,000 per day until the company complies. It also awarded King all of New Line's profits from the commercial exploitation of his name during the period of contempt and ordered New Line to pay the attorney's fees that King incurred.

New Line declined comment on the case.

Richard Harrington (*Washington Post*, 1992): "In the end, you'll wish the writers had either turned to King (who was not involved beyond selling his name for the title) or had signed up for some drug-and-VR sessions before submitting their script. Ultimately, it's the difference between Cyber-Being and nothingness."

Michael H. Price (*Fort Worth Star-Telegram*): "Fidelity to Stephen King goes well beyond the simplicity of the original 'Lawnmower Man' yarn, which figures as only a brief sequence in the film. The screenplay takes pains to capture the increasingly compassionate tone of King's general body of work."

Note: A sequel was produced, though not with King's name attached. *Lawnmower Man 2: Beyond Cyberspace* was released by New Line Cinema, starring Matt Frewer as Jobe. The basic plot of this 93-minute film: Jobe takes on the job of taking over the world but is foiled by computer hackers who, with the help of a scientist, stop him. (Don't bother to check this one out.)

The Stephen King Story,
by George Beahm

Originally published in 1991 in hardback by Andrews McMeel, this book was revised, expanded, and updated for its 1992 appearance as a trade paperback from the same company. A literary profile, the book includes the following:

Introduction, by Michael R. Collings
Preface, by George Beahm

Box for the *Stephen King's World of Horror* videotape, featuring a profile/interview of King.

Foreword by Chris Chesley
The Early Years
The College Years
The Long Walk
The Doubleday Days
America's Literary Boogeyman
Bestsellersaurus Rex
Stephen King's Golden Year
In a League of His Own
Stephen King in the Heart of Darkness: The Art of Writing
Afternote by Carroll F. Terrell
Afterword by Michael R. Collings
Appendices

Stephen King's World of Horror

Video profiles and interviews of horror writers and filmmakers, including King.

Stephen King's Year of Fear Calendar, 1986

The first official calendar tie-in, this wall calendar from NAL featured art from King's books and in the monthly calendar pages listed fictional dates that were important in his works. The cost was $7.95. (A second calendar was published in 1993.)

To promote the calendar, the publishers gave out free posters at the ABA conference in May 1986 showing a photo of King in front of his home in Bangor, and a year of months beneath.

Steve's Rag

A photocopied fanzine published in French that is the official publication of Club King Lille. The title is an allusion to *Dave's Rag*, a newspaper King's brother, David, published in the basement of their home in Durham, Maine. According to Douglas E. Winter, in *Stephen King: The Art of Darkness*, David would get phone calls while in the basement, printing his paper, but obviously couldn't take them. His mother would tell the caller that her son was on the rag and couldn't come to the phone.

Cover to *Stephen King's Year of Fear 1986 Calendar.*

Storm of the Century

Original screenplay by Stephen King.

An ABC miniseries (six hours) scheduled for 1999 with a basic plot that sounds similar to that of "The Mist." Liz Smith of *TV Guide* termed it "a killer storm paralyzing the state of Maine." In particular, the small town of Southwest Harbor, Maine, is hit hard, said King. Shooting on location in Toronto, King observed: "I wrote this two years before I ever heard of El Niño. And sometimes I think the whole El Niño thing might just be a Stephen King myth." As for the story: "I think we're going to shock a lot of people, as this is not like TV at all."

Storytelling

SK: "My idea has always been to tell a story, and the story is boss." (*Bare Bones.*)

"Storytelling—An Evening with King"

King's first major public talk in his hometown, on September 14, 1995, held to benefit the fund-raising campaign to restore the town library, "Renewing Today, Building Tomorrow." The restoration would cost an estimated $8.5 million; the campaign was chaired by Tabitha King. Tickets were five dollars.

The event raised $18,000 toward the drive. (The newspaper estimated 3,600 in attendance, but several hundred seats in the back rows were obviously empty.)

King spoke for an hour and 40 minutes, using his now-familiar format: speaking off the cuff, warming up the audience with anecdotes, reading from a work in progress (in this case, *Desperation*), and finally, answering questions from the audience.

Wearing his standard uniform—a Bangor High School letter jacket belonging to his son Owen, a pink T-shirt, jeans, and Converse sneakers—King cited *The Dead Zone* as his favorite book, cited *The Shawshank Redemption*, *Stand by Me*, and *Misery* as his favorite film adaptations, and got a loud round of applause when he said that when the snow began to fall that year, he'd write the long-awaited fourth *Dark Tower* novel. (And he did—

Grant published *The Dark Tower IV: Wizard and Glass* in August 1997.)

For those who wanted more to take away than a memory of the evening, autographed copies of *Rose Madder* were sold, raising additional money for the library drive.

Wanting to contribute to the fund-raising effort, Charlie Fried bought 50 tickets for free distribution to a worthy group. The tickets were donated to the Shaw House, Atrium House, and Bangor's Health and Welfare Department, benefiting homeless teenagers in the area. At the event, a special area was set aside up-front, behind chairperson Tabitha King, for the youths to sit.

Storytelling technique

SK: "I just try to create sympathy for my characters, then turn the monsters loose." (*Bare Bones.*)

"Story to order"

King has frequently said that he writes stories because it occurs to him to write them, but there was an exception: for a contest for *Cavalier* magazine, King wrote the first 500 words of a story based on "a photograph of a house-cat—a startling close-up of a snarling face, half black, half white," as he put it. The magazine ran King's 500 words, then challenged its readers to complete the story.

King's recollection was that the winning story "was pretty good." (*Castle Rock*, June 1985.)

The Strange Case of Dr. Jekyll and Mr. Hyde

A short novel by Robert Louis Stevenson.

Ruth King checked this book out of the local library and, at King's urging, read it to him.

"I lived and died with that story. . . . I can remember lying in bed, wakeful after that night's reading was done, and what I usually thought of was how Mr. Hyde walked over the little girl, back and forth, breaking her bones—it was such a terrible image. I thought, I have to do that, but I have to do that worse, because it was the only way to get back to normal again."

Stranglehold, by Jack Ketchum

SK: "He is, quite simply, one of the best in the business." "Be warned: Ketchum never stops, never flinches, never turns aside. He is . . . on a par with Clive Barker, James Ellroy, and Thomas Harris. You may be shocked, even revolted, by Jack Ketchum's hellish vision of the world, but you won't be able to dismiss or forget it."

"Strawberry Spring"

Originally published in *Ubris*, the UMO literary magazine (Fall 1968), this story was extensively revised for its republication in *Night Shift*, which was enhanced with added flashbacks.

King is fond of using unusual meteorological conditions to set the stage in introducing elements of the supernatural or real-world horror. In "The Mist," a strange mist brings with it unimaginable monsters. . . . In this story, the real monster is the narrator, who recalls the name Springheel Jack after a recent dismemberment of a college coed from New Sharon Teachers' College is reported in the paper. It triggers his memories of a rash of similar murders that took place eight years before, during a "dark and mist-blown strawberry spring" in which "Springheel Jack" made his first appearance.

This story got the attention of a newly minted lawyer, Douglas E. Winter, who was waiting for a quarter shoeshine at a storefront near the federal courthouse in St. Louis, Missouri, in the fall of 1975. As he tells it, in *Stephen King: The Art of Darkness*: "So it happened that I plucked forth an issue of *Cavalier*, and as I meandered through its ruined pages, the words 'Springheel Jack' caught my eye. And I began to read a peculiar short story —peculiar at first because it was neither about sex nor written with the tiresome, obsessive leer that passes for American eroticism; but primarily because it captured me . . . taking me away to a strawberry spring in New England where horror waited in every shadow. . . . That the writer of the story was named Stephen King was meaningless to me, as it would have been to most other readers; if anything, I assumed that the name was a pseudonym."

In due course, Winter would meet King at a convention and strike up a conversation. King, said Winter, had read and appreciated his review of *Firestarter*. It sparked an enduring friendship.

"Stud City"

Originally published in *Ubris* (fall 1969), this story was revised for its appearance as a story by Gordon Lachance within the story "The Body."

A pessimistic, slice-of-life story about Edward "Chico" May, who lives a dead-end life in a dead-end town. It's a study in contrast between his life and the lives of the more fortunate, who leave town.

In "The Body" (King's most autobiographical story), the narrator, Gordon Lachance (read: King), says that this story was a turning point for him as a writer, since it was the first one in which he felt his own fictional voice break through.

Success

"We have a mortgage like everybody else, but I don't have to worry about the payments. I feel we're as safe as anyone can be in this crazy world, but I'm not buying yachts. My only extravagances have been a canoe, a video recorder, and hardcover books." (Profile by Carol Lawson, "Behind the Best Sellers," in *NYTBR*, Sept. 23, 1979.)

"Suffer the Little Children"
(collected in *Nightmares & Dreamscapes*)

Originally published in *Cavalier* (February 1972), this is a story about a strict third-grade teacher, Miss Sidley, who notices that her students seem to be changing. She confronts one of them, Robert, who tells her that the other students are, like him, being taken over—an invasion of the body snatchers, as it were. Horrified, she breaks down and runs screaming out of the school. A month later, however, she's back, with a pistol to put an end to the infestation, taking each child to the sound-proof mimeograph room and killing him or her. She is stopped only when she's discovered by another teacher.

This Bradbury-esque story was originally sub-

"Suffer the Little Children" *continued*

mitted as part of the *Night Shift* collection, but the editor, Bill Thompson, elected to cut it for space considerations, according to King's notes in *Nightmares & Dreamscapes*.

Summers, Mark

A caricaturist whose work recalls that of Barry Moser (his work with scratchboard is a visual and artistic trademark), Summers has rendered dozens of portraits of literary figures for Barnes & Noble, at the urging of the chain's bookstore managers.

John Kelly, vice president and publisher of Barnes & Noble: "They started calling and saying, 'Hey, why can't we get King on a bag?'" They could . . . and did. The portrait of King, based on a dustjacket photo—showing King at his most photogenic—is now on a Barnes & Noble plastic bag.

"The Sun Dog"
(collected in *Four Past Midnight*)

The story does double duty in this collection of original novellas: it serves up an interesting little tale in its own right, and functions as a narrative bridge to the book that follows, *Needful Things*, set in Castle Rock, Maine.

Kevin Delevan turns 15 on September 15 and gets what he wants for his birthday: a Polaroid Sun 660 camera. But the first photo he takes is not what he expects. In fact, none of the pictures turn out, so to speak. Even Pop Merrill, the proprietor of Emporium Galorium, a "crackerbarrel philosopher and homespun Mr. Fixit," can't figure out what's *wrong* with the camera, though something clearly *is* wrong—terribly wrong, in fact.

Merrill puts the photos on videotape and what emerges is the image of a dog that, with each picture, comes closer to the photographer. The dog looks as if it wants to attack the cameraman. The supernatural Polaroid dog wants to escape the two-dimensional world, then kill. . . .

"Surviving Success: Best-selling Authors Tell (Almost All)"

A videotape recorded on April 10, 1994, at the Second Annual Oxford Conference for the Book, of a panel discussion between King and John Grisham, moderated by Barry Hannah.

This one-hour tape clearly demonstrates the differences between the two, despite the surface similarities of success: King is a writer, while Grisham is a storyteller only, which is to say, line for line, King writes better prose, understands and practices the art and craft of writing, and understands what makes a good story tick. Grisham, on the other hand, is concerned mostly with plot; his characters are clearly not fictionally rounded, and he is more in the tradition of a pulp writer grinding out lawyer-with-a-heart-takes-on-the-bad-guys stories.

King, who clearly was the most comfortable of the three in front of the camera, held the audience in his hand. Grisham, on the other hand, seemed wary, guarded, and on the verge of exasperation.

"Survivor Type" (collected in *Skeleton Crew*)

Originally published in *Terrors* (1982), this story goes for the gross-out and delivers in spades. A self-consuming man, Richard Pine, is a discredited surgeon and is all washed up. Shipwrecked on an island, his only asset is his will to live and two kilos of "pure heroin, worth about $350,000, New York street value." Both help him hold out, but as hope slips away and hunger takes its place, Pine must answer the question every med student asks himself: "How badly does the patient want to survive?"

Swannconn

The Fifth International Conference on the Fantastic in the Arts in Boca Raton, Florida, March 22–25, 1984, which, because of the presence of the noted academic Leslie Fiedler and the noted best-selling author Stephen King, drew its largest attendance to date, with 470 paid registrations and 100 guests.

Sword in the Darkness

Unpublished novel written by King.

Completed on April 30, 1970, this 150,000-word novel made the rounds on Publishers' Row in New York, represented by Patricia Shartle Myrer of McIntosh and Otis. A dozen publishers, including Doubleday, saw the novel but all rejected it. To date it remains unpublished, which is what King wishes.

Inspired by the Harrison High novels by John Farris, this novel is a downer tale: the story of a high school student, Arnie Kalowski, set against the background of a race riot.

Caroll Terrell read an early incomplete draft and, not knowing of King's financial difficulties at the time, told him after reading it that submitting it for publication "would do no harm, but it wouldn't do any good. I thought the book was potentially marketable, but not something in 1969 that a publisher would give an advance on. So I told him they'd read it, tell him it showed great promise, and invite him to send the completed version, but they wouldn't give an unknown either an advance or a contract."

Terrell was right. King later showed Terrell a rejection letter and said, "At least you hit the nail on the head."

consists of adaptations of four stories, only one of which is of a King story, the little-known "Cat from Hell." This story was the basis of a *Cavalier* contest, in which King wrote the first few pages and readers finished the story.

King, however, likes to tie up his loose ends, so he finished the story, which was adapted by George Romero.

In this film version, a cat from hell has killed several friends of Drogan, a millionaire who takes out a contract on the feline, which apparently has more than the usual allotment of nine lives. The killer, Halston, is himself killed by the cat and, in true E.C. Comics fashion, the appearance of the cat alive and crawling out of the dead killer's mouth is enough to give Drogan a heart attack. End of story.

Video movie, folks.

The Talisman

Hardback, 1984, 646 pages, Viking, $18.95.
First printing: 500,000.
Dedication: "This book is for Ruth King, Elvena Straub." [Stephen King's and Peter Straub's mothers]

King and Peter Straub had been kicking around the idea of collaborating on a novel, but contractual obligations kept interfering. When they finally were able to share a publisher, and the timing was right, the two collaborated on this long quest novel, using their modems to transmit text in a round-robin fashion from King's Wang to Straub's IBM Displaywriter. The result: an ambitious, much-heralded, eagerly anticipated novel and a one-time experiment for King, who prefers to work alone.

People magazine called the novel one of the worst of the year: "In horror fiction, two heads are better than one only if they're on the same body."

Twilight Zone magazine readers voted this the best novel of the year.

SK: "Either of us could have written *a* book. If someone had held a gun to one of my children's heads, and said, 'Write *The Talisman* by yourself,' I could have written *a Talisman*, but it wouldn't have been the same thing." (Quoted by William Goldstein, "A Coupl'a Authors Sittin' Around Talkin'," *PW*, May 11, 1984.)

Tabitha Spruce King Wing

The 6,000-square-foot addition to the Old Town Public Library, named after Tabitha King. Generous supporters of local libraries, the Kings donated $750,000 of the estimated $1.5 million needed for the expansion, completed in May 1991.

Valerie Osborne, librarian, on the matching funds the Kings gave: "Without that gift, we would have been on shaky ground. It's a real incentive to go out there and raise that money." (John Ripley, *BDN*, Sept. 6, 1989.)

Tabloids

Though King is clearly unhappy with the books being written about him, he has at least one consolation: None of the writers dig through his trash or look through his windows, or look for skeletons (if any) in his closet. In other words, the books are generally positive, eschewing the tabloid trash that is splashed on the front pages of those execrable publications. (King, in fact, makes fun of tabloids in "The Night Flier," in which the reporter-photographer works for *Inside View*.)

King can count his blessings; his Boswells aren't digging for kitty litter.

Tales from the Darkside (film), 1990

Billed on the movie poster as "four terrific tales in one horrific masterpiece," this anthology film

Teacher's Manual: Novels of Stephen King,
by Edward J. Zagorski

Published by NAL in 1981, this 48-page teacher's manual "will try to aid the teacher in preparing students to get their footing on the road to becoming, first, *avid* readers and, second, discriminating, *thinking* readers."

Zagorski, who has written other teacher's guides for NAL, is a former teacher, who now writes full time. (Teacher turned writer—sounds familiar.)

Contents
Preface
Purpose
Introduction

Teacher's Manual Novels of Stephen King

by Edward J. Zagorski

New American Library

Cover to *Teacher's Manual: Novels of Stephen* King, NAL's free publication designed for teachers to stimulate classroom discussion of King's fiction. Written by Edward J. Zagorski, it covers the Doubleday books.

Educational Application
The Novels [from *Carrie* to *Firestarter*]
The Short Fiction [*Night Shift* only]

Teague, Lewis

The director of *Cujo* who shot the film in "Little England," as the film community calls it, in northern California, which resembles New England. Shot on a $5 million budget, *Cujo* won high praise from King, who said, "It's one of the scariest things you'll ever see. It's terrifying!"

Teague subsequently directed another King project, *Cat's Eye*, which was not a critical or financial success.

"Teen Angel"

A 1959 song by Mark Dinning.

On the Rock Bottom Remainders tour, King suggested this song be added to the lineup. It was, and it became his signature song, especially after he playfully changed the lyrics, upsetting the song's owners, music publisher Acuff-Rose company, which threatened to sue if King repeated his performance. Acuff-Rose had heard King's improvised lyrics on the first printing of the BMG Video recorded at the Cowboy Boogie.

Telegram

King didn't have a telephone when Doubleday accepted *Carrie*, so William Thompson had to send a telegram, which read: 'CARRIE' OFFICIALLY A DOUBLEDAY BOOK. $2,500 ADVANCE AGAINST ROYALTIES. CONGRATS, KID—THE FUTURE LIES AHEAD. BILL.

Ten-dollar bet

When UMO classmate Flip Thompson criticized King for writing macho stories and saying that he couldn't write a novel about a woman, King wrote *Carrie* . . . and won the bet.

Tender, by Mark Childress

SK: "*Tender* is a big, all-American, Technicolor dreamboat of a book, as vital and as intense as anything I've read in the last ten years.

"This is the first novel I've ever read in my life that is more *inside* rock and roll than *about* it. Beneath that cool prose line of this minimalist epic there is the same raw and feverish drive that propelled the early rockabilly stars as they created a new kind of music.

"*Tender* is going to knock your socks off. This is a great novel." (Copy from the back cover of the advance reading copy of *Tender*.)

Ten favorite fantasy-horror novels of King

The list below is taken from J. N. Williamson's *How to Write Tales of Horror, Fantasy & Science Fiction*:

Ray Bradbury, *Something Wicked This Way Comes* (King did an unpublished screenplay for this book.)

Ramsey Campbell, *The Doll Who Ate His Mother* (In a review of Campbell's first book, King praised the work and said that, of the new British writers in the field, Campbell showed a lot of promise.)

Jack Finney, *The Body Snatchers*

Shirley Jackson, *The Haunting of Hill House* (A book that inspired *The Shining*.)

T. E. D. Klein, *The Ceremonies*

Robert Marasco, *Burnt Offerings* (King reviewed this book for *Horror: Best 100*.)

Richard Matheson, *I Am Legend* (Matheson is a big influence on King stylistically.)

Anne Rice, *Interview with the Vampire*

Curt Siodmak, *Donovan's Brain*

Peter Straub, *Ghost Story*

"The Ten O'Clock People"
(collected in *Nightmares & Dreamscapes*)

In his book notes on this story, King states that the idea for it came to him during a trip to Boston when he observed groups of people, from janitors to executives, smoking outside, members of what he calls a "sub-tribe" or "Lost Tribe" in the story. Living in a non-smokers' world, they must attend to their nicotine fix outdoors.

Pearson, standing in such a group outside of the First Mercantile Bank in Boston, stifles a scream as he observes a "thing in a dark-gray Andre Cyr suit" walk by him, whose "head had been *in motion*, different parts moving in different directions, like the bands of exotic gases surrounding some planetary giant."

One of the others in the group explains that he sees it, too, but doesn't want to let on, doesn't want that thing to know *he* knows.

The monsters go unseen among the population, except for the Ten O' Clock People, who can see the "bat" people, who have infiltrated society by assuming positions of power in the social stratum.

Retired Professor and Northern Lights publisher Carroll F. Terrell (UMO), who taught King as an undergraduate. (Terrell wrote and self-published *Stephen King: Man and Artist*.)

The Ten O'Clock People band to fight the "bat" people, first in Boston, then across the U.S., since the monsters have—like cigarettes—infiltrated everywhere.

A plot summary cannot do this story justice; you have to read it to appreciate the bizarreness of this tale, King's take on "The Invasion of the Body Snatchers."

Terrell, Carroll F.

College professor at the University of Maine at Orono who taught King. Founder of Northern Lights, a small press affiliated with the university. Terrell wrote *Stephen King: Man and Artist*.

Theft of King books

In the *Wall Street Journal* (Aug. 25, 1988), an article by Kim Clark cited the high incidence of King books disappearing from libraries, notably Maine libraries. Her explanation: "Maybe it has them in the sewers. Maybe the Tommyknockers have taken them away into space. Or maybe ol' Cujo is eating them."

The simple truth: King's books are so collectible that unscrupulous citizens would rather check a King book out and report it as "lost"—especially in the case of the Grant editions of *The Dark Tower*—than buy it from a second-hand book dealer.

Clark said that at Bangor's public library, of the 100 copies of King's books, almost 25 percent are missing.

Theodore "Ted" Sturgeon

SK on Sturgeon: "He fulfilled the pulp dictum to create story before all else." (*Isaac Asimov's Science Fiction Magazine*, January 1986.)

Thinner

Hardback, 1984, 309 pages, NAL, $12.95
First print run: 26,000
Dedication: None.
Contents: 27 chapters

Thinner, a Richard Bachman novel, was originally intended as a King novel, to be followed in time with *Misery*, which King felt would be Bachman's breakthrough book. The twenty-seventh chapter, "Gypsy Pie," was the book's original title.

Although the first four Bachman books, all published in paperback, helped build a small group of devoted readers, this book—published in hardback, with a major launch—commanded attention from the booksellers; in fact, at the American Booksellers Association convention that year, you could *not* ignore it.

Tongue in cheek, NAL gamely promoted Bachman as an exciting new voice, a major talent on the verge of breaking through, while never ac-

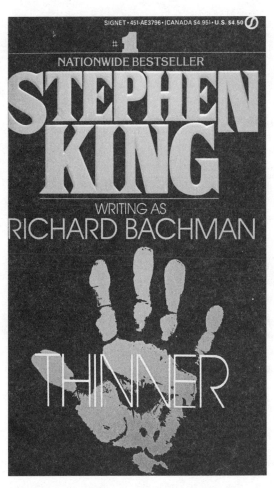

Cover to the mass market paperback edition of *Thinner* by Richard Bachman. (Note how large King's name is, in comparison to the Bachman name.)

Thinner continued

knowledging that the book was in fact authored by its best-selling author.

Like Dean Koontz's books written under the Leigh Nichols pseudonym, which started selling a million copies in paperback, *Thinner* became a best-seller, but only *after* King admitted he had written the book as Bachman; this immediately increased its sales tenfold, from 28,000 to 280,000.

Thinner is the story of Billy Halleck, an overweight attorney who accidentally runs down a gypsy woman and is put under a curse by her father, to literally waste away. *Thinner* is an admittedly dark novel, as Halleck's life spirals out of control, dragging those around him down into the abyss.

Like Johnny Smith in *The Dead Zone*, Billy Halleck is a victim of the wheel of fate.

Before a Literary Guild reader had known King was Bachman, he wrote, "This is what King would write like if King could really write."

Thinner (film), 1996

This Bachman novel never struck me as being anything more than a novella. It's about an overweight attorney who, haunted by a gypsy curse, seems destined to waste away to literally nothing.

How, you ask, can a movie be made of such thin gruel?

Well, it can't, but that didn't stop Richard P. Rubinstein from attempting to make a movie.

Early on it was clear that the movie was having problems. King had seen the final film and was reportedly unhappy with what he saw, so it was reshot and released later that year.

Whether or not he was pleased, I can't say, but the film certainly can't be on his or anyone else's list of favorite films—it just wasn't memorable cinematic fare.

To be fair to those involved in its production, they had an almost insurmountable task: In order to be successful, the movie would have to be padded; and in order to please King, it would have to be faithful to the book. The result: A film that tried to please everyone . . . and pleased very few people in the end.

Box design for the videotape *Thinner*. (Note: It says "Stephen King's Thinner," with no mention of Bachman.)

Thompson, William

The book editor who discovered Stephen King. At Doubleday when King submitted *Carrie*, Thompson subsequently moved to Everest House as its editor and solicited King to write a nonfiction overview of the horror field. King agreed and *Danse Macabre* was published, his first nonfiction title.

Three stages of King

Ralph Vincinanza, a literary agent who handles King's foreign rights to his books, feels that there are three stages to King's career, gauged in hardback book sales:

◆ The 1970s—King was a popular paperback writer, but not in hardback.

◆ The early 1980s—King sold hundreds of thousands of copies in hardback.

◆ From 1983 to present—King made publishing history, selling in numbers exceeding a half million to over a million in hardback.

Time magazine

King got star treatment in *Time*'s October 6, 1986, issue. He was on the cover and there was a lengthy, photo-illustrated profile.

Written by Stefan Kanfer, the piece confirmed that King was "the indisputable King of horror, a demon fabulist who raises gooseflesh for fun and profit."

The single best overview of King's career, Kanfer's piece covers the horror field, King's relationship to that field, and his seemingly inevitable rise to the top.

The Tommyknockers

Hardback, 1987, 560 pages, Putnam, $27.95
Dedication: "For Tabitha King, . . . promises to keep."
Contents
Book I. The Ship in the Earth
Book II. Tales of Haven
Book III. The Tommyknockers
A long book—in fact, *too* long, agreed the critics—*The Tommyknockers*, set in Haven, Maine, is at heart a novel about morality (or the lack thereof) in a technological age when weapons of mass destruction are at our fingertips. We hold them with our careless hands. For instance, when the U.S. Army in the fifties wanted to gauge the effects of an atomic blast on people, they lined up troopers in the open . . . wearing sunglasses for protection, as if that were enough.

Roberta ("Bobbie") Anderson stumbles across three inches of metal protruding from the ground. She touches it and it emits a faint vibration. She doesn't know that it's an alien spaceship that has been buried for 50 million years, and harbors the Tommyknockers, which soon exert their influence on the town's inhabitants.

Haven, Maine, as it turns out, is no safe harbor for its townsfolk, but instead a haven for the aliens, whose influence changes the townsfolk, first physiologically, then psychologically.

The spaceship, in short, is a technological boogeyman, and its influence—the process of "becoming"—turns into concrete reality, the wonky gadgets the town's people dream up to resolve their immediate problems, but not without cost: They don't realize that their inventions and actions have ramifications that go far beyond what they could possibly imagine. For instance, Hilly Brown constructs a magic kit with parts from Radio Shack, but when used on his brother, it zaps him to Altair-4, a planet light-years from Earth.

Sensing Roberta Anderson is in danger, her former lover, Jim Gardner, comes to Haven. Unaffected by the alien emanations, Anderson is the only hope for a town now enslaved by the Tommyknockers, who have brought them together in a collective consciousness. Resistance, after all, was futile.

It's Anderson against the aliens, Earth versus the Flying Saucers, and this time, don't look to the skies but to the ground, where the gigantic alien ship lies buried, exerting its malignant influence over the unsuspecting townspeople.

When asked by an interviewer for Waldenbooks if the threat of nuclear war is a subject that concerns King a lot, he responded: "Sure. It concerns me a lot and that's what the book tries to say—and not in any preachy way. I never wrote a book to espouse a principle or a theme. I never did anything but write to entertain myself. But what usually happens is that halfway through a book, there comes a time when you say to yourself, 'Wait a minute! *That's* what I'm writing about.' In the case of *The Tommyknockers*, what I was writing about were gadgets. I had to write this book to realize that all of these things—the Minuteman, the Skyhawk, the Polaris submarine—are nothing but gadgets. If we kill ourselves, that's what we're going to do with it: a lot of Disneyworld gadgets of the sort that kids build with chemistry sets."

Top Ten List

On April 27, 1989, King was the subject of David Letterman's Top Ten List on *Late Night with David Letterman*.

Top Ten List *continued*

"Top Ten Lines from SK Novels": Number ten was "Oh, there's nothing in the attic," and number one was "I've been a veterinarian for thirty years and I'm telling you—that's no ordinary poodle."

King, who has appeared on the show, made an interesting guest. Either Letterman didn't read King, or didn't know what to ask, as the chemistry between the two fizzled out.

"Tough Talk and Tootsies, Just 25 Cents"

Article in *USA Today* by King on the golden age of paperback originals, the days of the cheap paperback, when they cost only a quarter. A new King mass-market paperback novel now costs $6.99.

Tourists at King's house

They come from all over the world and stop at the most famous residence in Bangor, marked by its distinctive wrought-iron fence. They inevitably take pictures, usually of themselves posing in front of the bat-guarded gates.

Although the tourists come year-round, the traffic is heaviest on Halloween and during the summer, Maine's peak tourist season, when busloads of tourists show up, cameras dangling from their necks.

In *Castle Rock,* Stephanie Leonard, then King's secretary working out of his home office, wrote: "Why do they come by? To take a picture of the house, hoping to catch a glimpse of its residents coming and going? To get a book signed, or to knock on the door and hope to pass a word with the author of the books they carry? To see the house that is now familiar to them from magazines and calendar covers? All of the above."

Translations

King's books have sold 50 million copies overseas, and have been translated into 32 languages, according to Stuart Tinker of Betts Bookstore:
Bulgarian, Catalan, Chinese, Czech, Danish, Dutch, English, Finnish, French, German, Greek, Hebrew, Hungarian, Icelandic, Indonesian, Italian, Japanese, Korean, Latvian, Lithuanian, Norwegian, Polish, Portuguese, Rumanian, Russian, Serbo-Croatian, Slovak, Slovene, Spanish, Swedish, Turkish, and Ukrainian.

Transylvania Station

The novelized script to the Mohonk mystery weekend the Kings attended, put on by Donald and Abby Westlake in Mohonk, New York. It featured an introduction by King.

Naomi King (*Castle Rock*): "S.K.'s introduction gives insight to the character of Donald Westlake as well as some entertainment; it is probably the best part of the book."

Triad Publishing Company

Before there was Philtrum Press, there was Triad Publishing Company, which published King and Chris Chesley's *People, Places, and Things* in 1960. In 1964, the admittedly *very* small press self-published *The Star Invaders*, though the company had changed its name to Triad, Inc., and Gaslight Books.

Both "books" were mimeographed on David King's machine, which was also used to print the community newspaper, *Dave's Rag.* (Why was the company called "Triad"? There was no third party —only King and Chesley. Perhaps David King was included?)

Triskaidekaphobia

King suffers from this fear, which is fear of the number 13. In 1982 he told Phil Thomas, an AP Books editor, "I don't like thirteen at all. I don't like Friday the thirteenth, specifically, and I don't like the number generally. Thirteen seems to have an enchanted hold on me. Maybe, it's because of what I write. It seems that if you get successful, if you hit it big, then you get superstitious."

Trivia

Oddest accident while reading a King book: During a thunderstorm at night, a girl's bed was struck by lightning. (Was she reading *Firestarter*?)

Most expensive limited edition published (issue price): $2,200 for *My Pretty Pony*, in the Whitney Museum edition.

Most unusually bound King book: An asbestos-bound edition of *Firestarter*, from Phantasia Press. (The publisher likely got the idea after hearing about the asbestos-bound copy of *Fahrenheit 451*.)

Most copies printed of a small-press edition of a King book: 45,000 copies of *Dark Tower IV: Wizard and Glass*, the Grant edition.

Price paid for a letter typed by King in his early teens as a submission letter to *Famous Monsters of Filmland*: $440.

Longest book by King: *The Stand: The Complete and Uncut Edition* (1,153 pages).

Worst King film adaptation: *Children of the Corn.*

Best King adaptations: *Carrie, The Dead Zone, Stand by Me, Misery, The Shawshank Redemption.* (You can bet money that *The Green Mile* will join that list in due time.)

Most expensive King-related flop: The Broadway production of *Carrie.*

Estimated King books in print worldwide: 250 million (200 million in the U.S.).

Most prolific King critic: Dr. Michael R. Collings.

Most frequent occupations of King's main characters: Teacher and writer.

Most frequent fictional locale: Maine.

Best book about King: Douglas E. Winter's *Stephen King: the Art of Darkness.*

Most laughable proposed book on King: A collection of original stories featuring Stephen King as the main character. (Not surprisingly, King didn't think much of this idea and wrote to the editor to express his concerns, at which point the project was, thankfully, deep-sixed.)

"Trucks" (collected in *Night Shift*)

Appeared originally in *Cavalier* (June 1973). The hapless inhabitants of a truck stop are under siege by big trucks that have come to life and instead of serving man now want to be served *by* man, in an obscene inversion of the natural order. Humans are not served by technology but, in fact, must service the products of technology—the sentient, amoral 18-wheel trucks that pull into the truck

stop to get refueled . . . and refueled . . . and refueled, no matter the human cost or casualties.

This story was the basis for the movie *Maximum Overdrive*, which was originally titled *Trucks.*

Note: Roger Zelazny, a fantasy–sci-fi writer, wrote frequently on this theme. "The Devil Car" explores the notion of a marauding band of renegade cars that deliberately killed their drivers, allowing them to roam freely, to find new prey.

Trucks (film), 1997

USA Network made-for-TV movie based on the short story of the same name, which aired on October 29, November 1, and November 8, 1997.

Trunk books

Unpublished or aborted manuscripts that for various reasons will likely never see publication in any form. Most of these failed literary experiments, early efforts or projects that never quite jelled, are novels. In the fanzine *Skin*, Charlie Fried compiled a list of these projects, mentioned in various places over the years:

♦ *Blaze:* 50,000 words; novel completed on February 15, 1973. On deposit at the Special Collections at UMO.

♦ *The Cannibals:* Original title, *Under the Dome;* written in longhand when King was filming *Creepshow* in Philadelphia.

♦ *Sword in the Darkness:* Also called *Babylon Here;* 485 manuscript pages. A completed novel on deposit at the Special Collections at UMO.

♦ *The Corner:* An aborted 1976 novel. Source: Douglas E. Winter in *Stephen King: The Art of Darkness.*

♦ *The Doors:* An aborted novel. Source: Dr. Michael Collings.

♦ *The Milkman:* An aborted novel. Note: Two pieces from the novel were subsequently published in *Skeleton Crew.*

♦ *Welcome to Clearwater*: An aborted 1976 novel.

♦ *Weeds:* An aborted novel of which approximately 20,000 words were written.

♦ Untitled novel set in the West, aborted in 1989. "A few years ago," King said at a 1989 talk in California, "I tried very hard to write a Western, because it's a form I like. I wrote about 160 pages, but the only scene that really had any power was when the old guy got drunk outside a farmhouse and fell into the pigsty, and the pigs ate him. That one scene had some real drive and punch. That is what turned on my lights, for some reason I don't understand."

♦ *The Plant:* Three installments were published by Philtrum Press as Christmas greetings, but no more will likely appear, since the story was headed in the same direction as *The Little Shop of Horrors,* which killed King's incentive to finish it.

Fried also cites several works that fall into the category of "I have this idea and may write it someday." Books that King has mentioned in passing include the following:

♦ A sequel to *'Salem's Lot,* which picks up where that novel left off. Ben Mears, in London, gets an eerie phone call from his mother who tells him, "They're hurting me." He realizes that the horror isn't over . . . yet. (In an interview for *Fangoria* #58, King later said: "It has been too long. The kid's all grown up now, and the only way to do it would be to slug it back in time and set it up in 1980. At one time, that was something I wanted to do very much, but the time has gone by. It always does after a while. You either write it, or the time passes.")

♦ *Steel Machine:* Portions of this appeared under the Richard Stark byline in the text of *The Dark Half.* My guess: King will write this novel.

♦ An untitled "baseball" novel. For an article called "Field of Screams" by Daniel Golden, for the *Boston Globe,* King told Golden, "It's daunting. There are so many great baseball novels, like *The Natural* and *Bang the Drum Slowly.* But it will happen sooner or later."

♦ An untitled novel about a charismatic evangelist, a Christlike figure, in a Jonestown scenario.

♦ SK: A "story about a killer toilet, but I don't think anybody would publish it. I think it could be pretty good, if I could find a way to do it. After all, you're so vulnerable when . . . oh, never mind." (Quoted by Peter Strupp, Putnam publicity department, April 1985.)

♦ In a *USA Today* interview (May 10, 1985), King also mentioned an Elvis novel, a magic carpet novel, and a rock and roll novel.

Ubris

UMO literary magazine.

King published poetry and short stories in this journal. His first appearance was in its spring 1968 issue, with the publication of "Here There Be Tygers" and "Cain Rose Up."

Ultimate Unauthorized
Stephen King Trivia Challenge,
compiled by Robert W. Bly

Published in 1997 by Kensington Publishing Corp., this trade paperback is subtitled *Hundreds of Brainteasing Questions on Minute Details and Little-Known Facts About the World's Bestselling Author and His Work.* Written after Bly discovered that Stephen Spignesi's two trivia quiz books were out of print, Bly's book is marred with some technical errors, pointed out by members of SKE-MERs. In fact, the errors are sufficiently numerous that Betts Bookstore noted on its Web site that it is "probably the worst researched book on Steve we have ever seen! Many, many incorrect answers, but if a revised and corrected edition is ever done, you should have this one!" (Bly has made note of all the errors and promises to issue a revised edition in the future.)

"Umney's Last Case"
(collected in *Nightmares & Dreamscapes*)

First appearing on the Internet, then collected in *Nightmares & Dreamscapes,* this story was cited by King in his book notes as his favorite in this anthology. It was also published separately as a 95¢ paperback on the occasion of Penguin's sixtieth anniversary.

This homage to hard-bitten crime novels, the kind written by Raymond Chandler and Ross MacDonald, isn't merely an imitation, as you'd likely see in an anthology of homages, but an innovation. Like the holodeck in *Star Trek: The Next Generation,* which allows the crew of the *Enterprise* to interact with fictional constructs that come to life through computer imagery, this story is King's unique intersection between the creator and the created.

What appears to be another perfect day for a Los Angeles gumshoe, Clyde Umney, is anything

The cover to a Penguin paperback, reprinting as a separate book *Umney's Last Case.*

but: One by one, all of the familiar landmarks around him are changing, but he can't figure out why. The changes to his environment are unsettling because it's as if his world is literally shifting around him—his worst nightmare. Even his office is no refuge; his longtime secretary has split for home, and the building's interior is being repainted.

The mystery is solved when Samuel Landry makes his inevitable appearance, in a chapter appropriately titled "An Interview with God." The owner of the Fulwider Building, where Umney has his office, Landry in fact is the creator of Umney's fictional world. Afflicted with shingles, devastated by the death of his son and the suicide of his wife, Landry has come to escape the horrors of the real world. He's *had* it with reality, and has come to exchange lives with Umney.

A marvelously inventive story, "Umney's Last Case" makes you wish King would write more stories in this vein; not necessarily gumshoe fiction, but time-traveling story benders or fiction about fiction. It takes considerable imagination to pull it off, but King's got that in spades.

Uncollected stories

Stories not published in a trade King collection include the following:

Before the Play (*Whispers*, 1982)

Blind Willie (*Antaeus: The Final Volume*)

The Blue Air Compressor (*Onan*, 1971; *Heavy Metal*, July 1981, in a revised version)

The Cat from Hell (*Cavalier*, June 1977; revised for *Tales of Unknown Horror*, 1978)

The Crate (*Gallery*, 1979; published as a graphic story in *Creepshow* comic)

The Glass Floor (*Startling Mystery Stories*, fall 1967)

Jhonathan and the Witches (*First Words*)

The Killer (*Famous Monsters of Filmland*, spring 1994)

The Luckey Quarter (*USA Weekend*, Sunday supplement, 1995)

Lunch at the Gotham Café (*Dark Love*, ed. Nancy Collings et al.)

The Man in the Black Suit (*New Yorker*, Oct. 31, 1994)

Man with a Belly (*Cavalier*, December 1978)

Night of the Tiger (*The Magazine of Fantasy and Science Fiction*, 1978)

The Reploids (*Night Visions V*, 1988)

The Revelations of 'Becka Paulson (*Rolling Stone*, July 19–Aug. 2, 1984)

Squad D (forthcoming, *Last Dangerous Visions*, ed. Harlan Ellison)

Weeds (*Cavalier*, May 1976; published as a graphic story, "The Lonesome Death of Jordy Verrill," in *Creepshow* comic)

"Uncle Otto's Truck"
(collected in *Skeleton Crew*)

Originally published in *Yankee* magazine (1983), this story is based on a real scene, says Douglas E. Winter in his notes on the story in *Stephen King: The Art of Darkness*: Between Center Lovell and Bridgton, on Black Henry Road, there's a dilapidated truck in an open field with its nose pointed toward a one-room house across the road.

It's 1953 and two partners who went in on a land deal to buy 4,000 acres in Castle Rock for $10,000 are as drunk as the last lords of creation. George McCucheon's riding shotgun, and Uncle Otto is driving. But as they drive down the far side of Trinity Hill, Uncle Otto doesn't downshift, and the old Cresswell overheats. The truck runs off the road, its windshield covered by Diamond Gem Oil.

After its wheels are sold for $20 by McCucheon, there the truck sits, up on blocks, a permanent fixture of the land, just like the White Mountains in the background.

Two years later, though, McCucheon dies when the truck pitches forward off its blocks and crushes him. But it was no accident; it was murder, conceived by Uncle Otto, to benefit from a land deal with which he was at odds with his partner, McCucheon.

Uncle Otto had planted something in front of the truck, knowing his partner would bend over to pick it up; Otto, positioned behind the heavy truck, pushed it, pitching it forward, "Squotting him like a pumpkin."

After McCucheon dies, Uncle Otto sells the ill-gotten land at an obscene profit and becomes increasingly peculiar, downright eccentric, and finally as crazy as a shithouse rat, as the townsfolk said.

Otto offers the town the one-room building as a schoolhouse, but the town doesn't want it, one-room schoolhouses being a thing of the past. Otto spites the town by living in the building. Worth $7 million, the old man is living in the spurned building, with his stationary truck across the road to keep him company.

Otto claims that the truck is inching forward, trying to reach him, to kill him, which is discounted as mere babbling. But, the narrator recounts, when he visits to drop off groceries, he discovers Otto dead, with Diamond Gem Oil squirting from his nose and mouth—the same kind of oil that covered the windshield after the truck went off the road years earlier.

The narrator thinks it could all be dismissed, except for one fact: In Otto's mouth was a Champion spark plug, vintage 1920, the kind used in the ancient Cresswell.

Uncorrected proofs

The best way to promote a book is to provide an advance copy to key media, sometimes set in type as uncorrected galleys and sometimes photocopied from the manuscript itself. Proofs sent to reviewers bear the warning on the front or back cover, "Warning: if any material is to be quoted, it must be checked against the bound book."

Proofs of King's books are very collectible and care is taken in their distribution, since the publisher wants them to get into the hands of reviewers and sales staff, not collectors.

Underwood typewriter

A manual typewriter King used to type his early work, and also was used by David King to type mimeograph stencils for *Dave's Rag*.

In *Stephen King: The Art of Darkness*, there's a photo that shows King in his bedroom in Durham, hunched over the typewriter, with a copy of his first published short story propped on the typewriter.

Office model Underwood typewriter, similar to the kind King used up through college. (As the keys broke, King had to fill in the letters by hand.)

Undone, by Michael Kimball

SK: "Sly, sexy, suspenseful . . . and very, very moving."

Uniform

King almost always dresses casually, even for public appearances: Tee-shirt, jeans, and his Converse sneakers. Sometimes he dresses up for a special occasion, as he did for the world premiere of *Firestarter* or for formal functions out of town.

University of Maine at Orono

Land grant university in Orono, Maine, which Stephen and Tabitha King attended.

Stephen King has noted that although he did receive encouragement from the English department, for which he was grateful, the writing courses "constipated" him. He prefers to work alone, relying on his own sense of what's good and what's not. (How valid would the criticisms of fellow aspiring college writers be, anyway?)

King did get a thorough grounding in American literature—he collects first editions of John Steinbeck and William Faulkner—and an appreciation of poetry, which he writes, though as an undergraduate he was frustrated by the common perception that popular literature was trash. He later went back to teach for a year as a writer in residence.

The only undergraduate to ever teach a course at the school—a seminar on popular literature—King got his undergraduate degree with certification to teach at high school level, and got an honorary doctorate years later, after his career took off.

A generous benefactor of the college, King was the subject of a weekend seminar on his work, "Reading Stephen King," in October 1996.

University of Maine at Presque Isle

King gave a public talk on September 10, 1982, at the Wieden Gymnasium at UMPI, followed the next day by a book-signing session at the bookstore in Preble Hall.

For this second lecture in the Dr. George W. Bowman series UMPI faculty wanted a "national

Sign on campus of the University of Maine at Orono.

public figure who was the product of a liberal arts education and who possessed literary skills and talents." ("Stephen King to Lecture at U of M, Presque Isle," *Lewiston Daily Sun*, Aug. 26, 1982.)

University of Maine swimming program

After a cutback in the $4.3 million UM athletic budget in the late '90s, the Black Bear men's and women's varsity swimming and diving programs were adversely affected; King made an undisclosed donation to support the program. "I wanted to preserve my right to say two things. There's something wrong with a system where the hockey team can go to Los Angeles and the swimming team can't go to Bridgeport, Connecticut.... The other thing I wanted to say is the University of Maine has got to be able to do something for these kids. There's got to be a continuing effort to look around and help these programs that don't get on TV." (Quoted in Mike Dowd, "UM Swimming Program Kept Alive by King's Gift, *BDN*, Feb. 5, 1992.)

The Unseen King, by Tyson Blue

Published by Starmont House in 1989, this book has been superseded by Stephen Spignesi's authoritative book on the same subject, *The Lost Work of Stephen King.*

Contents
Introduction
1. Childhood and Other Early Work
2. The Maine Campus Years
3. Early Uncollected Short Stories
4. The "True" Limiteds
5. "The Plant": The Rarest King
6. The Poetry of King
7. Later Uncollected Short Stories
8. Screenplays
9. Editorials and Other Nonfiction
Conclusion: Under the Wire
List of Works Cited and Consulted
Index

USA Today Summer Fiction Series

An annual series of stories celebrating summer fiction that had appeared in *USA Today*. For 1995, six stories were published, leading off with King's "Luckey Quarter," which was inspired by a stop he made at a hotel in Carson City, Nevada, when he went on his coast-to-coast *Insomnia* tour. "My eye caught the housekeeper's 'honor envelope' propped up on the telephone, and the whole story just fell into my head," he told *USA Today*. King's story appeared in the June 30–July 2, 1995, issue.

The other contributors in the series were Alice Hoffman, Rita Dove, Julia Alvarez, Walter Mosley, and Gail Godwin.

Vacations

King likes to take a break from the word processor, on occasion. His most recent vacation: a ride across the Australian plains on a motorcycle, in November 1997.

Vandalism

In October 1986 and January 1987 issues of *The Bangor Daily News*, Bob Haskell wrote about the thefts from the King residence, including the bats and the gargoyle from the fence fronting the property.

The culprit was caught and gave up his ill-gotten goods.

Van Hise, James

A fan turned pro, prolific popular culture writer, and former editor for the comic zine *RB-CC*, Hise wrote two books on King: *Enterprise Incidents Presents Stephen King*, and *Stephen King/Clive Barker: The Illustrated Guide to the Masters of the Macabre*.

The publisher of *Midnight Graffiti*, Hise published "Rainy Season" in its pages and writes books on popular culture subjects for Pioneer Books of Las Vegas, Nevada.

Vasectomy

In the *Daily News Magazine* (July 13, 1985), King talked about his vasectomy. "I had this vasectomy done awhile ago and the guy doctor did something he shouldn't have, crossed some wires somewhere. See, they give you a local and then they do a little snip on you, in the office, fit it up with gauze pads and send you home, tell you to take it easy. So I thought, fine, I'll just sit in my chair and write, the study was downstairs at the time and I didn't have to move around a lot. I was working on *Firestarter* and it was going great."

Tabitha King added: "I found him working in a pool of blood. Anyone else would have been screaming, but he said, 'Hold on, let me just finish this paragraph!' "

Vehicles

King has owned numerous vehicles over the years, including two Mercedes (one for him and one for Tabitha), a Pinto, a Chevy van, a Chevy Blazer, a Cadillac convertible, and a Harley Davidson motorcycle.

The Village Vomit

A parody of his high school newspaper, King's satirical effort would normally have landed him a three-day suspension, but the authorities figured that the punishment should fit the crime, so he was "sentenced" to be a sportswriter for the local newspaper, the *Lisbon Enterprise*, for which he earned a half cent per word.

King credits its editor, John Gould, with showing him everything he needed to know about writing successfully: the art of rewriting.

"I was a journalist for a while. The first thing I was ever paid for was a sports column . . . I protested that I didn't know anything about sports and the guy says, 'Do you know how to write?' I said I thought I did. He said, 'We're going to find out.' He said if I could write, then I could learn about sports. So I wrote about bowling leagues and basketball games and stuff like that." (Quoted in Loukia Louka, "The Dispatch Talks with Writer King," *Maryland Coast Dispatch*, Aug. 8, 1986.)

Virginia Beach, Virginia

King gave a talk in this city on September 21, 1986. Prior to the talk, King signed hundreds of books, which were offered for sale. (Predictably, demand exceeded supply.)

Sponsored by Friends of the Virginia Beach Library, King's talk was well attended and well received. A videotape of the talk was broadcast on local cable channels, prompting criticism from conservatives who chided King for drinking beer in public in front of impressionable teens. (King had a sore throat and lubricated it with beer during the talk.)

A poster that promoted King's appearance in Virginia Beach, Virginia, on September 22, 1986.

house and when it was my turn to work on the book I would simply go up to my study and pound on my Wang. And that was good. And when I pounded on my Wang for a period of time I would call up Peter and say, 'It's ready.' And then I would send him what I had pounded." (*Fantasy Review*, November 1984.)

"Wanna read"

King's term for books he wanted to read, as he indicated in an article for *Seventeen* magazine; writers like John D. MacDonald (who would later write an introduction to King's *Night Shift*), Ed McBain, Shirley Jackson, Wilkie Collins, Ken Kesey, Tom Wolfe essays, Robert E. Howard (the creator of Conan), Andrew Norton, Jack London, Agatha Christie (a favorite of his mother's), *Gone with the Wind*, and comic books.

Web sites

The explosion of Web sites devoted to Stephen King attests to his growing popularity.

Ranging from text-only sites to elaborate, multimedia sites created by his Constant Readers and his publishers, the sites are the best way to keep informed in Stephen's kingdom, so to speak.

The Web is especially useful for reporting time-sensitive news, such as the imminent release of a forthcoming limited edition book by King.

Because of the large number of sites devoted exclusively to King—and their changing Web addresses—it's impractical to list them in this book. Your best option is to surf the Net and bookmark your favorite sites.

Web site: *Wizard and Glass*

Penguin, in collaboration with Headland Digital Media, created a web site to promote the fourth *Dark Tower* novel, *Wizard and Glass* (http://www.darktowerIV.com). This interactive site allowed visitors to test their knowledge in a "Dark Tower Trivia Challenge," talk on-line with other King fans, and register for a chance to win a trip for two to the Stanley Hotel in Estes Park, Colorado.

Waller, Robert James

Best-selling author of *The Bridges of Madison County*, which has sold more copies than any other novel in publishing history.

At Reading Stephen King, a conference in his honor, King gave a keynote address and talked about the "weird inverse ratio" of Waller's sales: Each successive book was better written than the last but sold less, a sharp contrast to King's readership, which mushroomed and then stabilized at predictable sales levels.

Wang Systems 5 word processor

The stand-alone word-processing machine King used for many years, until he retired it to write on Macintosh [Apple] computers, a Powerbook and a desktop, using Microsoft Word, which allows him to enlarge the type on the screen—necessary because of the macular degeneration with which he's afflicted. (The Wang also used large, eight-inch floppy disks, whereas the Apple computers use the standard 3.5-inch floppies.)

When King collaborated with Peter Straub on *The Talisman*, he explained to Douglas E. Winter, "We got word processors to do the book. That was his idea, and it was a good one. And we were hooked up by modems. He had an IBM and I had my big Wang. I had this big Wang at my

Maryann Palumbo, senior VP of marketing at Penguin Putnam: "The *Wizard and Glass* Web site is going to be a big draw for King fans around the world who have waited nearly six years for the next installment of this best-selling series. There's a huge community of King devotees, and many of them are already on-line from the tremendous response generated by *The Green Mile* on-line campaign last year. *The Wizard and Glass* Web site enables these fans to explore the books and its characters in a new way and at the same time to test their knowledge of the author and his work."

"The Wedding Gig"
(collected in *Skeleton Crew*)

Originally appearing in *Ellery Queen's Mystery Magazine* (1980), this story, set in 1927, tells of a jazz band that's invited to play at the wedding of Mike Scollay's sister. But it's not just any wedding gig, because Scollay is a "small-time racketeer" whose sister's weight has made her the butt of everyone's jokes—a very sore point with him. In fact, it proves to be Mike's undoing, because he's goaded by comments about his sister at her wedding and, in a blind rage, runs out into an ambush set by his nemesis, the Greek.

Payback, as they say, is a mother . . . and Mike's sister, Maureen, proves to be as bad as she is big, and "turned it [his operation] into a Prohibition empire that rivaled Capone's." And when she gets her hands on the Greek, "blubbering and pleading for his life," she executes him personally in a grisly and painful manner. (You don't want to know.)

King has an uncanny ability to recreate the milieu of the past with astonishing fidelity. The dialogue is dead-on, the slang's on the mark, and as far as that goes, King's writing is aces in my book.

"Weeds" (uncollected)

Originally published in *Cavalier*, May 1976.

Later adapted in comic book format for *Creepshow* ("The Lonesome Death of Jordy Verrill"), "Weeds" is the story of a New Hampshire hayseed, Jordy Verrill, who considers himself lucky —for once—after finding a meteor on his farm; he figures on selling it to the local university. But he accidentally breaks it open and liquid at its core spills out, transforming him from human to something plantlike, a weed monster of sorts, until he puts himself out of his misery.

Unfortunately, Jordy may be the only one who has escaped the effects of the fast-growing extraterrestrial weed, since it grows unchecked, toward the nearby town and, after that, presumably, engulfs an innocent world.

Welcome to Clearwater

Aborted novel begun in 1976.

West Broadway

Bangor's historic street with homes dating back to the turn of the century, when lumber barons made their fortunes.

King's Italianate house is located on this street.

"What would you have done?"

What the editors of *Midnight Graffiti* said when they got a new unsolicited King story, "Rainy Season," and a note asking if they wanted to publish it in their zine.

SK: "It's a story that means a lot to me, because it was the first good thing I managed to write after an unhappy year spent groping my way through a writer's block." (Letter to Michael Collings, May 24, 1989.)

Whelan, Michael

An award-winning artist in the fantasy field best known for his book cover illustrations.

Judging from his awards received, he is the most popular artist in the fantasy field. Whelan has published three collections of his art.

As for King material, Whelan's illustrated *The Dark Tower: The Gunslinger* for Grant and painted the art for the cover for the trade paperback edition of *The Dark Tower: The Gunslinger* and for the wraparound cover for the limited edition of

Michael Whelan *continued*

Firestarter, judged one of the finest fantasy illustrations in our time.

Photoprints of the painting for *Firestarter* and *The Dark Tower: The Gunslinger* were self-published; another firm published a lithographic print of *The Dark Tower: The Gunslinger.*

Whelan's prints can be purchased from: Glass Onion Graphics (P.O. Box 88, Brookfield, CT 06804), a mail-order company run by his wife, Audrey Price.

"When Buying Rare Books, Remember: Go for King, Not Galsworthy"

This article appeared in the *Wall Street Journal* (Jan. 14, 1985), urging investors buying books to cash in on King novels.

Thirteen years later, that's still good advice, as King collectors have found out.

"Whining About the Movies in Bangor: Take That, *Top Gun*"

In a guest column in *BDN,* King took umbrage at a story that ran in the paper, a phone interview with a patrician executive of General Cinema Corporation, who said that *Blue Velvet* and *A Room with a View* would show in the Bangor area, even though both would lose money; however, it would keep the populace from "whining" about not getting the quality films. (The sense I got was that he considered Maine to be a cultural wasteland, in the backwoods, and the rubes didn't understand the industry. Unfortunately, King lambasted the wrong company, for General Cinema did not operate theaters in Bangor or the surrounding area.)

King was understandably upset. Citing that the greater Bangor area supports a dozen theaters in a five-mile radius, he resented the Boston snobbery, saying that the "assertion that Bangor area residents won't support quality product is dumb."

Noting that Bangor typically misses out on independent films and grade-B movies as well, King—who has spent a lot of time in the film industry as screenwriter, producer, actor, and main advocate of shooting Maine films on location—explained that film distribution is a mystery to most people, and the less the people know about what gets selected and sent out to theaters, the happier the industry is as a whole. In the end, King notes, "We're just stuck with what they'll give us."

All of which explains the boom in video rentals, pay-per-view movies, and satellite dishes.

Whitney Museum of Art

Contemporary art museum in New York City, which through its in-house publishing program issued *My Pretty Pony,* the most expensive—and to King's mind, overpriced and overproduced—limited edition of his work published to date: a $2,200 book measuring 13.5 by 21 inches, with a stainless steel cover, sporting a digital clock (deliberately designed to run down).

My Pretty Pony was designed by Barbara Kruger, who worked on her own, by choice: "Not only didn't I want to go up to Maine, I didn't even ask to get from King any instructions on how to handle the text," she told *Artnews.*

The result: An oddly illustrated and designed book with a print run of only 280 copies.

For the book trade, Knopf issued a 68-page facsimile reprint—15,000 copies—that sold for $50. (It was published in a slightly smaller trim size: 9.25 by 13.5 inches.)

"Who Killed Bobby Ewing?"

In *TV Guide* (Aug. 30, 1986), King commented that an enemy of J. R. Ewing would reanimate Bobby—a classic King scenario, if I've ever heard of one!

"Why I Am for Gary Hart"

In the *New Republic* (June 4, 1984), King wrote a short essay on why he was for Gary Hart and against the incumbent, President Ronald Reagan. In a nutshell, King wrote that he believed Hart would make a difference, whereas Reagan was bad news. "It is, simply put, that Ronald Reagan is a bad President and must be turned out of office." King's distaste for Reagan was so strong that he echoed Michael McDowell's observation that he'd vote for a dead dog in the street, if he honestly thought the dog had a chance of beating Reagan.

King not only campaigned for and with Hart, but in November 1984 gave a public reception at his Bangor home that 150 people attended, paying $12.50 a head.

Wiener, Robert

General manager and partner in Donald M. Grant, Publisher. A longtime publisher in the fantasy-art field, Wiener's TK II and Archival Press published the work of noted fantasy artists Vaughn Bode, Jeffrey Jones, and Berni Wrightson, to name but a few.

Wiener has done an exceptionally fine job in publishing King's limited editions, notably the *Dark Tower* novels.

Willden, Nye

An editor at *Cavalier* magazine.

Nye Willden, on King's fiction: "I was very impressed, sensing that there was something very out of the ordinary about King's writing."

Those early years when *Cavalier* published his short stories, paying $250 to $300, were tough times for King. As Willden remembers, "He was having a difficult time financially." So difficult, in fact, that when King needed money badly, he would call, and get, an advance check for a story that normally would have been paid on publication only.

William Arnold House

Originally built in 1856 by William Arnold, it was sold to William H. Smith in 1857 for $6,148.93. The Kings bought the home in 1980 to use as their winter home. The home on Kezar Lake in the Lakes region of Maine is their summer home.

They spent four years renovating the interior and erecting a wrought-iron fence around the entire property, necessary because of the increasing crowds and a few crazies who trespassed.

With 23 rooms and an indoor swimming pool, the house serves as the home office for both Stephen and Tabitha King. It used to house the office staff, but they have since been moved to a separate office on the outskirts of Bangor.

Clearly the most famous house in Bangor—and one of the most distinctive, on a street with other architecturally interesting structures—the William Arnold House is now known as the King House.

Note: This was the first house built on West Broadway, and is the only Italianate villa.

Winter, Douglas E.

A prominent figure in the horror community, Winter published the first book about King, for Starmont House. That book was subsequently expanded and revised for its publication by NAL, which issued *Stephen King: The Art of Darkness* in hardback, trade paperback and mass-market paperback.

A seminal book, *Stephen King: The Art of Darkness* was the only book to be written with King's consent and cooperation, which allowed Winter to incorporate exclusive, illuminating interview material throughout the text.

Best known as a critic, anthologist (notably *Prime Evil* and *Revelations*), and interviewer, Winter is also a writer in his own right, publishing short stories and writing novels as well.

Douglas E. Winter: "I got a ton of letters when the book first came out; I would always get these letters from school kids, from teachers, from librarians, from federal prisoners—all telling me how much they enjoyed the book. Most of the letters would have a postscript: How can I find a copy of *The Dark Tower*? I really did receive some nice feedback from the book. There's obviously a tremendous number of Stephen King fans out there, and I think this was the sort of thing that they were waiting for, that was perfect for them, because it more or less organized the fiction and I think also served as a real companion, and I hope illuminated the books a great deal. That was the intent of it, to say: Here's not only some fiction that you've been reading for enjoyment, but there are messages, there are themes, there are subtexts here that are important. To me, that's always been

Douglas E. Winter, at his home in the Washington D.C. suburbs, displays his book, *Stephen King: The Art of Darkness*.

Douglas E. Winter *continued*

key: to consider what fiction is about and how it affects me and my thinking. I always hate it when people discount Steve as being just an entertainer, because he's not. The same thing's true about other major writers of horror fiction. And here was my opportunity in this book to make clear some very significant things that were going on." (Interview with George Beahm, 1988.)

Wizard and Glass Web site

The official site for the book, the Web site (*http://www.darktowerIV.com*) is your path to the world of *The Dark Tower*.

"The Woman in the Room"

(collected in *Night Shift*)

First published in this collection, this story is one of King's best, underscoring his frequent theme that death is the real boogeyman, and that sometimes death can be a blessing.

Drawing from his real-life experiences when he visited his mother at the hospital, when she was dying of cancer, King wrote his way through the pain by writing this story: Set in a hospital room at the Central Maine Hospital, the dying mother has one last request from her son—to help her ease the pain by putting her out of it permanently. Johnny, a good son, does his duty, in a loving act that serves as a final communion between them.

"The Woman in the Room" was a story that, as King explained, hit home hard. In an afternote to the story, collected in *The Year's Best Horror Fiction*, edited by Karl Wagner, King wrote that it was healing fiction, written in the wake of his mother's lingering death from cancer. Typically, fiction performs its healing powers for the reader; this time, it did so for its author.

The Woman in the Room (film), 1984

Stephen King's policy about student films is straightforward: In exchange for $1, a copy of the finished film, and a promise not to release the film commercially, King will grant one-time rights for a student to make a short film based on his short fiction (his novels are inevitably optioned for motion pictures).

So when a student named Frank Darabont contacted him about filming a short based on "The Woman in the Room," King granted permission and promptly forgot it. After all, it was just a student film . . . but *what* a film! The 32-minute film was later collected for home video release in *Stephen King's Night Shift Collection* (the "B" side was *The Boogeyman*).

The story, which closes *Night Shift* (the book), is simply told: John Elliott is at the bedside of his mother, at the Central Maine hospital in Lewiston. She is in great pain and is terminally ill, and wants her son to put an end to the pain, knowing it means prematurely ending her life as well. Living like this is a slow death for her, and is an ordeal for her son as well, and the son does his duty and gives his mother the Darvon Complex pills that put an end to her misery.

When it was completed, a videotape of the film was sent to King, who put it in his VHS machine, more out of curiosity than anyting else, not expecting much of anything.

Imagine his surprise when he saw what a masterful job Darabont had done, breathing new life into this personal story King had written.

This short film remains a personal favorite of King's, proving that big budgets and brand-name actors aren't as important as trying to transfer intact the feel of King from the printed page to the visual medium. A big budget is no substitute for imagination, insight, and empathy in the filmmaking process.

Eleven years passed . . . and the student director had turned pro, bringing to the screen another King film, *The Shawshank Redemption*, which was a critical success in the theaters and a critical and financial success in video stores.

Darabont expects to repeat history with his next King project, *The Green Mile*, which is, as King pointed out, likely to make him the director occupying the smallest niche in King-based films: period prison movies.

Now, if you're a betting soul, I'd like to make a wager: I'll bet you any amount of money that *The Green Mile*, starring Tom Hanks, will be a critical and financial success in the theaters. Bet your fur!

Wordaholic

SK: "Compulsive reading is a sickness and I've always wanted to be Typhoid Steve." (Quoted by Dawn Gagnon, "King Urges Keeping an Open Mind When Reading," *BDN*, Oct. 12, 1996.)

"Word Processor of the Gods"
(collected in *Skeleton Crew*)

Originally published in *Playboy* magazine (Jan. 1983), this story is about Richard Hagstrom and his modern-day genie's lamp, a makeshift word processor constructed by his nephew, Jon, who built it with whatever parts he could find, because his uncle couldn't afford a new machine.

The people to whom he was closest—his nephew Jonathan and his mother Belinda—are dead, killed in an auto accident at the hands of his late, drunken brother. Hagstrom, who dated Belinda years ago, feels that she should have been his wife, and Jonathan their child; instead, he's trapped in a loveless marriage with a verbally abusive wife and son and wishes he could magically restore Jonathan and Belinda to life and edit out his own wife and son.

Instead of that picture-perfect family, he's trapped in a loveless marriage that produced Seth, an obnoxious son who verbally abuses his father, just like his mother does. Like mother, like son. . .

Hagstrom, though, soon realizes after causing a picture on the wall to disappear, the word processor has the ability to literally change reality after he types whatever he wishes on the processor and hits the EXECUTE or DELETE buttons. He then edits his son out, then his wife, and inserts his nephew Jonathan and Belinda in their places, giving him the family he's always wanted.

The Word Processor of the Gods
(film), 1985

King, looking at the DELETE and ENTER buttons on his word processor, wondered what would happen if they literally got rid of whatever he

Word Processor of the Gods (film) *continued*
typed on the screen. The result: this short, effective piece that aired as an installment of *Tales from the Darkside*, a collaborative effort between George A. Romero and Richard Rubinstein of Laurel Entertainment.

In this story, Richard Hagstrom—a failed writer, not unlike Jack Torrance—edits his life to his satisfaction.

The Work of Stephen King: An Annotated Bibliography & Guide,
by Michael Collings

Published by Borgo Press in 1996, this guide is a must for King fans, teachers, students, academicians, and anyone else who needs authoritative information on primary and secondary publications by and about King.

An expansion of Collings's previously published bibliography, published by Starmont House, this book is the single best book of its kind.

Contents

Introduction: Not So Much to Tell, As to Let the Story Flow Through

A King Chronology

About Michael R. Collings

Part I. Primary Works

A. Books
B. Short Fiction [including excerpts from longer works]
C. Short Nonfiction
D. Poetry
E. Screenplays
F. Public and Screen Appearances
G. Visual Adaptations of King Materials
H. Audio Adaptations of King Materials

Part II. Secondary Works

I. Books and Book-Length Studies
J. Newsletters
K. Bibliographies and Filmographies
L. Profiles and Bio-Bibliographical Sketches
M. Interviews with King
N. Scholarly Essays
O. Articles in Popular and News Magazines
P. Media Magazines, Specialty Magazines, Fan Publications
Q. *Castle Rock: The Stephen King Newsletter* (1985–1989)
R. Newspaper Articles
S. Articles in Professional and Trade Journals
T. Selected Reviews of King Works
U. The King Archives, University of Maine, Orono
V. Unpublished Works
W. Parodies, Pastiches, Etc.
X. Honors and Awards
Y. Miscellanea

Quoth the Critics

Index: Primary Works

Index: Secondary Works

Index: Authors of Secondary Works and Miscellanea

Work schedule

According to King, as asserted in numerous interviews he has given over the years, he writes every day except on his birthday, the Fourth of July, and Christmas. Although he does maintain an office where his staff works, he prefers to write at home, producing 1,500 words daily.

After breakfast he takes a walk, then settles in for a morning of writing—his serious work, the paycheck books. He usually quits around noon and goes to the office by early afternoon to see what requires his attention.

In the evening he works on what he affectionately terms his "toy trucks," speculative projects that may or may not come to fruition.

That kind of wordage on a daily basis produces a published book a year, though King's prolificness—nonfiction, poetry, short fiction, screenplays—has in some years resulted in more than one book.

Writing

SK: "I am not a thoughtful writer; everything comes from the guts of me, heart in some of the better stuff, intestines in the rest." (Letter dated Aug. 3, 1985, to Michael Collings.)

Writing tools

King, unlike some writers, can write virtually anywhere, using whatever is on hand. His first typewriter was an office-model Underwood, used when he was a teenager up through the time he graduated from college. After graduation, he used this typewriter for writing the first *Dark Tower* novel.

King would later use a green IBM Selectric typewriter.

When traveling, King has written in notebooks, subsequently turned over to his secretaries for retyping into the computer at the office, which was linked to his home office, the site of the main CPU for his Wang word processor.

At the time the Wang was state of the art, like the IBM Displaywriter of its time, the machine preferred by Peter Straub when he was writing *The Talisman* with King. But times change, and King now uses Macintosh computers—a desktop and, for traveling, a Powerbook.

No matter what writing tool King uses, one thing is clear: It is the tale *and* the teller that count.

David King: "Steve was constantly at the typewriter. When I was home from college, he was always upstairs typing. And we always encouraged him. I remember how excited he was when he got his first check for 'The Glass Floor.' He got lots of rejection slips. If I remember correctly, there was a nail pounded in the wall up in the bedroom, and he's spear all the rejection slips on it." (*Shape.*)

World Fantasy Convention

Held in Ottawa, Canada, in 1984; King accepted awards on behalf of Richard Matheson and Peter Straub; Matheson won a World Fantasy Award, Straub a British Fantasy Award. Noted *Locus* magazine in December 1984: "King accepted the award for Matheson and gave a speech about his importance to the horror field as the man who moved horror into contemporary urban settings and is responsible for the tone of modern horror. There was a long ovation for either Matheson or King or both."

Writer's block

King, to my knowledge, has had only two extended periods of writer's block: in college and the prolonged period before he wrote "Rainy Season." Other than that, he's been cheerfully productive, pounding out 1,200 to 1,500 words daily on a year-round basis.

Wyman, Rev. Jasper

Chairman of the Civic League, who in 1986 spearheaded his organization's efforts to get a ban on the promotion and sale of pornographic material in Maine. Using the inflammatory slogan "Do it for the children," Wyman's efforts proved, in the end, to be insufficient. The referendum was overwhelmingly voted down in a primary election held on June 10—72 percent against the ban, 28 percent for it.

SK: "I'm against it because I don't know what it will do. . . . Pass a law like this and where does it stop? . . . I think the idea of making it a crime to sell obscene material is a bad one because it takes the responsibility of saying 'no' out of the hands of citizens and puts it into those of the police and the courts. I think it's a bad idea because it's undemocratic, high-handed, and frighteningly diffuse." (*Castle Rock.*)

WZON

An AM radio station (frequency 620) in Bangor that King bought, changing its format to hard rock. Later, the format changed to all-sports, with extensive coverage of local games. (King also owns a rock station, WKIT.)

WZON promotions

On April 12, 1985, station WZON sponsored a special midnight showing of *Cat's Eye* at the Brewer Cinema. The station gave away 62 pairs of tickets.

During the week of April 15, 1985, the station gave away 20 additional tickets for local showings, as well as a 10-pound bag of cat food to each winner. The winners were further entitled to a drawing for a cat's eye ring valued at $200, made by G. M. Pollack & Sons.

WZON now runs sports promotions.

Promotional T-shirt design for WZON, King's radio station.

The X-Files

King and *The X-Files*: A natural, right? But it took a chance encounter when the actor David Duchovny (Agent Mulder) met King backstage before their appearance on *Jeopardy*.

Unlike his three children, King had not watched the show on a regular basis, but after meeting Duchovny he did begin watching, and he liked what he saw.

Predictably, with his penchant for characterization, King loved the interaction between the two main characters.

"I love the chemistry between the characters and the reverse psychology. Mulder has the feminine characteristics, and [Agent] Scully [Gillian Anderson] is the tough male," he told Jefferson Graham of *USA Today* (Feb. 6, 1998).

The result: A collaborative script, initially written by King and rewritten by *X-Files* creator Chris Carter.

Chinga revolves around a young girl possessing and possessed by an evil doll fished out of Maine waters. Agent Scully rents a convertible with the Maine license plate bearing the ironic legend "Maine is Vacation Land," and wears a T-shirt with the same message, but vacationing in King's Maine is no vacation for anyone, least of all an FBI agent who reluctantly steps in to assist the local authorities to solve a rash of bizarre deaths linked to the demonic doll.

Of Carter's rewrite, King observed in *USA Today*, "If he hadn't rewritten the script, I would have felt like a geek, like the one kid in school who was different from the others."

King also said, "What people say about books—'I keep meaning to read that'—I say about TV. I keep meaning to watch shows like *The X-Files*, but I just never get around to it." ("Kitsching à la King," AOL, Aug. 5, 1995.)

King told *USA Today* that he had another idea for a script, so we may see another visit to King's Vacation Land.

"X, the Dreaded"

A long essay on film ratings that made its only print appearance in a double issue of *Castle Rock* (Dec. 1986/Jan. 1987).

In the piece, King discusses—in light of his recent experiences as director of *Maximum Overdrive*—the American and British film rating systems and concludes that it's time to rethink the American ratings system. His five recommendations include (1) mandatory ratings of all films, (2) adopt the British system of rating, which favors "intent and effect" as opposed to the U.S. system of "content and extent," (3) create a new rating of "AV" to prohibit anyone under the age of eighteen from viewing the film in question because of its violent content, (4) create a new rating of "AS" to prohibit anyone under the age of eighteen from viewing the film in question because of its sexual content, and (5) impose an escalating rating fee—on the low end "G" (for general) and on the high end "AV" or "AS" or, if brought back, an "X" rating.

"You Know They Got a Hell of a Band"
(collected in *Nightmares & Dreamscapes*)

Readers often pose the question to writers: Where do you get your ideas? As any writer will tell you, it's not the *idea* that's important but the *treatment* of the idea—that is to say, how the writer handles the idea and fleshes it out from a barebones idea to an engaging, imaginary narrative.

In the back of *Nightmares & Dreamscapes*, King takes the time to write "Notes," telling the story behind each of his stories.

For instance, the genesis of "You Know They Got a Hell of a Band" takes its literary inspiration from King's observation that "What I felt here—the impetus for the story—was how authentically creepy it is that so many rockers have died young, or under nasty circumstances; it's an actuarial expert's nightmare."

It is indeed, but it's an intriguing premise for a work of fiction, as this story clearly shows.

An appropriate epigram for this story would be James Dean's dictum: live fast, die young, and make a pretty corpse. Like Dean, a lot of rockers—whether intentionally self-destructing or unintentionally finding themselves in the wrong place at the wrong time, like Buddy Holly—were like shooting stars that blazed across the heavens, only to die out prematurely.

This story is what King terms a "peculiar town" tale. In other words, the characters, whether by choice or design, have ended up in a town that by all rights shouldn't exist—but it does. Recalling "Children of the Corn" and "Rainy Season," this story is cut from the same cloth—a different take on a familiar subject: What if you put ordinary people in extraordinary circumstances? Will they succumb—or fight?

Originally published in *Shock Rock*, an anthology of original stories, "You Know They Got a Hell of a Band" is the story of Mary and Clark, who left Portland, Oregon, and, after getting off the main road, pull into a small town curiously named Rock and Roll Heaven.

Now, it there were such a thing as a Rock and Roll Heaven, wouldn't you think they'd have one hell of a band?

Of course. And, unfortunately, it does.

In sharp contrast to her husband's fascination with the town's restaurant, Mary knows something is wrong, very wrong, but doesn't realize until it's too late that the staff in the restaurant don't just *look* and *sound* like rock icons Janis Joplin (a waitress) and Ricky Nelson (the cook), but they *are* the rock-and-roll legends. It is a town filled with rock iconography with Elvis Presley as its mayor.

Like others who innocently found their way to Rock and Roll Heaven, Mary and Clark are forced to attend the nightly concerts in Rock and Roll Heaven, Oregon, where they become, in every sense of the phrase, a captive audience.

ZBS Productions

A small company specializing in audio dramatizations that recorded "The Mist" in "3-D Sound."

A ninety-minute dramatization of "The Mist," directed by Bill Raymond with assistance provided by writer Dennis Etchison, was recorded in 1984 and released on chrome audiotape. Scored by Tim Clark, the recording process heightened the eerie story. Utilizing the Kunstkopf Binaural system, the recording—especially when listening with headphones on—creates an aural dimension that surrounds the listener.

Publishers Weekly noted that the recording is a "frighteningly real and unreal 3-D production, which lets conversation among characters, special effects and eerie music—rather than endless narration—do the work of scaring us. Chockful of sounds you don't want to know . . . this is easily the most successful [one] of the 3-D sound productions. . . ."

King, who grew up listening to radio shows that tapped into the listener's imagination—wrote in *Danse Macabre* that he was "of the last quarter of the last generation that remembers radio drama as an active force—a dramatic art form with its own set of reality. . . . They died, all right, one by one, the last handful of radio programs."

I*se Macabre,* King also remembers with fondness *Suspense, Inner Sanctum,* and *Mystery The-* ater—radio shows that play in what King likes to term skull cinema, the movie projector inside your head.

Interestingly, three film options on the "The Mist" were picked up and subsequently dropped, after the difficulty of generating realistic (and affordable) special effects made film versions too difficult (or expensive) to produce. In contrast, the ZBS production, with modest budget and using no special effects, pulls off what no film of "The Mist" can do: put the audience in the middle of the action. The listener is immersed in Stephen King country, in Bridgton, Maine, where the Draytons experience nature's fury as a sudden summer storm hammers them.

After the storm subsides, the horror seems to be over, but in truth it's just beginning: the storm heralds the coming of the mist, which brings with it unimaginable monsters—gigantic beasts that attack the hapless townsfolk barricaded in a supermarket; they wonder whether to make their stand or make a run for it.

A first-class production of a quintessential King story, the ZBS production of "The Mist" is the benchmark by which other audio dramatizations can be measured.

The compact disc for *The Mist,* published by Simon & Schuster, with appropriately buglike illustrations.

IT IS THE TALE,
NOT HE WHO TELLS IT.

That's been a good guide to me in life,
and I think it would make a good epitaph
for my tombstone. Just that and no name.

Stephen King (*Playboy* interview, 1983)